Walter Savage Landor, William Branford Shubrick Clymer

Selections from the writings of Walter Savage Landor

Walter Savage Landor, William Branford Shubrick Clymer

Selections from the writings of Walter Savage Landor

ISBN/EAN: 9783337275389

Printed in Europe, USA, Canada, Australia, Japan

Cover: Foto ©Andreas Hilbeck / pixelio.de

More available books at **www.hansebooks.com**

Athenæum Press Series

SELECTIONS

FROM THE WRITINGS OF

WALTER SAVAGE LANDOR

EDITED WITH INTRODUCTION AND NOTES

BY

W. B. SHUBRICK CLYMER

BOSTON, U.S.A.
GINN & COMPANY, PUBLISHERS
The Athenæum Press
1898

PREFACE.

THE first edition of John Forster's *Life* of Landor was published by Chapman and Hall, in two volumes, in 1869; in 1876, abridged, it formed the first volume of Forster's eight-volume edition of *The Works and Life of Walter Savage Landor;* in 1895 the second edition was reprinted. In this biography is stored almost all the information of any consequence relating to Landor; and Forster's is the standard text of the collected writings. The ample material in the biography is not especially well put together, nor is the appraisal always closely accurate. To a special student of the subject, however, the book is invaluable. Mr. Sidney Colvin's *Landor* (*English Men of Letters*) gives as full an account as any one but a special student cares for. In his volume of *Selections* (*Golden Treasury Series*) he attains, by rare skill in choice and arrangement, and by means of a really luminous preface and notes, that high point of critical merit which entitles him to the commendation bestowed by Landor on one who praises an author "becomingly." Mr. Charles G. Crump's comparatively recent *variorum* edition of the writings, with instructive critical notes, is based on Forster. In 1897 appeared *Letters and Other Unpublished Writings of Walter Savage Landor*, edited by Mr. Stephen Wheeler. The new material is not particularly important; but the editor's work is done with such good taste and judgment that the book cannot fail to interest an admirer of Landor. It has a well-made bibliography. The *Scott Library* contains, in convenient form, a good assortment of *Imaginary Conversations*, the *Pentameron*, and *Pericles and Aspasia*. The fullest American reprint of the prose is that published by Roberts Brothers.

Mr. Swinburne's article on Landor in the *Encyclopædia Britannica*, so strangely stimulating a blend of dithyramb and discernment as no other mortal could ever have produced, is to be read with mental reservations and qualifications. His *Song for the Centenary of Walter Savage Landor* is an encomium, in detail, of pretty much everything Landor wrote. In sharp contrast to Mr. Swinburne's apotheosis is Mr. Leslie Stephen's searching, and in some degree destructive, analysis (*Hours in a Library*). Irritating though the sarcastically depreciatory manner of the essay may be to youthful enthusiasm, yet the estimate is in the main so sound that mature and dispassionate reflection overlooks the lack of sympathy. It is by odds the cleverest thing in print on Landor. The article in the *Dictionary of National Biography*, also by Mr. Leslie Stephen, states the facts concisely, and concludes with an admirably just summing up of Landor as man and writer.

Among occasional contributions to the subject are Mrs. Browning's (then Miss Barrett) essay in Horne's *New Spirit of the Age* (1844); Miss Kate Field's three articles in the *Atlantic Monthly* (1866); Mrs. Linton's article in *Fraser's Magazine* (July, 1870); Lord Houghton's *Monograph* (1873); Mr. Horace E. Scudder's characterisation (*Men and Letters*); Professor Dowden's essay (*Studies in Literature*); Professor G. E. Woodberry's (*Studies in Letters and Life*); Mr. Aubrey de Vere's (*Essays, chiefly on Poetry*); M. Gabriel Sarrazin's (*Poètes modernes de l'Angleterre*); and two articles by J. R. Lowell (*Massachusetts Quarterly*, 1848; *Century Magazine*, 1888). Mr. E. W. Evans's academic *Study* of Landor is systematic and thorough. Landor is treated at some

length in Mrs. Oliphant's *Victorian Age of English Literature* and in Mr. Stedman's *Victorian Poets ;* and a few pages
are given to him in Professor Saintsbury's book on the
English literature of this century.

This small volume of selections, differing in plan both
from Mr. Hillard's and from Mr. Colvin's, contains some
of the dramatic and some of the discursive Conversations, a
considerable part of the last Day of the *Pentameron,* a small
number of letters from *Pericles and Aspasia,* and a few of
the best short poems. It has been difficult to find among
the dramatic Conversations good ones not already included
by Mr. Colvin ; among the non-dramatic it has been easy,
for he usually makes but short extracts from them. Only
one of these last is here given entire ; from others are made
excerpts long enough to serve as samples of the trend and
manner of the discussion. The letters taken from *Pericles
and Aspasia,* as well as the poems which follow them, though
totally inadequate to give an idea of the full value of the
classes of work they represent, are, at all events, characteristic. The order in which the selections are placed is
determined by considerations of congruity and contrast, not
chronology.

The slight biographical outline follows Mr. Colvin, my
indebtedness to whom at every turn in the preparation of
this book is obvious. The omission to mention in it Landor's idiosyncrasies of spelling is because they are matter
rather of curiosity than of serious literary interest. They
are discussed in full, along with various linguistic matters,
in Conversations between Johnson and Horne Tooke and
between Landor and Archdeacon Hare.

The notes, furnishing little of the information supplied
by dictionaries of biography and mythology, not minutely
analysing, touching only incidentally on technical details of
style, chiefly strive, by cursory suggestion of matters more

or less pertinent, to invite the reader to meet in a friendly spirit this somewhat uncompromising writer, whose acquaintance is so well worth making.

I take pleasure in thanking several friends for valuable aid, and the editor of *Scribner's Magazine* for his courtesy in consenting to the repetition, in the Introduction, of a few paragraphs from a previous article of my own.

W. B. S. C.

May, 1898.

CONTENTS.

		PAGE
INTRODUCTION	. . . .	xiii
DATES	. . . .	xxxix

IMAGINARY CONVERSATIONS.

I.	ACHILLES AND HELENA	.	3
II.	ÆSOP AND RHODOPÈ	. .	9
III.	TIBERIUS AND VIPSANIA	. .	19
IV.	METELLUS AND MARIUS	. .	23
V.	MARCELLUS AND HANNIBAL		28
VI.	HENRY VIII. AND ANNE BOLEYN	. .	33
VII.	ROGER ASCHAM AND LADY JANE GREY	.	41
VIII.	PRINCESS MARY AND PRINCESS ELIZABETH	.	44
IX.	ESSEX AND SPENSER	. .	54
X.	LEOFRIC AND GODIVA	. . . .	59
XI.	THE LADY LISLE AND ELIZABETH GAUNT	.	65
XII.	THE EMPRESS CATHARINE AND PRINCESS DASHKOF	.	69
XIII.	JOHN OF GAUNT AND JOANNA OF KENT	.	77
XIV.	TANCREDI AND CONSTANTIA	. .	82
XV.	THE MAID OF ORLEANS AND AGNES SOREL		87
XVI.	BOSSUET AND THE DUCHESS DE FONTANGES	.	96
XVII.	DANTE AND BEATRICE	.	104
XVIII.	BENIOWSKI AND APHANASIA	. .	113
XIX.	LEONORA DI ESTE AND FATHER PANIGAROLA	.	118

x

CONTENTS.

PAGE

XX. ADMIRAL BLAKE AND HUMPHREY BLAKE . . 120

XXI. RHADAMISTUS AND ZENOBIA . . 124

XXII. EPICURUS, LEONTION, AND TERNISSA . 129

XXIII. WALTON, COTTON, AND OLDWAYS . . 138

XXIV. WILLIAM PENN AND LORD PETERBOROUGH . 155

XXV. EPICTETUS AND SENECA . . . 167

XXVI. LUCULLUS AND CÆSAR 172

XXVII. THE APOLOGUE OF CRITOBULUS . . . 180

THE PENTAMERON.

XXVIII. FIFTH DAY'S INTERVIEW . . 183

PERICLES AND ASPASIA.

XXIX. SELECTED LETTERS . . . 200

POEMS.

HELLENICS.

XXX. THE HAMADRYAD 215

XXXI. ACON AND RHODOPÈ; OR, INCONSTANCY . 224

XXXII. THE DEATH OF ARTEMIDORA . . . 228

MISCELLANEOUS.

XXXIII. THE WRESTLING MATCH (from *Gebir*). . 229

XXXIV. TO IANTHE

    1. "IT OFTEN COMES INTO MY HEAD" . 232

    2. "IANTHE! YOU ARE CALL'D". . 232

    3. "YOUR PLEASURES SPRING" . 233

    4. "WELL I REMEMBER" . . 233

XXXV. ROSE AYLMER 233

XXXVI. A FIESOLAN IDYL . . 234

XXXVII. UPON A SWEET-BRIAR . . 236

PAGE

XXXVIII. The Maid's Lament . . . 237

XXXIX. To Robert Browning . . . 238

XL. To the Sister of Elia 238

XLI. On Dirce 239

XLII. "I will not love!" 239

OLD AGE AND DEATH.

XLIII. "How many voices" 239

XLIV. "The place where soon" . 240

XLV. To Age 240

XLVI. On his Seventy-fifth Birthday . 241

XLVII. On his Eightieth Birthday . 241

XLVIII. "Death stands above me" . . 241

Notes 243

INTRODUCTION.

———

Walter Savage Landor was born at Warwick, on January 30, 1775. His father, Dr. Landor, a practising physician at Warwick, reputed to have been a "polished, sociable, agreeable, somewhat choleric gentleman, more accomplished and better educated, as his profession required, than most of those with whom he associated, but otherwise dining, coursing, telling his story and drinking his bottle without particular distinction among the rest," had married two heiresses. Of the seven children by the second wife, Elizabeth Savage, a member of a Warwickshire family, Walter was the eldest. By entail he became heir, at birth, to two estates belonging to his mother's family — Ipsley Court and Tachbrook in Warwickshire; to a share in the reversionary interest in a third — Hughenden Manor in Buckinghamshire;[1] and to the family property of his father in Staffordshire. "No one, it should seem," says his latest biographer, "ever entered life under happier conditions. To the gifts of breeding and of fortune there were added at his birth the gifts of genius and of strength. But there had been evil god-mothers beside the cradle as well as good, and in the composition of this powerful nature pride, anger, and pre-

[1] Subsequently the country seat of another man of literary fame, Benjamin Disraeli, who in 1848 purchased the place, and on the refusal by his executors of the offer of a public funeral and Westminster Abbey was, in accordance with his express directions, buried there beside Lady Beaconsfield in 1881.

cipitancy had been too largely mixed, to the prejudice of a noble intellect and tender heart, and to the disturbance of all his relations with his fellow-men."

Landor went, at ten, to Rugby, and, during the six years he stayed there, was equally reckless in riding and in defiance of authority; regardless of bounds; proficient in his studies — "all except arithmetic"; deep in Latin and English literature, and skilful in turning verses in Latin and English; fond of reading at night, and of wandering by day beside streams. Illustrative of his readiness in Latin — of which he once said, in extreme old age, "I am sometimes at a loss for an English word, never for a Latin" — is a story told by Charles Reade's father, who was at Rugby at the same time. Dr. James, the master, found him eating an apple in school, and told him to bring it to his desk. As Landor was turning to go back to his seat, the doctor said, "Now, if you want that again, you had better make me a short line on the occasion"; whereupon, after thinking a moment, Landor replied:

Esuriens doctor dulcia poma rapit.

"What do you mean by *esuriens doctor?*" said the master. "The gormandizing doctor." "Take it, sir," said the doctor, delighted with his pupil. Another story is that once, when there were seven boys at Rugby named Hill, he got a half-holiday for the school by writing a copy of verses in which he compared Rugby to Rome because it was built on seven hills. "I don't ask you who wrote this," said the doctor, "for there is only one of you with the brains to do it." But Landor and the master were not always on amicable terms, and one day they differed over a Latin quantity. Landor is said to have been right about the quantity, but he conducted himself in so insubordinate a way that his removal was requested.

After two years with a tutor, he went, in 1793, to Trinity College, Oxford. Southey was then at Balliol. Though they did not know each other, they both made themselves conspicuous by avowing their republican sentiments in such practices as appearing in public with their hair unpowdered, and Landor by still more extreme insults to orthodox English opinion. "His Jacobinism," says Southey, "would have made me seek his acquaintance, but for his madness." An absurd freak led to his rustication. He quarreled with his father, whose politics were the reverse of his own, and, finding it impossible to live at home, established himself, in 1794, in lodgings in London. Here he published, in 1795, a small volume of poems, of which one was an ode *To Washington*.

Next he went to South Wales, where, he says, he lived "chiefly among woods," and appears to have been in the best spirits, though "not exchanging twelve sentences with men." With women, however, he may be supposed to have exchanged more, for he wrote poetry about two — Ionè, whose prose name was Jones, and Ianthè, which means Jane. The latter was an Irish lady, Sophia Jane Swift, who afterwards became Countess de Molandé, and always remained Landor's friend.[1] *Gebir*, in English and in Latin, suggested by a so-

[1] Mr. Colvin gives the following summary of the subsequent life of Ianthè :

" To this lady Landor's somewhat roving affections during his life at Bath (about 1800–1806) were principally devoted, and he held her in great honour and affection ever after. Her first husband, a collateral descendant of the Dean of St. Patrick's, died in 1812, and she soon afterwards married M. de Molandé, a French *Émigré* of high family. . After the Restoration, Madame de Molandé, who had children by both marriages, went to live with her second husband in Paris. Being left once more a widow, she spent two years (1829–31) with her children in Florence, and passed the remainder of her life between England and France, dying in Paris [Versailles] in 1851."

In Mr. Wheeler's recently published book are further details about her and her daughters, as well as about Ionè.

called Arabian story of Clara Reeve's, was the poetic fruit of Landor's out-of-door life in Wales. Ignored by the many, it has been admired by a few for a century. Southey found in it "miraculous beauties." The first edition of the English version appeared in 1798, the year of the *Lyrical Ballads* and of Lamb's *Rosamund Gray*. The date marks not inaccurately a point in the ideal divisional line between eighteenth-century and nineteenth-century English literature. The blank verse of *Gebir* is one sign of the growing reaction from the correct couplets of the preceding age. The question which has been suggested whether *The Ancient Mariner*, *Tintern Abbey*, or *Gebir* was "really the weightiest portent of the new day" seems, however, too remotely eccentric for special consideration here.

After contributing political articles to the *Courier* for a while, Landor made a visit to Paris, where he conceived a hatred of all things French. "As to the cause of liberty," he writes in 1802, "this cursed nation has ruined it forever." He includes the language in his dislike, though he was fond of a number of French writers. Ronsard, he says, "would have been a great poet if he had not been a Frenchman."

In 1805, on the death of his father, he succeeded, at thirty, to the family estates. He was in need of money, for, what with wandering from place to place, everywhere buying such expensive things as horses and pictures, and living generally on a scale which the limited sale of his unpopular writings could far from maintain, he had for some time been spending more than his allowance.

His life at Bath during the next few years was as near to dissipation as Landor's ever came. Though careless in dress and awkward in dancing, he was, as was natural, a favourite in society. He continued to buy horses and pictures, and to keep up an establishment beyond even his ample means. Personally of abstemious habits, he was yet sociable

and impressionable. As the owner of large landed properties, he was a conspicuous figure in so small a place. Of his
doings at Bath several stories are told on which it is needless to dwell. His friends were anxious that he should
marry ; and in his letters and his verses there are indica-
tions of dissatisfaction with the sort of life he had adopted,
of a craving for something more congenial to his refined
tastes than he found in the rather empty days and nights
of a rich but aimless young man of fashion.

"This conventional existence"— to quote from Lord
Houghton —"was interrupted by a resolve to join the
British army in Spain in 1808." He actually equipped and
commanded a thousand volunteers in the uprising against
Napoleon's attempt to convert Spain and Portugal into
dependencies of France. For this service, which lasted
some three months, the honorary rank of colonel in the
Spanish army was conferred on him — a title which he
afterward relinquished. His experience in Spain gave the
impulse for *Count Julian*, his principal drama in verse, of
which De Quincey, by a strange vagary, ranked the character of the hero with Milton's Satan and with the Prometheus
of Æschylus.

Not less characteristic than his espousal of the Spanish
cause was his scheme of restoring the border priory of
Llanthony, in Wales, and there establishing himself as the
benefactor and reformer of the neighbourhood. He sold
one of his estates to buy the property, instituted gigantic
operations to make it accessible and habitable, went to live
there with his wife (a young beauty whom he fell in love
with at first sight at a ball at Bath and married out-of-hand
in the course of a few months), got into trouble with every
one he had dealings with, and finally was forced to turn
about and leave England, after having wasted seventy
thousand pounds in the fruitless enterprise.

"It is small reproach to any woman," says Lord Houghton, "that she did not possess a sufficient union of charm, tact, and intelligence to suit Landor as a wife. He demanded beauty in woman just as imperatively as honesty in man, yet was hardly submissive to its influence." Mrs. Landor, on the other hand, had, as another critic puts it, "none of the gifts of the domestic artist ; she was not of those fine spirits who study to create, out of the circumstances and characters with which they have to deal, the best attainable ideal of a home ; but a commonplace provincial beauty enough, although lively and agreeable in her way." She and the lion were ill mated. He married her for her wonderful golden hair, and because she was penniless and without accomplishments. Her reasons for marrying him were probably no better. At any rate, he was not the man to bear being twitted by her with their difference in age of sixteen years. Accordingly, one night, unable to stay with her any longer, he walked across the island of Jersey, where they were living, and embarked for France.[1]

---

[1] It was a year after Landor's luckless marriage that the first husband of Ianthè died. Mrs. Lynn Linton, whose article (*Fraser's Magazine*, July, 1870) on Landor's latter years is of peculiar interest, represents him as sighing that he had not waited that year before marrying. What, one wonders, would have been his fate if he had waited? He certainly would not have married as he did. But would he have married Ianthè? It is not unlikely that he would, for, Mrs. Linton goes on to say, "of all his four great loves, Ianthè was the one to which his memory turned most constantly and most fondly. After he had told me the whole story, she, then an old woman, came to Bath with her grandchildren ; and we used to go regularly every day to pay her a visit. She was sweet and gentle, evidently very proud of her old lover's affection, very fond of him, and somewhat afraid. And his behaviour to her was perfect. He was at his best when with her. Tender, respectful, playful, with his old-world courtesy which sat so well on him, it was easy to understand why she had loved him so passionately in the fresh far-away past, and why she loved him still in

The incidents of the next few years may be mentioned very briefly. Landor went to Tours, where, a few months later, his wife rejoined him. Here began, in 1814, his acquaintance with Francis Hare,[1] who became and remained his fast friend. From Tours Mr. and Mrs. Landor went to Como, where their first boy was born. Here, as always, he kept up a constant correspondence with Southey, and sent him many valuable books which, once read, had served their purpose. He was continually buying and giving away good books and, in his later years, bad pictures. He had a visit from Southey, who was much entertained by his droll stories, and by his echoing laughter as he told them in the cool church of Sant' Abondio. Driven from Como by a quarrel, he went to Pisa. Characteristically, though Shelley was there at the same time, Landor avoided meeting him.

In 1821 he removed to Florence, where he lived for five years in the Palazzo Medici, and for three in the Villa Castiglione, a short distance out of Florence, devoting himself mainly during the whole period to the writing of the *Imaginary Conversations.* The first two volumes, containing thirty-six Conversations, were published first in 1824, by Taylor and Hessey, who were just about that time giving up the publication of the *London Magazine*, in which the *Opium Eater* and the *Essays of Elia* had appeared two or

the worn and withered present. All children were specially dear to Landor; but of all, her grandchildren were the dearest."

[1] Elder brother of the authors of *Guesses at Truth.* His son, Mr. A. J. C. Hare, author of *Walks in Rome*, etc., gives, in *The Story of My Life*, a number of personal reminiscences of Landor. In a letter written a few months before Landor's death, after speaking of his broken health, Mr. Hare tells how he used still to like to "say over the old names, — 'Francis, Augustus, Julius, i miei tre imperatori. I have never known any family I loved so much as yours. I loved Francis most, then Julius, then Augustus. But I loved them all. Francis was the best friend I ever had.'"

three years before.   The number of Conversations written and published between 1821 and 1829 is about eighty; the whole number produced before Landor's death, not quite one hundred and fifty.

During the Florentine period Landor led, despite certain annoying difficulties incident to the publishing of his books, a pretty tranquil and satisfactory life.   He was doing, in agreeable surroundings, the work he most enjoyed; his increasing reputation as a literary figure attracted to him many of the men best worth knowing; he had several dear friends; his wife appears to have been less vexatious than usual ; and in his children he took unbounded delight.

At Fiesole, where he next lived for some years in a villa bought with money advanced by a friend, he continued to romp with his children, to tend his flowers, to make companions of his numerous pets, to write poetry, to revise, enlarge, and add to his Conversations.   Several of his poems, especially *A Fiesolan Idyl*, suggest the beauty of the place and the charm of his life there.   In 1832, while on a short visit to England, he saw Crabb Robinson, Flaxman, Lamb, Coleridge, Julius Hare, Southey, and Wordsworth.   It was at Fiesole, whither he returned in 1833, that he composed the *Citation and Examination of William Shakespeare, Pericles and Aspasia*, and, in part, the *Pentameron*, which relate respectively, as their names show, to the three great periods of Elizabethan England, classic Greece, and Italy on the verge of the Renaissance.   The last two, of which the subjects were especially congenial to him, and the best of the Conversations establish his title to high rank as a writer of prose.

Before the appearance of the *Pentameron*, Landor and his wife had again separated, this time definitively, by mutual consent.   For two years he drifted from place to place in Italy and England.   At length, in 1837, he took up his abode at Bath, there to live for twenty years, writing diligently, frequently going up to London to meet the fashionable literary people whom Lady Blessington and Count D'Orsay entertained at Gore House, taking daily walks with his bright-eyed, yellow-tailed Pomeranian dog,[1] gradually towards the latter years losing his mental strength, until finally, in 1858, he was forced to escape by flight the consequences of a suit for libel in which his tempestuous quixotism had involved him. The story of the squabble at Bath is somewhat piteous, though also, as told by Forster, unintentionally amusing. Landor, eighty-four years old, running away from the entanglements of an imprudent intimacy with a young girl, was discovered by Dickens at Forster's house in London, where he had taken refuge for the night while Forster was giving a dinner party. Dickens, who had left the table to go to cheer the old man, came back laughing, and saying that he " found him very jovial, and that his whole conversation was upon the characters of Catullus, Tibullus, and other Latin poets."[2]

It was at Bath that *Andrea of Hungary, Giovanna of Naples*, and *Fra Rupert* were written, a trilogy which, by reason of the author's inability to conceive of the necessity

[1] No notice of Landor should omit mention of his dogs, Parigi, Pomero, and Giallo, his constant companions, with whom he never quarreled. Pomero's death is commemorated in a letter to Miss Boyle published by Mr. Lowell in the *Century* (February, 1888). In Mr. Colvin's *Landor* (p. 212) are some pretty lines to Giallo, Pomero's successor.

[2] It may be well to mention, in connection with the whole scandal, Mrs. Linton's indignant denial of the truth of the version commonly received. " Of one thing," she says, " I am *sure*, that his affection for ' Erminie ' was not the feeling his enemies have made it out to be. In his madness he wrote some bad things enough about the matter; but he never wilfully said a word that could shock the most sensitive girl; and I am as certain as of my own existence that he never showed any feeling whatsoever of the kind I mean."

of plot to a play, it is exceedingly difficult to understand. The character of Giovanna is in accordance with his own pleasure, not with Sismondi's history. There are scenes in which she lives, but they are not so knit together as to present a clear idea of the character as a whole. Another play, the *Siege of Ancona*, soon followed. Interesting and scholarly criticisms on Theocritus, Catullus, and Petrarch belong to the same period. And a few years afterward came the *Hellenics*, for the genuinely Greek tone of which some critics vouch. They are undoubtedly the crowning literary performance of Landor's later life.

Still he kept on writing to the end. As late as 1863 he published a volume, and even after that he wrote dialogues in prose and in verse. There is little to tell of the closing years. Penniless and mentally enfeebled, he received great kindness from Browning, and lived for a time at Siena with W. W. Story. Afterward he went again to live in Florence, whither, in 1864, Mr. Swinburne, aged twenty-seven,

> " — came as one whose thoughts half linger,
>   Half run before,
>   The youngest to the oldest singer
>   That England bore."

It was not very long after this visit that, on Sept. 17, 1864, the " unsubduable old Roman " was at last subdued.

During three-quarters of a life of almost ninety years, extending from before the Battle of Lexington to within a few months of Lee's surrender, Landor might have said with Walt Whitman, " I understand the large hearts of heroes," for his companions were mainly the illustrious men and women of the past. From the point of view of literary production, his life falls into three periods, thus marked off by Mr. Colvin :

1795–1821, *Poems, Gebir, Count Julian, Idyllia Heroica.*

1821–1837, *Imaginary Conversations, Examination of Shakespeare, Pericles and Aspasia, Pentameron.*

1837–1863, miscellaneous prose and verse. In this period the *Hellenics* are foremost in importance and beauty.

Since it is as a writer of prose that he is chiefly memorable, the general remarks which follow will deal for the most part with the work produced during the sixteen years immediately preceding the accession of Queen Victoria.

Forster, whose profusion of enthusiasm somewhat weakens his indispensable work in behalf of Landor, thus describes the literary character of the plan of the Conversations : " All the leading shapes of the past, the most familiar and the most august, were to be called up again. Modes of thinking the most various, and events the most distant, were proposed for his theme. Beside the fires of the present, the ashes of the past were to be rekindled and to shoot again into warmth and brightness.- The scene was to be shifting as life, but continuous as time. Down it were to pass successions of statesmen, lawyers, and churchmen ; wits and men of letters ; party men, soldiers, and kings ; the most tender, delicate, and noble women ; figures fresh from the schools of Athens and the courts of Rome ; philosophers philosophising, and politicians discussing questions of state ; poets talking of poetry, men of the world of matters worldly, and English, Italians, and French of their respective literatures and manners. . . . The requisites for it were such as no other existing writer possessed in the same degree as he did. Nothing had been indifferent to him that affected humanity. Poetry and history had delivered up to him their treasures, and the secrets of antiquity were his."

The usual classification of the Conversations as dramatic and non-dramatic is convenient. Of the first class a list may easily be made of a score or more of scenes which in a restricted and qualified sense are really dramatic. The speakers, that is to say, are felt behind the words, and the effect of each speech is felt in calling forth the reply. In some of these scenes, moreover, there is, if not dramatic development, at least dramatic movement: action, though not mentioned, is sometimes implied. Instances will occur to every reader. The beautiful Conversation between Walton, Cotton, and Oldways, a gem not so well known as it deserves to be, contains a good deal of such implied incident, as well as a little implied landscape. In such scenes Landor shows at their best what Mr. Gosse happily terms his "dramatic aptitudes." In others, although, as was once said of Sir Henry Irving, he does not get quite out of himself, he yet gets pretty completely into the character. Irving's "Louis XI." and his "Hamlet" may serve roughly to illustrate the distinction : the one is the French king as you feel he must have been ; the other is the English actor impersonating the Danish prince. So Leofric and Godiva live as individually as you or I ; whereas Epictetus and Epicurus are little else than Landor's mouthpieces — interesting mouthpieces, and to some degree dramatically conceived, but not, like the Lord of Coventry and his Lady, inevitable creations. Still other Conversations do not move at all. Some of these contain engaging matter ;[1] but some are dull and heavy discussions which

---

[1] Sometimes — in the opinion of at least two judicious and fair-minded men of the present day, one eminent in law, the other in letters — valuable matter. Writing in the *Fortnightly* in 1890, Sir Frederick Pollock casually mentions the Conversations between Southey and Landor as being "the best commentary on Milton's poetical workmanship yet produced." And Professor Dowden, who, being a staunch

there is no more occasion to read than there is to read *Sordello* — a task that an intelligent man may indefinitely defer without thereby disqualifying himself to speak aright meanwhile of the author of *Men and Women*.

Any one may likewise be excused from reading the *Examination of Shakespeare,*[1] for it is rather tedious, and lacks satiric verisimilitude. It contains, to be sure, several good bits; but, on the whole, Landor's remarks on Plato's wit apply to this and other attempts of his own to be funny: "What painful twisting of unelastic stuff !" he makes Lucian, who was frankly and naturally amusing, say; and again: "He sadly mistook the qualities of his mind in attempting the facetious; or rather he fancied he possessed one quality more than belonged to him." The style, moreover, is, for the most part, laboriously imitative.

Pericles and Aspasia, on the other hand, throbs with beauty which it is the custom to call Greek. Whether the clear, simple, straightforward, dignified, graceful treatment of Athenian life is Attic, perhaps admits of discussion. In the face of Goethe's opinion that *Samson Agonistes* was the only modern work which had "caught fire from the breath of the antique spirit," it may be prudent to think twice before accepting the hasty judgment of every stripling reviewer as to the Greek or Homeric character of much recent work. Pains have been taken to show that Kingsley's *Andromeda,* and that Mr. Swinburne's *Atalanta,* and particularly his *Erechtheus,* are Greek. All three are delightful; the last,

Wordsworthian, is free from prepossessions in Landor's favour, refers to his criticism of Wordsworth in the dialogue of Southey and Porson as if he thought it worth considering.

[1] Lamb, who died the year of its publication, made a careless remark to the effect that nobody else but Shakespeare could have written it; Tennyson, going to the other extreme, is reported by a friend to have despised it.

especially, is no less than a splendidly successful imitation. But whether it, or any such attempt to embody in English the Greek spirit, can rightly be called more than an imitation, may be questioned.   It is true that the author of some of the most pertinent criticism of Homer written in the past forty years calls Clough Homeric, and that one of the authors of the translation of Homer accepted by the present generation of Englishmen calls Dumas Homeric, and that each makes out a fairly good case.   But it is unlikely that Homer would have suggested Dumas to Arnold or Clough to Mr. Lang.   The contention is not that there are no points of resemblance, but that the bandying about of such epithets by tiros tends to blur real distinctions, and so to perplex criticism.   It does not necessarily enhance the value of a work to call it Greek, nor help us to understand its value.   If a Homeric Clough and a Homeric Dumas are difficult to accept together, it is still more difficult to reconcile either with Lowell's judicious remark that "between us and the Greeks lies the grave of their murdered paganism, making our minds and theirs irreconcilable."

As to the excellence of style of *Pericles and Aspasia*, there is less room for two opinions.   "Though not alien to the treatment of modern life," writes Lord Houghton, a critic of Landor at once sympathetic and discreet, "it [his style] is undoubtedly more at home in the old world; and in such 'Conversations' as those of Lucullus and Cæsar, Epictetus and Seneca, Epicurus and the Grecian Maidens, Marcus Tullius and Quinctus Cicero, and in the 'Epistles' of *Pericles and Aspasia*, there is a sense of fitness of language that suggests the desire to see them restored, as it were, to the original tongues."   And he goes on to say that they would be the best possible things from which to select passages for translation into Latin and Greek, so at one are the thought and the expression of it.   This praise of

Lord Houghton's comes perilously near to suggesting the presence of that sophomoric hybrid known to teachers as "translation English" — native or naturalised words so combined as to give to the style a foreign cast. In Landor may doubtless be found instances of that sort of solecism; but one would not be apt to look for such crudity in *Pericles and Aspasia*, the appropriate phrasing of which shows easy mastery of idiom. In none of his writings, indeed, is the style more essentially and naturally English, more harmoniously dignified, freer from the faults commonly imputed to it, richer in positive merits.

In *Pericles and Aspasia* there are dull passages, which any one is at liberty to skip; and there are anachronisms, inaccuracy in detail, and such like handles for pedants, which none else need grasp. The story, which is slight, is in the temper of the time; it is founded, in the main, on incidents recorded of the classic lovers, and to these are added others which are in keeping. The passion is pagan and free from self-consciousness, deep in tranquillity of expression, absolute in devotion, restrained, as in Shakespeare's Sonnets, by a sense of beauty. The vitality of the book is to some degree shown by a comparison of it with Becker's *Charicles* and *Gallus*, with Hamerling's *Aspasia*, and with numerous other clever and learned archæological exercises that might be named, which are all, by contrast, dead restorations of the past. The spirit of its period quickens none of these as intrinsic beauty — Hellenic and Landorian fused — quickens a great part of *Pericles and Aspasia*. It may be added, as a crown of grace, that here, for once, despite irrelevance and digression, Landor constructs well.

In the *Pentameron* it is likewise a fact that tedious passages occur — from which escape is as simple as in the other case. Perhaps it offers fewer temptations to skip than *Pericles and Aspasia*. The most obvious handle for pedants is the perverse estimate of Dante. The delight the book affords arises from the great charm of the relation between the two friends, from the exquisite picture set in an exquisite frame, from the episodical characters introduced now and then with a skill unusual in Landor, from occasional passages unsurpassed even by himself, from the quality of the English throughout. Whether or not the temper be Tuscan, the language assuredly is a web of gold, closely woven, strong, flexible, brilliant, visible in every detail of texture, in every detail disclosing new beauties the more carefully it is examined. Landor too frequently shares with Emerson a "formidable tendency to the lapidary style"; in parts of the *Pentameron*, however, he comes nearer than almost anywhere else to that "warm glow, blithe movement, and soft pliancy of life" which Arnold finds in the Attic style.

To read Landor's poetry after reading much of his prose is to perceive that he was right in regarding it as the less serious and complete expression of himself. "Poetry was always," he writes, "my amusement, prose my study and business." Though he could produce verse easily, his thoughts do not "voluntary move harmonious numbers,"[1] nor does "harmonious madness" flow from his lips, nor does he pour "the unpremeditated lay." His poetry is, for the most part, rather the work of a master of speech, as has been said, than of song. The long narrative and dramatic poems contain, it is true, fine flights. Parts of *Gebir*, in particular, bear a close external likeness to Milton. De Quincey speaks in flamboyant phrase of certain passages in *Count Julian* "to which, for their solemn grandeur, one raises one's hat as at night in walking under the Coliseum," and of others "which, for their luxury of loveliness, should

---

[1] Milton's phrase is almost identical with Carlyle's definition of poetry as "*musical Thought*," and of the poet as one "who *thinks* in that manner." See *The Hero as Poet.*

be inscribed on the phylacteries of brides, or upon the frescoes of Ionia, illustrated by the gorgeous allegories of Rubens." But neither are these long poems so well sustained as some of the long Conversations, nor is their verbal pattern so deftly woven. Effort is so obvious as to fatigue. In short occasional poems, on the other hand, not requiring such continuous attention, success is frequent, for in them the perfect turn of phrase often perfectly fits the thought. Some of the *Hellenics*, again, have an idyllic quality which leads one critic to say that they "would hardly have been written otherwise at Alexandria in the days of Theocritus" — a quality concisely described in Mr. Swinburne's much-quoted lines :

> " And through the trumpet of a child of Rome
> Rang the pure music of the flutes of Greece."

Their charm is, indeed, unique in English.[1] Yet even in the best of them one feels, recalling the exquisite allegories of the *Pentameron*, that the delicate strain of sentiment running through and idealising them might have been as adequately expressed in prose — in *Landor's* prose. Landor in verse seldom, to put it in one word, transports ;[2] so that it is not obvious what Mr. Swinburne means in ranking him as a poet between Byron and Shelley. In prose he not infrequently does transport, as truly as they do in verse.

---

[1] Professor Dowden, in an interesting page, ingeniously discriminates between the *Hellenics* and André Chénier's *Poésies Antiques*, likening the English poems to " designs upon Greek urns," the French to " paintings upon Pompeian walls, but nobler."

[2] Non satis est pulchra esse poemata ; dulcia sunto,
Et, quocumque volent, animum auditoris agunto.
Ars Poetica.

Horace's idea has been felicitously rendered :

> Form, grace will not suffice ; the poet's art
> Must stir the passions, and subdue the heart.

Nor is the reason of this particular difference between his poetry and that of his romantic contemporaries to be found in the fact that he was, as it is always said of him, and truly said, classic. He was Greek in a sense in which, for instance, Keats,[1] who is sometimes called so, was not. His method is to present the object undraped ; Keats, whose love of beauty, though essentially different, was not more disinterested than his, presents the object clad in the drapery of modern association and personal feeling. The effect of the one method is totally unlike that of the other, as Keats's *Hyperion* and Landor's *Hellenics* sufficiently show. The greater popularity of Keats's method is explained by Landor in the line, " Most have an eye for colour, few for form." The classic form of the *Hellenics* is, however, no reason why they should not throb and glow with vitality to as high a degree as *Hyperion :* surely nothing is more classic and nothing more alive with emotion than Greek sculpture and Greek drama. Yet that vitality one does not find in the *Hellenics*. One finds in them classic workman-ship, and the beauty resulting from the exercise of that workmanship on subjects of captivating grace and lasting charm — beauty of a high order, but not deeply moving. The secret of the failure of Landor's poetry to reach the pitch of his best prose is simply that verse was to him a less natural mode of utterance than prose. Technically, the verse and the prose are much alike and, at their best, equally flawless. The superiority of the prose lies in Lan-dor's closer affinity to the rhythm of prose than to that of verse. When he had a deep feeling to put into words, he habitually used prose ; for a beautiful fancy he often used verse of consummate charm. The lines to Mary Lamb,

[1] Landor writes to Forster : " Keats was no more pagan than Words-worth himself. Between you and me, the style of Keats is extremely far removed from the very boundaries of Greece."

written on the day he heard of her brother's death, and sent in a letter to Crabb Robinson, are perhaps alone in his poetry — not even excepting *Rose Aylmer*, "the most enchanting of his minor poems" — as the spontaneous expression of a deep feeling which could not conceivably have been so well expressed in prose; and but little of his poetry approaches those verses in the special power to move that so distinguishes poets, both classic and romantic, whose instinctive utterance is not, as Landor's is, in "the other harmony of prose."

"A classic writing in a romantic age,"[1] Landor has had scant appreciation. Only a few of his contemporaries cared much for his work, and now that he has been dead above a third of a century, he is read by but a small portion of even literary folk. That is natural enough, for he is rather bulky, and by no means always interesting. The dialogue is a form not attractive to the cursory reader. Moreover, the subjects which most interested Landor do not, as a rule, allure any but historical or classical scholars. Nor is his style so inviting and ingratiating as Lamb's, for instance, or De Quincey's, or Ruskin's, or Newman's. He is a little difficult of approach, for he does not meet the reader half-way. He professed sincerely not to care for popularity; it is wholly likely that he will never have it. That is as it should be. He ought not to be popular, for he was out of sympathy with the time he lived in, and is as much aloof as ever from the present or from any future time that can be foreseen. He came charged with no "message" to the

---

[1] For suggestive discussion of the classical and romantic spirits, see the last essay in Walter Pater's *Appreciations;* also the preface to Colvin's *Selections from Landor.* Landor's Epistle *To the Author of "Festus" (Last Fruit,* 1853) contains his own mature reflections on the subject, together with remarks on some of his predecessors and contemporaries.

world; his thoughts do not form a philosophy of life; he does not directly encourage or console; he neither prompts to action nor lightens the burden of the weary.

Carried along by the scientific drift of the day, certain critics of Landor have sought to define his relation to his predecessors and to his successors. They trace his literary pedigree and issue, with all the affinities and hereditary influences implied by that investigation. The result is neither very clear nor very fruitful. When the patent facts have been stated that he owed much to the Greek and Latin classics and to Milton, less to Cowper[1] and one or two others, that analogies exist between his prose and Ben Jonson's,[2] that the effect of his style on a few of his contemporaries may be fancied in some of their collateral literary descendants, there remains little further to say on that score. In reality, the complexity of nineteenth-century literature is so great that any recent writer of original power is far more difficult to account for than a writer of the age, for instance, of Elizabeth. The playwrights from Marlowe to Webster exemplify the theory of literary evolution with a

---

[1] That he thought highly of Cowper is shown by sundry bits of criticism uttered by characters in different Conversations. For instance, in one Cowper is "more diversified in his poetry and more classical than any since"; and again, "in some passages, he stands quite unrivalled by any recent poet of this century," and "nothing of his is out of place or out of season"; and elsewhere, "Cowper is worthy of his succession to Goldsmith; more animated, more energetic, more diversified. Sometimes he is playful, oftener serious; and you go with him in either path with equal satisfaction." There are more good remarks to like effect, all presumably giving Landor's own opinion of the poet by whom he said that he was first moved to care for poetry, and whom he called "the only modern poet who is so little of a mannerist as I am."

[2] He writes, in 1850, to Forster: "Ben Jonson I have studied, principally for the purity of his English. Had it not been for him and Shakespeare, our language would have fallen into ruin."

definiteness not found in the poets from, let us say, Wordsworth to Tennyson. The half-century of English romantic
drama is developed from adolescence, through maturity, to
decay. The century of English romantic poetry shows no
such organic unity and completeness ; an era rather of
individuality than of solidarity, it has been constantly
increasing in diversity. Professional critics busily arrange
and classify, only to prepare the way for the facile rearrange-
ments and reclassifications of new experts. Such work is
tempting and charming, it may be, and occasionally valuable. Yet, when all is done, the words with which that
accomplished dilettante, the late J. A. Symonds, closes his
comparison of Victorian with Elizabethan poetry are still
worth pondering. "This intimate and pungent personality,"
he writes from amid the snows of Davos, "settling the
poet's attitude toward things, moulding his moral sympathies,
flavouring his philosophy of life and conduct, colouring his
style, separating him from fellow-workers, is the leading
characteristic of Victorian literature — that which distinguishes it most markedly from the Elizabethan." If that
be measurably true of a literature essentially romantic in its
main current (a literature of which the vitality consists in
the romantic spirit that differently inspired Wordsworth,
Coleridge, Scott, Byron, Keats, Shelley, Browning, Tennyson), do not the words apply with double force to so strongly
marked a personality as Landor's, who was not of his time,
but, to an extreme degree, a man apart, an exception, an
individual ? Even allowing him to have been, as Mr. Aubrey
de Vere calls him, "the earliest of our modern poets specially
characterised by their devotion to ideal beauty and to classical associations," he was, at most, a forerunner without a
following. Tonic as may be the effect of his writings on an
admiring student who does not blindly adore, their direct
impress on the literature of the century is almost as

indiscernible as the effect of the seiches in the Lake of Geneva on the level of the water in the Gulf of Lyons.

Yet the artistic value of his best work is of a high order. Professor Saintsbury, echoing Forster, is right in saying that "if we tried to do without Landor, we should lose something with which no one else could supply us"; so is Mr. Crump in saying that at death he left "a gap in literature not yet filled up"; and most especially right is Emerson in calling him "one of the foremost of that small band who make good in the nineteenth century the claims of pure literature." Precisely what meaning attaches to the term "pure literature" does not especially matter. In a vague sort of way Emerson may have been thinking of him as one of those writers whose appeal to the æsthetic sense is so immediate and strong as to leave no place for regret that that is the only appeal they make. Such is, at least, a perfectly legitimate feeling about Landor's best work. His genius for style and his devotion to literature on the æsthetic side give him a position from which all possible talk about high purpose or practical aim, or the like, cannot budge him. Those are side issues of literary criticism. The literature that lasts may or may not have been originally inspired by love of humanity or by other lofty motive. That which has its spring in love of beauty stands at least a fair chance of lasting while man's thirst for art shall remain unquenched.

Landor is impelled by just such love of beauty of form as few people — even educated people — are likely to sympathise with, for his instinct is highly special. Lacking ability to bring large masses into subordination to a controlling purpose, he yet has exceptional skill in expressing his love of beauty of form in detail. Herein resides much of the strong, if circumscribed, originality on which he so plumed himself as to reject ideas or phrases that he suspected himself of having got from other writers, to use only imagery of his own invention, to shun quotation. Shakespeare, indifferent to the source of his material, unblushingly appropriated whatever happened to come to hand. "Yet," as Landor says of him, "he was more original than the originals. He breathed upon dead bodies and brought them into life." His may be regarded as the most broadly human type of originality. Landor's, on the other hand, is near of kin, in its aristocratic fastidiousness, to his constitutional repugnance to the world at large. With an austerity free from the relentless asceticism of Flaubert's style, a sensitiveness less sinuously feminine than that of Newman's, a classic amplitude distinct from the antique scope of Leopardi's, the style of Landor is so exclusively his own, uncopied and inimitable, that it not only scarcely resembles, but seldom even momentarily recalls any other.

Though essences so volatile as the personality and the voice of any style worth analysing elude analysis, yet various remarks of Landor's indicate his aim and define some of the salient features of his own style. "I hate," he says, "false words, and seek with care, difficulty, and moroseness those that fit the thing." His sense of the etymological force and the literary value of words, and his skilful use of a wide and varied vocabulary are foundation stones of his style, which shows as high a regard as Swift's for "proper words in proper places." Such discrimination in the employment of them is a natural result of the intellectual faculty which determines also the logical construction, giving to his sentences, even when stripped of usual connectives, the stable equilibrium and close coherence of Greek architecture, which stands without mortar, through sheer structural propriety in accordance with natural law. For not Flaubert himself gave more solicitous heed to order and proportion, to due distribution of emphasis, to contour of sentence. Many of Landor's sentences are, it is true, too closely modelled on inflected Latin grammatical forms for perfect flexibility in uninflected English; the passion for excision of the superfluous and for compactness leads often to omission of the requisite, and so to discontinuity, abruptness, and even obscurity. But Landor, unlike some writers called obscure, is pretty sure to know his own meaning, however little he may sometimes consider a reader's need of help. In such cases, then, the fundamental logic of construction may usually be relied on to guide an attentive reader through the dark places to a point of sympathy where he can see the beauties. As unerring verbal fitness and unswaying structural firmness are masculine attributes, masculine, too, are those higher beauties appropriate to them. No characteristic of Landor's style is more marked than the abounding wealth of picture words and of fresh concrete imagery — a tissue of simile and of expressed or implied metaphor which forms an integral part of its substance. Sometimes over-elaborated, this figurative language never degenerates into meretricious or merely exterior adornment, but springs naturally from the subject, and gives to the stately pages which might otherwise seem formal and inert the glow of imaginative life; it has interpretative value, too, and tends to lucidity. Rhythmic modulation of parts, clause answering to clause, is the crowning merit, the final charm, contenting the ear as the structural adaptation satisfies the mind, and justifying Landor's maxim that "whatever is rightly said, sounds rightly." Those are, very briefly stated, the main heads under which the mechanism of the style may best be studied. The total effect — so far, at least, as a few inexact adjectives can delineate the impalpable — is of a regulated and succinct style, uniform without mannerism, at once sturdy and rich, euphonious and finely tempered, indefeasibly original both in its merits and in its faults — a style which, even when its kinship to Greek or to Latin is closest, remains always intrinsically English.

It is to be understood that a passage embodying such qualities as those just mentioned, turning up anywhere throughout Landor's writings, is liable at any point to be broken by a dull passage, for his instinct for form and for beauty by no means invariably sustains him to the end of a long flight. Though visible logical structure is seldom lacking, true correlation of parts often is. The musical sentence, "A bell warbles the more mellifluously in the air when the sound of the stroke is over, and when another swims out from underneath it, and pants upon the element that gave it birth," may easily win admiration and nestle in the memory. Yet nothing is more frequent in Landor than that just such a lovely image should be immediately succeeded — as, in fact, this one is — by a comparatively tame explanation or application of the figurative language. The aim of this volume is to show the most characteristic traits of a richly gifted writer whose complete works few readers care to confront. For, though essentially original in substance and varied and charming in detail, the work as a whole is, if not technically, at least in power to hold the attention, uneven. Organic unity throughout a long composition was usually beyond Landor's reach ; rare quality in short passages, or even in passages of several pages, he attains constantly. Those numerous beautiful pages, detached and collected, though incompletely representing his unceasing literary activity, yet suffice permanently to mark his solitary place among the imaginative writers of this century as one of eminent distinction.

Guy de Maupassant draws a picture, tremulous with artistic conviction and personal quality, of the limitation set by a writer's nature on his work. Life, he says, no words can depict; a man can make in words but a partial image of life as he sees it, for each one of us is the dupe of a self-generated illusion. The literary critic's sole business is, then, to point out what illusion of life possesses the writer criticised, and with what success he brings the reader under its spell. Applied in a more general sense than the literary, this theory contains an element of psychologic truth which is strikingly exemplified in the case of Landor, who from boyhood to the end of his life rebelled against life's conditions, and never even tried to learn the lesson of submission to restraint. Strong, noble, ardent, sincere, generous, and high as were his ideals of life and art, he saw life, at any rate, through the smoked glass of his own impetuous temperament. That he "strove with none" is palpably untrue; though it is literally a fact that he thought "none was worth [his] strife," he was, in another sense than Browning, "ever a fighter." His disposition was intractable, his imagination masterful, his originality scornful. Impatience of control ended in isolating the idealist of liberty from his fellows; disdain of the common-place was carried so far as to repel sympathy. Thus did the imp of haughtily autocratic self-reliance sport with this independent genius proudly trusting in his own power, whose work remains the lonely monument to a unique mixture of elements in the man. Destitute of the insinuatingly persuasive strain which was lacking in his temper, but with superb loftiness of bearing, and severe beauty of the type that he most highly prized, Landor's writing finds, alike by its strength and by its weakness, an analogue in his character. Together with much that, though characteristic, is not vital, he fashioned, in conformity to laws imposed only by his own nature and by the nature of his material, certain works of art almost precisely matching his illusion of life.

DATES.

1775. Landor born at Warwick, January 30.
1785. Rugby.
1793. Trinity College, Oxford.
1794. Rusticated.
1795. *Poems.*
1798. *Gebir.*
1800. *Poems from the Arabic and Persian.*
1806. *Simonidea.* (The only copy is in the Forster Collection at the South Kensington Museum.)
1808. Purchases Llanthony Abbey ; joins army in Spain.
1811. Marries Julia Thuillier.
1812. *Count Julian.*
1815. *Idyllia nova quinque Heroum atque Heroidum.*
1820. *Idyllia Heroica decem.*
1824. *Imaginary Conversations of Literary Men and Statesmen,* vols. i. and ii.
1828. *Imaginary Conversations, etc.,* vol. iii.
1829. Villa Gherardesca ; *Imaginary Conversations, etc.,* vols. iv. and v.
1834. *Citation and Examination of William Shakespeare, etc.*
1836. *Pericles and Aspasia.*
1837. *The Pentameron and Pentalogia.*
1839. *Andrea of Hungary,* and *Giovanna of Naples.*
1841. *Fra Rupert.*
1846. Collected Edition of *Works,* including *Hellenics.*
1847. *Poemata et Inscriptiones. The Hellenics, enlarged and completed.*
1853. *Imaginary Conversations of Greeks and Romans. The Last Fruit off an Old Tree.*
1859. *The Hellenics. New edition, enlarged.*
1863. *Heroic Idyls, with additional Poems.*
1864. Dies in Florence, September 17.

SELECTIONS FROM LANDOR.

I claim no place in the world of letters; I am alone; and will be alone, as long as I live, and after.

. LANDOR.

. . . in the life
Where thou art not
We find none like thee.

SWINBURNE.

SELECTIONS FROM LANDOR.

IMAGINARY CONVERSATIONS.

I.

ACHILLES AND HELENA.

Helena.   Where am I?   Desert me not, O ye blessed from above! ye twain who brought me hither!

Was it a dream?

Stranger! thou seemest thoughtful; couldst thou answer me?   Why so silent?   I beseech and implore thee, speak.

Achilles.   Neither thy feet nor the feet of mules have borne thee where thou standest.   Whether in the hour of departing sleep, or at what hour of the morning, I know not, O Helena! but Aphroditè and Thetis, inclining to my prayer, have, as thou art conscious, led thee into these solitudes.   To me also have they shown the way, that I might behold the pride of Sparta, the marvel of the earth, and — how my heart swells and agonizes at the thought! — the cause of innumerable woes to Hellas.

Helena.   Stranger! thou art indeed one whom the goddesses or gods might lead, and glory in; such is thy stature, thy voice, and thy demeanour; but who, if earthly, art thou?

Achilles.   Before thee, O Helena! stands Achilles, son of Peleus.   Tremble not, turn not pale, bend not thy knees, O Helena!

Helena.   Spare me, thou goddess-born! thou cherished and only son of silver-footed Thetis! Chryseïs and Briseïs ought to soften and content thy heart. Lead not me also into captivity. Woes too surely have I brought down on Hellas; but woes have been mine alike, and will for ever be.

Achilles.   Daughter of Zeus! what word hast thou spoken! Chryseïs, child of the aged priest who performs in this land due sacrifices to Apollo, fell to the lot of another; an insolent and unworthy man, who hath already brought more sorrows upon our people than thou hast; so that dogs and vultures prey on the brave who sank without a wound. Briseïs is indeed mine; the lovely and dutiful Briseïs. He, unjust and contumelious, proud at once and base, would tear her from me. But, gods above! in what region has the wolf with impunity dared to seize upon the kid which the lion hath taken?

Talk not of being led into servitude. Could mortal be guilty of such impiety? Hath it never thundered on these mountain-heads? Doth Zeus, the wide-seeing, see all the earth but Ida? doth he watch over all but his own? Capaneus and Typhöeus less offended him, than would the wretch whose grasp should violate the golden hair of Helena. And dost thou still tremble? irresolute and distrustful!

Helena.   I must tremble; and more and more.

Achilles.   Take my hand: be confident; be comforted.

Helena.   May I take it? may I hold it? I am comforted.

Achilles.   The scene around us, calm and silent as the sky itself, tranquillizes thee; and so it ought. Turnest thou to survey it? perhaps it is unknown to thee.

Helena.   Truly; for since my arrival I have never gone beyond the walls of the city.

Achilles. Look then around thee freely, perplexed no longer. Pleasant is this level eminence, surrounded by broom and myrtle, and crisp-leaved beech and broad dark pine above. Pleasant the short slender grass, bent by insects as they alight on it or climb along it, and shining up into our eyes, interrupted by tall sisterhoods of gray lavender, and by dark-eyed cistus, and by lightsome citisus, and by little troops of serpolet running in disorder here and there.

Helena. Wonderful! how didst thou ever learn to name so many plants?

Achilles. Chiron taught me them, when I walked at his side while he was culling herbs for the benefit of his brethren. All these he taught me, and at least twenty more; for wondrous was his wisdom, boundless his knowledge, and I was proud to learn.

Ah, look again! look at those little yellow poppies; they appear to be just come out to catch all that the sun will throw into their cups: they appear in their joyance and incipient dance to call upon the lyre to sing among them.

Helena. Childish! for one with such a spear against his shoulder; terrific even its shadow: it seems to make a chasm across the plain.

Achilles. To talk or to think like a child is not always a proof of folly: it may sometimes push aside heavy griefs where the strength of wisdom fails. What art thou pondering, Helena?

Helena. Recollecting the names of the plants. Several of them I do believe I had heard before, but had quite forgotten; my memory will be better now.

Achilles. Better now? in the midst of war and tumult?

Helena. I am sure it will be, for didst thou not say that Chiron taught them?

Achilles.   He sang to me over the lyre the lives of Narcissus and Hyacynthus, brought back by the beautiful Hours, of silent unwearied feet, regular as the stars in their courses.   Many of the trees and bright-eyed flowers once lived and moved, and spoke as we are speaking. They may yet have memories, although they have cares no longer.

Helena.   Ah! then they have no memories; and they see their own beauty only.

Achilles.   Helena! thou turnest pale, and droopest.

Helena.   The odour of the blossoms, or of the gums, or the height of the place, or something else, makes me dizzy. Can it be the wind in my ears?

Achilles.   There is none.

Helena.   I could wish there were a little.

Achilles.   Be seated, O Helena!

Helena.   The feeble are obedient; the weary may rest even in the presence of the powerful.

Achilles.   On this very ground where we are now reposing, they who conducted us hither told me, the fatal prize of beauty was awarded.   One of them smiled the other, whom in duty I love the most, looked anxious, and let fall some tears.

Helena.   Yet she was not one of the vanquished.

Achilles.   Goddesses contended for it; Helena was afar.

Helena.   Fatal was the decision of the arbiter!

But could not the venerable Peleus, nor Pyrrhus the infant so beautiful and so helpless, detain thee, O Achilles, from this sad, sad war?

Achilles.   No reverence or kindness for the race of Atreus brought me against Troy : I detest and abhor both brothers; but another man is more hateful to me still.   Forbear we to name him.   The valiant, holding the hearth as sacred as the temple, is never a violator of hospitality.   He carries not away the gold he finds in the house; he folds not up the purple linen worked for solemnities, about to convey it from the cedar chest to the dark ship, together with the wife confided to his protection in her husband's absence, and sitting close and expectant by the altar of the gods.

It was no merit in Menelaüs to love thee; it was a crime in another — I will not say to love, for even Priam or Nestor might love thee — but to avow it, and act on the avowal.

Helena.　Menelaüs, it is true, was fond of me, when Paris was sent by Aphroditè to our house. It would have been very wrong to break my vow to Menelaüs; but Aphroditè urged me by day and by night, telling me that to make her break hers to Paris would be quite inexpiable. She told Paris the same thing at the same hour; and as often. He repeated it to me every morning: his dreams tallied with mine exactly. At last —

Achilles.　The last is not yet come. Helena, by the Immortals! if ever I meet him in battle I transfix him with this spear.

Helena.　Pray do not. Aphroditè would be angry and never forgive thee.

Achilles.　I am not sure of that; she soon pardons. Variable as Iris, one day she favours and the next day she forsakes.

Helena.　She may then forsake *me.*

Achilles.　Other deities, O Helena, watch over and protect thee. Thy two brave brothers are with those deities now, and never are absent from their higher festivals.

Helena.　They could protect me were they living, and they would. Oh that thou couldst but have seen them!

Achilles.　Companions of my father on the borders of the Phasis, they became his guests before they went all three to hunt the boar in the brakes of Kalydon. Thence too the beauty of a woman brought many sorrows into brave men's breasts, and caused many tears to hang long and heavily on the eyelashes of matrons.

Helena.   Horrible creatures !— boars I mean.

Didst thou indeed see my brothers at that season?   Yes, certainly.

Achilles.   I saw them not, desirous though I always was of seeing them, that I might have learned from them, and might have practised with them, whatever is laudable and manly.. But my father, fearing my impetuosity, as he said, and my inexperience, sent me away. Soothsayers had foretold some mischief to me from an arrow: and among the brakes many arrows might fly wide, glancing from trees.

Helena.   I wish thou hadst seen them, were it only once. Three such youths together the blessed sun will never shine upon again.

O my sweet brothers! how they tended me! how they loved me! how often they wished me to mount their horses and to hurl their javelins ! They could only teach me to swim with them; and when I had well learned it I was more afraid than at first. It gratified me to be praised for anything but swimming.

Happy, happy hours ! soon over! Does happiness always go away before beauty? It must go then: surely it might stay that little while.   Alas ! dear Kastor! and dearer Polydeukès! often shall I think of you as ye were (and oh ! as I was) on the banks of the Eurotas.

Brave, noble creatures ! they were as tall, as terrible, and almost as beautiful, as thou art. Be not wroth! Blush no more for me !

Achilles.   Helena ! Helena ! wife of Menelaüs ! my mother is reported to have left about me only one place vulnerable: I have at last found where it is.   Farewell !

Helena. Oh leave me not! Earnestly I entreat and implore thee, leave me not alone! These solitudes are terrible: there must be wild beasts among them; there certainly are Fauns and Satyrs. And there is Cybelè, who carries towers and temples on her head; who hates and abhors Aphroditè, who persecutes those *she* favours, and whose priests are so cruel as to be cruel even to themselves.

Achilles. According to their promise, the goddesses who brought thee hither in a cloud will in a cloud reconduct thee, safely and unseen, into the city.

Again, O daughter of Leda and of Zeus, farewell!

II.

ÆSOP AND RHODOPE.

Rhodopè. You perplex me exceedingly; but I would not disquiet you at present with more questions. Let mé pause and consider a little, if you please. I begin to suspect that, as gods formerly did, you have been turning men into beasts, and beasts into men. But, Æsop, you should never say the thing that is untrue.

Æsop. We say and do and look no other all our lives.

Rhodopè. Do we never know better?

Æsop. Yes; when we cease to please, and to wish it; when death is settling the features, and the cerements are ready to render them unchangeable.

Rhodopè. Alas! alas!

Æsop. Breathe, Rhodopè! breathe again those painless sighs: they belong to thy vernal season. May thy summer of life be calm, thy autumn calmer, and thy winter never come!

Rhodopè. I must die then earlier.

Æsop. Laodameia died; Helen died; Leda, the beloved of Jupiter, went before. It is better to repose in the earth betimes than to sit up late; better, than to cling pertinaciously to what we feel crumbling under us, and to protract an inevitable fall. We may enjoy the present while we are insensible of infirmity and decay : but the present, like a note of music, is nothing but as it appertains to what is past and what is to come. There are no fields of amaranth on this side of the grave ; there are no voices, O Rhodopè, that are not soon mute, however tuneful; there is no name, with whatever emphasis of passionate love repeated, of which the echo is not faint at last.

Rhodopè. O Æsop! let me rest my head on yours : it throbs and pains me.

Æsop. What are these ideas to thee ?

Rhodopè. Sad, sorrowful.

Æsop. Harrows that break the soil, preparing it for wisdom. Many flowers must perish ere a grain of corn be ripened. And now remove thy head : the cheek is cool enough after its little shower of tears.

Rhodopè. How impatient you are of the least pressure !

Æsop. There is nothing so difficult to support imperturbably as the head of a lovely girl, except her grief. Again upon mine, forgetful one ! Raise it, remove it, I say! Why wert thou reluctant ? why wert thou disobedient ? Nay, look not so. It is I (and thou shalt know it) who should look reproachfully.

Rhodopè. Reproachfully? did I ? I was only wishing you would love me better, that I might come and see you often.

Æsop. Come often and see me, if thou wilt ; but expect no love from me.

Rhodopè. Yet how gently and gracefully you have spoken and acted, all the time we have been together. You have rendered the most abstruse things intelligible, without once grasping my hand, or putting your fingers among my curls.

Æsop. I should have feared to encounter the displeasure of two persons if I had.

Rhodopè. And well you might. They would scourge you, and scold me.

Æsop. That is not the worst.

Rhodopè. The stocks too, perhaps.

Æsop. All these are small matters to the slave.

Rhodopè. If they befell you, I would tear my hair and my cheeks, and put my knees under your ancles. Of whom should you have been afraid?

Æsop. Of Rhodopè and of Æsop. Modesty in man, O Rhodopè, is perhaps the rarest and most difficult of virtues : but intolerable pain is the pursuer of its infringement. Then follow days without content, nights without sleep, throughout a stormy season ; a season of impetuous deluge which no fertility succeeds.

Rhodopè. My mother often told me to learn modesty, when I was at play among the boys.

Æsop. Modesty in girls is not an acquirement, but a gift of nature; and it costs as much trouble and pain in the possessor to eradicate, as the fullest and firmest lock of hair would do.

Rhodopè. Never shall I be induced to believe that men at all value it in themselves, or much in us ; although from idleness or from rancour they would take it away from us whenever they can.

Æsop. And very few of you are pertinacious : if you run after them, as you often do, it is not to get it back.

Rhodopè. I would never run after any one, not even you; I would only ask you, again and again, to love me.

Æsop. Expect no love from me. I will impart to thee all my wisdom, such as it is: but girls like our folly best. Thou shalt never get a particle of mine from me.

Rhodopè. Is love foolish?

Æsop.   At thy age and at mine.   I do not love thee: if I did, I would the more forbid thee ever to love *me.*

Rhodopè.   Strange man!

Æsop.   Strange, indeed!   When a traveller is about to wander on a desert, it is strange to lead him away from it; strange to point out to him the verdant path he should pursue, where the tamarisk and lentisk and acacia wave overhead, where the reseda is cool and tender to the foot that presses it, and where a thousand colours sparkle in the sunshine, on fountains incessantly gushing forth.

Rhodopè.   Xanthus has all these; and I could be amid them in a moment.

Æsop.   Why art not thou?

Rhodopè.   I know not exactly.   Another day perhaps. I am afraid of snakes this morning.   Beside, I think it may be sultry out of doors.   Does not the wind blow from Libya?

Æsop.   It blows as it did yesterday when I came over, fresh across the Ægean, and from Thrace.   Thou mayest venture into the morning air.

Rhodopè.   No hours are so adapted to study as those of the morning.   But will you teach me?   I shall so love you if you will.

Æsop.   If thou wilt *not* love me, I will teach thee.

Rhodopè.   Unreasonable man!

Æsop.   Art thou aware what those mischievous little hands are doing?

Rhodopè.   They are tearing off the golden hem from the bottom of my robe; but it is stiff and difficult to detach.

Æsop.   Why tear it off?

Rhodopè.   To buy your freedom.   Do you spring up, and turn away, and cover your face from me?

Æsop.   My freedom!   Go, Rhodopè!   Rhodopè!   This, of all things, I shall never owe to thee.

Rhodopè. Proud man! and you tell me to go, do you? do you? Answer me at least! Must I? and so soon?

Æsop. Child! begone!

Rhodopè. O Æsop! you are already more my master than Xanthus is. I will run and tell him so; and I will implore of him, upon my knees, never to impose on *you* a command so hard to obey.

*   *   *   *

Æsop. Recollect a little. I can be patient with this hand in mine.

Rhodopè. I am not certain that yours is any help to recollection.

Æsop. Shall I remove it?

Rhodopè. O! now I think I can recall the whole story. What did you say? did you ask any question?

Æsop. None, excepting what thou hast answered.

Rhodopè. Never shall I forget the morning when my father, sitting in the coolest part of the house, exchanged his last measure of grain for a chlamys of scarlet cloth fringed with silver. He watched the merchant out of the door, and then looked wistfully into the corn-chest. I, who thought there was something worth seeing, looked in also, and, finding it empty, expressed my disappointment, not thinking however about the corn. A faint and transient smile came over his countenance at the sight of mine. He unfolded the chlamys, stretched it out with both hands before me, and then cast it over my shoulders. I looked down on the glittering fringe and screamed with joy. He then went out; and I know not what flowers he gathered, but he gathered many; and some he placed in my bosom, and some in my hair. But I told him with captious pride, first that I could arrange them better, and again that I would have only the white. However, when he had selected all the white, and I had placed a few of them according to my fancy, I told him (rising in my slipper) he might crown me with the remainder. The splendour of my apparel gave me a sensation of authority. Soon as the flowers had taken their station on my head, I expressed a dignified satisfaction at the taste displayed by my father, just as if I could have seen how they appeared! But he knew that there was at least as much pleasure as pride in it, and perhaps we divided the latter (alas! not both) pretty equally. He now took me into the market place, where a concourse of people was waiting for the purchase of slaves. Merchants came and looked at me; some commending, others disparaging; but all agreeing that I was slender and delicate, that I could not live long, and that I should give much trouble. Many would have bought the chlamys, but there was something less saleable in the child and flowers.

Æsop. Had thy features been coarse and thy voice rustic, they would all have patted thy cheeks and found no fault in thee.

Rhodopè. As it was, every one had bought exactly such another in time past, and been a loser by it. At these speeches I perceived the flowers tremble slightly on my bosom, from my father's agitation. Although he scoffed at them, knowing my healthiness, he was troubled internally, and said many short prayers, not very unlike imprecations, turning his head aside. Proud was I, prouder than ever, when at last several talents were offered for me, and by the very man who in the beginning had undervalued me the most, and prophesied the worst of me. My father scowled at him, and refused the money. I thought he was playing a game, and began to wonder what it could be, since I never had seen it played before. Then I fancied it might be some celebration because plenty had returned to the city, insomuch that my father had bartered the last of the corn he hoarded. I grew more and more delighted at the sport. But soon there advanced an elderly man, who said gravely, "Thou hast stolen this child: her vesture alone is worth above a hundred drachmas. Carry her home again to her parents, and do it directly, or Nemesis and the Eumenides will overtake thee." Knowing the estimation in which my father had always been holden by his fellow-citizens, I laughed again, and pinched his ear. He, although naturally choleric, burst forth into no resentment at these reproaches, but said calmly, "I think I know thee by name, O guest! Surely thou art Xanthus the Samian. Deliver this child from famine."

Again I laughed aloud and heartily; and, thinking it was now my part of the game, I held out both my arms and protruded my whole body towards the stranger. He would not receive me from my father's neck, but he asked me with benignity and solicitude if I was hungry; at which I laughed again, and more than ever: for it was early in the morning, soon after the first meal, and my father had nourished me most carefully and plentifully in all the days of the famine. But Xanthus, waiting for no answer, took out of a sack, which one of his slaves carried at his side, a cake of wheaten bread and a piece of honey-comb, and gave them to me. I held the honey-comb to my father's mouth, thinking it the most of a dainty. He dashed it to the ground; but, seizing the bread, he began to devour it ferociously. This also I thought was in play; and I clapped my hands at his distortions. But Xanthus looked on him like one afraid, and smote the cake from him, crying aloud, "Name the price." My father now placed me in his arms, naming a price much below what the other had offered, saying, "The gods are ever with thee, O Xanthus! therefore to thee do I consign my child." But while Xanthus was counting out the silver, my father seized the cake again, which the slave had taken up and was about to replace in the wallet. His hunger was exasperated by the taste and the delay. Suddenly there arose much tumult. Turning round in the old woman's bosom who had received me from Xanthus, I saw my beloved father struggling on the ground, livid and speechless. The more violent my cries, the more rapidly they hurried me away; and many were soon between us. Little was I suspicious that he had suffered the pangs of famine long before: alas! and he had suffered them for me. Do I weep while I am telling you they ended? I could not have closed his eyes; I was too young: but I might have received his last breath, the only comfort of an' orphan's bosom. Do you now think him blamable, O Æsop?

Æsop. It was sublime humanity: it was forbearance and self-denial which even the immortal gods have never shown us. He could endure to perish by those torments which alone are both acute and slow; he could number the steps of death and miss not one: but he could never see thy tears, nor let thee see his. O weakness above all fortitude! Glory to the man who rather bears a grief corroding his breast, than permits it to prowl beyond, and to prey on the tender and compassionate! Women commiserate the brave, and men the beautiful. The dominion of Pity has usually this extent, no wider. Thy father was exposed to the obloquy not only of the malicious, but also of the ignorant and thoughtless, who condemn in the unfortunate what they applaud in the prosperous. There is no shame in poverty or in slavery, if we neither make ourselves poor by our improvidence nor slaves by our venality. The lowest and highest of the human race are sold: most of the intermediate are also slaves, but slaves who bring no money in the market.

Rhodopè. Surely the great and powerful are never to be purchased, are they?

Æsop. It may be a defect in my vision, but I cannot see

greatness on the earth.   What they tell me is great and aspiring, to me seems little and crawling.   Let me meet thy question with another.   What monarch gives his daughter for nothing?   Either he receives stone walls and unwilling cities in return, or he barters her for a parcel of spears and horses and horsemen, waving away from his declining and helpless age young joyous life, and trampling down the freshest and the sweetest memories.   Midas in the height of prosperity would have given his daughter to Lycaon, rather than to the gentlest, the most virtuous, the most intelligent of his subjects.   Thy father threw wealth aside, and, placing thee under the protection of Virtue, rose up from the house of Famine to partake in the festivals of the gods.

Release my neck, O Rhodopè! for I have other questions to ask of thee about him.

Rhodopè.   To hear thee converse on him in such a manner, I can do even that.

Æsop.   Before the day of separation was he never sorrowful?   Did he never by tears or silence reveal the secret of his soul?

Rhodopè.   I was too infantine to perceive or imagine his intention.   The night before I became the slave of Xanthus, he sat on the edge of my bed.   I pretended to be asleep: he moved away silently and softly.   I saw him collect in the hollow of his hand the crumbs I had wasted on the floor, and then eat them, and then look if any were remaining. I thought he did so out of fondness for me, remembering that, even before the famine, he had often swept up off the table the bread I had broken, and had made me put it between his lips.   I would not dissemble very long, but said,—

"Come, now you have wakened me, you must sing me asleep again, as you did when I was little."

He smiled faintly at this, and, after some delay, when he had walked up and down the chamber, thus began:—

"I will sing to thee one song more, my wakeful Rhodopè! my chirping bird! over whom is no mother's wing! That it may lull thee asleep, I will celebrate no longer, as in the days of wine and plenteousness, the glory of Mars, guiding in their invisibly rapid onset the dappled steeds of Rhæsus. What hast thou to do, my little one, with arrows tired of clustering in the quiver? How much quieter is thy pallet than the tents which whitened the plain of Simöis? What knowest thou about the river Eurotas? What knowest thou about its ancient palace, once trodden by assembled gods, and then polluted by the Phrygian? What knowest thou of perfidious men or of sanguinary deeds?

"Pardon me, O goddess who presidest in Cythera! I am not irreverent to thee, but ever grateful. May she upon whose brow I lay my hand praise and bless thee for evermore!

"Ah yes! continue to hold up above the coverlet those fresh and rosy palms clasped together: her benefits have descended on thy beauteous head, my child! The Fates also have sung, beyond thy hearing, of pleasanter scenes than snow-fed Hebrus; of more than dim grottoes and sky-bright waters. Even now a low murmur swells upward to my ear: and not from the spindle comes the sound, but from those who sing slowly over it, bending all three their tremulous heads together. I wish thou could'st hear it; for seldom are their voices so sweet. Thy pillow intercepts the song perhaps: lie down again, lie down, my Rhodopè! I will repeat what they are saying:—

"'Happier shalt thou be, nor less glorious, than even she, the truly beloved, for whose return to the distaff and the lyre the portals of Tænarus flew open. In the woody dells of Ismarus, and when she bathed among the swans of Strymon, the nymphs called her Eurydicè. Thou shalt behold that fairest and that fondest one hereafter. But first thou must go unto the land of the lotos, where famine never cometh, and where alone the works of man are immortal.'

"O my child! the undeceiving Fates have uttered this. Other powers have visited me, and have strengthened my heart with dreams and visions. We shall meet again, my Rhodopè! in shady groves and verdant meadows, and we shall sit by the side of those who loved us."

He was rising: I threw my arms about his neck, and, before I would let him go, I made him promise to place me, not by the side, but between them; for I thought of her who had left us. At that time there were but two, O Æsop!

You ponder: you are about to reprove my assurance in having thus repeated my own praises. I would have omitted some of the words, only that it might have disturbed the measure and cadences, and have put me out. They are the very words my dearest father sang; and they are the last. Yet, shame upon me! the nurse (the same who stood listening near, who attended me into this country) could remember them more perfectly: it is from her I have learned them since; she often sings them, even by herself.

III.

TIBERIUS AND VIPSANIA.

Tiberius. Vipsania, my Vipsania, whither art thou walking?

Vipsania. Whom do I see? — my Tiberius?

Tiberius. Ah! no, no, no! but thou seest the father of thy little Drusus. Press him to thy heart the more closely for this meeting, and give him —

Vipsania. Tiberius! the altars, the gods, the destinies, are between us — I will take it from this hand; thus, thus shall he receive it.

Tiberius. Raise up thy face, my beloved! I must not shed tears. Augustus! Livia! ye shall not extort them from me. Vipsania! I may kiss thy head — for I have saved it. Thou sayest nothing. I have wronged thee; ay?

Vipsania. Ambition does not see the earth she treads on; the rock and the herbage are of one substance to her. Let me excuse you to my heart, O Tiberius. It has many wants; this is the first and greatest.

Tiberius. My ambition, I swear by the immortal gods, placed not the bar of severance between us. A stronger hand, the hand that composes Rome and sways the world —

Vipsania. — Overawed Tiberius. I know it; Augustus willed and commanded it.

Tiberius. And overawed Tiberius! Power bent, Death terrified, a Nero! What is our race, that any should look down on us and spurn us? Augustus, my benefactor, I have wronged thee! Livia, my mother, this one cruel deed was thine! To reign, forsooth, is a lovely thing. O womanly appetite! Who would have been before me, though the palace of Cæsar cracked and split with emperors, while I, sitting in idleness on a cliff of Rhodes, eyed the sun as he swang his golden censer athwart the heavens, or his image as it overstrode the sea? I have it before me; and, though it seems falling on me, I can smile at it, — just as I did from my little favourite skiff, painted round with the marriage of Thetis, when the sailors drew their long shaggy hair across their eyes, many a stadium away from it, to mitigate its effulgence.

These too were happy days: days of happiness like these I could recall and look back upon with unaching brow.

O land of Greece! Tiberius blesses thee, bidding thee rejoice and flourish.

Why cannot one hour, Vipsania, beauteous and light as we have led, return?

Vipsania.　Tiberius! is it to me that you were speaking?
I would not interrupt you; but I thought I heard my name
as you walked away and looked up toward the East. So
silent!

Tiberius.　Who dared to call thee? Thou wert mine
before the gods — do they deny it? Was it my fault —

Vipsania.　Since we are separated, and for ever, O
Tiberius, let us think no more on the cause of it. Let
neither of us believe that the other was to blame: so shall
separation be less painful.

Tiberius.　O mother! and did I not tell thee what she
was? — patient in injury, proud in innocence, serene in
grief!

Vipsania.　Did you say that too? But I think it was so :
I had felt little. One vast wave has washed away the impression of smaller from my memory. Could Livia, could
your mother, could she who was so kind to me —

Tiberius.　The wife of Cæsar did it. But hear me now!
hear me: be calm as I am. No weaknesses are such as
those of a mother who loves her only son immoderately;
and none are so easily worked upon from without. Who
knows what impulses she received? She is very, very
kind; but she regards me only, and that which at her bidding is to encompass and adorn me. All the weak look
after Power, protectress of weakness. Thou art a woman,
O Vipsania! is there nothing in thee to excuse my mother?
So good she ever was to me! so loving.

Vipsania.　I quite forgive her: be tranquil, O Tiberius!

Tiberius.　Never can I know peace — never can I pardon
— any one. Threaten me with thy exile, thy separation,
thy seclusion! Remind me that another climate might
endanger thy health! — There death met me and turned me
round. Threaten me to take our son from us, — our one
boy, our helpless little one, — him whom we made cry

because we kissed him both together!   Rememberest thou?
Or dost thou not hear? turning thus away from me!

Vipsania.   I hear; I hear.   Oh cease, my sweet Tiberius!
Stamp not upon that stone : my heart lies under it.

Tiberius.   Ay, there again death, and more than death,
stood before me.   Oh she maddened me, my mother did,
she maddened me — she threw me to where I am at one
breath.   The gods cannot replace me where I was, nor
atone to me, nor console me, nor restore my senses.   To
whom can I fly? to whom can I open my heart? to whom
speak plainly?   There was upon the earth a man I could
converse with and fear nothing ; there was a woman too I
could love, and fear nothing.   What a soldier, what a
Roman, was thy father, O my young bride!   How could
those who never saw him have discoursed so rightly upon
virtue!

Vipsania.   These words cool my breast like pressing his
urn against it.   He was brave: shall Tiberius want courage?

Tiberius.   My enemies scorn me.   I am a garland dropped
from a triumphal car, and taken up and looked on for the
place I occupied ; and tossed away and laughed at.   Senators! laugh, laugh!   Your merits may be yet rewarded — be
of good cheer!   Counsel me, in your wisdom, what services
I can render you, conscript fathers !

Vipsania.   This seems mockery: Tiberius did not smile
so, once.

Tiberius.   They had not then congratulated me.

Vipsania.   On what?

Tiberius.   And it was not because she was beautiful, as
they thought her, and virtuous, as I know she is; but
because the flowers on the altar were to be tied together by
my heart-string.   On this they congratulated me.   Their
day will come.   Their sons and daughters are what I would
wish them to be : worthy to succeed them.

Vipsania. Where is that quietude, that resignation, that sanctity, that heart of true tenderness?

Tiberius. Where is my love? — my love?

Vipsania. Cry not thus aloud, Tiberius! there is an echo in the place. Soldiers and slaves may burst in upon us.

Tiberius. And see my tears? There is no echo, Vipsania; why alarm and shake me so? We are too high here for the echoes: the city is below us. Methinks it trembles and totters: would it did! from the marble quays of the Tiber to this rock. There is a strange buzz and murmur in my brain; but I should listen so intensely, I should hear the rattle of its roofs, and shout with joy.

Vipsania. Calm, O my life! calm this horrible transport.

Tiberius. Spake I so loud? Did I indeed then send my voice after a lost sound, to bring it back; and thou fanciedest it an echo? Wilt not thou laugh with me, as thou wert wont to do, at such an error? What was I saying to thee, my tender love, when I commanded — I know not whom — to stand back, on pain of death? Why starest thou on me in such agony? Have I hurt thy fingers, child? I loose them; now let me look! Thou turnest thine eyes away from me. Oh! oh! I hear my crime! Immortal gods! I cursed then audibly, and before the sun, my mother!

IV.

METELLUS AND MARIUS.

Metellus. Well met, Caius Marius! My orders are to find instantly a centurion who shall mount the walls; one capable of observation, acute in remark, prompt, calm, active, intrepid. The Numantians are sacrificing to the gods in secrecy; they have sounded the horn once only, — and hoarsely, and low, and mournfully.

Marius. Was that ladder I see yonder among the caper-bushes and purple lilies, under where the fig-tree grows out of the rampart, left for me?

Metellus. Even so, wert thou willing. Wouldst thou mount it?

Marius. Rejoicingly. If none are below or near, may I explore the state of things by entering the city?

Metellus. Use thy discretion in that.

What seest thou? Wouldst thou leap down? Lift the ladder.

Marius. Are there spikes in it where it sticks in the turf? I should slip else.

Metellus. How! bravest of our centurions, art even thou afraid? Seest thou any one by?

Marius. Ay; some hundreds close beneath me.

Metellus. Retire, then. Hasten back; I will protect thy descent.

Marius. May I speak, O Metellus, without an offence to discipline?

Metellus. Say.

Marius. Listen! Dost thou not hear?

Metellus. Shame on thee! alight, alight! my shield shall cover thee.

Marius. There is a murmur like the hum of bees in the beanfield of Cereate;* for the sun is hot, and the ground is thirsty. When will it have drunk up for me the blood that has run, and is yet oozing on it, from those fresh bodies!

Metellus. How! We have not fought for many days; what bodies, then, are fresh ones?

Marius. Close beneath the wall are those of infants and of girls; in the middle of the road are youths, emaciated; some either unwounded or wounded months ago; some on their spears, others on their swords: no few have received

* The farm of Marius, near Arpinum.

in mutual death the last interchange of friendship; their
daggers unite them, hilt to hilt, bosom to bosom.

Metellus. Mark rather the living, — what are they about?

Marius. About the sacrifice, which portends them, I
conjecture, but little good, — it burns sullenly and slowly.
The victim will lie upon the pyre till morning, and still be
unconsumed, unless they bring more fuel.

I will leap down and walk on cautiously, and return with
tidings, if death should spare me.

Never was any race of mortals so unmilitary as these
Numantians: no watch, no stations, no palisades across the
streets.

Metellus. Did they want, then, all the wood for the
altar?

Marius. It appears so, — I will return anon.

Metellus. The gods speed thee, my brave, honest
Marius!

Marius (returned). The ladder should have been better
spiked for that slippery ground. I am down again safe,
however. Here a man may walk securely, and without
picking his steps.

Metellus. Tell me, Caius, what thou sawest.

Marius. The streets of Numantia.

Metellus. Doubtless; but what else?

Marius. The temples and markets and places of exercise and fountains.

Metellus. Art thou crazed, centurion? what more? Speak
plainly, at once, and briefly.

Marius. I beheld, then, all Numantia.

Metellus. Has terror maddened thee? hast thou descried
nothing of the inhabitants but those carcasses under the
ramparts?

Marius. Those, O Metellus, lie scattered, although not
indeed far asunder. The greater part of the soldiers and

citizens — of the fathers, husbands, widows, wives, espoused — were assembled together.

Metellus.   About the altar?

Marius.   Upon it.

Metellus.   So busy and earnest in devotion! but how all upon it?

Marius.   It blazed under them, and over them, and round about them.

Metellus.   Immortal gods!   Art thou sane, Caius Marius? Thy visage is scorched: thy speech may wander after such an enterprise; thy shield burns my hand.

Marius.   I thought it had cooled again.   Why, truly, it seems hot: I now feel it.

Metellus.   Wipe off those embers. ·

Marius.   'T were better: there will be none opposite to shake them upon, for some time.

The funereal horn, that sounded with such feebleness, sounded not so from the faint heart of him who blew it. Him I saw; him only of the living.   Should I say it? there was another: there was one child whom its parent could not kill, could not part from.   She had hidden it in her robe, I suspect; and, when the fire had reached it, either it shrieked or she did.   For suddenly a cry pierced through the crackling pinewood, and something of round in figure fell from brand to brand, until it reached the pavement, at the feet of him who had blown the horn.   I rushed toward him, for I wanted to hear the whole story, and felt the pressure of time.   Condemn not my weakness, O Cæcilius! I wished an enemy to live an hour longer ; for my orders were to explore and bring intelligence.   When I gazed on him, in height almost gigantic, I wondered not that the blast of his trumpet was so weak: rather did I wonder that Famine, whose hand had indented every limb and feature, had left him any voice articulate.   I rushed toward him, however, ere my eyes had measured either his form or strength. He held the child against me, and staggered under it.

"Behold," he exclaimed, "the glorious ornament of a Roman triumph!"

I stood horror-stricken; when suddenly drops, as of rain, pattered down from the pyre. I looked; and many were the precious stones, many were the amulets and rings and bracelets, and other barbaric ornaments, unknown to me in form or purpose, that tinkled on the hardened and black branches, from mothers and wives and betrothed maids; and some, too, I can imagine, from robuster arms, — things of joyance, won in battle. The crowd of incumbent bodies was so dense and heavy, that neither the fire nor the smoke could penetrate upward from among them; and they sank, whole and at once, into the smouldering cavern eaten out below. He at whose neck hung the trumpet felt this, and started.

"There is yet room," he cried, "and there is strength enough yet, both in the element and in me."

He extended his withered arms, he thrust forward the gaunt links of his throat, and upon gnarled knees, that smote each other audibly, tottered into the civic fire. It — like some hungry and strangest beast' on the innermost wild of Africa, pierced, broken, prostrate, motionless, gazed at by its hunter in the impatience of glory, in the delight of awe — panted once more, and seized him.

I have seen within this hour, O Metellus, what Rome in the cycle of her triumphs will never see, what the Sun in his eternal course can never show her, what the Earth has borne but now, and must never rear again for her, what Victory herself has envied her — a Numantian.

Metellus. We shall feast to-morrow. Hope, Caius Marius, to become a tribune : trust in fortune.

Marius.   Auguries are surer: surest of all is perseverance.

Metellus.   I hope the wine has not grown vapid in my tent: I have kept it waiting, and must now report to Scipio the intelligence of our discovery.   Come after me, Caius.

Marius (alone).   The tribune is the discoverer! the centurion is the scout!   Caius Marius must enter more Numantias.   Light-hearted Cæcilius, thou mayest perhaps hereafter, and not with humbled but with exulting pride, take orders from this hand.   If Scipio's words are fate, and to me they sound so, the portals of the Capitol may shake before my chariot, as my horses plunge back at the applauses of the people, and Jove in his high domicile may welcome the citizen of Arpinum.

V.

MARCELLUS AND HANNIBAL.

Hannibal.   Could a Numidian horseman ride no faster? Marcellus! ho! Marcellus!   He moves not — he is dead. Did he not stir his fingers?   Stand wide, soldiers — wide, forty paces — give him air — bring water — halt!   Gather those broad leaves, and all the rest, growing under the brushwood — unbrace his armour.   Loose the helmet first — his breast rises.   I fancied his eyes were fixed on me — they have rolled back again.   Who presumed to touch my shoulder?   This horse?   It was surely the horse of Marcellus!   Let no man mount him.   Ha! ha! the Romans too sink into luxury: here is gold about the charger.

Gaulish Chieftain.   Execrable thief!   The golden chain of our king under a beast's grinders!   The vengeance of the gods hath overtaken the impure —

Hannibal.   We will talk about vengeance when we have entered Rome, and about purity among the priests, if they will hear us.   Sound for the surgeon.   That arrow may be extracted from the side, deep as it is. — The conqueror of Syracuse lies before me. — Send a vessel off to Carthage. Say Hannibal is at the gates of Rome. — Marcellus, who stood alone between us, fallen. Brave man! I would rejoice and cannot. — How awfully serene a countenance! Such as we hear are in the islands of the Blessed. And how glorious a form and stature! Such too was theirs! They also once lay thus upon the earth wet with their blood — few other enter there. And what plain armour!

Gaulish Chieftain. My party slew him — indeed I think I slew him myself. I claim the chain: it belongs to my king: the glory of Gaul requires it. Never will she endure to see another take it: rather would she lose her last man. We swear! we swear!

Hannibal. My friend, the glory of Marcellus did not require him to wear it. When he suspended the arms of your brave king in the temple, he thought such a trinket unworthy of himself and of Jupiter. The shield he battered down, the breast-plate he pierced with his sword, — these he showed to the people and to the gods; hardly his wife and little children saw this, ere his horse wore it.

Gaulish Chieftain. Hear me, O Hannibal!

Hannibal. What! when Marcellus lies before me? when his life may perhaps be recalled? when I may lead him in triumph to Carthage? when Italy, Sicily, Greece, Asia, wait to obey me? Content thee! I will give thee mine own bridle, worth ten such.

Gaulish Chieftain. For myself?

Hannibal. For thyself.

Gaulish Chieftain. And these rubies and emeralds, and that scarlet —

Hannibal. Yes, yes.

Gaulish Chieftain. O glorious Hannibal! unconquerable hero! O my happy country! to have such an ally and defender.   I swear eternal gratitude — yes, gratitude, lóve, devotion, beyond eternity.

Hannibal.   In all treaties we fix the time: I could hardly ask a longer.   Go back to thy station. — I would see what the surgeon is about, and hear what he thinks.   The life of Marcellus! the triumph of Hannibal! what else has the world in it?   Only Rome and Carthage: these follow.

Surgeon.   Hardly an hour of life is left.

Marcellus.   I must die then!   The gods be praised!   The commander of a Roman army is no captive.

Hannibal (to the Surgeon).   Could not he bear a sea-voyage?   Extract the arrow.

Surgeon.   He expires that moment.

Marcellus.   It pains me: extract it.

Hannibal.   Marcellus, I see no expression of pain on your countenance, and never will I consent to hasten the death of an enemy in my power.   Since your recovery is hopeless, you say truly you are no captive.

(*To the Surgeon*)   Is there nothing, man, that can assuage the mortal pain? for, suppress the signs of it as he may, he must feel it.   Is there nothing to alleviate and allay it?

Marcellus.   Hannibal, give me thy hand — thou hast found it and brought it me, compassion.

(*To the Surgeon.*)   Go, friend; others want thy aid; several fell around me.

Hannibal.   Recommend to your country, O Marcellus, while time permits it, reconciliation and peace with me, informing the Senate of my superiority in force, and the impossibility of resistance.   The tablet is ready: let me take off this ring — try to write, to sign it at least.   Oh, what satisfaction I feel at seeing you able to rest upon the elbow, and even to smile!

Marcellus. Within an hour or less, with how severe a brow would Minos say to me, " Marcellus, is this thy writing ? "

Rome loses one man: she hath lost many such, and she still hath many left.

Hannibal. Afraid as you are of falsehood, say you this? I confess in shame the ferocity of my countrymen. Unfortunately, too, the nearer posts are occupied by Gauls, infinitely more cruel. The Numidians are so in revenge; the Gauls both in revenge and in sport. My presence is required at a distance, and I apprehend the barbarity of one or other, learning, as they must do, your refusal to execute my wishes for the common good, and feeling that by this refusal you deprive them of their country, after so long an absence.

Marcellus. Hannibal, thou art not dying.

Hannibal. What then? What mean you?

Marcellus. That thou mayest, and very justly, have many things yet to apprehend: I can have none. The barbarity of thy soldiers is nothing to me: mine would not dare be cruel. Hannibal is forced to be absent; and his authority goes away with his horse. On this turf lies defaced the semblance of a general; but Marcellus is yet the regulator of his army. Dost thou abdicate a power conferred on thee by thy nation? Or wouldst thou acknowledge it to have become, by thy own sole fault, less plenary than thy adversary's?

I have spoken too much: let me rest; this mantle oppresses me.

Hannibal. I placed my mantle on your head when the helmet was first removed, and while you were lying in the sun. Let me fold it under, and then replace the ring.

Marcellus. Take it, Hannibal. It was given me by a poor woman who flew to me at Syracuse, and who covered it with her hair, torn off in desperation that she had no other gift to offer. Little thought I that her gift and her words should be mine. How suddenly may the most power-

ful be in the situation of the most helpless! Let that ring
and the mantle under my head be the exchange of guests at
parting. The time may come, Hannibal, when thou (and
the gods alone know whether as conqueror or conquered)
mayest sit under the roof of my children, and in either case
it shall serve thee. In thy adverse fortune, they will remember on whose pillow their father breathed his last; in
thy prosperous (Heaven grant it may shine upon thee in
some other country!) it will rejoice thee to protect them.
We feel ourselves the most exempt from affliction when we
relieve it, although we are then the most conscious that it
may befall us.

There is one thing here which is not at the disposal of
either.

Hannibal.   What?

Marcellus.   This body.

Hannibal.   Whither would you be lifted?   Men are
ready.

Marcellus.   I meant not so.   My strength is failing.   I
seem to hear rather what is within than what is without.
My sight and my other senses are in confusion.   I would
have said — This body, when a few bubbles of air shall
have left it, is no more worthy of thy notice than of mine;
but thy glory will not let thee refuse it to the piety of my
family.

Hannibal.   You would ask something else.   I perceive
an inquietude not visible till now.

Marcellus.   Duty and Death make us think of home
sometimes.

Hannibal.   Thitherward the thoughts of the conqueror
and of the conquered fly together.

Marcellus.   Hast thou any prisoners from my escort?

Hannibal.   A few dying lie about — and let them lie —
they are Tuscans.   The remainder I saw at a distance,

flying, and but one brave man among them — he appeared a Roman — a youth who turned back, though wounded. They surrounded and dragged him away, spurring his horse with their swords. These Etrurians measure their courage carefully, and tack it well together before they put it on, but throw it off again with lordly ease.

Marcellus, why think about them? or does aught else disquiet your thoughts?

Marcellus. I have suppressed it long enough. My son — my beloved son!

Hannibal. Where is he? Can it be? Was he with you?

Marcellus. He would have shared my fate — and has not. Gods of my country! beneficent throughout life to me, in death surpassingly beneficent, I render you, for the last time, thanks.

VI.

HENRY VIII. AND ANNE BOLEYN.

Henry. Dost thou know me, Nanny, in this yeoman's dress? 'S blood! does it require so long and vacant a stare to recollect a husband after a week or two? No tragedy-tricks with me! a scream, a sob, or thy kerchief a trifle the wetter, were enough. Why, verily the little fool faints in earnest. These whey faces, like their kinsfolk the ghosts, give us no warning. (*Sprinkling water over her.*) Hast had water enough upon thee? Take that, then : art thyself again?

Anne. Father of mercies! do I meet again my husband, as was my last prayer on earth? Do I behold my beloved lord — in peace — and pardoned, my partner in eternal bliss? It was his voice. I cannot see him : why cannot I ? Oh why do these pangs interrupt the transports of the blessed?

Henry. Thou openest thy arms: faith! I came for that. Nanny, thou art a sweet slut. Thou groanest, wench: art in labour? Faith! among the mistakes of the night, I am ready to think almost that thou hast been drinking, and that I have not.

Anne. God preserve your Highness: grant me your forgiveness for one slight offence. My eyes were heavy; I fell asleep while I was reading. I did not know of your presence at first; and, when I did, I could not speak. I strove for utterance: I wanted no respect for my liege and husband.

Henry. My pretty warm nestling, thou wilt then lie! Thou wert reading, and aloud too, with thy saintly cup of water by thee, and — what! thou art still girlishly fond of those dried cherries!

Anne. I had no other fruit to offer your Highness the first time I saw you, and you were then pleased to invent for me some reason why they should be acceptable. I did not dry these: may I present them, such as they are? We shall have fresh next month.

Henry. Thou art always driving away from the discourse. One moment it suits thee to know me, another not.

Anne. Remember, it is hardly three months since I miscarried: I am weak, and liable to swoons.

Henry. Thou hast, however, thy bridal cheeks, with lustre upon them when there is none elsewhere, and obstinate lips resisting all impression; but, now thou talkest about miscarrying, who is the father of the boy?

Anne. The Father is yours and mine; he who hath taken him to his own home, before (like me) he could struggle or cry for it.

Henry. Pagan, or worse, to talk so! He did not come into the world alive: there was no baptism.

Anne. I thought only of our loss: my senses are confounded. I did not give him my milk, and yet I loved him tenderly; for I often fancied, had he lived, how contented and joyful he would have made you and England.

Henry. No subterfuges and escapes. I warrant, thou canst not say whether at my entrance thou wert waking or wandering.

Anne. Faintness and drowsiness came upon me suddenly.

Henry. Well, since thou really and truly sleepedst, what didst dream of?

Anne. I begin to doubt whether I did indeed sleep.

Henry. Ha! false one — never two sentences of truth together! But come, what didst think about, asleep or awake?

Anne. I thought that God had pardoned me my offences, and had received me unto him.

Henry. And nothing more?

Anne. That my prayers had been heard and my wishes were accomplishing : the angels alone can enjoy more beatitude than this.

Henry. Vexatious little devil! she says nothing now about me, merely from perverseness. Hast thou never thought about me, nor about thy falsehood and adultery?

Anne. If I had committed any kind of falsehood, in regard to you or not, I should never have rested until I had thrown myself at your feet and obtained your pardon ; but, if ever I had been guilty of that other crime, I know not whether I should have dared to implore it, even of God's mercy.

Henry. Thou hast heretofore cast some soft glances upon Smeaton ; hast thou not?

Anne. He taught me to play on the virginals, as you know, when I was little, and thereby to please your Highness.

Henry. And Brereton and Norris, what have they taught thee?

Anne. They are your servants, and trusty ones.

Henry.   Has not Weston told thee plainly that he loved thee?

Anne.   Yes ; and —

Henry.   What didst thou ?

Anne.   I defied him.

Henry.   Is that all ?

Anne.   I could have done no more if he had told me that he hated me.   Then, indeed, I should have incurred more justly the reproaches of your Highness : I should have smiled.

Henry.   We have proofs abundant : the fellows shall one and all confront thee. — Ay, clap thy hands and kiss thy sleeve, harlot !

Anne.   Oh, that so great a favour is vouchsafed me !   My honour is secure ; my husband will be happy again ; he will see my innocence.

Henry.   Give me now an account of the moneys thou hast received from me within these nine months.   I want them not back : they are letters of gold in record of thy guilt. Thou hast had no fewer than fifteen thousand pounds in that period, without even thy asking ; what hast done with it, wanton ?

Anne.   I have regularly placed it out to interest.

Henry.   Where ? I demand of thee.

Anne.   Among the needy and ailing. My Lord Archbishop has the account of it, sealed by him weekly.   I also had a copy myself: those who took away my papers may easily find it ; for there are few others, and they lie open.

Henry.   Think on my munificence to thee ; recollect who made thee.   Dost sigh for what thou hast lost ?

Anne.   I do, indeed.

Henry.   I never thought thee ambitious ; but thy vices creep out one by one.

Anne.   I do not regret that I have been a queen and am no longer one ; nor that my innocence is called in question by those who never knew me : but I lament that the good people who loved me so cordially, hate and curse me ; that those who pointed me out to their daughters for imitation, check them when they speak about me ; and that he whom next to God I have served with most devotion is my accuser.

Henry. Wast thou conning over something in that dingy book for thy defence ? Come, tell me, what wast thou reading?

Anne. This ancient chronicle. I was looking for some one in my own condition, and must have missed the page. Surely in so many hundred years there shall have been other young maidens, first too happy for exaltation, and after too exalted for happiness, — not, perchance, doomed to die upon a scaffold, by those they ever honoured and served faithfully: that, indeed, I did not look for nor think of ; but my heart was bounding for any one I could love and pity. She would be unto me as a sister dead and gone ; but hearing me, seeing me, consoling me, and being consoled. O my husband ! it is so heavenly a thing —

Henry. To whine and whimper, no doubt, is vastly heavenly.

Anne. I said not so ; but those, if there be any such, who never weep, have nothing in them of heavenly or of earthly. The plants, the trees, the very rocks and unsunned clouds, show us at least the semblances of weeping ; and there is not an aspect of the globe we live on, nor of the waters and skies around it, without a reference and a similitude to our joys or sorrows.

Henry. I do not remember that notion anywhere. Take care no enemy rake out of it something of materialism. Guard well thy empty hot brain : it may hatch more evil. As for those odd words, I myself would fain see no great harm in them, knowing that grief and frenzy strike out many things which would else lie still, and neither spirt nor sparkle. I also know that thou hast never read any thing but Bible and history, — the two worst books in the world for young people, and the most certain to lead astray both prince and subject. For which reason I have interdicted and entirely put down the one, and will (by the blessing of the Virgin and of holy Paul) commit the other to a rigid censor. If it behooves us kings to enact what our people shall eat and drink, — of which the most unruly and rebellious spirit can entertain no doubt, — greatly more doth it behoove us to examine what they read and think. The body is moved according to the mind and will: we must take care that the movement be a right one, on pain of God's anger in this life and the next.

Anne. O my dear husband! it must be a naughty thing, indeed, that makes him angry beyond remission. Did you ever try how pleasant it is to forgive any one? There is nothing else wherein we can resemble God perfectly and easily.

Henry. Resemble God perfectly and easily! Do vile creatures talk thus of the Creator?

Anne. No, Henry, when his creatures talk thus of him, they are no longer vile creatures! When they know that he is good, they love him; and, when they love him, they are good themselves. O Henry! my husband and King! the judgments of our Heavenly Father are righteous: on this, . surely, we must think alike.

Henry. And what, then? Speak out: again I command thee, speak plainly! thy tongue was not so torpid but this moment. Art ready? Must I wait?

Anne. If any doubt remains upon your royal mind of your equity in this business; should it haply seem possible to you that passion or prejudice, in yourself or another, may have warped so strong an understanding, — do but supplicate the Almighty to strengthen and enlighten it, and he will hear you.

Henry. What ! thou wouldst fain change thy quarters, ay?

Anne. My spirit is detached and ready, and I shall change them shortly, whatever your Highness may determine. Ah ! my native Bickling is a pleasant place. May I go back to it ? Does that kind smile say, *Yes*? Do the hounds ever run that way now? The fruit-trees must be all in full blossom, and the gorse on the hill above quite dazzling. How good it was in you to plant your park at Greenwich after my childish notion, tree for tree, the very same as at Bickling ! Has the hard winter killed them, or the winds loosened the stakes about them?

Henry. Silly child ! as if thou shouldst see them any more.

Anne. Alas, what strange things happen ! But they and I are nearly of the same age ; young alike, and without hold upon any thing.

Henry. Yet thou appearest hale and resolute, and (they tell me) smirkest and smilest to everybody.

Anne. The withered leaf catches the sun sometimes, little as it can profit by it ; and I have heard stories of the breeze in other climates that sets in when daylight is about to close, and how constant it is, and how refreshing. My heart, indeed, is now sustained strangely : it became the more sensibly so from that time forward, when power and grandeur and all things terrestrial were sunk from sight. Every act of kindness in those about me gives me satisfaction and pleasure, such as I did not feel formerly. I was worse before God chastened me ; yet I was never an ingrate. What pains have I taken to find out the village-girls who placed their posies in my chamber ere I arose in the morning ! How gladly would I have recompensed the forester who lit up a brake on my birthnight, which else had warmed him half the winter ! But these are times past: I was not Queen of England.

Henry. Nor adulterous, nor heretical.

Anne.   God be praised !

Henry.   Learned saint ! thou knowest nothing of the lighter, but perhaps canst inform me about the graver, of them.

Anne.   Which may it be, my liege ?

Henry.   Which may it be ?   Pestilence !   I marvel that the walls of this tower do not crack around thee at such impiety.

Anne.   I would be instructed by the wisest of theologians : such is your Highness.

Henry.   Are the sins of the body, foul as they are, comparable to those of the soul ?

Anne.   When they are united, they must be worse.

Henry.   Go on, go on : thou pushest thy own breast against the sword.   God hath deprived thee of thy reason for thy punishment.   I must hear more : proceed, I charge thee.

Anne.   An aptitude to believe one thing rather than another, from ignorance or weakness, or from the more persuasive manner of the teacher, or from his purity of life, or from the strong impression of a particular text at a particular time, and various things beside, may influence and decide our opinion ; and the hand of the Almighty, let us hope, will fall gently on human fallibility.

Henry.   Opinion in matters of faith ! rare wisdom ! rare religion !   Troth, Anne ! thou hast well sobered me.   I came rather warmly and lovingly ; but these light ringlets, by the holy rood, shall not shade this shoulder much longer.   Nay, do not start ; I tap it for the last time, my sweetest.   If the Church permitted it, thou shouldst set forth on thy long journey with the eucharist between thy teeth, however loath.

Anne.   Love your Elizabeth, my honoured lord, and God bless you !   She will soon forget to call me.   Do not chide her : think how young she is.

Could I, could I kiss her, but once again ! it would comfort my heart, — or break it.

VII.

ROGER ASCHAM AND LADY JANE GREY.

Ascham.   Thou art going, my dear young lady, into a most awful state; thou art passing into matrimony and great wealth.   God hath willed it : submit in thankfulness.

Thy affections are rightly placed and well distributed. Love is a secondary passion in those who love most; a primary in those who love least.   He who is inspired by it in a high degree is inspired by honour in a higher: it never reaches its plenitude of growth and perfection but in the most exalted minds.   Alas! alas!

Jane.   What aileth my virtuous Ascham?   What is amiss? Why do I tremble?

Ascham.   I remember a sort of prophecy, made three years ago : it is a prophecy of my condition and of my feelings on it.   Recollectest thou who wrote, sitting upon the sea-beach the evening after an excursion to the Isle of Wight, these verses? —

> "Invisibly bright water !   so like air,
> On looking down I feared thou couldst not bear
> My little bark, of all light barks most light,
> And look'd again, and drew me from the sight,
> And, hanging back, breath'd each fresh gale aghast,
> And held the bench, not to go on so fast."

Jane.   I was very childish when I composed them; and, if I had thought any more about the matter, I should have hoped you had been too generous to keep them in your memory as witnesses against me.

Ascham.   Nay, they are not much amiss for so young a girl; and, there being so few of them, I did not reprove thee.   Half an hour, I thought, might have been spent more unprofitably; and I now shall believe it firmly, if thou wilt but be led by them to meditate a little on the similarity of situation in which thou then wert to what thou art now in.

Jane. I will do it, and whatever else you command; for I am weak by nature and very timorous, unless where a strong sense of duty holdeth and supporteth me. There God acteth, and not his creature.

Those were with me at sea who would have been attentive to me if I had seemed to be afraid, even though worshipful men and women were in the company; so that something more powerful threw my fear overboard. Yet I never will go again upon the water.

Ascham. Exercise that beauteous couple, that mind and body, much and variously : but at home, at home, Jane! indoors, and about things indoors; for God is there too. We have rocks and quicksands on the banks of our Thames, O lady! such as ocean never heard of ; and many (who knows how soon?) may be engulfed in the current under their garden-walls.

Jane. Thoroughly do I now understand you. Yes, indeed, I have read evil things of courts ; but I think nobody can go out bad who entereth good, if timely and true warning shall have been given.

Ascham. I see perils on perils which thou dost not see, albeit thou art wiser than thy poor old master. And it is not because Love hath blinded thee, for that surpasseth his supposed omnipotence ; but it is because thy tender heart, having always leaned affectionately upon good, hath felt and known nothing of evil.

I once persuaded thee to reflect much : let me now persuade thee to avoid the habitude of reflection, to lay aside books, and to gaze carefully and steadfastly on what is under and before thee.

Jane. I have well bethought me of my duties. Oh how extensive they are! what a goodly and fair inheritance!

But, tell me, would you command me never more to read Cicero and Epictetus and Plutarch and Polybius? The others I do resign ; they are good for the arbour and for the gravel-walk : yet leave unto me, I beseech you, my friend and father,—leave unto me for my fireside and for my pillow,— truth, eloquence, courage, constancy.

Ascham.   Read them on thy marriage-bed, on thy child-bed, on thy death-bed. Thou spotless, undrooping lily, they have fenced thee right well. These are the men for men : these are to fashion the bright and blessed creatures whom God one day shall smile upon in thy chaste bosom. Mind thou thy husband.

Jane.   I sincerely love the youth who hath espoused me ; I love him with the fondest, the most solicitous affection : I pray to the Almighty for his goodness and happiness, and do forget at times — unworthy supplicant !— the prayers I should have offered for myself. Never fear that I will disparage my kind religious teacher, by disobedience to my husband in the most trying duties.

Ascham.   Gentle is he, gentle and virtuous : but time will harden him ; time must harden even thee, sweet Jane ! Do thou, complacently and indirectly, lead him from ambition.

Jane.   He is contented with me and with home.

Ascham.   Ah Jane ! Jane ! men of high estate grow tired of contentedness.

Jane.   He told me he never liked books unless I read them to him : I will read them to him every evening ; I will open new worlds to him, richer than those discovered by the Spaniard ; I will conduct him to treasures — Oh what treasures !— on which he may sleep in innocence and peace.

Ascham.   Rather do thou walk him, ride with him, play with him, be his fairy, his page, his everything that love and poetry have invented : but watch him well ; sport with his fancies; turn them about like the ringlets round his cheek; and, if ever he meditate on power, go toss up thy baby to his brow, and bring back his thoughts into his heart by the music of thy discourse.

Teach him to live unto God and unto thee; and he will discover that women, like the plants in woods, derive their softness and tenderness from the shade.

VIII.

PRINCESS MARY AND PRINCESS ELIZABETH.

Mary.   My dear, dear sister! it is long, very long, since we met.

Elizabeth.   Methinks it was about the time they chopped off our Uncle Seymour's head for him.   Not that he was *our* uncle, though : he was only Edward's.

Mary.   The Lord Protector, if not your uncle, was always doatingly fond of you; and he often declared to me, even within your hearing, he thought you very beautiful.

Elizabeth.   He said as much of you, if that is all; and he told me why : "*not to vex me,*" — as if, instead of vexing me, it would not charm me.   I beseech your Highness is there any thing remarkable or singular in thinking me — what he thought me?

Mary.   No, indeed; for so you are.   But why call me *Highness*, drawing back and losing half your stature in the circumference of the courtesy.

Elizabeth.   Because you are now, at this blessed hour, my lawful Queen.

Mary.   Hush, prithee, hush!   The Parliament has voted otherwise.

Elizabeth.   They would choose you.

Mary.   What would they do with me?

Elizabeth.   Trump you.

Mary.   I am still at a loss.

Elizabeth.   Bamboozle you.

Mary.   Really, my dear sister, you have been so courted by the gallants, that you condescend to adopt their language in place of graver.

Elizabeth.   Cheat you, then : will that do?

Mary.   Comprehensibly.

Elizabeth.   I always speak as the thing spoken of requires.   To the point.   Would our father have minded the caitiffs?

Mary.   Naming our father, I should have said, *our father now in bliss;* for surely he must be, having been a . rock of defence against the torrent of irreligion.

Elizabeth.   Well ; in bliss or out, there, here, or anywhere, would he, royal soul ! have minded Parliament ? No such fool he.   There were laws before there were parliaments ; and there were kings before there were laws.   Were I in your Majesty's place (God forbid the thought should ever enter my poor weak head even in a dream !)I would try the mettle of my subjects : I would mount my horse, and head them.

Mary.   Elizabeth, you were always a better horsewoman than I am : I should be ashamed to get a fall among th soldiers.

Elizabeth.   Pish ! pish ! it would be among knights and nobles—the worst come to the worst.   Lord o' mercy ! do you think they never saw such a thing before?

Mary.   I must hear of no resistance to the powers that be.   Beside, I am but a weak woman.

Elizabeth.   I do not see why women should be weak, unless they like.

Mary.   Not only the Commons, but likewise the peers, have sworn allegiance.

Elizabeth.   Did you ever in your lifetime, in any chronicle or commentary, read of any parliament that was not as ready to be foresworn as to swear?

Mary.   Alas !

Elizabeth.   If ever you did, the book is a rare one, kept in an out-of-the-way library, in a cedar chest all to itself, with golden locks and amber seals thereto.

Mary.   I would not willingly think so ill of men.

Elizabeth.   For my part, I can't abide 'em.   All that can be said is, some are not so bad as others.   You smile, and deem the speech a silly and superfluous one.   We may live, Sister Mary, to see and acknowledge that it is not quite so sure and flat a verity as it now appears to us.   I never come near a primrose but I suspect an adder under it; and, · the sunnier the day, the more misgivings.

Mary.   But we are now, by the settlement of the monarchy, farther out of harm's way than ever.

Elizabeth.   If the wench has children to-morrow, as she may have, they will inherit.

Mary.   No doubt they would.

Elizabeth.   No doubt?   I will doubt : and others shall doubt, too.   The heirs of my body — yours first — God prosper them !   Parliament may be constrained to retrace its steps.   One half sees no harm in taking bribes ; the other, no guilt in taking fright.   Corruption is odious and costly; but, when people have yielded to compulsion, conscience is fain to acquiesce.   Men say they were forced, and what is done under force is invalid.

Mary.   There is nothing like compulsion.

Elizabeth.   Then let there be.   Let the few yield to the many, and all to the throne.   Now is your time to stir. The furnace is mere smut, and no bellows to blow the embers.   Parliament is without a leader.   Three or four turnspits are crouching to leap upon the wheel; but, while they are snarling and snapping one at another, what becomes of the roast? Take them by the scuff, and out with 'em. The people will applaud you. They want bread within doors, and honesty without. They have seen enough of partisans and parliaments.

Mary. We cannot do without one.

Elizabeth. Convoke it, then ; but call it with sound of trumpet. Such a body is unlikely to find a head. There is little encouragement for an honest knight or gentleman to take the station. The Commons slink away with lowered shoulders, and bear hateful compunction against the very names and memory of those braver men who, in dangerous times and before stern, authoritative, warlike sovereigns, supported their pretensions. Kings, who peradventure would have strangled such ringleaders, well remember and well respect them ; their fellows would disown their bene- factors and maintainers. Kings abominate their example ; clowns would efface the images on their sepulchres. What forbearance on our part can such knaves expect, or what succor from the people ?

Mary. What is done is done.

Elizabeth. Oftentimes it is easier to undo than to do. I should rather be glad than mortified at what has been done yonder. In addition to those churls and chapmen in the lower House, there are also among the peers no few who voted most audaciously.

Mary. The majority of them was of opinion that the Lady Jane should be invested with royal state and dignity.

Elizabeth. The majority ! so much the better, — so much the better, say I. I would find certain folk who should make sharp inquest into their title-deeds, and spell the indentures syllable by syllable. Certain lands were granted for certain services, which services have been neglected. I would not in such wise neglect the lands in question, but annex them to my royal domains.

Mary. Sister! sister! you forget that the Lady Jane Grey (as was) is now queen of the realm.

Elizabeth. Forget it, indeed! The vile woman! I am minded to call her as such vile women are called out of doors.

Mary. Pray, abstain ; not only forasmuch as it would be unseemly in those sweet, slender, delicate lips of yours, but also by reason that she is adorned with every grace and virtue, bating (which, indeed, outvalues them all) the true religion. Sister, I hope and believe I in this my speech have given you no offence ; for your own eyes, I know, are opened. Indeed, who that is not wilfully blind can err in so straight a road, even if so gentle and so sure a guidance were wanting? The mind, sister, the mind itself, must be crooked which deviates a hair's-breadth. Ay, that intelligent nod would alone suffice to set my bosom quite at rest thereupon. Should it not?

Elizabeth. It were imprudent in me to declare my real opinion at this juncture : we must step warily when we walk among cocatrices. I am barely a saint, — indeed, far from it ; and I am much too young to be a martyr. But that odious monster, who pretends an affection for reformation, and a reverence for learning, is counting the jewels in the crown, while you fancy she is repeating her prayers or conning her Greek.

Sister Mary, as God is in heaven, I hold nothing so detestable in a woman as hypocrisy, — add thereunto, as you fairly may, avarice, man-hunting, lasciviousness. The least atom of the least among these vices is heavy enough to weigh down the soul to the bottomless pit.

Mary. Unless divine grace —

Elizabeth. Don't talk to me. Don't spread the filth fine.

Now could not that empty fool, Dudley, have found some other young person of equal rank with Mistress Jane, and of higher beauty? Not that any other such, pretty as the boy is, would listen to his idle discourse.

And, pray, who are these Dudleys? The first of them was made a man of by our grandfather. And what was the man, after all? Nothing better than a huge smelting-pot, with a commodious screw at the colder end of the ladle.

I have no patience with the bold harlotry.

Mary. I see you have not, sister!

Elizabeth. No, nor have the people. They are on tip-toe for rising in all parts of the kingdom.

Mary. What can they do? God help them !

Elizabeth. Sister Mary! good Sister Mary! did you say, *God help them?* I am trembling into a heap. It is well you have uttered such words to safe and kindred ears. If they should ever come whispered at the Privy Council, it might end badly.

I believe my visit hath been of as long continuance as may seem befitting. I must be gone.

Mary. Before your departure, let me correct a few of your opinions in regard to our gentle kinswoman and most gracious Queen. She hath nobly enlarged my poor alimony. Look here! to begin.

Elizabeth. What ! all golden pieces? I have not ten groats in the world.

Mary. Be sure she will grant unto you plenteously. She hath condescended to advise me of her intent. Meanwhile, I do entreat you will take home with you the purse you are stroking down, thinking about other things.

Elizabeth. Not I, not I, if it comes from such a creature.

Mary. You accept it from me.

Elizabeth. Then, indeed, unreservedly. Passing through your hands, the soil has been wiped away. However, as I live, I will carefully wash every piece in it with soap and water.   Do you believe they can lose any thing of their weight thereby?

Mary.   Nothing material.

Elizabeth.   I may reflect and cogitate upon it.   I would not fain offer anybody light money.

Truth ! I fear the purse, although of chamois and double stitched, is insufficient to sustain the weight of the gold, which must be shaken violently on the road as I return. Dear Sister Mary, as you probably are not about to wear that head-tire, could you, commodiously to yourself, lend me it awhile, just to deposit a certain part of the moneys therein? for the velvet is stout, and the Venetian netting close and stiff : I can hardly bend the threads.   I shall have more leisure to admire its workmanship at home.

Mary.   Elizabeth, I see you are grown forgiving.   In the commencement of our discourse, I suggested a slight alteration of manner in speaking of our father.   Do you pray for the repose of his soul morning and night?

Elizabeth.   The doubt is injurious.

Mary.   Pardon me ! I feel it.   But the voices of children, O Elizabeth, come to the ear of God above all other voices. The best want intercession.   Pray for him, Elizabeth ; pray for him.

Elizabeth.   Why not?   He did indeed — but he was in a passion — order my mother up the three black stairs, and he left her pretty head on the landing ; but I bear him no malice for it.

Mary.   Malice ! The baneful word hath shot up from hell in many places, but never between child and parent. In the space of that one span, on that single sod from Paradise, the serpent never trailed.   Husband and wife were severed by him, then again clashed together ; brother slew brother : but parent and child stand where their Creator first placed them, and drink at the only source of pure, untroubled love.

Elizabeth. Beside, you know, being King, he had clearly a right to do it, plea or no plea.

Mary. We will converse no longer on so dolorous a subject.

Elizabeth. I will converse on it as long as such is my pleasure.

Mary. Being my visitor, you command here.

Elizabeth. I command nowhere. I am blown about like a leaf : I am yielding as a feather in a cushion, only one among a million. But I tell you, honestly and plainly, I do not approve of it, anyhow ! It may have grown into a trick and habit with him : no matter for that ; in my view of the business, it is not what a husband ought to do with a wife. And, if she did — but she did not ; and I say it.

Mary. It seems, indeed, severe.

Elizabeth. Yea, afore God, methinks it smacks a trifle of the tart.

Mary. Our father was God's vicegerent. Probably it is for the good of her soul, poor lady ! Better suffer here than hereafter. We ought to kiss the rod, and be thankful.

Elizabeth. Kiss the rod, forsooth ! I have been con-strained erewhile even unto that ; and no such a child nei-ther. But I would rather have kissed it fresh and fair, with all its buds and knots upon it, than after it had bestowed on me, in such a roundabout way, such a deal of its embroidery and lace-work. I thank my father for all that. I hope his soul lies easier than my skin did.

Mary. The wish is kind ; but prayers would much help it. Our father, of blessed memory, now (let us hope) among the saints, was somewhat sore in his visitations ; but they tended heavenward.

Elizabeth. Yea, when he cursed and cuffed and kicked us.

Mary.   He did kick, poor man !

Elizabeth.   Kick !   Fifty folks, young and old, have seen the marks his kicking left behind.

Mary.   We should conceal all such his infirmities.   They arose from an irritation in the foot, whereof he died.

Elizabeth.   I only know I could hardly dance or ride for them ; chiefly caught, as I was, fleeing from his wrath.   He seldom vouchsafed to visit me : when he did, he pinched my ear so bitterly I was fain to squeal.   And then he said I should turn out like my mother : calling me by such a name, moreover, as is heard but about the kennel ; and even there it is never given to the young.

Mary.   There was choler in him at certain times and seasons.   Those who have much will, have their choler excited when opposite breath blows against it.

Elizabeth.   Let them have will ; let them have choler too, in God's name: but it is none the better, as gout is, for flying to hand or foot.

Mary.   I have seen — now do, pray, forgive me —

Elizabeth.   Well, what have you seen ?

Mary.   My sweet little sister lift up the most delicate of all delicate white hands, and with their tiny narrow pink nails tear off ruffs and caps, and take sundry unerring aims at eyes and noses.

Elizabeth.   Was that any impediment or hindrance to riding and dancing ?   I would always make people do their duty, and always will.   Remember (for your memory seems accurate enough) that, whenever I scratched anybody's face, I permitted my hand to be kissed by the offender within a day or two.

Mary.   Undeniable.

Elizabeth.   I may, peradventure, have been hasty in my childhood : but all great hearts are warm ; all good ones are relenting.   If, in combing my hair, the hussy lugged it, I

obeyed God's command and referred to the *lex talionis.* I
have not too much of it ; and every soul on earth sees its
beauty. A single one would be a public loss. Uncle Seymour — but what boots it ? There are others who can see
perhaps as far as Uncle Seymour.

Mary. I do remember his saying that he watched its
growth as he would a melon's. And how fondly did those
little, sharp, gray eyes of his look and wink when you
blushed and chided his flattery !

Elizabeth. Never let any man dare to flatter me : I am
above it. Only the weak and ugly want the refreshment of
that perfumed fan. I take but my own ; and touch it who
dares !

Really, it is pleasant to see in what a pear-form fashion
both purse and caul are hanging. Faith ! they are heavy :
I could hardly lift them from the back of the chair.

Mary. Let me call an attendant to carry them for you.

Elizabeth. Are you mad? They are unsealed, and
ill-tied : any one could slip his hand in.

And so that — the word was well nigh out of my mouth —
gave you all this gold ?

Mary. For shame ! Oh, for shame !

Elizabeth. I feel shame only for her. It turns my cheeks
red, — together with some anger upon it. But I cannot keep
my eyes off that book — if book it may be — on which the
purse was lying.

Mary. Somewhat irreverently, God forgive me ! But it
was sent at the same time by the same fair creature, with
many kind words. It had always been kept in our father's
bedroom closet, and was removed from Edward's by those
unhappy men who superintended his education.

Elizabeth. She must have thought all those stones are
garnets : to me they look like rubies, one and all. Yet,
over so large a cover, they cannot all be rubies.

Mary. I believe they are ; excepting the glory in the centre, which is composed of chrysolites. Our father was an excellent judge in jewelry, as in every thing else; and he spared no expenditure in objects of devotion.

Elizabeth. What creature could fail in devotion with an object such as that before the eyes? Let me kiss it, — partly for my Saviour's and partly for my father's sake.

Mary. How it comforts me, O Elizabeth, to see you thus press it to your bosom!. Its spirit, I am confident, has entered there. Disregard the pebbles : take it home ; cherish it evermore. May there be virtue, as some think there is, even in the stones about it. God bless you, strengthen you, lead you aright, and finally bring you to everlasting glory !

Elizabeth (going). The Popish puss !

IX.

ESSEX AND SPENSER.

Spenser. Interrogate me, my lord, that I may answer each question distinctly, my mind being in sad confusion at what I have seen and undergone.

Essex. Give me thy account and opinion of these very affairs as thou leftest them; for I would rather know one part well than all imperfectly ; and the violences of which I have heard within the day surpass belief.

Why weepest thou, my gentle Spenser? Have the rebels sacked thy house?

Spenser. They have plundered and utterly destroyed it.

Essex. I grieve for thee, and will see thee righted.

Spenser. In this they have little harmed me.

Essex. How ! I have heard it reported that thy grounds are fertile, and thy mansion large and pleasant.

Spenser. If river and lake and meadow-ground and mountain could render any place the abode of pleasantness, pleasant was mine, indeed !

On the lovely banks of Mulla I found deep contentment. Under the dark alders did I muse and meditate. Innocent hopes were my gravest cares, and my playfullest fancy was with kindly wishes. Ah ! surely of all cruelties the worst is to extinguish our kindness. Mine is gone : I love the people and the land no longer. My lord, ask me not about them : I may speak injuriously.

Essex. Think rather, then, of thy happier hours and busier occupations; these likewise may instruct me.

Spenser. The first seeds I sowed in the garden, ere the old castle was made habitable for my lovely bride, were acorns from Penshurst. I planted a little oak before my mansion at the birth of each child. My sons, I said to myself, shall often play in the shade of them when I am gone; and every year shall they take the measure of their growth, as fondly as I take theirs.

Essex. Well, well; but let not this thought make thee weep so bitterly.

Spenser. Poison may ooze from beautiful plants; deadly grief from dearest reminiscences.

I *must* grieve, I *must* weep: it seems the law of God, and the only one that men are not disposed to contravene. In the performance of this alone do they effectually aid one another.

Essex. Spenser ! I wish I had at hand any arguments or persuasions, of force sufficient to remove thy sorrow ; but, really, I am not in the habit of seeing men grieve at any thing except the loss of favour at court, or of a hawk, or of a buck-hound. And were I to swear out my condolences to a man of thy discernment, in the same round roll-call phrases we employ with one another upon these occasions, I should be guilty, not of insincerity, but of insolence. True grief hath ever something sacred in it; and, when it visiteth a wise man and a brave one, is most holy.

Nay, kiss not my hand: he whom God smiteth hath God with him. In his presence what am I?

Spenser. Never so great, my lord, as at this hour, when you see aright who is greater. May he guide your counsels, and preserve your life and glory!

Essex. Where are thy friends? Are they with thee?

Spenser. Ah, where, indeed! Generous, true-hearted Philip! where art thou, whose presence was unto me peace and safety; whose smile was contentment, and whose praise renown? My lord! I cannot but think of him among still heavier losses: he was my earliest friend, and would have taught me wisdom.

Essex. Pastoral poetry, my dear Spenser, doth not require tears and lamentations. Dry thine eyes; rebuild thine house: the Queen and Council, I venture to promise thee, will make ample amends for every evil thou hast sustained. What! does that enforce thee to wail yet louder?

Spenser. Pardon me, bear with me, most noble heart! I have lost what no Council, no Queen, no Essex, can restore.

Essex. We will see that. There are other swords, and other arms to wield them, beside a Leicester's and a Raleigh's. Others can crush their enemies, and serve their friends.

Spenser. O my sweet child! And of many so powerful, many so wise and so beneficent, was there none to save thee? None! none!

Essex. I now perceive that thou lamentest what almost every father is destined to lament. Happiness must be bought, although the payment may be delayed. Consider; the same calamity might have befallen thee here in London.

Neither the houses of ambassadors, nor the palaces of kings, nor the altars of God himself, are asylums against death. How do I know but under this very roof there may sleep some latent calamity, that in an instant shall cover with gloom every inmate of the house, and every far dependent?

Spenser. God avert it.

Essex. Every day, every hour of the year, do hundreds mourn what thou mournest.

Spenser. Oh, no, no, no! Calamities there are around us; calamities there are all over the earth; calamities there are in all seasons: but none in any season, none in any place, like mine.

Essex. So say all fathers, so say all husbands. Look at any old mansion-house, and let the sun shine as gloriously as it may on the golden vanes, or the arms recently quartered over the gateway or the embayed window, and on the happy pair that haply is toying at it: nevertheless, thou mayest say that of a certainty the same fabric hath seen much sorrow within its chambers, and heard many wailings; and each time this was the heaviest stroke of all. Funerals have passed along through the stout-hearted knights upon the wainscot, and amid the laughing nymphs upon the arras. Old servants have shaken their heads as if somebody had deceived them, when they found that beauty and nobility could perish.

Edmund! the things that are too true pass by us as if they were not true at all; and when they have singled us out, then only do they strike us. Thou and I must go too. Perhaps the next year may blow us away with its fallen leaves.*

Spenser. For you, my lord, many years (I trust) are waiting: I never shall see those fallen leaves. No leaf, no bud, will spring upon the earth before I sink into her breast for ever.

* It happened so.

Essex. Thou, who art wiser than most men, shouldst bear with patience, equanimity, and courage what is common to all.

Spenser. Enough, enough, enough ! have all men seen their infant burned to ashes before their eyes?

Essex. Gracious God ! Merciful Father ! what is this?

Spenser. Burned alive ! burned to ashes ! burned to ashes ! The flames dart their serpent tongues through the nursery-window. I cannot quit thee, my Elizabeth ! I cannot lay down our Edmund ! Oh, these flames ! They persecute, they enthrall me ; they curl round my temples ; they hiss upon my brain ; they taunt me with their fierce, foul voices ; they carp at me, they wither me, they consume me, throwing back to me a little of life to roll and suffer in, with their fangs upon me. Ask me, my lord, the things you wish to know from me : I may answer them ; I am now composed again. Command me, my gracious lord ! I would yet serve you : soon I shall be unable. You have stooped to raise me up ; you have borne with me ; you have pitied me, even like one not powerful. You have brought comfort, and will leave it with me ; for gratitude is comfort.

·Oh ! my memory stands all a tip-toe on one burning point : when it drops from it, then it perishes. Spare me : ask me nothing ; let me weep before you in peace, — the kindest act of greatness.

Essex. I should rather have dared to mount into the midst of the conflagration than I now dare entreat thee not to weep. The tears that overflow thy heart, my Spenser, will staunch and heal it in their sacred stream ; but not without hope in God.

Spenser. My hope in God is that I may soon see again what he has taken from me. Amid the myriads of angels, there is not one so beautiful ; and even he (if there be any) who is appointed my guardian could never love me so.

Ah! these are idle thoughts, vain wanderings, distempered dreams. If there ever were guardian angels, he who so wanted one — my helpless boy — would not have left these arms upon my knees.

Essex. God help and sustain thee, too gentle Spenser! I never will desert thee. But what am I? Great they have called me! Alas, how powerless then and infantile is greatness in the presence of calamity!

Come, give me thy hand : let us walk up and down the gallery. Bravely done! I will envy no more a Sydney or a Raleigh.

X.

LEOFRIC AND GODIVA.

Godiva. There is a dearth in the land, my sweet Leofric! Remember how many weeks of drought we have had, even in the deep pastures of Leicestershire ; and how many Sundays we have heard the same prayers for rain, and supplications that it would please the Lord in his mercy to turn aside his anger from the poor, pining cattle. You, my dear husband, have imprisoned more than one malefactor for leaving his dead ox in the public way; and other hinds have fled before you out of the traces, in which they, and their sons and their daughters, and haply their old fathers and mothers, were dragging the abandoned wain homeward. Although we were accompanied by many brave spearmen and skilful archers, it was perilous to pass the creatures which the farm-yard dogs, driven from the hearth by the poverty of their masters, were tearing and devouring; while others, bitten and lamed, filled the air either with long and deep howls or sharp and quick barkings, as they struggled with hunger and feebleness, or were exasperated by heat and pain. Nor could the thyme from the heath, nor the bruised branches of the fir-tree, extinguish or abate the foul odour.

Leofric.   And now, Godiva, my darling, thou art afraid we should be eaten up before we enter the gates of Coventry; or perchance that in the gardens there are no roses to greet thee, no sweet herbs for thy mat and pillow.

Godiva.   Leofric, I have no such fears. This is the month of roses: I find them everywhere since my blessed marriage. They, and all other sweet herbs, I know not why, seem to greet me wherever I look at them, as though they knew and expected me. Surely they cannot feel that I am fond of them.

Leofric.   O light, laughing simpleton! But what wouldst thou? I came not hither to pray; and yet if praying would satisfy thee, or remove the drought, I would ride up straightway to St. Michael's and pray until morning.

Godiva.   I would do the same, O Leofric! but God hath turned away his ear from holier lips than mine. Would my own dear husband hear me, if I implored him for what is easier to accomplish, — what he can do like God?

Leofric.   How! what is it?

Godiva.   I would not, in the first hurry of your wrath, appeal to you, my loving Lord, in behalf of these unhappy men who have offended you.

Leofric.   Unhappy! is that all?

Godiva.   Unhappy they must surely be, to have offended you so grievously. What a soft air breathes over us! how quiet and serene and still an evening! how calm are the heavens and the earth! — Shall none enjoy them; not even we, my Leofric? The sun is ready to set : let it never set, O Leofric, on your anger. These are not my words: they are better than mine. Should they lose their virtue from my unworthiness in uttering them?

Leofric.   Godiva, wouldst thou plead to me for rebels?

Godiva.   They have, then, drawn the sword against you? Indeed, I knew it not.

Leofric. They have omitted to send me my dues, established by my ancestors, well knowing of our nuptials, and of the charges and festivities they require, and that in a season of such scarcity my own lands are insufficient.

Godiva. If they were starving, as they said they were —

Leofric. Must I starve too? Is it not enough to lose my vassals?

Godiva. Enough? O God! too much! too much! May you never lose them! Give them life, peace, comfort, contentment. There are those among them who kissed me in my infancy, and who blessed me at the baptismal font. Leofric, Leofric! the first old man I meet I shall think is one of those; and I shall think on the blessing he gave, and (ah me!) on the blessing I bring back to him. My heart will bleed, will burst; and he will weep at it! he will weep, poor soul, for the wife of a cruel lord who denounces vengeance on him, who carries death into his family!

Leofric. We must hold solemn festivals.

Godiva. We must, indeed.

Leofric. Well, then?

Godiva. Is the clamourousness that succeeds the death of God's dumb creatures, are crowded halls, are slaughtered cattle, festivals? — are maddening songs, and giddy dances, and hireling praises from parti-coloured coats? Can the voice of a minstrel tell us better things of ourselves than our own internal one might tell us; or can his breath make our breath softer in sleep? O my beloved! let every thing be a joyance to us : it will, if we will. Sad is the day, and worse must follow, when we hear the blackbird in the garden, and do not throb with joy. But, Leofric, the high festival is strown by the servant of God upon the heart of man. It is gladness, it is thanksgiving; it is the orphan, the starveling, pressed to the bosom, and bidden as its first commandment to remember its benefactor. We will hold this festival; the guests are ready: we may keep it up for weeks, and months, and years together, and always be the happier and the richer for it. The beverage of this feast, O Leofric, is sweeter than bee or flower or vine can give us: it flows from heaven; and in heaven will it abundantly be poured out again to him who pours it out here unsparingly.

Leofric. Thou art wild.

Godiva. I have, indeed, lost myself. Some Power, some good kind Power, melts me (body and soul and voice) into tenderness and love. O my husband, we must obey it. Look upon me! look upon me! lift your sweet eyes from the ground! I will not cease to supplicate; I dare not.

Leofric. We may think upon it.

Godiva. Never say that! What! think upon goodness when you can be good? Let not the infants cry for sustenance! The mother of our blessed Lord will hear them; us never, never afterward.

Leofric. Here comes the Bishop: we are but one mile from the walls. Why dismountest thou? no bishop can expect it. Godiva! my honour and rank among men are humbled by this. Earl Godwin will hear of it. Up! up! The Bishop hath seen it: he urgeth his horse onward. Dost thou not hear him now upon the solid turf behind thee?

Godiva. Never, no, never will I rise, O Leofric, until you remit this most impious tax, — this tax on hard labour, on hard life.

Leofric. Turn round: look how the fat nag canters, as to the tune of a sinner's psalm, slow and hard-breathing. What reason or right can the people have to complain, while their bishop's steed is so sleek and well caparisoned? Inclination to change, desire to abolish old usages. — Up! up! for shame! They shall smart for it, idlers! Sir Bishop, I must blush for my young bride.

Godiva.	My husband, my husband! will you pardon the city?

Leofric.	Sir Bishop!	I could not think you would have seen her in this plight.	Will I pardon?	Yea, Godiva, by the holy rood, will I pardon the city, when thou ridest naked at noontide through the streets!

Godiva.	O my dear, cruel Leofric, where is the heart you gave me?	It was not so: can mine have hardened it?

Bishop.	Earl, thou abashest thy spouse; she turneth pale, and weepeth.	Lady Godiva, peace be with thee.

Godiva.	Thanks, holy man! peace will be with me when peace is with your city.	Did you hear my Lord's cruel word?

Bishop.	I did, lady.

Godiva.	Will you remember it, and pray against it?

Bishop.	Wilt *thou* forget it, daughter?

Godiva.	I am not offended.

Bishop.	Angel of peace and purity!

Godiva.	But treasure it up in your heart: deem it an incense, good only when it is consumed and spent, ascending with prayer and sacrifice.	And, now, what was it?

Bishop.	Christ save us! that he will pardon the city when thou ridest naked through the streets at noon.

Godiva.	Did he not swear an oath?

Bishop.	He sware by the holy rood.

Godiva. My Redeemer, thou hast heard it! save the city!

Leofric.	We are now upon the beginning of the pavement: these are the suburbs.	Let us think of feasting: we may pray afterward; to-morrow we shall rest.

Godiva.	No judgments, then, to-morrow, Leofric?

Leofric.	None: we will carouse.

Godiva.	The saints of heaven have given me strength and confidence; my prayers are heard; the heart of my beloved is now softened.

Leofric (aside). Ay, ay — they shall smart, though.

Godiva. Say, dearest Leofric, is there indeed no other hope, no other mediation?

Leofric. I have sworn. Beside, thou hast made me redden and turn my face away from thee, and all the knaves have seen it: this adds to the city's crime.

Godiva. I have blushed too, Leofric, and was not rash nor obdurate.

Leofric. But thou, my sweetest, art given to blushing: there is no conquering it in thee. I wish thou hadst not alighted so hastily and roughly : it hath shaken down a sheaf of thy hair. Take heed thou sit not upon it, lest it anguish thee. Well done ! it mingleth now sweetly with the cloth of gold upon the saddle, running here and there, as if it had life and faculties and business, and were working thereupon some newer and cunninger device. O my beauteous Eve ! there is a Paradise about thee ! the world is refreshed as thou movest and breathest on it. I cannot see or think of evil where thou art. I could throw my arms even here about thee. No signs for me ! no shaking of sunbeams ! no reproof or frown or wonderment. — I *will* say it — now, then, for worse — I could close with my kisses thy half-open lips, ay, and those lovely and loving eyes, before the people.

Godiva. To-morrow you shall kiss me, and they shall bless you for it. I shall be very pale, for to-night I must fast and pray.

Leofric. I do not hear thee ; the voices of the folk are so loud under this archway.

Godiva (to herself). God help them ! good kind souls ! I hope they will not crowd about me so to-morrow. O Leofric ! could my name be forgotten, and yours alone remembered ! But perhaps my innocence may save me from reproach ; and how many as innocent are in fear and famine! No eye will open on me but fresh from tears. What a young mother for so large a family! Shall my youth harm me! Under God's hand it gives me courage. Ah, when will the morning come! ah, when will the noon be over!

The story of Godiva, at one of whose festivals or fairs I was present in my boyhood, has always much interested me; and I wrote a poem on it, sitting, I remember, by the *square pool* at Rugby. When I showed it to the friend in whom I had most confidence, he began to scoff at the subject; and, on his reaching the last line, his laughter was loud and immoderate. This Conversation has brought both laughter and stanza back to me, and the earnestness with which I entreated and implored my friend *not to tell the lads;* so heart-strickenly and desperately was I ashamed. The verses are these, if any one else should wish another laugh at me :—

<blockquote>
In every hour, in every mood,
O lady, it is sweet and good
  To bathe the soul in prayer ;
And, at the close of such a day,
When we have ceased to bless and pray,
  To dream on thy long hair.
</blockquote>

May the peppermint be still growing on the bank in that place!

W. S. L.

XI.

THE LADY LISLE AND ELIZABETH GAUNT.

Lady Lisle. Madam, I am confident you will pardon me; for affliction teaches forgiveness.

Elizabeth Gaunt. From the cell of the condemned we are going, unless my hopes mislead me, where alone we can receive it.

Tell me, I beseech you, lady! in what matter or manner do you think you can have offended a poor sinner such as I am. Surely we come into this dismal place for our offences; and it is not here that any can be given or taken.

Lady Lisle.   Just now, when I entered the prison, I saw your countenance serene and cheerful ; you looked upon me for a time with an unaltered eye : you turned away from me, as I fancied, only to utter some expressions of devotion ; and again you looked upon me, and tears rolled down your face.   Alas that I should, by any circumstance, any action or recollection, make another unhappy!   Alas that I should deepen the gloom in the very shadow of death !

Elizabeth Gaunt.   Be comforted : you have not done it. Grief softens and melts and flows away with tears.

I wept because another was greatly more wretched than myself.   I wept at that black attire, — at that attire of modesty and of widowhood.

Lady Lisle.   It covers a wounded, almost a broken, heart, — an unworthy offering to our blessed Redeemer.

Elizabeth Gaunt.   In his name let us now rejoice !   Let us offer our prayers and our thanks at once together !   We may yield up our souls, perhaps, at the same hour.

Lady Lisle.   Is mine so pure ?   Have I bemoaned, as I should have done, the faults I have committed ?   Have my sighs arisen for the unmerited mercies of my God ; and not rather for him, the beloved of my heart, the adviser and sustainer I have lost ?

Open, O gates of Death !

Smile on me, approve my last action in this world, O virtuous husband !   O saint and martyr ! my brave, compassionate, and loving Lisle.

Elizabeth Gaunt.   And cannot you too smile, sweet lady ? Are not you with him even now ?   Doth body, doth clay, doth air, separate and estrange free spirits ?   Bethink you of his gladness, of his glory ; and begin to partake them.

Oh ! how could an Englishman, how could twelve, condemn to death — condemn to so great an evil as they thought it and may find it — this innocent and helpless widow ?

Lady Lisle.   Blame not *that* jury!—blame not the jury which brought against me the verdict of guilty.   I was so: I received in my house a wanderer who had fought under the rash and giddy Monmouth.   He was hungry and thirsty, and I took him in.   My Saviour had commanded, my King had forbidden, it.

Yet the twelve would not have delivered me over to death, unless the judge had threatened them with an accusation of treason in default of it.   Terror made them unanimous: they redeemed their properties and lives at the stated price.

Elizabeth Gaunt.   I hope, at least, the unfortunate man whom you received in the hour of danger may avoid his penalty.

Lady Lisle.   Let us hope it.

Elizabeth Gaunt.   I, too, am imprisoned for the same offence; and I have little expectation that he who was concealed by me hath any chance of happiness, although he hath escaped.   Could I find the means of conveying to him a small pittance, I should leave the world the more comfortably.

Lady Lisle.   Trust in God; not in one thing or another, but in all.   Resign the care of this wanderer to *his* guidance.

Elizabeth Gaunt.   He abandoned that guidance.

Lady Lisle.   Unfortunate! how can money then avail him?

Elizabeth Gaunt.   It might save him from distress and from despair, from the taunts of the hard-hearted and from the inclemency of the godly.

Lady Lisle.   In godliness, O my friend! there cannot be inclemency.

Elizabeth Gaunt.   You are thinking of perfection, my dear lady; and I marvel not at it, for what else hath ever occupied your thoughts! But godliness, in almost the best of us, often is austere, often uncompliant and rigid, — proner to reprove than to pardon, to drag back or thrust aside than to invite and help onward.

Poor man! I never knew him before; I cannot tell how he shall endure his self-reproach, or whether it will bring him to calmer thoughts hereafter.

Lady Lisle. I am not a busy idler in curiosity; nor, if I were, is there time enough left me for indulging in it; yet gladly would I learn the history of events, at the first appearance so resembling those in mine.

Elizabeth Gaunt. The person's name I never may disclose; which would be the worst thing I could betray of the trust he placed in me. He took refuge in my humble dwelling, imploring me in the name of Christ to harbour him for a season. Food and raiment were afforded him unsparingly; yet his fears made him shiver through them. Whatever I could urge of prayer and exhortation was not wanting; still, although he prayed, he was disquieted. Soon came to my ears the declaration of the King, that his Majesty would rather pardon a rebel than the concealer of a rebel. The hope was a faint one; but it *was* a hope, and I gave it him. His thanksgivings were now more ardent, his prayers more humble, and oftener repeated. They did not strengthen his heart: it was unpurified and unprepared for them. Poor creature! he consented with it to betray me; and I am condemned to be burned alive. Can we believe, can we encourage the hope, that in his weary way through life he will find those only who will conceal from him the knowledge of this execution? Heavily, too heavily, must it weigh on so irresolute and infirm a breast.

Let it not move you to weeping.

Lady Lisle. It does not; oh! it does not.

Elizabeth Gaunt.   What, then ?

Lady Lisle.   Your saintly tenderness, your heavenly tranquillity.

Elizabeth Gaunt.   No, no : abstain ! abstain ! It was I who grieved ; it was I who doubted.   Let us now be firmer : we have both the same rock to rest upon.   See ! I shed no tears.

I saved his life, an unprofitable and (I fear) a joyless one ; he, by God's grace, has thrown open to me, and at an earlier hour than ever I ventured to expect it, the avenue to eternal bliss.

Lady Lisle.   O my good angel ! that bestrewest with fresh flowers a path already smooth and pleasant to me, may those timorous men who have betrayed, and those misguided ones who have persecuted, us, be conscious on their death-beds that we have entered it ! and they too will at last find rest.

XII.

THE EMPRESS CATHARINE AND PRINCESS DASHKOF.

Catharine.   Into his heart ! into his heart ! If he escapes, we perish.

Do you think, Dashkof, they can hear me through the double door ?   Yes ; hark ! they heard me : they have done it.

What bubbling and gurgling ! he groaned but once.

Listen ! his blood is busier now than it ever was before. I should not have thought it could have splashed so loud upon the floor, although our bed, indeed, is rather of the highest.

Put your ear against the lock.

Dashkof.   I hear nothing.

Catharine.   My ears are quicker than yours, and know these notes better.   Let me come. — Hear nothing !   You did not wait long enough, nor with coolness and patience. There ! — there again ! The drops are now like lead : every half-minute they penetrate the eider-down and the mattress. — How now ! which of these fools has brought his dog with him ? What tramping and lapping ! the creature will carry the marks all about the palace with his feet and muzzle.

Dashkof. Oh, heavens !

Catharine. Are you afraid ?

Dashkof. There is a horror that surpasses fear, and will have none of it. I knew not this before.

Catharine. You turn pale and tremble. You should have supported me, in case I had required it.

Dashkof. I thought only of the tyrant. Neither in life nor in death could any one of these miscreants make me tremble. But the husband slain by his wife ! — I saw not into my heart ; I looked not into it, and it chastises me.

Catharine. Dashkof, are you, then, really unwell ?

Dashkof. What will Russia, what will Europe, say ?

Catharine. Russia has no more voice than a whale. She may toss about in her turbulence ; but my artillery (for now, indeed, I can safely call it mine) shall stun and quiet her.

Dashkof. God grant —

Catharine. I cannot but laugh at thee, my pretty Dash-kof ! God grant, forsooth ! He has granted all we wanted from him at present, — the safe removal of this odious Peter.

Dashkof. Yet Peter loved *you ;* and even the worst husband must leave, surely, the recollection of some sweet moments. The sternest must have trembled, both with apprehension and with hope, at the first alteration in the health of his consort ; at the first promise of true union, imperfect without progeny. Then, there are thanks rendered together to heaven, and satisfactions communicated,

and infant words interpreted ; and when the one has failed
to pacify the sharp cries of . babyhood, pettish and impatient
as sovereignty itself, the success of the other in calming it,
and the unenvied triumph of this exquisite ambition, and
the calm gazes that it wins upon it.

Catharine. Are these, my sweet friend, your lessons from
the Stoic school ? Are not they, rather, the pale-faced
reflections of some kind epithalamiast from Livonia or Bessa-
rabia? Come, come away. I am to know nothing at
present of the deplorable occurrence. Did not you wish
his death ?

Dashkof. It is not his death that shocks me.

Catharine. I understand you : beside, you said as much
before.

Dashkof. I fear for your renown. ·

Catharine. And for your own good name, — ay, Dashkof ?

Dashkof. He was not, nor did I ever wish him to be, my
friend.

Catharine. You hated him.

Dashkof. Even hatred may be plucked up too roughly.

Catharine. Europe shall be informed of my reasons, if
she should ever find out that I countenanced the conspiracy.
She shall be persuaded that her repose made the step necessary ; that my own life was in danger ; that I fell upon my
knees to soften the conspirators ; that, only when I had
fainted, the horrible deed was done. She knows already
that Peter was always ordering new exercises and uniforms ;
and my ministers can evince at the first audience my
womanly love of peace.

Dashkof. Europe may be more easily subjugated than
duped.

Catharine. She shall be both, God willing.

Dashkof. The majesty of thrones will seem endangered
by this open violence.

Catharine. The majesty of thrones is never in jeopardy by those who sit upon them. A sovereign may cover one with blood more safely than a subject can pluck a feather out of the cushion. It is only when the people does the violence that we hear an ill report of it. Kings poison and stab one another in pure legitimacy. Do your republican ideas revolt from such a doctrine?

Dashkof. I do not question this right of theirs, and never will oppose their exercise of it. But if you prove to the people how easy a matter it is to extinguish an emperor, and how pleasantly and prosperously we may live after it, is it not probable that they also will now and then try the experiment; particularly, if any one in Russia should here-after hear of glory and honour, and how immortal are these by the consent of mankind, in all countries and ages, in him who releases the world, or any part of it, from a lawless and ungovernable despot? The chances of escape are many, and the greater if he should have no accomplices. Of his renown there is no doubt at all: that is placed above chance and beyond time, by the sword he hath exercised so righteously.

Catharine. True; but we must reason like democrats no longer. Republicanism is the best thing we can have, when we cannot have power; but no one ever held the two together. I am now autocrat.

Dashkof. Truly, then, may I congratulate you. The dignity is the highest a mortal can attain.

Catharine. I know and feel it.

Dashkof. I wish you always may.

Catharine. I doubt not the stability of power: I can make constant both fortune and love. My Dashkof smiles at this conceit: she has here the same advantage, and does not envy her friend even the autocracy.

Dashkof. Indeed I do, and most heartily.

Catharine. How?

Dashkof. I know very well what those intended who first composed the word ; but they blundered egregiously. In spite of them, it signifies power over oneself, — of all power the most enviable, and the least consistent with power over others.

I hope and trust there is no danger to you from any member of the council-board inflaming the guards or other soldiery.

Catharine. The members of the council-board did not sit *at* it, but *upon* it ; and their tactics were performed cross-legged. What partisans are to be dreaded of that commander-in-chief whose chief command is over pantaloons and facings, whose utmost glory is perched on loops and feathers, and who fancies that battles are to be won rather by pointing the hat than the cannon?

Dashkof. Peter was not insensible to glory; few men are : but wiser heads than his have been perplexed in the road to it, and many have lost it by their ardour to attain it. I have always said that, unless we devote ourselves to the public good, we may perhaps be celebrated; but it is beyond the power of fortune, or even of genius, to exalt us above the dust.

Catharine. Dashkof, you are a sensible, sweet creature ; but rather too romantic on *principle*, and rather too visionary on glory. I shall always both esteem and love you ; but no other woman in Europe will be great enough to endure you, and you will really put the men *hors de combat.* Thinking is an enemy to beauty, and no friend to tenderness. Men can ill brook it one in another; in women it renders them what they would fain call "scornful" (vain assumption of high prerogative!) and what you would find bestial and outrageous. As for my reputation, which I know is dear to you, I can purchase all the best writers in Europe with a snuffbox each, and all the remainder with its contents.

Not a gentleman of the Academy but is enchanted by a toothpick, if I deign to send it him.   A brilliant makes me Semiramis ; a watch-chain, Venus ; a ring, Juno.   Voltaire is my friend.

Dashkof.   He was Frederick's.

Catharine.   I shall be the *Pucelle* of Russia.   No ! I had forgotten : he has treated her scandalously.

Dashkof.   Does your Majesty value the flatteries of a writer who ridicules the most virtuous and glorious of his nation ; who crouched before that monster of infamy, Louis XV. ; and that worse monster, the king his predecessor?   He reviled, with every indignity and indecency, the woman who rescued France ; and who alone, of all that ever led the armies of that kingdom, made its conquerors — the English — tremble.   Its monarchs and marshals cried and ran like capons, flapping their fine crests from wall to wall, and cackling at one breath defiance and sur- render.   The village girl drew them back into battle, and placed the heavens themselves against the enemies of Charles.   She seemed supernatural : the English recruits deserted ; they would not fight against God.

Catharine.   Fools and bigots !

Dashkof.   The whole world contained none other, except- ing those who fed upon them.   The Maid of Orleans was pious and sincere : her life asserted it : her death confirmed it.   Glory to her, Catharine, if you love glory.   Detestation to him who has profaned the memory of this most holy martyr, — the guide and avenger of her king, the redeemer and saviour of her country.

Catharine.   Be it so ; but Voltaire buoys me up above some impertinent, troublesome qualms.

Dashkof.   If Deism had been prevalent in Europe, he would have been the champion of Christianity ; and, if the French had been Protestants, he would have shed tears upon the papal slipper.   He buoys up no one ; for he gives no one hope.   He may amuse : dulness itself must be amused, indeed, by the versatility and brilliancy of his wit.

Catharine.   While I was meditating on the great action I have now so happily accomplished, I sometimes thought his wit feeble.   This idea, no doubt, originated from the littleness of every thing in comparison with my undertaking.

Dashkof.   Alas ! we lose much when we lose the capacity of being delighted by men of genius, and gain little when we are forced to run to them for incredulity.

Catharine.   I shall make some use of my philosopher at Ferney.   I detest him as much as you do ; but where will you find me another who writes so pointedly?   You really, then, fancy that people care for truth?   Innocent Dashkof ! Believe me, there is nothing so delightful in life as to find a liar in a person of repute.   Have you never heard good folks rejoicing at it?   Or, rather, can you mention to me any one who has not been in raptures when he could communicate such glad tidings?   The goutiest man would go on foot without a crutch to tell his friend of it at midnight ; and would cross the Neva for the purpose, when he doubted whether the ice would bear him.   Men, in general, are so weak in truth, that they are obliged to put their bravery under it to prop it.   Why do they pride themselves, think you, on their courage, when the bravest of them is by many degrees less courageous than a mastiff-bitch in the straw? It is only that they may be rogues without hearing it, and make their fortunes without rendering an account of them.

Now we chat again as we used to do.   Your spirits and your enthusiasm have returned.   Courage, my sweet Dashkof ; do not begin to sigh again.   We never can want husbands while we are young and lively.   Alas! I cannot always be so.   Heigho !   But serfs and preferment will do : none shall refuse me at ninety, — Paphos or Tobolsk.

Have not you a song for me?

Dashkof.   German or Russian?

Catharine.   Neither, neither.   Some frightful word might drop — might remind me — no, nothing shall remind me. French, rather: French songs are the liveliest in the world.

Is the rouge off my face?

Dashkof.   It is rather in streaks and mottles; excepting just under the eyes, where it sits as it should do.

Catharine.   I am heated and thirsty: I cannot imagine how.   I think we have not yet taken our coffee.   Was it so strong?   What am I dreaming of? I could eat only a slice of melon at breakfast; my duty urged me *then*, and dinner is yet to come.   Remember, I am to faint at the midst of it when the intelligence comes in, or rather when, in despite of every effort to conceal it from me, the awful truth has flashed upon my mind.   Remember, too, you are to catch me, and to cry for help, and to tear those fine flaxen hairs which we laid up together on the toilet; and we are both to be as inconsolable as we can be for the life of us.   Not now, child, not now.   Come, sing.   I know not how to fill up the interval.   Two long hours yet! — how stupid and tiresome!   I wish all things of the sort could be done and be over in a day.   They are mightily disagreeable when by nature one is not cruel.   People little know my character. I have the tenderest heart upon earth.   I am courageous, but I am full of weaknesses.   I possess in perfection the higher part of men, and — to a friend I may say it — the most amiable part of women.   Ho, ho! at last you smile: now, your thoughts upon that.

Dashkof.   I have heard fifty men swear it.

Catharine.   They lied, the knaves!   I hardly knew them by sight.   We were talking of the sad necessity. — Ivan must follow next: he is heir to the throne.   I have a wild, impetuous, pleasant little *protégé*, who shall attempt to rescue him. I will have him persuaded and incited to it, and assured of pardon on the scaffold. He can never know the trick we play him; unless his head, like a bottle of Bordeaux, ripens its contents in the sawdust. Orders are given that Ivan be dispatched at the first disturbance in the precincts of the castle; in short, at the fire of the sentry. But not now, — another time :· two such scenes together, and without some interlude, would perplex people.

I thought we spoke of singing: do not make me wait, my dearest creature! Now cannot you sing as usual, without smoothing your dove's-throat with your handkerchief, and taking off your necklace? Give it me, then; give it me. I will hold it for you: I must play with something.

Sing, sing; I am quite impatient.

XIII.

JOHN OF GAUNT AND JOANNA OF KENT.

Joanna. How is this, my cousin, that you are besieged in your own house, by the citizens of London? I thought you were their idol.

Gaunt. If their idol, madam, I am one which they may tread on as they list when down; but which, by my soul and knighthood! the ten best battle-axes among them shall find it hard work to unshrine.

Pardon me: I have no right perhaps to take or touch this hand; yet, my sister, bricks and stones and arrows are not presents fit for you. Let me conduct you some paces hence.

Joanna. I will speak to those below in the street. Quit my hand: they shall obey me.

Gaunt. If you intend to order my death, madam, your guards who have entered my court, and whose spurs and halberts I hear upon the staircase, may overpower my domestics ; and, seeing no such escape as becomes my dignity, I submit to you. Behold my sword at your feet ! Some formalities, I trust, will be used in the proceedings against me.   Entitle me, in my attainder, not John of Gaunt, not Duke of Lancaster, not King of Castile ; nor commemorate my father, the most glorious of princes, the vanquisher and pardoner of the most powerful ; nor style me, what those who loved or who flattered me did when I was happier, cousin to the Fair Maid of Kent. Joanna, those days are over !   But no enemy, no law, no eternity can take away from me, or move further off, my affinity in blood to the conqueror· in the field of Crecy, of Poitiers, and Najora. Edward was my brother when he was but your cousin : and the edge of my shield has clinked on his in many a battle. Yes, we were ever near, — if not in worth, in danger.

Joanna.   Attainder ! God avert it ! Duke of Lancaster, what dark thought — alas ! that the Regency should have known it ! I came hither, sir, for no such purpose as to ensnare or incriminate or alarm you.

These weeds might surely have protected me from the fresh tears you have drawn forth.

Gaunt.   Sister, be comforted ! this visor, too, has felt them.

Joanna.   O my Edward ! my own so lately ! Thy memory — thy beloved image — which never hath abandoned me, makes me bold : I dare not say "generous ;" for in saying it I should cease to be so, — and who could be called generous by the side of thee ?   I will rescue from perdition the enemy of my son.

Cousin, you loved your brother. Love, then, what was dearer to him than his life : protect what he, valiant as you have seen him, cannot ! The father, who foiled so many, hath left no enemies ; the innocent child, who can injure no one, finds them.

Why have you unlaced and laid aside your visor? Do not expose your body to those missiles. Hold your shield before yourself, and step aside. I need it not. I am resolved —

Gaunt. On what, my cousin? Speak, and by the Lord! it shall be done. This breast is your shield; this arm is mine.

Joanna. Heavens! who could have hurled those masses of stone from below? they stunned me. Did they descend all of them together; or did they split into fragments on hitting the pavement?

Gaunt. Truly, I was not looking that way: they came, I must believe, while you were speaking.

Joanna. Aside, aside! further back! disregard *me!* Look! that last arrow sticks half its head deep in the wain-scot. It shook so violently I did not see the feather at first.

No, no, Lancaster! I will not permit it. Take your shield up again; and keep it all before you. Now step aside: I am resolved to prove whether the people will hear me.

Gaunt. Then, madam, by your leave —

Joanna. Hold! forbear! Come hither! hither, — not forward.

Gaunt. Villains! take back to your kitchen those spits and skewers that you forsooth would fain call swords and arrows; and keep your bricks and stones for your graves!

Joanna. Imprudent man! who can save you? I shall be frightened: I must speak at once.

O good kind people! ye who so greatly loved me, when I am sure I had done nothing to deserve it, have I (unhappy me!) no merit with you now, when I would assuage your anger, protect your fair fame, and send you home contented with yourselves and me? Who is he, worthy citizens, whom ye would drag to slaughter?

True, indeed, he did revile some one. Neither I nor you can say whom, — some feaster and rioter, it seems, who had little right (he thought) tó carry sword or bow, and who, to show it, hath slunk away. And then another raised his anger: he was indignant that, under his roof, a woman should be exposed to stoning. Which of you would not be as choleric in a like affront? In the house of which among you, should I not be protected as resolutely?

No, no: I never can believe those angry cries. Let none ever tell me again he is the enemy of my son, of his king, your darling child, Richard. Are your fears more lively than a poor weak female's? than a mother's? yours, whom he hath so often led to victory, and praised to his father, naming each, — he, John of Gaunt, the defender of the helpless, the comforter of the desolate, the rallying signal of the desperately brave!

Retire, Duke of Lancaster! This is no time —

Gaunt. Madam, I obey; but not through terror of that puddle at the house-door, which my handful of dust would dry up. Deign to command me!

Joanna. In the name of my son, then, retire!

Gaunt. Angelic goodness! I must fairly win it.

Joanna. I think I know his voice that crieth out, "Who will answer for him?" An honest and loyal man's, one who would counsel and save me in any difficulty and danger. With what pleasure and satisfaction, with what perfect joy and confidence, do I answer our right-trusty and well-judging friend!

"Let Lancaster bring his sureties," say you, "and we separate." A moment yet before we separate; if I might delay you so long, to receive your sanction of those sureties: for, in such grave matters, it would ill become us to be over-hasty. I could bring fifty, I could bring a hundred, not from among soldiers, not from among courtiers; but selected from yourselves, were it equitable and fair to show such partialities, or decorous in the parent and guardian of a king to offer any other than herself.

Raised by the hand of the Almighty from amidst you, but still one of you, if the mother of a family is a part of it, here I stand surety for John of Gaunt, Duke of Lancaster, for his loyalty and allegiance.

Gaunt (running toward Joanna).   Are the rioters, then, bursting into the chamber through the windows?   .

Joanna.   The windows and doors of this solid edifice rattled and shook at the people's acclamation.   My word is given for you : this was theirs in return.   Lancaster! what a voice have the people when they speak out!   It shakes me with astonishment, almost with consternation, while it establishes the throne: what must it be when it is lifted up in vengeance!

Gaunt.   Wind; vapour —

Joanna.   Which none can wield nor hold.   Need I say this to my cousin of Lancaster?

Gaunt.   Rather say, madam, that there is always one star above which can tranquillize and control them.

Joanna.   Go, cousin! another time more sincerity!

Gaunt.   You have this day saved my life from the people ; for I now see my danger better, when it is no longer close before me.   My Christ! if ever I forget —

Joanna.   Swear not: every man in England hath sworn what you would swear.   But if you abandon my Richard, my brave and beautiful child, may — Oh! I could never curse, nor wish an evil ; but, if you desert him in the hour of need, you will think of those who have not deserted you, and your own great heart will lie heavy on you, Lancaster!

Am I graver than I ought to be, that you look dejected? Come, then, gentle cousin, lead me to my horse, and accompany me home.　Richard will embrace us tenderly.　Every one is dear to every other upon rising out fresh from peril; affectionately then will he look, sweet boy, upon his mother and his uncle !　Never mind how many questions he may ask you, nor how strange ones.　His only displeasure, if he has any, will be that he stood not against the rioters or among them.

Gaunt.　Older than he have been as fond of mischief, and as fickle in the choice of a party.

I shall tell him that, coming to blows, the assailant is often in the right; that the assailed is always.

XIV.

TANCREDI AND CONSTANTIA.

Constantia.　Is this in mockery, sir?　Do you place me under a canopy, and upon what (no doubt) you presume to call a throne, for derision ?

Tancredi.　Madonna, if it never were a throne before, henceforward let none approach it but with reverence.　The greatest, the most virtuous, of queens and empresses (it were indecorous in such an inferior as I am to praise in your presence aught else in you that raises men's admiration) leaves a throne for homage wherever she has rested.

Constantia.　Count Tancredi ! your past conduct ill accords with your present speech.　Your courtesy, great as it is, would have been much greater, if you yourself had taken me captive, and had not turned your horse and rode back, on purpose that villanous hands might seize me.

Tancredi.　Knightly hands (I speak it with all submission) are not villanous.　I could not in my heart command you to surrender; and I would not deprive a brave man, a man distinguished for deference and loyalty, of the pleasure he was about to enjoy in encountering your two barons. I am confident he never was discourteous.

Constantia. He was; he took my horse's bridle by the bit, turned his back on me, and would not let me go.

Tancredi. War sometimes is guilty of such enormities, and even worse.

Constantia. I would rather have surrendered myself to the most courageous knight in Italy.

Tancredi. Which may that be?

Constantia. By universal consent, Tancredi, Count of Lecce.

Tancredi. To possess the highest courage is but small glory; to be without it is a great disgrace.

Constantia. Loyalty, not only to ladies, but to princes, is the true and solid foundation of it. Count of Lecce! am I not the daughter of your king?

Tancredi. I recognise in the Lady Constantia the daughter of our late sovereign lord, King William, of glorious memory.

Constantia. Recognise, then, your Queen.

Tancredi. Our laws, and the supporters of these laws, forbid it.

Constantia. Is that memory a glorious one, as you call it, which a single year is sufficient to erase? And did not my father nominate me his heir?

Tancredi. A kingdom is not among the chattels of a king. A people is paled within laws, and not within parks and chases: the powerfullest have no privilege to sport in that enclosure. The barons of the realm and the knights and the people assembled in Palermo, and there by acclamation called and appointed me to govern the State. Certainly, the Lady Constantia is nearer to the throne in blood, and much worthier: I said so then. The unanimous reply was, that Sicily should be independent of all other lands, and that neither German kings nor Roman emperors should control her.

Constantia. You must be aware, sir, that an armed resistance to the Emperor is presumptuous and traitorous.

Tancredi. He has carried fire and sword into my country, and has excited the Genoese and Pisans — men speaking the same language as ourselves — to debark on our coasts, to demolish our villages, and to consume our harvests.

Constantia. Being a sovereign, he possesses the undoubted right.

Tancredi. Being a Sicilian, I have no less a right to resist him.

Constantia. Right? Do rights appertain to vassals?

Tancredi. Even to them; and this one particularly. Were I still a vassal, I should remember that I am a king by election, by birth a Sicilian, and by descent a Norman.

Constantia. All these fine titles give no right whatever to the throne, from which an insuperable bar precludes you.

Tancredi. What bar can there be which my sword and my people's love are unable to bear down?

Constantia. Excuse my answer.

Tancredi. Deign me one, I entreat you, Madonna; although the voice of my country may be more persuasive with me even than yours.

Constantia. Count Lecce, you are worthy of all honour, excepting that alone which can spring only from lawful descent.

Tancredi. My father was the first-born of the Norman conqueror, King of Sicily; my mother, in her own right, Countess of Lecce. I have no reason to blush at my birth; nor did ever the noble breast which gave me nourishment heave with a sense of ignominy as she pressed me to it. She thought the blessing of the poor equivalent to the blessing of the priest.

Constantia.   I would not refer to her ungently ; but she by her alliance set at nought our Holy Father.

Tancredi.   In all her paths, in all her words and actions, she obeyed him.

Constantia.   Our Holy Father?

Tancredi.   Our holiest, our only holy one, — "our Father which art in heaven." She wants no apology: precedent is nothing ; but remember our ancestors — I say *ours ;* for I glory in the thought that they are the same, and so near. Among the early dukes of Normandy, vanquishers of France, and (what is greater) conquerors of England, fewer were born within the pale of wedlock than without. Nevertheless, the ladies of our nation were always as faithful to love and duty as if hoods and surplices and psalms had gone before them, and the Church had been the vestibule to the bedchamber.

Constantia. My cousin the Countess was irreproachable, and her virtues have rendered you as popular as your exploits.

Who is this pretty boy, who holds down his head so, with the salver in his hand?

Tancredi.   He is my son.

Constantia.   Why, then, does he kneel before me ?

Tancredi.   To teach his father his duty.

Constantia.   You acknowledge the rights of my husband ?

Tancredi.   To a fairer possession than fair Sicily.

Constantia.   I must no longer hear this language.

Tancredi.   I utter it from the depths of a heart as pure as the coldest.

Constantia (to the boy).   Yes, my sweet child, I accept the refreshments you have been holding so patiently and present so gracefully. But you should have risen from your knees : such a posture is undue to a captive.

Boy.   Papa ! what did the lady say ?   Do you ever make ladies captives ?

(*To Constantia.*)　Run away !　I will hold his hands for him.

Constantia.　I intend to run away ; but you are quite as dangerous as your father.　Count, you must name my ransom.

Tancredi.　Madonna, I received it when you presented your royal hand to my respectful homage.　The barons who accompanied you are mounted at the door, in order to reconduct you ; and the most noble and the most venerable of mine will be proud of the same permission.

Constantia.　I also am a Sicilian, Tancredi !　I also am sensible to the glories of the Norman race.　Never shall my husband, if I have any influence over him, be the enemy of so courteous a knight.　I could almost say, Prosper ! prosper ! for the defence, the happiness, the example, of our Sicily.

Tancredi.　We may be deprived of territory and power, but never of knighthood.　The brave alone can merit it ; the brave alone can confer it ; the recreant alone can lose it.　So long as there is Norman blood in my veins, I am a knight ; and our blood and our knighthood are given us to defend the sex. — Insensate !　I had almost said the weaker ! and with your eyes before me !

Constantia.　He cannot be a rebel, nor a false, bad man.

Tancredi.　Lady, the sword which I humbly lay at your feet was, a few years ago, a black misshapen mass of metal : the gold that surrounds it, the jewel that surmounts it, the victories it hath gained, constitute now its least value ; it owes the greatest to its position.

XV.

THE MAID OF ORLEANS AND AGNES SOREL.

Agnes. If a boy could ever be found so beautiful and so bashful, I should have taken you for a boy about fifteen years old. Really and without flattery, I think you very lovely.

Jeanne. I hope I shall be greatly more so.

Agnes. Nay, nay: do not expect to improve, except a little in manner. Manner is the fruit, blushes are the blossom: these must fall off before the fruit sets.

Jeanne. By God's help, I may be soon more comely in the eyes of men.

Agnes. Ha, ha! even in piety there is a spice of vanity. The woman can only cease to be the woman when angels have disrobed her in Paradise.

Jeanne. I shall be far from loveliness, even in my own eyes, until I execute the will of God in the deliverance of his people.

Agnes. Never hope it.

Jeanne. The deliverance that is never hoped, seldom comes. We conquer by hope and trust.

Agnes. Be content to have humbled the proud islanders. Oh, how I rejoice that a mere child has done so!

Jeanne. A child of my age, or younger, chastised the Philistines, and smote down the giant their leader.

Agnes. But Talbot is a giant of another mould: his will is immovable; his power is irresistible; his word of command is, *Conquer.*

Jeanne. It shall be heard no longer. The tempest of battle drowns it in English blood.

Agnes. Poor simpleton! The English will recover from the stupor of their fright, believing thee no longer to be a sorceress.　　Did ever sword or spear intimidate them? Hast thou never heard of Crecy? Hast thou never heard of Agincourt? Hast thou never heard of Poitiers, where the chivalry of France was utterly vanquished by sick and starving men, one against five? The French are the eagle's plume; the English are his talon.

Jeanne.　·The talon and the plume shall change places.

Agnes.　Too confident!

Jeanne.　O lady! is any one too confident in God?

Agnes.　We may mistake his guidance. Already, not only the whole host of the English, but many of our wisest and most authoritative Churchmen, believe you on their consciences to act under the instigation of Satan.

Jeanne.　What country or what creature has the Evil One ever saved? With what has he tempted me? — with reproaches, with scorn, with weary days, with slumberless nights, with doubts, distrusts, and dangers, with absence from all who cherish me, with immodest, soldierly language, and perhaps an untimely and a cruel death.

Agnes.　But you are not afraid.

Jeanne.　Healthy and strong, yet always too timorous, a few seasons ago I fled away from the lowings of a young steer, if he ran opposite; I awaited not the butting of a full-grown kid; the barking of a house-dog at our neighbour's gate turned me pale as ashes; and (shame upon me!) I scarcely dared kiss the child, when he called on me with burning tongue in the pestilence of a fever.

Agnes.　No wonder! A creature in a fever! what a frightful thing!

Jeanne.　It would be, were it not so piteous.

Agnes.　And did you kiss it? Did you really kiss the lips?

Jeanne.　I fancied mine would refresh them a little.

Agnes.　And did they? I should have thought mine could do but trifling good in such cases. ·

Jeanne.   Alas ! when I believed I had quite cooled them, it was death had done it.

Agnes.   Ah ! this is courage.

Jeanne.   The courage of the weaker sex, inherent in us all, but as deficient in me as in any until an infant taught me my duty by its cries.   Yet never have I quailed in the front of the fight, where I directed our ranks against the bravest.   God pardon me, if I err ! but I believe his Spirit flamed within my breast, strengthened my arm, and led me on to victory.

Agnes.   Say not so, or they will burn thee alive, poor child !

Why fallest thou before me ?   I have some power, indeed ; but in this extremity I could little help thee : the priest never releases the victim.

What ! how ! thy countenance is radiant with a heavenly joy : thy humility is like an angel's at the feet of God ; I am unworthy to behold it.

Rise, Jeanne, rise !

Jeanne.   Martyrdom too !   The reward were too great for such an easy and glad obedience.   France will become just and righteous ; France will praise the Lord for her deliverance.

Agnes.   Sweet enthusiast !   I am confident, I am certain, of thy innocence.

Jeanne.   O Lady Agnes !

Agnes.   Why fixest thou thy eyes on me so piteously ? Why sobbest thou, — thou, to whom the representation of an imminent death to be apprehended for thee left untroubled, joyous, exulting ?   Speak ; tell me.

Jeanne.   I must.   This also is commanded me.   You believe me innocent ?

Agnes.   In truth, I do ; why, then, look abashed ?   Alas ! alas ! could I mistake the reason ?   I spoke of innocence !

Leave me, leave me. Return another time. Follow thy vocation.

Jeanne.   Agnes Sorel ! be thou more than innocent, if innocence is denied thee. In the name of the Almighty, I call on thee to earn his mercy.

Agnes.   I implore it incessantly, by day, by night. ·

Jeanne.   Serve him as thou mayest best serve him ; and thy tears, I 'promise thee, shall soon be less bitter than those which are dropping on this jewelled hand, and on the rude one which has dared to press it.

Agnes.   What can I, — what can I do ?

Jeanne.   Lead the King back to his kingdom.

Agnes.   The King is in France.

Jeanne.   No, no, no !

Agnes.   Upon my word of honour.

Jeanne.   And at such a time, O Heaven ! in idleness and sloth ?

Agnes.   Indeed, no. He is busy (this is the hour) in feeding and instructing two young hawks. Could you but see the little miscreants, how they dare to bite and claw and tug at him ! He never hurts or scolds them for it; he is so good-natured : he even lets them draw blood ; he is so very brave !

Running away from France ! Who could have raised such a report ? Indeed, he is here. He never thought of leaving the country ; and his affairs are becoming more and more prosperous ever since the battle. Can you not take my asseverations ? Must I say it ? he is now in this very house.

Jeanne.   Then, not in France. In France, all love their country. Others of our kings, old men tell us, have been captives ; but less ignominiously. Their enemies have respected their misfortunes and their honour.

Agnes.   The English have always been merciful and generous.

Jeanne.   And will you be less generous, less merciful?

Agnes.   I?

Jeanne.   You; the beloved of Charles.

Agnes.   This is too confident.   No, no, do not draw back; it is not too confident: it is only too reproachful. But your actions have given you authority.   I have, nevertheless, a right to demand of you what creature on earth I have ever treated ignominiously or unkindly.

Jeanne.   Your beloved; your King.

Agnes.   Never.   I owe to him all I have, all I am.

Jeanne.   Too true!   But let him in return owe to you, O Lady Agnes, eternal happiness, eternal glory.   Condescend to labour with the humble handmaiden of the Lord, in fixing his throne and delivering his people.

Agnes.   I cannot fight; I abominate war.

Jeanne.   Not more than I do; but men love it.

Agnes.   Too much.

Jeanne.   Often too much, for often unjustly.   But when God's right hand is visible in the vanguard, we who are called must follow.

Agnes.   I dare not; indeed, I dare not.

Jeanne.   You dare not?—you who dare withhold the King from his duty!

Agnes.   We must never talk of their duties to our princes.

Jeanne.   Then, we omit to do much of our own.   It is now mine; but, above all, it is yours.

Agnes.   There are learned and religious men who might more properly.

Jeanne.   Are these learned and religious men in the court?   Pray tell me : since, if they are, seeing how poorly they have sped, I may peradventure, however unwillingly, however blamably, abate a little of my reverence for learning, and look for pure religion in lower places.

Agnes. They are modest ; and they usually ask of me in what manner they may best please their master.

Jeanne. They believe, then, that your affection is proportional to the power you possess over him. I have heard complaints that it is usually quite the contrary. But can such great men be loved ? And do you love him ? Why do you sigh so ?

Agnes. Life is but sighs; and, when they cease, 't is over.

Jeanne. Now deign to answer me : do you truly love him ?

Agnes. From my soul, and above it.

Jeanne. Then, save him !

Lady, I am grieved at your sorrow, although it will hereafter be a source of joy unto you. The purest water runs from the hardest rock. Neither worth nor wisdom come without an effort; and patience and piety and salutary knowledge spring up and ripen from under the harrow of affliction. Before there is wine or there is oil, the grape must be trodden and the olive must be pressed.

I see you are framing in your heart the resolution.

Agnes. My heart can admit nothing but his image.

Jeanne. It must fall thence at last.

Agnes. Alas ! alas ! Time loosens man's affections. I may become unworthy. In the sweetest flower there is much that is not fragrance, and which transpires when the freshness has passed away.

Alas, if he should ever cease to love me !

Jeanne. Alas, if God should !

Agnes. Then, indeed, he might afflict me with so grievous a calamity.

Jeanne. And none worse after ?

Agnes. What can there be ?

O Heaven ! mercy ! mercy !

Jeanne. Resolve to earn it: one hour suffices.

Agnes. I am lost. Leave me, leave me.

Jeanne. Do we leave the lost? Are they beyond our care? Remember who died for them, and them only.

Agnes. You subdue me. Spare me: I would only collect my thoughts.

Jeanne. Cast them away. Fresh herbage springs from under the withered. Be strong; and, if you love, be generous. Is it more glorious to make a captive than to redeem one?

Agnes. Is he in danger? Oh!—you see all things— is he? is he? is he?

Jeanne. From none but you.

Agnes. God, it is evident, has given to thee alone the power of rescuing both him and France. He has bestowed on thee the mightiness of virtue.

Jeanne. Believe, and prove thy belief, that he has left no little of it still in thee.

Agnes. When we have lost our chastity, we have lost all, in his sight and in man's. But man is unforgiving; God is merciful.

Jeanne. I am so ignorant, I know only a part of my duties: yet those which my Maker has taught me I am earnest to perform. He teaches me that divine love has less influence over the heart than human; He teaches me that it ought to have more; finally, He commands me to announce to thee, not His anger, but His will.

Agnes. Declare it; Oh! declare it. I do believe His holy word is deposited in thy bosom.

Jeanne. Encourage the King to lead his vassals to the field.

Agnes. When the season is milder.

Jeanne. And bid him leave you for ever.

Agnes. Leave me! one whole campaign! one entire

summer! Oh, anguish! it sounded in my ears as if you said, "for ever."

Jeanne. I say it again.

Agnes. Thy power is superhuman ; mine is not.

Jeanne. It ought to be, in setting God at defiance. The mightiest of the angels rued it.

Agnes. We did not make our hearts.

Jeanne. But we can mend them.

Agnes. Oh! mine (God knows it) bleeds.

Jeanne. Say rather it expels from it the last stagnant drop of its rebellious sin. Salutary pangs may be pain-fuller than mortal ones.

Agnes. Bid him leave me! wish it! permit it! think it near! believe it ever can be! Go, go. — I am lost eternally.

Jeanne. And Charles too.

Agnes. Hush! hush! What has he done that other men have not done also?

Jeanne. He has left undone what others do. Other men fight for their country.

I always thought it was pleasant to the young and beautiful to see those they love victorious and applauded. Twice in my lifetime I have been present at wakes, where prizes were contended for, — what prizes I quite forget ; certainly not kingdoms. The winner was made happy ; but there was one made happier. Village maids love truly : ay, they love glory too ; and not their own. The tenderest heart loves best the courageous one : the gentle voice says, " Why wert thou so hazardous ? " The deeper-toned replies, " For thee, for thee."

Agnes. But if the saints of heaven are offended, as I fear they may be, it would be presumptuous in the King to expose his person in battle until we have supplicated and appeased them.

Jeanne. One hour of self-denial, one hour of stern exertion against the assaults of passion, outvalues a life of prayer.

Agnes. Prayer, if many others will pray with us, can do all things. I will venture to raise up that arm which has only one place for its repose ; I will steal away from that undivided pillow, fragrant with fresh and unextinguishable love.

Jeanne. Sad earthly thoughts !

Agnes. You make them sad ; you cannot make them earthly. There is a divinity in a love descending from on high, in theirs who can see into the heart and mould it to their will.

Jeanne. Has man that power ?

Agnes. Happy, happy girl ! to ask it, and unfeignedly.

Jeanne. Be happy too.

Agnes. How? how ?

Jeanne. By passing resolutely through unhappiness. It must be done.

Agnes. I will throw myself on the pavement, and pray until no star is in the heavens. Oh, I will so pray, so weep !

Jeanne. Unless you save the tears of others, in vain you shed your own.

Agnes. Again I ask you, What *can* I do ?

Jeanne. When God has told you what you ought to do, he has already told you what you can.

Agnes. I will think about it seriously.

Jeanne. Serious thoughts are folded up, chested, and unlooked-at : lighter, like dust, settle all about the chamber. The promise to think seriously dismisses and closes the door on the thought. Adieu ! God pity and pardon you. Through you the wrath of Heaven will fall upon the kingdom.

Agnes. Denouncer of just vengeance, recall the sentence ! I tremble before that countenance severely radiant :

I sink amid that calm, more appalling than the tempest. Look not into my heart with those gentle eyes ! Oh, how they penetrate ! They ought to see no sin : sadly must it pain them.

Jeanne. Think not of me ; pursue thy destination ; save France.

Agnes (after a long pause). Glorious privilege ! divine appointment ! Is it thus, O my Redeemer, my crimes are visited ?

Come with me, blessed Jeanne ! come instantly with me to the King : come to him whom thy virtue and valour have rescued.

Jeanne. Not now ; nor ever with thee. Again I shall behold him, — a conqueror at Orleans, a king at Rheims. Regenerate Agnes ! be this thy glory, if there be any that is not God's.

XVI.

BOSSUET AND THE DUCHESS DE FONTANGES.*

Bossuet. Mademoiselle, it is the King's desire that I compliment you on the elevation you have attained.

Fontanges. O monseigneur, I know very well what you mean. His Majesty is kind and polite to everybody. The last thing he said to me was, " Angélique ! do not forget to compliment Monseigneur the Bishop on the dignity I have conferred upon him, of almoner to the Dauphiness. I desired the appointment for him only that he might be of rank sufficient to confess you, now you are Duchess. Let him be your confessor, my little girl. He has fine manners."

Bossuet. I dare not presume to ask you, mademoiselle, what was your gracious reply to the condescension of our royal master.

---

* The Abbé de Choisy says that she was "*belle comme un ange, mais sotte comme un panier.*"

Fontanges. Oh, yes ! you may. I told him I was almost sure I should be ashamed of confessing such naughty things to a person of high rank, who writes like an angel.

Bossuet. The observation was inspired, mademoiselle, by your goodness and modesty.

Fontanges. You are so agreeable a man, monseigneur, I will confess to you, directly, if you like.

Bossuet. Have you brought yourself to a proper frame of mind, young lady?

Fontanges. What is that?

Bossuet. Do you hate sin?

Fontanges. Very much.

Bossuet. Are you resolved to leave it off?

Fontanges. I have left it off entirely since the King began to love me. I have never said a spiteful word of anybody since.

Bossuet. In your opinion, mademoiselle, are there no other sins than malice?

Fontanges. I never stole any thing; I never committed adultery; I never coveted my neighbour's wife; I never killed any person, though several have told me they should die for me.

Bossuet. Vain, idle talk! Did you listen to it?

Fontanges. Indeed I did, with both ears; it seemed so funny.

Bossuet. You have something to answer for, then.

Fontanges. No, indeed, I have not, monseigneur. I have asked many times after them, and found they were all alive; which mortified me.

Bossuet. So, then! you would really have them die for you?

Fontanges. Oh, no, no! but I wanted to see whether they were in earnest, or told me fibs; for, if they told me fibs, I would never trust them again. I do not care about them; for the King told me I was only to mind *him.*

Bossuet. Lowest and highest, we all owe to his Majesty our duty and submission.

Fontanges. I am sure he has mine : so you need not blame me or question me on that. At first, indeed, when he entered the folding-doors, I was in such a flurry I could hear my heart beat across the chamber ; by degrees I cared little about the matter ; and at last, when I grew used to it, I liked it rather than not. Now, if this is not confession, what is ?

Bossuet. We must abstract the soul from every low mundane thought. Do you hate the world, mademoiselle?

Fontanges. A good deal of it : all Picardy, for example, and all Sologne ; nothing is uglier, — and, oh my life ! what frightful men and women !

Bossuet. I would say, in plain language, do you hate the flesh and the Devil?

Fontanges. Who does not hate the Devil? If you will hold my hand the while, I will tell him so. — I hate you, beast ! There now. As for flesh, I never could bear a fat man. Such people can neither dance nor hunt, nor do anything that I know of.

Bossuet. Mademoiselle Marie-Angélique de Scoraille de Rousille, Duchess de Fontanges ! do you hate titles and dignities and yourself?

Fontanges. Myself ! does any one hate me? Why should I be the first ? Hatred is the worst thing in the world : it makes one so very ugly.

Bossuet. To love God, we must hate ourselves. We must detest our bodies, if we would save our souls.

Fontanges. That is hard : how can I do it ? I see nothing so detestable in mine. Do you? To love is easier. I love God whenever I think of him, he has been so very good to me ; but I cannot hate myself, if I would. As God hath not hated me, why should I ? Beside, it was he who made the King to love me ; for I heard you say in a sermon that the hearts of kings are in his rule and governance. As for titles and dignities, I do not care much about them while His Majesty loves me, and calls me his Angélique. They make people more civil about us ; and therefore it must be a simpleton who hates or disregards them, and a hypocrite who pretends it. I am glad to be a duchess. Manon and Lisette have never tied my garter so as to hurt me since, nor has the mischievous old La Grange said anything cross or bold : on the contrary, she told me what a fine colour and what a plumpness it gave me. Would not you rather be a duchess than a waiting-maid or a nun, if the King gave you your choice ?

Bossuet. Pardon me, mademoiselle, I am confounded at the levity of your question.

Fontanges. I am in earnest, as you see.

Bossuet. Flattery will come before you in other and more dangerous forms : you will be commended for excellences which do not belong to you ; and this you will find as injurious to your repose as to your virtue. An ingenuous mind feels in unmerited praise the bitterest reproof. If you reject it, you are unhappy ; if you accept it, you are undone. The compliments of a king are of themselves sufficient to pervert your intellect.

Fontanges. There you are mistaken twice over. It is not my person that pleases him so greatly: it is my spirit, my wit, my talents, my genius, and that very thing which you have mentioned — what was it? my intellect. He never complimented me the least upon my beauty. Others have said that I am the most beautiful young creature under heaven ; a blossom of Paradise, a nymph, an angel ; worth (let me whisper it in your ear — do I lean too hard ?) a thousand Montespans. But his Majesty never said more on the occasion than that I was *imparagonable !* (what is that ?) and

that he adored me ; holding my hand and sitting quite still.
when he might have romped with me and kissed me.

Bossuet.   I would aspire to the glory of converting you.

Fontanges.   You may do anything with me but convert
me : you must not do that; I am a Catholic born.   M. de
Turenne and Mademoiselle de Duras were heretics : you
did right there.   The King told the chancellor that he prepared them, that the business was arranged for you, and
that you had nothing to do but to get ready the arguments
and responses, which you did gallantly, — did not you?
And yet Mademoiselle de Duras was very awkward for a
long while afterward in crossing herself, and was once
remarked to beat her breast in the litany with the points of
two fingers at a time, when every one is taught to use only
the second, whether it has a ring upon it or not.   I am
sorry she did so ; for people might think her insincere in
her conversion, and pretend that she kept a finger for each
religion.

Bossuet.   It would be as uncharitable to doubt the conviction of Mademoiselle de Duras as that of M. le Maréchal.

Fontanges.   I have heard some fine verses, I can assure
you, monseigneur, in which you are called the conqueror of
Turenne.   I should like to have been his conqueror myself,
he was so great a man.   I understand that you have lately
done a much more difficult thing.

Bossuet.   To what do you refer, mademoiselle?

Fontanges.   That you have overcome quietism.   Now, in
the name of wonder, how could you manage that?

Bossuet.   By the grace of God.

Fontanges.   Yes, indeed ; but never until now did God give
any preacher so much of his grace as to subdue this pest.

Bossuet.   It has appeared among us but lately.

Fontanges.   Oh, dear me ! I have always been subject to
it dreadfully, from a child.

Bossuet.   Really! I never heard so.

Fontanges.   I checked myself as well as I could, although they constantly told me I looked well in it.

Bossuet.   In what, mademoiselle?

Fontanges.   In quietism; that is, when I fell asleep at sermon-time. I am ashamed that such a learned and pious man as M. de Fénélon should incline to it, as they say he does.

Bossuet.   Mademoiselle, you quite mistake the matter.

Fontanges.   Is not then M. de Fénélon thought a very pious and learned person?

Bossuet.   And justly.

Fontanges.   I have read a great way in a romance he has begun, about a knight-errant in search of a father. The King says there are many such about his court; but I never saw them nor heard of them before. The Marchioness de la Motte, his relative, brought it to me, written out in a charming hand, as much as the copy-book would hold; and I got through, I know not how far. If he had gone on with the nymphs in the grotto, I never should have been tired of him; but he quite forgot his own story, and left them at once; in a hurry (I suppose) to set out upon his mission to Saintonge in the *pays d'Aunis*, where the King has promised him a famous *heretic-hunt*. He is, I do assure you, a wonderful creature: he understands so much Latin and Greek, and knows all the tricks of the sorceresses. Yet you keep him under.

Bossuet.   Mademoiselle, if you really have anything to confess, and if you desire that I should have the honour of absolving you, it would be better to proceed in it, than to oppress me with unmerited eulogies on my humble labours.

Fontanges.   You must first direct me, monseigneur: I have nothing particular. The King assures me there is no harm whatever in his love toward me.

Bossuet.   That depends on your thoughts at the moment. If you abstract the mind from the body, and turn your heart toward heaven —

Fontanges.   O monseigneur, I always did so — every time but once — you quite make me blush. Let us converse about something else, or I shall grow too serious, just as you made me the other day at the funeral sermon. And now let me tell you, my Lord, you compose such pretty funeral sermons, I hope I shall have the pleasure of hearing you preach mine.

Bossuet.   Rather let us hope, mademoiselle, that the hour is yet far distant when so melancholy a service will be performed for you. May he who is unborn be the sad announcer of your departure hence !* May he indicate to those around him many virtues not perhaps yet full-blown in you, and point triumphantly to many faults and foibles checked by you in their early growth, and lying dead on the open road you shall have left behind you ! To me the painful duty will, I trust, be spared : I am advanced in age ; you are a child.

Fontanges.   Oh, no ! I am seventeen.

Bossuet.   I should have supposed you younger by two years at least. But do you collect nothing from your own reflection, which raises so many in my breast ? You think it possible that I, aged as I am, may preach a sermon on your funeral. Alas, it is so ! such things have been. There is, however, no funeral so sad to follow as the funeral of our own youth, which we have been pampering with fond desires, ambitious hopes, and all the bright berries that hang in poisonous clusters over the path of life.

Fontanges.   I never minded them : I like peaches better ; and one a day is quite enough for me.

---

* Bossuet was in his fifty-fourth year ; Mademoiselle de Fontanges died in child-bed the year following : he survived her twenty-three.

Bossuet. We say that our days are few; and, saying it, we say too much. Marie-Angélique, we have but one: the past are not ours, and who can promise us the future? This in which we live is ours only while we live in it; the next moment may strike it off from us; the next sentence I would utter may be broken and fall between us. The beauty that has made a thousand hearts to beat at one instant, at the succeeding has been without pulse and colour, without admirer, friend, companion, follower. She by whose eyes the march of victory shall have been directed, whose name shall have animated armies at the extremities of the earth, drops into one of its crevices and mingles with its dust. Duchess de Fontanges! think on this! Lady! so live as to think on it undisturbed!

Fontanges. O God! I am quite alarmed. Do not talk thus gravely. It is in vain that you speak to me in so sweet a voice. I am frightened even at the rattle of the beads about my neck: take them off, and let us talk on other things. What was it that dropped on the floor as you were speaking? It seemed to shake the room, though it sounded like a pin or button.

Bossuet. Never mind it: leave it there; I pray you, I implore you, madame!

Fontanges. Why do you rise? Why do you run? Why not let me? I am nimbler. So, your ring fell from your hand, my Lord Bishop! How quick you are! Could not you have trusted me to pick it up?

Bossuet. Madame is too condescending: had this happened, I should have been overwhelmed with confusion. My hand is shrivelled: the ring has ceased to fit it. A mere accident may draw us into perdition; a mere accident may bestow on us the means of grace. A pebble has moved you more than my words.

Fontanges. It pleases me vastly: I admire rubies. I will

ask the King for one exactly like it.   This is the time he usually comes from the chase.   I am sorry you cannot be present to hear how prettily I shall ask him: but that is impossible, you know; for I shall do it just when I am certain he would give me any thing.   He said so himself: he said but yesterday, —

"Such a sweet creature is worth a world;"

and no actor on the stage was more like a king than his Majesty was when he spoke it, if he had but kept his wig and robe on.   And yet you know he is rather stiff and wrinkled for so great a monarch; and his eyes, I am afraid, are beginning to fail him, he looks so close at things.

Bossuet.   Mademoiselle, such is the duty of a prince who desires to conciliate our regard and love.

Fontanges.   Well, I think so too, though I did not like it in him at first.   I am sure he will order the ring for me, and I will confess to you with it upon my finger.   But first I must be cautious and particular to know of him how much it is his royal will that I should say.

XVII.

DANTE AND BEATRICE.

Dante.   When you saw me profoundly pierced with love, and reddening and trembling, did it become you, did it become you, you whom I have always called *the most gentle Bice*, to join in the heartless laughter of those girls around you?   Answer me.   Reply unhesitatingly.   Requires it so long a space for dissimulation and duplicity?   Pardon! pardon! pardon!   My senses have left me: my heart being gone, they follow.

Beatrice.   Childish man! pursuing the impossible.

Dante. And was it this you laughed at ? We cannot touch the hem of God's garment; yet we fall at his feet, and weep.

Beatrice. But weep not, gentle Dante! fall not before the weakest of his creatures, willing to comfort, unable to relieve, you. Consider a little. Is laughter at all times the signal or the precursor of derision? I smiled, let me avow. it, from the pride I felt in your preference of me ; and, if I laughed, it was to conceal my sentiments. Did you never cover sweet fruit with worthless leaves? Come, do not drop again so soon so faint a smile. I will not have you grave, nor very serious. I pity you ; I must not love you : if I might, I would.

Dante. Yet how much love is due to me, O Bice, who have loved you, as you well remember, even from your tenth year ! But it is reported, and your words confirm it, that you are going to be married.

Beatrice. If so, and if I could have laughed at that, and if my laughter would have estranged you from me, would you blame me?

Dante. Tell me the truth.

Beatrice. The report is general.

Dante. The truth ! the truth! Tell me, Bice.

Beatrice. Marriages, it is said, are made in heaven.

Dante. Is heaven, then, under the paternal roof?

Beatrice. It has been to me, hitherto.

Dante. And now you seek it elsewhere.

Beatrice. I seek it not. The wiser choose for the weaker. Nay, do not sigh so. What would you have, my grave, pensive Dante? What can I do?

Dante. Love me.

Beatrice. I always did.

Dante. Love me? Oh, bliss of heaven !

Beatrice. No, no, no ! Forbear ! Men's kisses are always

mischievous and hurtful; everybody says it. If you truly loved me, you would never think of doing so.

Dante. Nor even this?

Beatrice. You forget that you are no longer a boy; and that it is not thought proper at your time of life to continue the arm at all about the waist. Beside, I think you would better not put your head against my bosom; it beats too much to be pleasant to you. Why do you wish it? Why fancy it can do you any good? It grows no cooler: it seems to grow even hotter. Oh, how it burns! Go, go; it hurts me too: it struggles, it aches, it throbs. Thank you, my gentle friend, for removing your brow away: your hair is very thick and long; and it began to heat me more than you can imagine. While it was there, I could not see your face so well, nor talk with you quietly.

Dante. Oh! when shall we talk so quietly in future?

Beatrice. When I am married. I shall often come to visit my father. He has always been solitary since my mother's death, which happened in my infancy, long before you knew me.

Dante. How can he endure the solitude of his house when you have left it?

Beatrice. The very question I asked him.

Dante. You did not then wish to — to — go away?

Beatrice. Ah, no! It is sad to be an outcast at fifteen.

Dante. An outcast?

Beatrice. Forced to leave a home.

Dante. For another?

Beatrice. Childhood can never have a second.

Dante. But childhood is now over.

Beatrice. I wonder who was so malicious as to tell my father that? He wanted me to be married a whole year ago.

Dante. And, Bice, you hesitated?

Beatrice. No ; I only wept. He is a dear, good father. I never disobeyed him but in those wicked tears ; and they ran the faster the more he reprehended them.

Dante. Say, who is the happy youth?

Beatrice. I know not who ought to be happy, if you are not.

Dante. I?

Beatrice. Surely, you deserve all happiness.

Dante. Happiness! any happiness is denied me. Ah, hours of childhood! bright hours! what fragrant blossoms ye unfold! what bitter fruits to ripen!

Beatrice. Now cannot you continue to sit under that old fig-tree at the corner of the garden? It is always delightful to me to think of it.

Dante. Again you smile : I wish I could smile too.

Beatrice. You were usually more grave than I, although very often, two years ago, you told me I was the graver. Perhaps I *was* then, indeed ; and perhaps I ought to be now : but, really, I must smile at the recollection, and make you smile with me.

Dante. Recollection of what, in particular?

Beatrice. Of your ignorance that a fig-tree is the brittlest of trees, especially when it is in leaf ; and, moreover, of your tumble, when your head was just above the wall, and your hand (with the verses in it) on the very coping-stone. Nobody suspected that I went every day to the bottom of our garden, to hear you repeat your poetry on the other side ; nobody but yourself : you soon found me out. But on that occasion I thought you might have been hurt ; and I clambered up our high peach-tree in the grass-plot nearest the place ; and thence I saw Messer Dante, with his white sleeve reddened by the fig-juice, and the seeds sticking to it pertinaciously, and Messer blushing, and trying to conceal his calamity, and still holding the verses. They were all about me.

Dante. Never shall any verse of mine be uttered from my lips, or from the lips of others, without the memorial of Bice.

Beatrice. Sweet Dante ! in the purity of your soul shall Bice live ; as (we are told by the goat-herds and foresters) poor creatures have been found preserved in the serene and lofty regions of the Alps, many years after the breath of life had left them. Already you rival Guido Cavalcanti and Cino da Pistoja : you must attempt — nor perhaps shall it be vainly — to surpass them in celebrity.

Dante. If ever I am above them, — and I must be, — I know already what angel's hand will have helped me up the ladder. Beatrice, I vow to heaven, shall stand higher than Selvaggia, high and glorious and immortal as that name will be. You have given me joy and sorrow ; for the worst of these (I will not say the least) I will confer on you all the generations of our Italy, all the ages of our world. But, first (alas, from me you must not have it !) may happiness, long happiness, attend you !

Beatrice. Ah ! those words rend your bosom ! Why should they ?

Dante. I could go away contented, or almost contented, were I sure of it. Hope is nearly as strong as despair, and greatly more pertinacious and enduring. You have made me see clearly that you never can be mine in this world ; but at the same time, O Beatrice, you have made me see quite as clearly that you may and must be mine in another. I am older than you : precedency is given to age, and not to worthiness, in our way to heaven. I will watch over you ; I will pray for you when I am nearer to God, and purified from the stains of earth and mortality. He will permit me to behold you lovely as when I left you. Angels in vain should call me onward.

Beatrice. Hush, sweetest Dante ! hush !

Dante. It is there, where I shall have caught the first glimpse of you again, that I wish all my portion of Paradise to be assigned me ; and there, if far below you, yet within the sight of you, to establish my perdurable abode.

Beatrice. Is this piety? Is this wisdom? O Dante! And may not I be called away first?

Dante. Alas! alas! how many small feet have swept off the early dew of life, leaving the path black behind them! But to think that you should go before me! It almost sends me forward on my way, to receive and welcome you. If indeed, O Beatrice! such should be God's immutable will, sometimes look down on me when the song to him is suspended. Oh! look often on me with prayer and pity; for there all prayers are accepted, and all pity is devoid of pain. Why are you silent?

Beatrice. It is very sinful not to love all creatures in the world. But is it true, O Dante! that we always love those the most who make us the most unhappy?

Dante. The remark, I fear, is just.

Beatrice. Then, unless the Virgin be pleased to change my inclinations, I shall begin at last to love my betrothed; for already the very idea of him renders me sad, wearisome, and comfortless. Yesterday, he sent me a bunch of violets. When I took them up, delighted as I felt at that sweetest of odours, which you and I once inhaled together —

Dante. And only once.

Beatrice. You know why. Be quiet now, and hear me. I dropped the posy ; for around it, hidden by various kinds of foliage, was twined the bridal necklace of pearls. O Dante! how worthless are the finest of them (and there are many fine ones) in comparison with those little pebbles, some of which (for perhaps I may not have gathered up all) may be still lying under the peach-tree, and some (do I blush to say it?) under the fig! Tell me not who threw these, nor for what. But you know you were always thoughtful, and sometimes reading, sometimes writing, and sometimes forgetting me, while I waited to see the crimson cap, and the two bay-leaves I fastened in it, rise above the garden-wall. How silently you are listening, if you do listen !

Dante. Oh, could my thoughts incessantly and eternally dwell among these recollections, undisturbed by any other voice, — undisturbed by any other presence ! Soon must they abide with me alone, and be repeated by none but me, — repeated in the accents of anguish and despair ! Why could you not have held in the sad home of your heart that necklace and those violets?

Beatrice. My Dante ! we must all obey : I, my father; you, your God. He will never abandon you.

Dante. I have ever sung, and will for ever sing, the most glorious of his works : and yet, O Bice ! he abandons me, he casts me off ; and he uses your hand for this infliction.

Beatrice. Men travel far and wide, and see many on whom to fix or transfer their affections ; but we maidens have neither the power nor the will. Casting our eyes on the ground, we walk along the straight and narrow road prescribed for us ; and, doing thus, we avoid in great measure the thorns and entanglements of life. We know we are performing our duty; and the fruit of this knowledge is contentment. Season after season, day after day, you have made me serious, pensive, meditative, and almost wise. Being so little a girl, I was proud that you, so much taller, should lean on my shoulder to overlook my work. And greatly more proud was I when in time you taught me several Latin words, and then whole sentences, both in prose and verse ; pasting a strip of paper over, or obscuring with impenetrable ink, those passages in the poets which were beyond my comprehension, and might perplex me. But proudest of all was I when you began to reason with me. What will now be my pride, if you are convinced by the first arguments I ever have opposed to you ; or if you only take them up and try if they are applicable. Certainly do I know (indeed, indeed I do) that even the patience to consider them will make you happier. Will it not, then, make me so? I entertain no other wish. Is not this true love?

Dante. Ah, yes ! the truest, the purest, the least perishable ; but not the sweetest. Here are the rue and the hyssop ; but where the rose?

Beatrice. Wicked must be whatever torments you ; and will you let love do it? Love is the gentlest and kindest breath of God. Are you willing that the Tempter should intercept it, and respire it polluted into your ear? Do not make me hesitate to pray to the Virgin for you, nor tremble lest she look down on you with a reproachful pity. To her alone, O Dante ! dare I confide all my thoughts. Lessen not my confidence in my only refuge.

Dante. God annihilate a power so criminal ! Oh, could my love flow into your breast with hers ! It should flow with equal purity.

Beatrice. You have stored my little mind with many thoughts ; dear because they are yours, and because they are virtuous. May I not, O my Dante ! bring some of them back again to your bosom ; as the *Contadina* lets down the string from the cottage-beam in winter, and culls a few bunches of the soundest for the master of the vineyard? You have not given me glory that the world should shudder at its eclipse. To prove that I am worthy of the smallest part of it, I must obey God ; and, under God, my father. Surely, the voice of Heaven comes to us audibly from a parent's lips. You will be great, and, what is above all greatness, good.

Dante.   Rightly and wisely, my sweet Beatrice, have you spoken in this estimate.   Greatness is to goodness what gravel is to porphyry : the one is a movable accumulation, swept along the surface of the earth ; the other stands fixed and solid and alone, above the violence of war and of the tempest, above all that is residuous of a wasted world. Little men build up great ones ; but the snow colossus soon melts.   The good stand under the eye of God ; and therefore stand.

Beatrice.   Now you are calm and reasonable, listen to Bice.   You must marry.

Dante.   Marry ?

Beatrice.   Unless you do, how can we meet again, unreservedly?   Worse, worse than ever !   I cannot bear to see those large, heavy tears following one another, heavy and slow as nuns at the funeral of a sister.   Come, I will kiss off one, if you will promise me faithfully to shed no more. Be tranquil, be tranquil; only hear reason.   There are many who know you ; and all who know you must love you. Don't you hear me?   Why turn aside? and why go further off ?   I will have that hand.   It twists about as if it hated its confinement.   Perverse and peevish creature ! you have no more reason to be sorry than I have ; and you have many to the contrary which I have not.   Being a man, you are at liberty to admire a variety, and to make a choice.   Is that no comfort to you ?

Dante.

> Bid this bosom cease to grieve ?
>   Bid these eyes fresh objects see ?
> Where 's the comfort to believe
>   None might once have rivall'd me ?
> What ! my freedom to receive !
>   Broken hearts, are they the free ?
> For another can I live
>   When I may not live for thee ?

Beatrice. I will never be fond of you again, if you are so violent. We have been together too long, and we may be noticed.

Dante. Is this our last meeting? If it is — and that it is, my heart has told me — you will not, surely you will not refuse —

Beatrice. Dante! Dante! they make the heart sad after : do not wish it. But prayers — oh, how much better are they ! how much quieter and lighter they render it ! They carry it up to heaven with them ; and those we love are left behind no longer.

XVIII.

BENIOWSKI AND APHANASIA.

Aphanasia. You are leaving us ! you are leaving us ! O Maurice ! in these vast wildernesses are you, then, the only thing cruel ?

Beniowski. Aphanasia ! who, in the name of Heaven, could have told you this ?

Aphanasia. Your sighs when we met at lesson.

Beniowski. And may not an exile sigh ? Does the merciless Catharine, the murderer of her husband, — does even she forbid it ? Loss of rank, of estate, of liberty, of country ! —

Aphanasia. You had lost them, and still were happy. Did not you tell me that our studies were your consolation, and that Aphanasia was your heart's content ?

Beniowski. Innocence and youth should ever be unsuspicious.

Aphanasia. I am, then, wicked in your eyes ! Hear me ! hear me ! It was no suspicion in me. Fly, Maurice ! fly, my beloved Maurice ! my father knows your intention, — fly, fly !

Beniowski.   Impossible ! how know it ? how suspect it ? Speak, my sweet girl ! be calm.

Aphanasia.   Only do not go while there is nothing under heaven but the snows and sea.   Where will you find food ?   Who will chafe your hands ?   Who will warn you not to sleep lest you should die ?   And whose voice, can you tell me, will help your smiles to waken you ?   Maurice, dear Maurice, only stay until the summer : my father will then have ceased to suspect you, and I may learn from you how to bear it.   March, April, May — three months are little — you have been here three months — one fagot's blaze !   Do promise me.   I will throw myself on the floor, and ask my good, kind father to let you leave us.

Beniowski.   Aphanasia ! are you wild ?   My dearest girl, abandon the idea ! you ruin me ; you cause my imprisonment, my deprivation of you, my death.   Listen to me : I swear to do nothing without you.

Aphanasia.   Oh, yes ! you go without me.   .

Beniowski.   Painfullest of my thoughts !   No ; here let me live, — here, lost, degraded, useless ; and Aphanasia be the witness of nothing but my ignominy.   O God ! was I born for this : is mine a light to set in this horizon ?

Aphanasia.   I do not understand you : did you pray ? May the saints of heaven direct you ! but not to leave me !

Beniowski.   O Aphanasia !   I thought you were too reasonable and too courageous to shed tears : you did not weep before ; why do you now ?   .

Aphanasia.   Ah ! why did you read to me, once, of those two lovers who were buried in the same grave ?

Beniowski.   What two ? there have been several.

Aphanasia.   Dearest, dearest Maurice ! are lovers, then, often so happy to the last ?   God will be as good to us as to any ; for surely we trust in him as much.   Come, come along : let us run to the sea the whole way.   There is fondness in your sweet, compassionate face ; and yet, I pray you, do not look, — oh do not look, at me ! I am so ashamed. Take me, take me with you : let us away this instant ! Loose me from your arms, dear Maurice : let me go ; I will return again directly. Forgive me ! *but* forgive me ! Do not think me vile ! You do not : I know you do not, now you kiss me.

Beniowski. Never will I consent to loose you, light of my deliverance ! Let this unite us eternally, my sweet espoused Aphanasia !

Aphanasia. Espoused ! O blessed day ! O light from heaven ! I could no longer be silent ; I could not speak otherwise. The seas are very wide, they tell me, and covered with rocks of ice and mountains of snow for many versts, upon which there is not an aspen or birch or alder to catch at, if the wind should blow hard. There is no rye, nor berries, nor little birds tamed by the frost, nor beasts asleep ; and many days, and many long, stormy nights must be endured upon the waves without food. Could you bear this quite alone ?

Beniowski. Could *you* bear it, Aphanasia ?

Aphanasia. Alone, I could not.

Beniowski. Could you with me ? Think again : we both must suffer.

Aphanasia. How can we, Maurice ? Shall not we die together ? Why do you clasp me so hard ?

Beniowski. Could you endure to see, hour after hour, the deaths and the agonies of the brave ? — how many deaths ! what dreadful agonies ! The fury of thirst, the desperation of hunger ? To hear their bodies plunged nightly into the unhallowed deep ; but first, Aphanasia, to hear them curse me as the author of their sufferings, the deluder of an innocent and inexperienced girl, dragging her with me to a watery grave, famished and ghastly, so lovely and so joyous but the other day?   O my Aphanasia ! there are things which you have never heard, never should have heard, and must hear.   You have read about the works of God in the creation ?

Aphanasia.   My father could teach me thus far : it is in the Bible.

Beniowski.   You have read, " In his image created he man."

Aphanasia.   I thought it strange, until I saw you, Maurice !

Beniowski.   Strange, then, will you think it that man himself breaks this image in his brother.

Aphanasia.   Cain did, and was accursed for it.

Beniowski.   We do, and are honoured ; dishonoured, if we do not.   This is yet distant from the scope of my discourse. You have heard the wolves and bears howl about our sheds ?

Aphanasia.   Oh, yes ! and I have been told that they come upon the ice into the sea.   But I am not afraid of them : I will give you a signal when they are near us.

Beniowski.   Hunger is sometimes so intolerable, it compels them to kill and devour one another.

Aphanasia.   They are violent and hurtful creatures ; but that shocks me.

Beniowski.   What, if men did it ?

Aphanasia.   Merciful Redeemer !   You do not mean, devour each other ?

Beniowski.   Hunger has driven men to this extremity. You doubt my words : astonishment turns you pale, — paler than ever.

Aphanasia.   I do believe you. — Was I then so pale ?   I know they kill one another when they are not famished ; can I wonder that they eat one another when they are ? The cruelty would be less, even without the compulsion ; but the killing did not seem so strange to me, because I had heard of it before.

Beniowski.   Think ! our mariners may draw lots for the victim, or may seize the weakest.

Aphanasia.   I am the weakest ; what can you say now ? O foolish girl to have spoken it !   You have hurt, you have hurt your forehead !   Do not stride away from me thus wildly !   Do not throw back on me those reproaching, those terrifying glances !   Have .the sailors no better hopes of living, strong as they are, and accustomed to the hardships and dangers of the ocean ?

Beniowski.   Hopes there are always.

Aphanasia.   Why, then, do you try to frighten me with what is not and may not ever be?   .Why look as if it pained you to be kind to me ?   Do you retract the promise yet warm upon your lips ?   Would you render the sea itself more horrible than it is ?   Am I ignorant that it has whirl-pools and monsters in its bosom ; and storms and tempests that will never let it rest ; and revengeful and remorseless men, that mix each other's blood in its salt waters, when cities and solitudes are not vast enough to receive it ?   The sea is indeed a very frightful thing : I will look away from it.   I protest to you I never will be sad or frightened at it, if you will but let me go with you.   If you will not, O Maurice, I shall die with fear ; I shall never see you again, though you return, — and you will so wish to see me !   For you will grow kinder when you are away.

Beniowski.   O Aphanasia ! little know you me or yourself.

Aphanasia.   While you are with me, I know how dearly I love you ; when you are absent, I cannot think it half, so many sighs and sorrows interrupt me !   And you will love me very much when you are gone !   Even this might pain you : do not let it !   No ! you have promised ; 't was I who had forgotten it, not you.

How your heart beats !   These are your tears upon my hair and shoulders.

Beniowski.   May they be the last we shall mingle .

Aphanasia.   Let me run, then, and embrace my father :
if he does not bless me, you ought not.

Beniowski.   Aphanasia, I will not refuse you even what
would disunite us.   Let me, too, stay and perish !

Aphanasia.   Ah, my most tender, most confiding father !
must you then weep for me, or must you hate me ?

Beniowski.   We shall meet again ; and soon, perhaps.   I
promise it.   The seas will spare us.   He who inspires the
heart of Aphanasia will preserve her days.

XIX.

LEONORA DI ESTE AND FATHER PANIGAROLA.

Leonora.   You have, then, seen him, father ?   Have you
been able — you who console so many, you who console
even me — to comfort poor Torquato ?

Panigarola.   Madonna, the ears of the unhappy man are
quickened by his solitude and his sorrow.   He seemed
aware, or suspicious at least, that somebody was listening
at his prison-door ; and the cell is so narrow, that every
sound in it is audible to those who stand outside.

Leonora.   He might have whispered.

Panigarola.   It would have been most imprudent.

Leonora.   Said he nothing ? not a word ? — to prove — to
prove that he had not lost his memory ?   His memory — of
what ? of reading his verses to me, and of my listening to
them.   Lucrezia listened to them as attentively as I did,
until she observed his waiting for my applause first.   When
she applauded, he bowed so gracefully ; when I applauded,
he only held down his head.   I was not angry at the difference.   But tell me, good father ! tell me, pray, whether he
gave no sign of sorrow at hearing how soon I am to leave

the world.   Did you forget to mention it ; or did you fear
to pain him ?

Panigarola.   I mentioned it plainly, fully.

Leonora.   And was he, was gentle Torquato, very
sorry ?

Panigarola.   Be less anxious.   He bore it like a Christian.   He said deliberately, — but he trembled and sighed,
as Christians should sigh and tremble, — that, although he
grieved at your illness, yet that to write, either in verse or
prose, on such a visitation of Providence, was repugnant to
his nature.

Leonora.   *He* said so ? could *he* say it ?   But I thought
you told me he feared a listener.   Perhaps, too, he feared
to awaken in me the sentiments he once excited.   However
it may be, already I feel the chilliness of the grave : his
words breathe it over me.   I would have entreated him to
forget me ; but to be forgotten before I had entreated it !
— O father, father!

Panigarola.   Human vanity still is lingering on the precincts of the tomb.   Is it criminal, is it censurable in him,
to anticipate your wishes ?

Leonora.   Knowing the certainty and the nearness of my
departure, he might at least have told me through you that
he lamented to lose me.

Panigarola.   Is there no voice within your heart that
clearly tells you so ?

Leonora.   That voice is too indistinct, too troubled with
the throbbings round about it.   We women want sometimes
to hear what we know ; we die unless we hear what we
doubt.

Panigarola.   Madonna, this is too passionate for the
hour.   But the tears you are shedding are a proof of your
compunction.   May the Virgin and the saints around her
throne accept and ratify it!

Leonora. Father! what were you saying? What were you asking me? Whether no voice whispered to me, assured me? I know not. I am weary of thinking. He must love me. It is not in the nature of such men ever to cease from loving. Was genius ever ungrateful? Mere talents are dry leaves, tossed up and down by gusts of passion, and scattered and swept away ; but Genius lies on the bosom of Memory, and Gratitude at her feet.

Panigarola. Be composed, be calm, be resigned to the will of Heaven ; be ready for that journey's end, where the happier who have gone before, and the enduring who soon must follow, will meet.

Leonora. I am prepared to depart : for I have struggled (God knows) to surmount what is insurmountable ; and the wings of Hope will sustain and raise me, seeing my descent toward earth too swift, too unresisted, and too prone. Pray, father, for my deliverance ; pray also for poor Torquato's : do not separate us in your prayers. Oh, could he leave his prison as surely and as speedily as I shall mine, it would not be more thankfully ! Oh that bars of iron were as fragile as bars of clay ! Oh that princes were as merciful as death ! But tell him, tell Torquato, — go again ; entreat, persuade, command him, — to forget me.

Panigarola. Alas ! even the command, even the command from you and from above, might not avail perhaps. You smile, Madonna !

Leonora. I die happy.

XX.

ADMIRAL BLAKE AND HUMPHREY BLAKE.

Blake. Humphrey ! it hath pleased God, upon this day, to vouchsafe unto the English arms a signal victory. Brother ! it grieves my heart that neither of us can rejoice in it as we should do. Evening is closing on the waters: our crews are returning thanks and offering up prayers to the Almighty. Alas! Alas! that we, who ought to be the most grateful for his protection, and for the spirit he hath breathed into our people, should be the only men in this vast armament whom he hath sorely chastened! — that we of all others should be ashamed to approach the throne of grace among our countrymen and comrades! There are those who accuse you, and they are brave and honest men — there are those, O Humphrey! Humphrey! — was the sound ever heard in our father's house? — who accuse you, brother! brother! — how can I ever find utterance for the word? — yea, of cowardice.

Stand off! I want no help: let me be.

Humphrey. To-day, for the first time in my life, I was in the midst of many ships of superior force firing upon mine, at once and incessantly.

Blake. The very position where most intrepidity was required. Were none with you? — were none in the same danger? Shame, shame! You owed many an example, and you defrauded them of it. They could not gain promotion, the poor seamen! they could not hope for glory in the wide world: example they might have hoped for. You would not have robbed them of their prize-money —

Humphrey. Brother! was ever act of dishonesty imputed to a Blake?

Blake. — Until now. You have robbed them even of the chance they had of winning it; you have robbed them of the pride, the just and chastened pride, awaiting them at home; you have robbed their children of their richest inheritance, a father's good repute.

Humphrey. Despite of calumniators, there are worthy men ready to speak in my favour, at least in extenuation —

Blake. I will hear them, as becomes me, although I myself am cognizant of your default; for during the conflict how anxiously, as often as I could, did I look toward your frigate! Especial care could not be fairly taken that aid at the trying moment should be at hand : other vessels were no less exposed than yours; and it was my duty to avoid all partiality in giving my support.

Humphrey. Grievous as my short-coming may be, surely I am not precluded from what benefit the testimony of my friends may afford me.

Blake. Friends!—ah, thou hast many, Humphrey! and many hast thou well deserved. In youth, in boyhood, in childhood, thy honied temper brought ever warm friends about thee. Easiness of disposition conciliates bad and good alike ; it draws affections to it, and relaxes enmities : but that same easiness renders us, too often, negligent of our graver duties. God knows, I may without the same excuse (if it is any) be impeached of negligence in many of mine ; but never where the honour or safety of my country was concerned. Wherefore the Almighty's hand, in this last battle, as in others no less prosperous, hath conducted and sustained me.

Humphrey! did thy heart wax faint within thee through want of confidence in our sole Deliverer?

Humphrey. Truly I have no such plea.

Blake. It were none ; it were an aggravation.

Humphrey. I confess I am quite unable to offer any adequate defence for my backwardness, my misconduct. Oh! could the hour return, the battle rage again! How many things are worse than death ! — how few things better ! I am twelve years younger than you are, brother, and want your experience.

Blake. Is that your only want? Deplorable is it to know, as now I know, that you will never have it, and that you will have a country which you can never serve.

Humphrey.   Deplorable it is, indeed.   God help me!

Blake.   Worse evil soon may follow, — worse to me, remembering thy childhood.   Merciful Father! after all the blood that hath been shed this day, must I devote a brother's? .

Humphrey.   O Robert! — always compassionate, always kind and generous! — do not inflict on yourself so lasting a calamity, so unavailing a regret.

Listen! — not to me — but listen.   I hear under· your bow the sound of oars.   I hear them drawn into boats : verily do I believe that several of the captains are come to intercede for me, as they said they would do.

Blake.   Intercession is vain.   Honourable men shall judge you.   A man to be honourable must be strictly just, at the least.   Will brave men spare you?   It lies with them.   Whatever be their sentence, my duty is (God give me strength!) to execute it.

Gentlemen! who sent for you?   [*Officers come aboard.*

Senior Officer.   General! we, the captains of your fleet, come before you upon the most painful of duties.

Blake (to himself).   I said so : his doom is sealed.   (*To Senior Officer.*)   Speak, sir! speak out, I say.   A man who hath fought so bravely as you have fought to-day ought never to hesitate and falter.

Senior Officer.   General! we grieve to say that Captain Humphrey Blake, commanding a frigate in the service of the Commonwealth, is accused of remissness in his duty.

Blake.   I know it.   Where is the accuser?   What! no answer from any of you?   Then I am he.   Captain Humphrey Blake is here impleaded of neglecting to perform his uttermost in the seizure or destruction of the enemy's galleons.   Is the crime — write it, write it down! — no need to speak it here — capital?   Negligence? no worse?   But worse can there be ?

Senior Officer.   We would humbly represent —

Blake. Representations, if made at all, must be made elsewhere. He goes forthwith to England. Return each of you to his vessel. Delinquency, grave delinquency, there hath been, of what nature and to what extent you must decide. Take him away. (*Alone.*) Just God ! am I the guilty man, that I should drink to the very dregs such a cup of bitterness ?

Forgive, forgive, O Lord ! the sinful cry of thy servant ! Thy will be done ! Thou hast shown thy power this day, O Lord ! now show, and make me worthy of, thy mercy !

Various and arduous as were Blake's duties, such on all occasions were his circumspection and discretion, that no fault could be detected or invented in him. His victories were won against all calculation but his own. Recollecting, however late, his services ; recollecting that in private life, in political, in military, his purity was ever the same, — England will place Robert Blake the foremost and the highest of her defenders. He was the archetype of her Nelsons, Collingwoods, and Pellews. Of all the men that ever bore a sword, none was worthier of that awful trust.

XXI.

RHADAMISTUS AND ZENOBIA.

Zenobia. My beloved ! my beloved ! I can endure the motion of the horse no longer ; his weariness makes his pace so tiresome to me. Surely we have ridden far, very far, from home ; and how shall we ever pass the wide and rocky stream, among the whirlpools of the rapid and the deep Araxes ? From the first sight of it, O my husband, you have been silent ; you have looked at me at one time intensely, at another wildly : have you mistaken the road, or the ford, or the ferry ?

Rhadamistus. Tired, tired, did you say ? — ay, thou must be. Here thou shalt rest : this before us is the place for it. Alight ; drop into my arms : art thou within them ?

Zenobia. Always in fear. for me, my tender, thoughtful Rhadamistus !

Rhadamistus. Rhadamistus, then, once more embraces his Zenobia !

Zenobia. And presses her to his bosom as with the first embrace.

Rhadamistus. What is the first to the last ?

Zenobia. Nay, this is not the last.

Rhadamistus. Not quite (oh, agony !), not quite ; once more.

Zenobia. So, with a kiss : which you forget to take.

Rhadamistus (aside). And shall this shake my purpose ? It may my limbs, my heart, my brain ; but what my soul so deeply determined it shall strengthen, as winds do trees in forests.

Zenobia. Come, come ! cheer up. How good you are to be persuaded by me : back again at one word ! Hark ! where are those drums and bugles ? On which side are these echoes ?

Rhadamistus. Alight, dear, dear Zenobia ! and does Rhadamistus, then, press thee to his bosom ? Can it be ?

Zenobia. *Can it cease to be ?* you would have said, my Rhadamistus ! Hark ! again those trumpets ? On which bank of the water are they ? Now they seem to come from the mountains, and now along the river. Men's voices too ! threats and yells ! You, my Rhadamistus, could escape.

Rhadamistus. Wherefore ? with whom ? and whither in all Asia ?

Zenobia. Fly ! there are armed men climbing up the cliffs.

Rhadamistus. It was only the sound of the waves in the hollows of them, and the masses of pebbles that rolled down from under you as you knelt to listen.

Zenobia. Turn round ; look behind ! is it dust yonder, or smoke ? And is it the sun, or what is it, shining so crimson ? — not shining any longer now, but deep, and dull purple, embodying into gloom.

Rhadamistus.   It is the sun, about to set at mid-day : we shall soon see no more of him.

Zenobia.   Indeed ! what an ill omen !   But how can you tell that?   Do you think it?   I do not.   Alas ! alas ! the dust and the sounds are nearer.

Rhadamistus.   Prepare, then, my Zenobia !

Zenobia.   I was always prepared for it.

Rhadamistus.   What reason, O unconfiding girl, from the day of our union, have I ever given you to accuse or to suspect me?

Zenobia.   None, none :   your love, even in these sad moments, raises me above the reach of fortune.   How can it pain me so ?   Do I repine ?   Worse may it pain me ; but let that love never pass away !

Rhadamistus.   Was it, then, the loss of power and kingdom for which Zenobia was prepared?

Zenobia.   The kingdom was lost when Rhadamistus lost the affection of his subjects.   Why did they not love you? How could they not?   Tell me so strange a thing.

Rhadamistus.   Fables, fables ! about the death of Mithridates and his children ; declamations, out-cries, as if it were as easy to bring men to life again as — I know not what — to call after them.

Zenobia.   But about the children ?

Rhadamistus.   In all governments there are secrets.

Zenobia.   Between us ?

Rhadamistus.   No longer : time presses ; not a moment is left us, not a refuge, not a hope !

Zenobia.   Then, why draw the sword ?

Rhadamistus.   Wanted I courage ?   Did I not fight as becomes a king ?

Zenobia.   True, most true.

Rhadamistus. Is my resolution lost to me? Did I but dream I had it?

Zenobia. Nobody is very near yet; nor can they cross the dell where we did. Those are fled who could have shown the pathway. Think not of defending me. Listen! look! what thousands are coming! The protecting blade above my head can only provoke the enemy. And do you still keep it there? You grasp my arm too hard. Can you look unkindly? Can it be? Oh! think again and spare me, Rhadamistus! From the vengeance of man, from the judgments of heaven, the unborn may preserve my husband.

Rhadamistus. We must die! They advance; they see us; they rush forward!

Zenobia. Me, me would you strike? Rather let me leap from the precipice.

Rhadamistus. Hold! Whither would thy desperation? Art thou again within my grasp?

Zenobia. O my beloved! never let me call you cruel. Let me love you in the last hour of seeing you as in the first. I must, I must; and be it my thought in death that you love me so! I would have cast away my life to save you from remorse : it may do that and more, preserved by you. Listen! listen! among those who pursue us there are many fathers; childless by his own hand, none. Do not kill our baby — the best of our hopes when we had many — the baby not yet ours! Who shall then plead for you, my unhappy husband?

Rhadamistus. My honour; and before me, sole arbiter and sole audience of our cause. Bethink thee, Zenobia, of the indignities, — not bearing on my fortunes, but imminent over thy beauty! What said I? — did I bid thee think of them? Rather die than imagine, or than question me, what they are! Let me endure two deaths before my own, crueller than wounds or than age or than servitude could inflict on me, rather than make me name them.

Zenobia. Strike ! Lose not a moment so precious ! Why hesitate now, my generous, brave defender ?

Rhadamistus. Zenobia, dost thou bid it ?

Zenobia. Courage is no longer a crime in you. Hear the shouts, the threats, the imprecations ! Hear them, my beloved ! let *me*, no more.

Rhadamistus. Embrace me not, Zenobia ! Loose me, loose me !

Zenobia. I cannot : thrust me away ! Divorce — but with death — the disobedient wife, no longer your Zenobia. (*He strikes.*) Oh ! oh ! one innocent head — in how few days — should have reposed — no, not upon this blood. Swim across ! Is there a descent — an easy one, a safe one, anywhere ? I might have found it for you ! Ill-spent time ! heedless woman !

Rhadamistus. An arrow hath pierced me : more are showering round us. Go, my life's flower ! the blighted branch drops after. Away ! forth into the stream ! strength is yet left me for it. (*He throws her into the river.*) She sinks not ! Oh, last calamity ! She sinks ! she sinks ! Now both are well, and fearless ! One look more ! grant one more look ! On what ? where was it ? which whirl ? which ripple ? they are gone too. How calm is the haven of the most troubled life ! I enter it ! Rebels ! traitors ! slaves ! subjects ! why gape ye ? why halt ye ? On, on, dastards ! Oh that ye dared to follow ! (*He plunges, armed, into the Araxes.*)

XXII.

EPICURUS, LEONTION, AND TERNISSA.

Epicurus. The place commands, in my opinion, a most perfect view.

Leontion. Of what, pray?

Epicurus. Of itself ; seeming to indicate that we, Leontion, who philosophize, should do the same.

Leontion. Go on, go on! say what you please : I will not hate any thing yet. Why have you torn up by the root all these little mountain ash-trees? This is the season of their beauty : come, Ternissa, let us make ourselves necklaces and armlets, such as may captivate old Sylvanus and Pan ; you shall have your choice. But why have you torn them up?

Epicurus. On the contrary, they were brought hither this morning. Sosimenes is spending large sums of money on an olive-ground, and has uprooted some hundreds of them, of all ages and sizes. I shall cover the rougher part of the hill with them, setting the clematis and vine and honey-suckle against them, to unite them.

Ternissa. Oh what a pleasant thing it is to walk in the green light of the vine-leaves, and to breathe the sweet odour of their invisible flowers !

Epicurus. The scent of them is so delicate that it requires a sigh to inhale it ; and this, being accompanied and followed by enjoyment, renders the fragrance so exquisite. Ternissa, it is this, my sweet friend, that made you remember the green light of the foliage, and think of the invisible flowers as you would of some blessing from heaven.

Ternissa. I see feathers flying at certain distances just above the middle of the promontory : what can they mean?

Epicurus. Cannot you imagine them to be feathers from the wings of Zethes and Calaïs, who came hither out of

Thrace to behold the favourite haunts of their mother Oreith-yia? From the precipice that hangs over the sea a few paces from the pinasters she is reported to have been carried off by Boreas; and these remains of the primeval forest have always been held sacred on that belief.

Leontion. The story is an idle one.

Ternissa. O no, Leontion! the story is very true.

Leontion. Indeed?

Ternissa. I have heard not only odes, but sacred and most ancient hymns, upon it; and the voice of Boreas is often audible here, and the screams of Oreithyia.

Leontion. The feathers then really may belong to Caläis and Zethes.

Ternissa. I don't believe it; the winds would have car-ried them away.

Leontion. The gods, to manifest their power as they often do by miracles, could as easily fix a feather eternally on the most tempestuous promontory, as the mark of their feet upon the flint.

Ternissa. They could indeed; but we know the one to a certainty, and have no such authority for the other. I have seen these pinasters from the extremity of the Piræus, and have heard mention of the altar raised to Boreas: where is it?

Epicurus. As it stands in the centre of the platform, we cannot see it from hence; there is the only piece of level ground in the place.

Leontion. Ternissa intends the altar to prove the truth of the story.

Epicurus. Ternissa is slow to admit that even the young can deceive, much less the old; the gay, much less the serious.

Leontion. It is as wise to moderate our belief as our desires.

Epicurus.   Some minds require much belief, some thrive on little.   Rather an exuberance of it is feminine and beautiful.   It acts differently on different hearts ; it troubles some, it consoles others : in the generous it is the nurse of tenderness and kindness, of heroism and self-devotion ; in the ungenerous it fosters pride, impatience of contradiction and appeal, and, like some waters, what it finds a dry stick or hollow straw, it leaves a stone.

Ternissa.   We want it chiefly to make the way of death an easy one.

Epicurus.   There is no easy path leading out of life, and few are the easy ones that lie within it.   I would adorn and smoothen the declivity, and make my residence as commodious as its situation and dimensions may allow ; but principally I would cast underfoot the empty fear of death.

Ternissa.   Oh ! how can you?

Epicurus.   By many arguments already laid down : then by thinking that some perhaps, in almost every age, have been timid and delicate as Ternissa ; and yet have slept soundly, have felt no parent's or friend's tear upon their faces, no throb against their breasts : in short, have been in the calmest of all possible conditions, while those around were in the most deplorable and desperate.

Ternissa.   It would pain me to die, if it were only at the idea that any one I love would grieve too much for me.

Epicurus.   Let the loss of our friends be our only grief, and the apprehension of displeasing them our only fear.

Leontion.   No apostrophes ! no interjections !   Your argument was unsound ; your means futile.

Epicurus.   Tell me, then, whether the horse of a rider on the road should not be spurred forward if he started at a shadow.

Leontion.   Yes.

Epicurus.   I thought so : it would however be better to

guide him quietly up to it, and to show him that it was one. Death is less than a shadow : it represents nothing, even imperfectly.

Leontion.   Then at the best what is it ? why care about it, think about it, or remind us that it must befall us? Would you take the same trouble, when you see my hair entwined with ivy, to make me remember that, although the leaves are green and pliable, the stem is fragile and rough, and that before I go to bed I shall have many knots and entanglements to extricate ?   Let me have them ; but let me not hear of them until the time is come.

Epicurus.   I would never think of death as an embarrassment, but as a blessing.

Ternissa.   How ! a blessing?

Epicurus.   What, if it makes our enemies cease to hate us ? what, if it makes our friends love us the more ?

Leontion.   Us?   According to your doctrine, we shall not exist at all.

Epicurus.   I spoke of that which is consolatory while we are here, and of that which in plain reason ought to render us contented to stay no longer.   You, Leontion, would make others better ; and better they certainly will be, when their hostilities languish in an empty field, and their rancour is tired with treading upon dust.   The generous affections stir about us at the dreary hour of death, as the blossoms of the Median apple swell and diffuse their fragrance in the cold.

Ternissa.   I cannot bear to think of passing the Styx, lest Charon should touch me ; he is so old and wilful, so cross and ugly.

Epicurus.   Ternissa ! Ternissa ! I would accompany you thither, and stand between.   Would you not too, Leontion ?

Leontion.   I don't know.

Ternissa.   Oh ! that we could go together !

Leontion.   Indeed !

Ternissa.   All three, I mean — I said — or was going to say it.   How ill-natured you are, Leontion, to misinterpret me ; I could almost cry.

Leontion.   Do not, do not, Ternissa !   Should that tear drop from your eyelash you would look less beautiful.

Epicurus.   Whenever I see a tear on a beautiful young face, twenty of mine run to meet it.   If it is well to conquer a world, it is better to conquer two.

Ternissa.   That is what Alexander of Macedon wept because he could not accomplish.

Epicurus.   Ternissa ! we three can accomplish it ; or any one of us.

Ternissa.   How ? pray !

Epicurus.   We can conquer this world and the next ; for you will have another, and nothing should be refused you.

Ternissa.   The next by piety : but this, in what manner ?

Epicurus.   By indifference to all who are indifferent to us ; by taking joyfully the benefit that comes spontaneously ; by wishing no more intensely for what is a hair's breadth beyond our reach than for a draught of water from the Ganges ; and by fearing nothing in another life.

Ternissa.   This, O Epicurus ! is the grand impossibility.

Epicurus.   Do you believe the gods to be as benevolent and good as you are ? or do you not ?

Ternissa.   Much kinder, much better in every way.

Epicurus.   Would you kill or hurt the sparrow that you keep in your little dressing-room with a string around the leg, because he hath flown where you did not wish him to fly ?

Ternissa.   No ! it would be cruel ; the string about the leg of so little and weak a creature is enough.

Epicurus.   You think so ; I think so ; God thinks so. This I may say confidently : for whenever there is a sentiment in which strict justice and pure benevolence unite, it must be His.

* * * *

Epicurus. Leontion and Ternissa, those eyes of yours brighten at inquiry, as if they carried a light within them for a guidance.

Leontion. No flattery!

Ternissa. No flattery! Come, teach us!

Epicurus. Will you hear me through in silence?

Leontion. We promise.

Epicurus. Sweet girls! the calm pleasures, such as I hope you will ever find in your walks among these gardens, will improve your beauty, animate your discourse, and correct the little that may hereafter rise up for correction in your dispositions. The smiling ideas left in our bosoms from our infancy, that many plants are the favourites of the gods, and that others were even the objects of their love, — having once been invested with the human form, beautiful and lively and happy as yourselves, — give them an interest beyond the vision ; yes, and a station — let me say it — on the vestibule of our affections. Resign your ingenuous hearts to simple pleasures ; and there is none in man, where men are Attic, that will not follow and outstrip their movements.

Ternissa. O Epicurus !

Epicurus. What said Ternissa?

Leontion. Some of those anemones, I do think, must be still in blossom. Ternissa's golden cup is at home ; but she has brought with her a little vase for the philter — and has filled it to the brim. — Do not hide your head behind my shoulder, Ternissa ; no, nor in my lap.

Epicurus. Yes, there let it lie, — the lovelier for that tendril of sunny brown hair upon it. How it falls and rises ! Which is the hair? which the shadow?

Leontion.   Let the hair rest.

Epicurus.   I must not, perhaps, clasp the shadow !

Leontion.   You philosophers are fond of such unsubstantial things.   Oh, you have taken my volume !   This is deceit.

You live so little in public, and entertain such a contempt for opinion, as to be both indifferent and ignorant what it is that people blame you for.

Epicurus.   I know what it is I should blame myself for, if I attended to them.   Prove them to be wiser and more disinterested in their wisdom than I am, and I will then go down to them and listen to them.   When I have well considered a thing, I deliver it, — regardless of what those think who neither take the time nor possess the faculty of considering any thing well, and who have always lived far remote from the scope of our speculations.

Leontion.   In the volume you snatched away from me so slily, I have defended a position of yours which many philosophers turn into ridicule; namely, that politeness is among the virtues.   I wish you yourself had spoken more at large upon the subject.

Epicurus.   It is one upon which a lady is likely to display more ingenuity and discernment.   If philosophers have ridiculed my sentiment, the reason is, it is among those virtues which in general they find most difficult to assume or counterfeit.

Leontion.   Surely life runs on the smoother for this equability and polish ; and the gratification it affords is more extensive than is afforded even by the highest virtue.   Courage, on nearly all occasions, inflicts as much of evil as it imparts of good.   It may be exerted in defence of our country, in defence of those who love us, in defence of the harmless and helpless ; but those against whom it is thus exerted may possess an equal share of it.   If they succeed, then manifestly the ill it produces is greater than the benefit; if they succumb, it is nearly as great. For many of their adversaries are first killed and maimed, and many of their own kindred are left to lament the consequences of the aggression.

Epicurus. You have spoken first of courage, as that virtue which attracts your sex principally.

Ternissa. Not me; I am always afraid of it. I love those best who can tell me the most things I never knew before, and who have patience with me, and look kindly while they teach me, and almost as if they were waiting for fresh questions. Now let me hear directly what you were about to say to Leontion.

Epicurus. I was proceeding to remark that temperance comes next; and temperance has then its highest merit when it is the support of civility and politeness. So that I think I am right and equitable in attributing to politeness a distinguished rank, not among the ornaments of life, but among the virtues. And you, Leontion and Ternissa, will have leaned the more propensely toward this opinion, if you considered, as I am sure you did, that the peace and concord of families, friends, and cities are preserved by it; in other terms, the harmony of the world.

Ternissa. Leontion spoke of courage, you of temperance; the next great virtue, in the division made by the philosophers, is justice.

Epicurus. Temperance includes it; for temperance is imperfect if it is only an abstinence from too much food, too much wine, too much conviviality or other luxury. It indicates every kind of forbearance. Justice is forbearance from what belongs to another. Giving to this one rightly what that one would hold wrongfully is justice in magistrature, not in the abstract, and is only a part of its office. The perfectly temperate man is also the perfectly just man; but the perfectly just man (as philosophers now define him) may not be the perfectly temperate one. I include the less in the greater.

Leontion. We hear of judges, and upright ones, too, being immoderate eaters and drinkers.

Epicurus. The Lacedemonians are temperate in food and courageous in battle; but men like these, if they existed in sufficient numbers, would devastate the universe. We alone, we Athenians, with less military skill perhaps, and certainly less rigid abstinence from voluptuousness and luxury, have set before it the only grand example of social government and of polished life. From us the seed is scattered; from us flow the streams that irrigate it; and ours are the hands, O Leontion, that collect it, cleanse it, deposit it, and convey and distribute it sound and weighty through every race and age. Exhausted as we are by war, we can do nothing better than lie down and doze while the weather is fine overhead, and dream (if we can) that we are affluent and free.

O sweet sea-air! how bland art thou and refreshing! breathe upon Leontion! breathe upon Ternissa! bring them health and spirits and serenity, many springs and many summers, and when the vine-leaves have reddened and rustle under their feet !

These, my beloved girls, are the children of Eternity: they played around Theseus and the beauteous Amazon; they gave to Pallas the bloom of Venus, and to Venus the animation of Pallas. Is it not better to enjoy by the hour their soft, salubrious influence, than to catch by fits the rancid breath of demagogues; than to swell and move under it without or against our will; than to acquire the semblance of eloquence by the bitterness of passion, the tone of philosophy by disappointment, or the credit of prudence by distrust? Can fortune, can industry, can desert itself, bestow on us any thing we have not here?

Leontion.   And when shall those three meet?   The gods have never united them, knowing that men would put them asunder at their first appearance.

Epicurus.   I am glad to leave the city as often as possible, full as it is of high and glorious reminiscences, and am inclined much rather to indulge in quieter scenes, whither the Graces and Friendship lead me.   I would not contend even with men able to contend with me.   You, Leontion, I see, think differently, and have composed at last your long-meditated work against the philosophy of Theophrastus.

Leontion. Why not? he has been praised above his merits.

Epicurus. My Leontion! you have inadvertently given me the reason and origin of all controversial writings.   They flow not from a love of truth or a regard for science, but from envy and ill-will.   Setting aside the evil of malignity — always hurtful to ourselves, not always to others — there is weakness in the argument you have adduced.   When a writer is praised above his merits in his own times, he is certain of being estimated below them in the times succeeding.   Paradox is dear to most people: it bears the appearance of originality, but is usually the talent of the superficial, the perverse, and the obstinate.

XXIII.

WALTON, COTTON, AND OLDWAYS.

Walton.   God be with thee and preserve thee, old Ashbourne! Thou art verily the pleasantest place upon His earth; I mean from May-day till Michaelmas.   Son Cotton, let us tarry a little here upon the bridge.   Did you ever see greener meadows than these on either hand?   And what says that fine lofty spire upon the left, a trowling-line's cast from us? It says methinks, "Blessed be the Lord for this bounty: come hither and repeat it beside me." How my jade winces! I wish the strawberry-spotted trout, and ash-coloured grayling under us, had the bree that plagues thee so, my merry wench! Look, my son, at the great venerable house opposite. You know these parts as well as I do, or better; are you acquainted with the worthy who lives over there?

Cotton. I cannot say I am.

Walton. You shall be then. He has resided here forty-five years, and knew intimately our good Doctor Donne, and (I hear) hath some of his verses, written when he was a stripling or little better, the which we come after.

Cotton. That, I imagine, must be he! — the man in black, walking above the house.

Walton. Truly said on both counts. Willy Oldways, sure enough; and he doth walk above his house-top. The gardens here, you observe, overhang the streets.

Cotton. Ashbourne, to my mind, is the prettiest town in England.

Walton. And there is nowhere between Trent and Tweed a sweeter stream for the trout, I do assure you, than the one our horses are bestriding. Those, in my opinion, were very wise men who consecrated certain streams to the Muses: I know not whether I can say so much of those who added the mountains. Whenever I am beside a river or rivulet on a sunny day, and think a little while, and let images warm into life about me, and joyous sounds increase and multiply in their innocence, the sun looks brighter and feels warmer, and I am readier to live, and less unready to die.

> Son Cotton! these light idle brooks,
> Peeping into so many nooks,
> Yet have not for their idlest wave
> The leisure you may think they have:

> No, not the little ones that run
> And hide behind the first big stone,
> When they have squirted in the eye
> Of their next neighbour passing by;
> Nor yonder curly sideling fellow
> Of tones than Pan's own flute more mellow,
> Who learns his tune and tries it over
> As girl who fain would please her lover.
> Something has each of them to say;
> He says it and then runs away,
> And says it in another place,
> Continuing the unthrifty chase.
> We have as many tales to tell,
> And look as gay and run as well,
> But leave another to pursue
> What we had promised we would do;
> Till in the order God has fated,
> One after one precipitated,
> Whether we *would* on, or would *not* on,
> Just like these idle waves, son Cotton!

And now I have taken you by surprise, I will have (finished or unfinished) the verses you snatched out of my hand, and promised me another time, when you awoke this morning.

Cotton.   If you must have them, here they are.

Walton (*reads*).

> Rocks under Okeover park-paling
> Better than Ashbourne suit the grayling.
> Reckless of people springs the trout,
> Tossing his vacant head about,
> And his distinction-stars, as one
> Not to be touched but looked upon,
> And smirks askance, as who should say
> " I 'd lay now (if I e'er *did* lay)
> The brightest fly that shines above,
> You know not what *I 'm* thinking of;
> What *you* are, I can plainly tell
> And so, my gentles, fare ye well! "

Heigh ! heigh ! what have we here ? — a double hook with a bait upon each side.   Faith ! son Cotton, if my friend Oldways had seen these, — not the verses I have been reading, but these others I have run over in silence, — he would have reproved me, in his mild amicable way, for my friendship with one who, at two-and-twenty, could either know so much or invent so much about a girl.   He remarked to me, the last time we met, that our climate was more backward and our youth more forward than anciently ; and, taking out a newspaper from under the cushion of his arm-chair, showed me a paragraph, with a cross in red ink, and seven or eight marks of admiration, — some on one side, some on the other, — in which there was mention made of a female servant, who, hardly seventeen years old, charged her master's son, who was barely two older —

Cotton.   Nonsense ! nonsense ! impossible !

Walton.   Why, he himself seemed to express a doubt ; for beneath was written, "Qu., if perjured — which God forbid !   May all turn out to His glory !"

Cotton.   But really I do not recollect that paper of mine, if mine it be, which appears to have stuck against the Okeover paling lines.

Walton.   Look ! they are both on the same scrap.   Truly, son, there are girls here and there who might have said as much as thou, their proctor, hast indicted for them : they have such froward tongues in their heads, some of them. A breath keeps them in motion, like a Jew's harp, God knows how long.   If you do not or will not recollect the verses on this endorsement, I will read them again, and aloud.

Cotton.   Pray do not balk your fancy.

Walton (*reads*).

> Where 's my apron ?   I will gather
> Daffodils and kingcups, rather

> Than have fifty silly souls,
> False as cats and dull as owls,
> Looking up into my eyes
> And half-blinding me with sighs.

Cats, forsooth !　*Owls*, and cry you mercy !　Have they no better words than those for civil people ?　Did any young woman really use the expressions, bating the metre, or can you have contrived them out of pure likelihood ?

Cotton.　I will not gratify your curiosity at present.

Walton.　Anon, then.

> Here I stretch myself along,
> Tell a tale or sing a song,
> By my cousin Sue or Bet —
> And, for dinner here I get
> Strawberries, curds, or what I please,
> With my bread upon my knees ;
> And, when I have had enough,
> Shake, and off to *blind-man's-buff*.

Spoken in the character of a maiden, it seems, who little knows, in her innocence, that *blind-man's-buff* is a perilous game.

You are looking, I perceive, from off the streamlet toward the church.　In its chancel lie the first and last of the Cockaynes.　Whole races of men have been exterminated by war and pestilence ; families and names have slipped down and lost themselves by slow and imperceptible decay : but I doubt whether any breed of fish, with heron and otter and angler in pursuit of it, hath been extinguished since the Heptarchy.　They might humble our pride a whit, methinks, though they hold their tongues.　The people here entertain a strange prejudice against the *nine-eyes*.

Cotton.　What, in the name of wonder, is that ?

Walton.　At your years, do not you know ?　It is a tiny kind of lamprey, a finger long ; it sticketh to the stones by its sucker, and, if you are not warier and more knowing than folks in general from the South, you might take it for a weed: it wriggles its whole body to and fro so regularly, and is of that dark colour which subaqueous weeds are often of, as though they were wet through; which they are not any more than land-weeds, if one may believe young Doctor Plott, who told me so in confidence.

Hold my mare, son Cotton. I will try whether my whip can reach the window, when I have mounted the bank.

Cotton. Curious! the middle of a street to be lower than the side by several feet. People would not believe it in London or Hull.

Walton. Ho! lass! tell the good parson, your master, or his wife if she be nearer at hand, that two friends would dine with him: Charles Cotton, kinsman of Mistress Cotton of the Peak, and his humble servant, Izaak Walton.

Girl. If you are come, gentles, to dine with my master, I will make another kidney-pudding first, while I am about it, and then tell him; not but we have enough and to spare, yet master and mistress love to see plenty, and to welcome with no such peacods as words.

Walton. Go, thou hearty jade; trip it, and tell him.

Cotton. I will answer for it, thy friend is a good soul: I perceive it in the heartiness and alacrity of the wench. She glories in his hospitality, and it renders her labour a delight.

Walton. He wants nothing, yet he keeps the grammar-school, and is ready to receive, as private tutor, any young gentleman in preparation for Oxford or Cambridge; but only one. They live like princes, converse like friends, and part like lovers.

Cotton. Here he comes: I never saw such a profusion of snow-white hair.

Walton. Let us go up and meet him.

Oldways.   Welcome, my friends ! will you walk back into the house, or sit awhile in the shade here ?

Walton.   We will sit down in the grass, on each side of your arm-chair, good master William.   Why, how is this ? here are tulips and other flowers by the thousand growing out of the turf.   You are all of a piece, my sunny saint : you are always concealing the best things about you, except your counsel, your raisin-wine, and your money.

Oldways.   The garden was once divided by borders.   A young gentleman, my private pupil, was fond of leaping : his heels ruined my choicest flowers, ten or twenty at a time. I remonstrated : he patted me on the shoulder, and said, " My dear Mr. Oldways, in these borders if you miss a flower you are uneasy ; now, if the whole garden were in turf, you would be delighted to discover one.   Turf it then, and leave the flowers to grow or not to grow, as may happen."   I mentioned it to my wife : " Suppose we do," said she.   It was done ; and the boy's remark, I have found by experience, is true.   .

Walton.   You have some very nice flies about the trees here, friend Oldways.   Charles, do prythee lay thy hand upon that green one.   He has it ! he has it ! bravely done, upon my life ! I never saw any thing achieved so admirably — not a wing nor an antenna the worse for it.   Put him into this box.   Thou art caught, but shalt catch others : lie softly.

Cotton.   The transport of Dad Walton will carry him off (I would lay a wager) from the object of his ride.

Oldways.   What was that, sir ?

Cotton.   Old Donne, I suspect, is nothing to such a fly.

Walton.   All things in their season.

Cotton.   Come, I carried the rods in my hand all the way.

Oldways.   I never could have believed, Master Izaak, that you would have trusted your tackle out of your own hand.

Walton. Without cogent reason, no, indeed : but — let me whisper.

I told youngster it was because I carried a hunting-whip, and could not hold that and rod too. But why did I carry it, bethink you?

Oldways. I cannot guess.

Walton. I must come behind your chair and whisper softlier. I have that in my pocket which might make the dogs inquisitive and troublesome, — a rare paste, of my own invention. When son Cotton sees me draw up gill after gill, and he can do nothing, he will respect me, — not that I have to complain of him as yet, — and he shall know the whole at supper, after the first day's sport.

Cotton. Have you asked ?

Walton. Anon : have patience..

Cotton. Will no reminding do? Not a rod or line, or fly of any colour, false or true, shall you have, Dad Izaak, before you have made to our kind host here your intended application.

Oldways. No ceremony with me, I desire. Speak, and have.

Walton. Oldways, I think you were curate to Master Donne ?

Oldways. When I was first in holy orders, and he was ready for another world.

Walton. I have heard it reported that you have some of his earlier poetry.

Oldways. I have (I believe) a trifle or two ; but, if he were living, he would not wish them to see the light.

Walton. Why not? — he had nothing to fear : his fame was established ; and he was a discreet and holy man.

Oldways. He was almost in his boyhood when he wrote it, being but in his twenty-third year, and subject to fits of love.

Cotton.   This passion, then, cannot have had for its object the daughter of Sir George More, whom he saw not until afterward.

Oldways.   No, nor was that worthy lady called Margaret, as was this ; who scattered so many pearls in his path, he was wont to say, that he trod uneasily on them, and could never skip them.

Walton.   Let us look at them in his poetry.

Oldways.   I know not whether he would consent thereto, were he living, the lines running so totally on the amorous.

Walton.   Faith and troth ! we mortals are odd fishes. We care not how many see us in choler, when we rave and bluster and make as much noise and bustle as we can ; but if the kindest and most generous affection comes across us, we suppress every sign of it, and hide ourselves in nooks and coverts.   Out with the drawer, my dear Oldways : we have seen Donne's sting ; in justice to him, let us now have a sample of his honey.

Oldways.   Strange that you never asked me before.

Walton.   I am fain to write his life, now one can sit by Dove-side and hold the paper upon one's knee, without fear that some unlucky catchpole of a rheumatism tip one upon the shoulder.   I have many things to say in Donne's favour : let me add to them, by your assistance, that he not only loved well and truly, as was proved in his marriage, — though like a good angler he changed his fly, and did not at all seasons cast his rod over the same water, — but that his heart opened early to the genial affections ; that his satire was only the overflowing of his wit ; that he made it administer to his duties ; that he ordered it to officiate as he would his curate, and perform half the service of the church for him.

Cotton.   Pray, who was the object of his affections ?

Oldways.   The damsel was Mistress Margaret Hayes.

Cotton. I am curious to know, if you will indulge my curiosity, what figure of a woman she might be.

Oldways. She was of lofty stature, red-haired (which some folks dislike), but with comely white eyebrows, a very slender transparent nose, and elegantly thin lips, covering with due astringency a treasure of pearls beyond price, which, as her lover would have it, she never ostentatiously displayed. Her chin was somewhat long, with what I should have simply called a sweet dimple in it, quite proportionate : but Donne said it was more than dimple ; that it was peculiar ; that her angelic face could not have existed without it, nor it without her angelic face, — that is, unless by a new dispensation. He was much taken thereby, and mused upon it deeply : calling it in moments of joyousness the cradle of all sweet fancies, and, in hours of suffering from her sedateness, the vale of death.

Walton. So ingenious are men when the spring torrent of passion shakes up and carries away their thoughts, covering (as it were) the green meadow of still homely life with pebbles and shingle, — some colourless and obtuse, some sharp and sparkling.

Cotton. I hope he was happy in her at last.

Oldways. Ha ! ha ! here we have 'em. Strong lines ! Happy, no ; he was not happy. He was forced to renounce her, by what he then called his evil destiny ; and wishing, if not to forget her, yet to assuage his grief under the impediments to their union, he made a voyage to Spain and the Azores with the Earl of Essex. When this passion first blazed out he was in his twentieth year ; for the physicians do tell us that where the genius is ardent the passions are precocious. The lady had profited by many more seasons than he had, and carried with her manifestly the fruits of circumspection. No benefice falling unto him, nor indeed there being fit preparation, she submitted to the will of

Providence. Howbeit, he could not bring his mind to reason until ten years after, when he married the daughter of the worshipful Sir George More.

Cotton. I do not know whether the arduous step of matrimony, on which many a poor fellow has broken his shin, is a step geometrically calculated for bringing us to reason ; but I have seen passion run up it in a minute, and down it in half a one.

Oldways. Young gentleman ! my patron the doctor was none of the light-hearted and oblivious.

Cotton. Truly I should think it a hard matter to forget such a beauty as his muse and his chaplain have described ; at least if one had ever stood upon the brink of matrimony with her. It is allowable, I hope, to be curious concerning the termination of so singular an attachment.

Oldways. She would listen to none other.

Cotton. Surely she must have had good ears to have heard one.

Oldways. No pretender had the hardihood to come forward too obtrusively. Donne had the misfortune, as he then thought it, to outlive her, after a courtship of about five years, which enabled him to contemplate her ripening beauties at leisure, and to bend over the opening flowers of her virtues and accomplishments. Alas! they were lost to the world (unless by example) in her forty-seventh spring.

Cotton. He might then leisurely bend over them, and quite as easily shake the seed out as smell them. Did she refuse him, then ?

Oldways. He dared not ask her.

Cotton. Why, verily, I should have boggled at that said vale (I think) myself.

Oldways. Izaak ! our young friend Master Cotton is not sedate enough yet, I suspect, for a right view and perception of poetry. I doubt whether these affecting verses on her loss will move him greatly ; somewhat, yes: there is in the beginning so much simplicity, in the middle so much reflection, in the close so much grandeur and sublimity, no scholar can peruse them without strong emotion. Take, and read them.

Cotton.   Come, come ; do not keep them to yourself, dad ! I have the heart of a man, and will bear the recitation as valiantly as may be.

Walton.   I will read aloud the best stanza only.   What strong language !

> " Her one hair would hold a dragon,
>   Her one eye would burn an earth :
> Fall, my tears ! fill each your flagon !
>   Millions fall !   A dearth ! a dearth ! "

Cotton.   The doctor must have been desperate about the fair Margaret.

Walton.   His verses are fine, indeed : one feels for him, poor man !

Cotton.   And wishes him nearer to Stourbridge, or some other glass-furnace.   He must have been at great charges.

Oldways.   Lord help the youth !   Tell him, Izaak, *that* is poetical, and means nothing.

Walton.   He has an inkling of it, I misgive me.

Cotton.   How could he write so smoothly in his affliction, when he exhibited nothing of the same knack afterward ?

Walton.   I don't know ; unless it may be that men's verses, like their knees, stiffen by age.

Oldways.   I do like vastly your glib verses ; but you cannot be at once easy and majestical.

Walton.   It is only our noble rivers that enjoy this privilege.   The greatest conqueror in the world never had so many triumphal arches erected to him as our middlesized brooks have.

Oldways.   Now, Master Izaak, by your leave, I do think you are wrong in calling them triumphal. The ancients would have it that arches over waters were signs of sub-jection.

Walton.   The ancients may have what they will, except-ing your good company for the evening, which (please God !) we shall keep to ourselves. They were mighty people for subjection and subjugation.

Oldways.   Virgil says, " Pontem indignatus Araxes."

Walton.   Araxes was testy enough under it, I dare to aver. But what have you to say about the matter, son Cotton ?

Cotton.   I dare not decide either against my father or mine host.

Oldways.   So, we are yet no friends.

Cotton.   Under favour, then, I would say that we but acknowledge the power of rivers and runlets in bridging them ; for without so doing we could not pass. We are obliged to offer them a crown or diadem as the price of their acquiescence.

Oldways.   Rather do I think that we are feudatory to them much in the same manner as the dukes of Normandy were to the kings of France ; pulling them out of their beds, or making them lie narrowly and uneasily therein.

Walton.   Is that between thy fingers, Will, another piece of honest old Donne's poetry ?

Oldways.   Yes ; these and one other are the only pieces I have kept : for we often throw away or neglect, in the lifetime of our friends, those things which in some following age are searched after through all the libraries in the world. What I am about to read he composed in the meridian heat of youth and genius.

> " She was so beautiful, had God but died
>   For her, and none beside,

> Reeling with holy joy from east to west
> Earth would have sunk down blest ;
> And, burning with bright zeal, the buoyant Sun
> Cried through his worlds, ' *Well done !* ' "

He must have had an eye on the Psalmist ; for I would not asseverate that he was inspired, Master Walton, in the theological sense of the word ; but I do verily believe I discover here a thread of the mantle.

Cotton. And with enough of the nap on it to keep him hot as a muffin when one slips the butter in.

Oldways. True. Nobody would dare to speak thus but from authority. The Greeks and Romans, he remarked, had neat baskets, but scanty simples ; and did not press them down so closely as they might have done, and were fonder of nosegays than of sweet-pots. He told me the rose of Paphos was of one species, the rose of Sharon of another. Whereat he burst forth to the purpose, —

> " Rather give me the lasting rose of Sharon :
> But dip it in the oil that oil'd thy beard, O Aaron ! "

Nevertheless, I could perceive that he was of so equal a mind that he liked them equally in their due season. These majestical verses —

Cotton. I am anxious to hear the last of 'em.

Oldways. No wonder : and I will joyfully gratify so laudable a wish. He wrote this among the earliest :—

> " Juno was proud, Minerva stern,
> Venus would rather toy than learn :
> What fault is there in Margaret Hayes ?
> Her high disdain and pointed stays."

I do not know whether, it being near our dinner-time, I ought to enter so deeply as I could into a criticism on it, which the doctor himself, in a single evening, taught me how to do. Charley is rather of the youngest ; but I will be

circumspect. That Juno was proud may be learned from
Virgil. The following passages in him and other Latin
poets —

Cotton. We will examine them all after dinner, my dear
sir.

Oldways. The nights are not mighty long; but we shall
find time, I trust.

" Minerva stern."

Excuse me a moment : my Homer is in the study, and my
memory is less exact than it was formerly.

Cotton. Oh, my good Mr. Oldways ! do not let us lose
a single moment of your precious company. Doctor Donne
could require no support from these heathens, when he had
the dean and chapter on his side.

Oldways. A few parallel passages. — One would wish to
write as other people have written.

Cotton. We must sleep at Uttoxeter.

Oldways. I hope not.

Walton. We must, indeed ; and, if we once get into
your learning, we shall be carried down the stream without
the power even of wishing to mount it.

Oldways. Well, I will draw in, then.

" Venus would rather toy than learn."

Now, Master Izaak, does that evince a knowledge of the
world, a knowledge of men and manners, or not ? In our
days we have nothing like it: exquisite wisdom ! Reason
and meditate as you ride along, and inform our young friend
here how the beautiful trust in their beauty, and how little
they learn from experience, and how they trifle and toy.
Certainly the Venus here is Venus Urania ; the Doctor
would dissertate upon none other ; yet even she, being a
Venus — the sex is the sex — ay, Izaak !

" Her high disdain and pointed stays."

Volumes and volumes are under these words. Briefly, he could find no other faults in his beloved than the defences of her virgin chastity against his marital and portly ardour. What can be more delicately or more learnedly expressed !

Walton. This is the poetry to reason upon from morning to night.

Cotton. By my conscience is it ! He wrongs it greatly who ventures to talk a word about it, unless after long reflection, or after the instruction of the profound author.

Oldways. Izaak, thou hast a son worthy of thee, or about to become so — the son here of thy adoption — how grave and thoughtful !

Walton. These verses are testimonials of a fine fancy in Donne ; and I like the man the better who admits Love into his study late and early : for which two reasons I seized the lines at first with some avidity. On second thoughts, however, I doubt whether I shall insert them in my biography, or indeed hint at the origin of them. In the whole story of his marriage with the daughter of Sir George More there is something so sacredly romantic, so full of that which bursts from the tenderest heart and from the purest, that I would admit no other light or landscape to the portraiture. For if there is aught, precedent or subsequent, that offends our view of an admirable character, or intercepts or lessens it, we may surely cast it down and suppress it, and neither be called injudicious nor disingenuous. I think it no more requisite to note every fit of anger or of love, than to chronicle the returns of a hiccup, or the times a man rubs between his fingers a sprig of sweet brier to extract its smell. Let the character be taken in the complex ; and let the more obvious and best peculiarities be marked plainly and distinctly, or (if those predominate) the worst. These latter I leave to others, of whom the school is full, who like anatomy the better because the subject of their incisions was hanged. When I would sit upon a bank in my angling, I look for the even turf, and do not trust myself so willingly to a rotten stump or a sharp one. I am not among those who, speaking ill of the virtuous, say, " Truth obliges me to confess — the interests of learning and of society demand from me — " and such things ; when this truth of theirs is the elder sister of malevolence, and teaches her half her tricks ; and when the interests of learning and of society may be found in the printer's ledger, under the author's name, by the side of shillings and pennies.

Oldways.   Friend Izaak, you are indeed exempt from all suspicion of malignity ; and I never heard you intimate that you carry in your pocket the *letters-patent* of society for the management of her interests in this world below. Verily do I believe that both society and learning will pardon you, though you never talk of *pursuing*, or *exposing*, or *laying bare*, or *cutting up ;* or employ any other term in their behalf drawn from the woods and forests, the chase and butchery. Donne fell into unhappiness by aiming at espousals with a person of higher condition than himself.

Walton.   His affections happened to alight upon one who was ; and in most cases I would recommend it rather than the contrary, for the advantage of the children in their manners and in their professions.

Light and worthless men, I have always observed, choose the society of those who are either much above or much below them ; and, like dust and loose feathers, are rarely to be found in their places. Donne was none such : he loved his equals, and would find them where he could ; when he could not find them, he could sit alone. This seems an easy matter ; and yet, masters, there are more people who could run along a rope from yonder spire to this grass-plot, than can do it.

Oldways. Come, gentles : the girl raps at the garden-gate. I hear the ladle against the lock : dinner waits for us.

XXIV.

WILLIAM PENN AND LORD PETERBOROUGH.

Penn. Friend Mordaunt, thou hast been silent the whole course of our ride hither ; and I should not even now interrupt thy cogitations, if the wood before us were not equally uncivil.

Peterborough. Cannot we push straight through it ?

Penn. Verily the thing may be done, after a time : but at present we have no direct business with the Pacific Ocean ; and I doubt whether the woodland terminates till those waters bid it.

Peterborough. And, in this manner, for the sake of liberty you run into a prison. I would not live in a country that does not open to me in all directions, and that I could not go through when I wish.

Penn. Where is such a country on earth ?

Peterborough. England or France.

Penn. Property lays those restrictions there which here are laid by Nature. Now it is right and proper to bow before each of them; but Nature is the more worthy of obedience, as being the elder, the more beauteous, the more powerful, and the more kindly. Thou couldst no sooner ride through thy neighbour's park, unless he permitted it, than through this forest ; and even a raspberry-bush in some ten feet border at Southampton would be an impediment for a time to thy free-will.

Peterborough. I should like rather more elbow-room than this, having gone so far for it.

Penn. Here we are stopped *before* we are tired ; and in

thy *rather more elbow-room* we should be stopped *when* we are, — a mighty advantage truly !   We run, thou sayest, into a prison, for the sake of liberty.   Alas, my friend ! such hath ever been the shortsightedness of mortals.   The liberty they have pursued is indeed the very worst of thraldom.   But neither am I disposed to preach nor thou to hear a preacher.

Here at least we are liberated from the habitudes and injunctions of semi-barbarous society.   We may cultivate, we may manipulate, we may manufacture, what we choose. Industry and thought, and the produce of both, are unrestricted.   We may open our hearts to God without offence to man : our brothers, we may call our brothers, and without a mockery.   If we are studious of wisdom, we may procure it at the maker's, and at prime cost; if we are ambitious of learning, we may gather it fresh and sound, slowly indeed, but surely and richly, and without holding out our beavers for it, in a beaten and dusty road, to some half-dozen old chatterers and dotards, who, by their quarrelsomeness and pertinacity, testify that they have little of a good quality to impart !

Peterborough.   All this is very well; but we cannot enlighten men if we shock their prejudices too violently.

Penn.   The shock comes first, the light follows.

Peterborough.   Most people will run away from both. Children are afraid of being left in the dark ; men are afraid of *not* being left in it.

Penn.   Well, then, let them stay where they are.   We will go forward, and hope to find the road of life easier and better.   In which hope, if we are disappointed, we will at least contribute our share of materials for mending it, and of labour in laying them where they are most wanted.

Prythee now, setting aside thy prepossessions, what thinkest thou, in regard to appearance and aspect, of our Pennsylvania ?

Peterborough.   Even in this country, like every one I have visited, there are some places where I fancy I could fix myself for life.   True, such a fancy lasts but for a moment: the wonder is that it should ever have arisen in me.

*   *   *   *

Penn.   God mend thee, madcap!   Wilt thou come and live with us?

Peterborough.   I confess I should be reluctant to exchange my native country for any other.

Penn.   Are there many parts of England thou hast never seen?

Peterborough.   Several: I was never in Yorkshire or Lancashire, never in Monmouthshire or Nottinghamshire, never in Lincolnshire or Rutland.

Penn.   Hast thou at no time felt a strong desire to visit them?

Peterborough.   Not I, indeed.

Penn.   Yet thy earnestness to come over into America was great: so that America had attractions for thee, in its least memorable parts, powerfuller than England in those that are the most.   York and Lancaster have stirring sounds about them, particularly for minds easily set in motion at the fluttering of banners.   Is the whole island of Britain thy native country, or only a section of it?   If all Britain is, all Ireland must be too; for both are under the same crown, though not under the same laws.   Perhaps not a river nor a channel, but a religion, makes the difference: then I, among millions more of English, am not thy countryman.   Consider a little, what portion or parcel of soil is our native land.

Peterborough.   Just as much of it as our friends stand upon.

Penn.   I would say more: I would say, just as much as supports our vanity in our shire.

Peterborough. I confess, the sort of patriotism which attaches most men to their country is neither a wiser nor a better feeling than the feeling of recluses and cats. Scourges and starvation do not cure them of their stupid love for localities. Mine is different : I like to see the desperate rides I have taken in the forest, and the places where nobody dared follow me. I like to feel and to make felt my superiority, not over tradespeople and farmers in their dull debates, but over lords and archbishops, over chancellors and kings. I would no more live where they are not, than have a mansion-house without a stable, or a paddock without a leaping-bar.

Penn. Superiority in wealth is communicated to many and partaken by thousands, and therefore men pardon it ; while superiority of rank is invidious, and the right to it is questioned in most instances. I would not for the world raise so many evil passions every time I walk in the street.

Peterborough. It would amuse me. I care not how much people hate me, nor how many, provided their hatred feed upon itself without a blow at me, or privation or hindrance. Great dogs fondle little dogs ; but little dogs hate them mortally, and lift up their ears and tails and spinal hairs to make themselves as high. Some people are unhappy unless they can display their superiority ; others are satisfied with a consciousness of it. The latter are incontestably the better ; the former are infinitely the more numerous, and, I will venture to say, the more useful : their vanity, call it nothing else, sets in motion all the activity of less men, and nearly all of greater.

Penn. Prove this activity to be beneficial, prove it only to be neutral, and we meet almost near enough for discussion. Not quite ; for vanity, which is called idle, is never inoperative : when it cannot by its position ramble far afield, it chokes the plant that nurtures it. Consciousness of superiority, kept at home and quiet, is the nurse of innocent meditations and of sound content.

Canst not thou feel and exhibit the same superiority at any distance?

Peterborough. I cannot make *them* feel it nor see it. What is it to be any thing, unless we enjoy the faculty of impressing our image at full length on the breast of others, and strongly too and deeply and (when we wish it) painfully; but mostly on those who, because their rank in court-calendars is the same or higher, imagine they are like me, equal to me, over me? I thank God that there are kings and princes: remove them, and you may leave me alone with swine and sheep.

Penn. I would not draw thee aside from bad company into worse : if indeed that may reasonably be called so, which allows thee greater room and more leisure for reflection, and which imparts to thee purer innocence and engages thee in usefuller occupations. That such is the case is evident. The poets, to whom thou often appealest for sound philosophy and right feeling, never lead shepherds into courts, but often lead the great among shepherds. If it were allowable for me to disdain or despise even the wickedest and vilest of God's creatures, in which condition a king peradventure as easily as any other may be, I think I could, without much perplexity or inquiry, find something in the multitude of his blessings quite as reasonable and proper to thank him for. With all thy contemptuousness, thou placest thy fortune and the means of thy advancement in the hands of such persons ; and they may ruin thee.

Peterborough. You place your money in the hands of bankers; and they may ruin you. The difference is, your ruiner may gain a good deal by it, and may run off ; mine has no such temptation, and should not run far. All titulars else must be produced by others, — a knight by a knight, a peer by a king, — while a gentleman is self-existent. Our country exhibits in every part of it what none in the world beside can do, — men at once of elegant manners, ripe and sound learning, unostentatious honour, unprofessional courage, confiding hospitality, courteous independence. If a Frenchman saw, as he might do any week in the winter, a hundred or two of our fox-hunters in velvet caps and scarlet coats, he would imagine he saw only a company of the rich and idle.

Penn. He would think rightly. Such gentlemen ought, willing or loath, to serve an apprenticeship of seven years to a rat-catcher.

Peterborough.   It would be no unwise thing to teach, if not gentlemen, at least the poor, in what manner to catch and exterminate every kind of noxious animal.   In our island it is not enough to have exterminated the wolves : we are liable to the censure of idleness and ill husbandry while an otter, a weasel, a rat, or a snake is upon it. Zoölogists may affirm that these and other vermin were created for some peculiar use. Voracious and venomous animals may be highly respectable in their own society ; and whenever it is proved that their service to the community is greater than the disadvantage, I will propose in parliament to import them again duty-free.

Penn. Rats come among us with almost every vessel ; and nothing is easier than to entice them to a particular spot, either for the purpose of conversation or destruction, as may seem fittest.

Peterborough. Release me from the traps, and permit me to follow the hounds again ; but previously to remark that probably a third of these fox-hunters is composed of well-educated men. Joining in the amusements of others is, in our social state, the next thing to sympathy in their distresses ; and even the slenderest bond that holds society together should rather be strengthened than snapped. I feel no horror at seeing the young clergyman in the field, by the side of his patron the squire and his parishioner the yeoman. Interests, falsely calculated, would keep men and classes separate, if amusements and recreations did not insensibly bring them close. If conviviality (which by your leave I call a virtue) is promoted by fox-hunting, I will drink to its success, whatever word in the formulary may follow or go before it. Nations have fallen by wanting, not unanimity in the hour of danger, so much as union in the hours preceding it. Our national feelings are healthy and strong by the closeness of their intertexture. What touches one rank is felt by another : it sounds on the rim of the glass, the hall rings with it, and it is well (you will say) if the drum and the trumpet do not catch it. Feelings are more easily communicated among us than manners. Every one disdains to imitate another : a grace is a peculiarity. Yet in a ride no longer than what we have been taking, how many objects excite our interest! By how many old mansion-houses should we have passed, within which there are lodged those virtues that constitute the power, stability, and dignity of a people ! We never see a flight of rooks or wood-pigeons without the certainty that in a few minutes they will alight on some grove where a brave man has been at his walk, or a wise man at his meditations. North America may one day be very rich and powerful ; she cannot be otherwise : but she never will gratify the imagination as Europe does. Her history will interest her inhabitants ; but there never will be another page in it so interesting as that which you yourself have left open for unadorned and simple narrative. The poet, the painter, the statuary, will awaken no enthusiasm in it ; not a ballad can be written on a *bale of goods :* and not only no artist, but no gentleman, is it likely that America will produce in many generations.

Penn.   She does not feel the need of them : she can do without 'em.

Peterborough.   Those who have corn may not care for roses ; and those who have dog-roses may not care for double ones.   I have a buttonhole that wants a posy.

Penn.   I do not conceal from thee my opinion of thy abilities, which probably is not a more favourable one than thy own ; since, however, the vices that accompany them rather than the virtues, thy ambition rather than thy honesty, thy violence rather than thy prudence, may push thee forward to the first station, it is my duty as a friend to forewarn thee that such promotion will render thee, and probably thy countrymen, less happy.

Peterborough.   I will not permit any thing to produce that effect on me : the moment it begins the operation, I resign it.   Happiness would overflow my heart, to see reduced to the condition of my lackeys the proudest of our priesthood and our peerage.   I should only have to regret that, my condition being equal to theirs, I could not so much enjoy their humiliation, as if my family and my connections were inferior.   When I discover men of high birth condescending to perform the petty tricks of party for the sake of obtaining a favour at court, I wish it were possible, by the usages of our country and the feelings of Englishmen, to elevate to the rank of prime minister some wrangling barrister, some impudent buffon, some lampooner from the cockpit, some zany from the theatre, that their backs might serve for his footstool.

Penn.   Was there ever in a Christian land a wish more irrational or more impious !

Peterborough.   The very kind of wish that we oftenest see accomplished.

Penn.   Never wilt thou see this.

Peterborough.   Be not over certain.

Penn. Charles, whose pleasures were low and vulgar, whose parliaments were corrupt and traitorous, chose ministers of some authority. The mob itself, that is amused by dancing dogs, is loath to be ridden by them. The hand that writeth songs on our street walls ought never to subscribe to the signature of our kings.

Peterborough. I speak of Parliament.

Penn. Thou speakest then worse still. A king wears its livery and eats its bread. Without a parliament he is but as the slough of a snake, hanging in a hedge : it retains the form and colours, but it wants the force of the creature ; it waves idly in the wind, and is fit only to frighten wrens and mice.

Thy opinions are aristocratical : yet never did I behold a man who despised the body and members of the aristocracy more haughtily and scornfully than thou dost.

Peterborough. Few have had better opportunities of knowing its composition.

Penn. Those who are older must have had better.

Peterborough. Say rather, may have had more : yet I have omitted few, unless the lady's choice lay below the chaplain ; for I was always select in my rivals. How many do you imagine of our nobility are not bastards, or sons or grandsons of bastards ? If you believe there are a few, I will send the titheman into the enclosure, and he shall levy his proportion in spite of you.

Aristocracy is not contemptible as a system of government ; in fact, it is the only one a true gentleman can acquiesce in. Give me any thing rather than the caldron, eternally bubbling and hissing, in which the scum of the sugar-baker has nought at the bottom of it but the poison of the lawyer's tongue and the bones of the poor reptiles he hath starved.

Enough for aristocracy ; now for aristocrats. Let me hold my hat before my face and look demurely while I say, and apply the saying to myself, that, to him whose survey is from any great elevation, all men below are of an equal size. Aristocrats and democrats, kings and scullions, present one form, one státure, one colour, and one gait. I see but·two classes of men, — those whose names are immortal, and those whose names are perishable. Of the immortal there is but one body ; all in it are so high as to seem on an equality, inasmuch as immortality admits of no degree : of the perishable there are several sets and classes, — kings and chamberlains, trumpeters and heralds, take up half their time in cutting them out and sticking them on blank paper. If I by fighting or writing could throw myself forward and gain futurity, I should think myself as much superior to our sovereign lord the king, as our sovereign lord the king is to any bell-wether in his park at Windsor.

Penn. Strange that men should toil for earthly glory, when the only difference between the lowest and highest is comprised in two letters : the one *in* a thousand, and the one *of* a· thousand, — an atom in the midst of atoms, take which thou wilt !

*   *   *   *

Peterborough. There are two reasons, however, why I never could become a member of your society: first, I never should be quiet or good enough ; secondly, supposing me to have acquired all the tranquillity and virtue requisite, my propensity toward the theatre and its fair actresses would seduce me.

Penn. Thy language is light and inconsequent. Thou couldst not indeed be quiet and good enough for any rational and sedate society, and oughtest not even to discourse with any confidence on virtue, unless thou hadst first subdued such an idle fantasy as that of mockery, and such vile affections as those for paint and fiddles, and wind-instruments and female ones.

Peterborough.   They who are to live in the world must see what the world is composed of, — its better and its worse.

Penn.   No doubt, he who is to live in a street must see the cleaner parts of the pavement and the dirtier ; but must he put his foot into them equally, or, according to thy system, step over the plain flagstone to splash into the filth ?

Peterborough.   Philosophers tell us our passions and follies should be displayed to us together with their evil consequences, that we may regulate and control them.

Penn.   In my opinion, who am no philosopher, we should grow as little familiar even with their faces as may be.   We ought to have nothing to do with such as are exhibited on the tragic stage; if they really exist, they are placed by Providence out of our range : they cannot hurt us unless we run after them on purpose.   Then do we want strange characters of less dimensions, such as can come under our doorway and affect us at home ?   We meet them everywhere ; nay, we cannot help it.

Peterborough.   Elevated sentiment is found in tragedy ; elegant reproof in comedy.

Penn.   Comedy is the aliment of childish malice ; tragedy of malice full-grown.   Comedy has made many fools, and tragedy many criminals.   Show me one man who hath been the wiser or the better for either, and I will show you twenty who have been made rogues and coxcombs by aping the only models of fashion they can find admittance to, and as many more who have grown indifferent and hard-hearted, and whatever else is reprehensible in higher life.

Who, being thoughtless, ignorant, self-sufficient, would not be moody, vindictive, unforgiving, if great monarchs set the example before him ? and who fears those chastisements at the end, which it would be a thousand times more difficult for him to run into than to avoid ?   There is only one thing in either kind of scenic representation which is sure enough never to hit him — the moral.

If, however, thou visitest the theatre for reflection, thou art the first that ever went there for it, although not the first that found it there. Reflection, from whatever quarry extracted, is the foundation of solid pleasures, which foundation, we think, cannot be laid too early in the season.

Peterborough. Solid pleasures, like other solid things, grow heavy and tiresome : I would rather have three or four lighter, of half the value, readily taken up, and as readily laid down again.

Penn. The time will come, young man, when thou wilt reason better, and wilt detest that wit, the rivet of sad consistency. Thou hast spoken, as thou fanciest, a smart and lively thing ; and, because thou hast spoken it, thou wilt tie thy body and soul to it.

Peterborough. Possibly the time may come, but it lies beyond my calculation, when the frame of my mind may be better adapted to those cubic joys you were proposing for me ; but I have observed that all who in their youthful days are the well-strapped, even-paced porters of them have been the first broken down by calamity or infirmity.

Penn. The greater sign of infirmity, the greater of calamity, is there apparent, where the intertexture of pleasures and duties seems intractable.

Peterborough. If the theatre were as hostile and rancourous against the church as the church in some countries is against the theatre, we should call it very immoral ; not because it had less justice on its side, but because it had more virulence. Splendour and processions and declamation and rodomontade are high delights to the multitude. Accompanied by lofty and generous sentiments, they do good ; accompanied by merriment and amusement, they do more good still : for lofty and generous sentiments are so ill-fitted to the heads and hearts of most men, that they fall off in getting through the crowd in the lobby ; but the amusement and merriment go to bed with man and wife, and something of them is left for the children the next morning at breakfast.   I have no greater objection to parade and stateliness in that theatre where the actors have been educated at the university, than in that where one can more easily be admitted behind the scenes : what I want is a little good-nature and good-manners, and that God should be thought as tolerant as my lord chamberlain.

The worst objection I myself could ever find against the theatre is, that I lose in it my original idea of such men as Cæsar and Coriolanus, and, where the loss affects me more deeply, of Juliet and Desdemona.   Alexander was a fool to wish for a second world to conquer : but no man is a fool who wishes for the enjoyment of two ; the real and ideal : nor is it any thing short of a misfortune, I had almost said of a calamity, to confound them.   This is done by the stage: it is likewise done by engravings in books, which have a great effect in weakening the imagination, and are serviceable only to those who have none, and who read negligently and idly.

XXV.

EPICTETUS AND SENECA.

Seneca.   Epictetus, I desired your master, Epaphroditus, to send you hither, having been much pleased with his report of your conduct, and much surprised at the ingenuity of your writings.

Epictetus.   Then I am afraid, my friend —

Seneca.   *My friend !* are these the expressions — Well, let it pass.   Philosophers must bear bravely.   The people expect it.

Epictetus.   Are philosophers, then, only philosophers for the people ; and, instead of instructing them, must they play tricks before them ? Give me rather the gravity of dancing dogs. Their motions are for the rabble ; their reverential eyes and pendant paws are under the pressure of awe at a master ; but they are dogs, and not below their destinies.

Seneca.   Epictetus! I will give you three talents to let me take that sentiment for my own.

Epictetus.   I would give thee twenty, if I had them, to make it thine.

Seneca.   You mean, by lending to it the graces of my language ?

Epictetus.   I mean, by lending it to thy conduct. And now let me console and comfort thee, under the calamity I brought on thee by calling thee *my friend.* If thou art not my friend, why send for me ? Enemy I can have none : being a slave, Fortune has now done with me.

Seneca.   Continue, then, your former observations. What were you saying ?

Epictetus.   That which thou interruptedst.

Seneca.   What was it?

Epictetus.   I should have remarked that, if thou foundest ingenuity in my writings, thou must have discovered in them some deviation from the plain, homely truths of Zeno and Cleanthes.

Seneca.   We all swerve a little from them.

Epictetus.   In practice too?

Seneca.   Yes, even in practice, I am afraid.

Epictetus.   Often?

Seneca.   Too often.

Epictetus.   Strange! I have been attentive, and yet have remarked but one difference among you great personages at Rome.

Seneca. What difference fell under your observation?

Epictetus. Crates and Zeno and Cleanthes taught us that our desires were to be subdued by philosophy alone. In this city, their acute and inventive scholars take us aside, and show us that there is not only one way, but two.

Seneca. Two ways?

Epictetus. They whisper in our ear, "These two ways are philosophy and enjoyment : the wiser man will take the readier, or, not finding it, the alternative." Thou reddenest.

Seneca. Monstrous degeneracy.

Epictetus. What magnificent rings! I did not notice them until thou liftedst up thy hands to heaven, in detestation of such effeminacy and impudence.

Seneca. The rings are not amiss; my rank rivets them upon my fingers : I am forced to wear them. Our emperor gave me one, Epaphroditus another, Tigellinus the third. I cannot lay them aside a single day, for fear of offending the gods, and those whom they love the most worthily.

Epictetus. Although they make thee stretch out thy fingers, like the arms and legs of one of us slaves upon a cross.

Seneca. Oh horrible! Find some other resemblance.

Epictetus. The extremities of a fig-leaf.

Seneca. Ignoble!

Epictetus. The claws of a toad, trodden on or stoned.

Seneca. You have great need, Epictetus, of an instructor in eloquence and rhetoric : you want topics and tropes and figures.

Epictetus. I have no room for them. They make such a buzz in the house, a man's own wife cannot understand what he says to her.

Seneca. Let us reason a little upon style. I would set you right, and remove from before you the prejudices of a somewhat rustic education. We may adorn the simplicity of the wisest.

Epictetus. Thou canst not adorn simplicity. What is naked or defective is susceptible of decoration ; what is decorated is simplicity no longer. Thou mayst give another thing in exchange for it ; but if thou wert master of it, thou wouldst preserve it inviolate. It is no wonder that we mortals, little able as we are to see truth, should be less able to express it.

Seneca. You have formed at present no idea of style.

Epictetus. I never think about it. First, I consider whether what I am about to say is true ; then whether I can say it with brevity, in such a manner as that others shall see it as clearly as I do in the light of truth ; for, if they survey it as an ingenuity, my desire is ungratified, my duty unfulfilled. I go not with those who dance round the image of Truth, less out of honour to her than to display their agility and address.

Seneca. We must attract the attention of readers by novelty and force and grandeur of expression.

Epictetus. We must. Nothing is so grand as truth, nothing so forcible, nothing so novel.

Seneca. Sonorous sentences are wanted to awaken the lethargy of indolence.

Epictetus. Awaken it to what? Here lies the question ; and a weighty one it is. If thou awakenest men when they can see nothing and do no work, it is better to let them rest : but will not they, thinkest thou, look up at a rainbow, unless they are called to it by a clap of thunder ?

Seneca. Your early youth, Epictetus, has been, I will not say neglected, but cultivated with rude instruments and unskilful hands.

Epictetus. I thank God for it. Those rude instruments have left the turf lying yet toward the sun ; and those unskilful hands have plucked out the docks.

Seneca. We hope and believe that we have attained a

vein of eloquence, brighter and more varied than has been hitherto laid open to the world.

Epictetus. Than any in the Greek?

Seneca. We trust so.

Epictetus. Than your Cicero's?

Seneca. If the declaration may be made without an offence to modesty. Surely, you cannot estimate or value the eloquence of that noble pleader?

Epictetus. Imperfectly, not being born in Italy; and the noble pleader is a much less man with me than the noble philosopher. I regret that, having farms and villas, he would not keep his distance from the pumping up of foul words against thieves, cutthroats, and other rogues; and that he lied, sweated, and thumped his head and thighs, in behalf of those who were no better.

Seneca. Senators must have clients, and must protect them.

Epictetus. Innocent or guilty?

Seneca. Doubtless.

Epictetus. If it becomes a philosopher to regret at all, and if I regret what is and might not be, I may regret more what both is and must be. However, it is an amiable thing, and no small merit in the wealthy, even to trifle and play at their leisure hours with philosophy. It cannot be expected that such a personage should espouse her, or should recommend her as an inseparable mate to his heir.

Seneca. I would.

Epictetus. Yes, Seneca, but thou hast no son to make the match for; and thy recommendation, I suspect, would be given him before he could consummate the marriage. Every man wishes his sons to be philosophers while they are young; but takes especial care, as they grow older, to teach them its insufficiency and unfitness for their intercourse with mankind. The paternal voice says, "You must

not be particular; you are about to have a profession to live
by: follow those who have thriven the best in it." Now,
among these, whatever be the profession, canst thou point
out to me one single philosopher?

Seneca. Not just now. Nor, upon reflection, do I think
it feasible.

Epictetus. Thou indeed mayest live much to thy ease
and satisfaction with philosophy, having (they say) two
thousand talents.

Seneca. And a trifle to spare — pressed upon me by that
god-like youth, my pupil Nero.

Epictetus. Seneca! where God hath placed a mine he
hath placed the materials of an earthquake.

Seneca. A true philosopher is beyond the reach of Fortune.

Epictetus. The false one thinks himself so. Fortune
cares little about philosophers; but she remembers where
she hath set a rich man, and she laughs to see the Destinies
at his door.

XXVI.

LUCULLUS AND CÆSAR.

Lucullus. You are surveying the little lake beside us. It
contains no fish, birds never alight on it, the water is extremely pure and cold; the walk round is pleasant, not only
because there is always a gentle breeze from it, but because
the turf is fine, and the surface of the mountain on this
summit is perfectly on a level to a great extent in length, —
not a trifling advantage to me, who walk often and am weak.
I have no alley, no garden, no inclosure; the park is in the
vale below, where a brook supplies the ponds, and where
my servants are lodged; for here I have only twelve in
attendance.

Cæsar. What is that so white, toward the Adriatic?

Lucullus. The Adriatic itself. Turn round and you may descry the Tuscan Sea. Our situation is reported to be among the highest of the Apennines. — Marcipor has made the sign to me that dinner is ready. Pass this way.

Cæsar. What a library is here! Ah, Marcus Tullius! I salute thy image. Why frownest thou upon me, — collecting the consular robe, and uplifting the right arm, as when Rome stood firm again, and Catiline fled before thee?

Lucullus. Just so; such was the action the statuary chose, as adding a new endearment to the memory of my absent friend.

Cæsar. Sylla, who honoured you above all men, is not here.

Lucullus. I have his *Commentaries:* he inscribed them, as you know, to me. Something even of our benefactors may be forgotten, and gratitude be unreproved.

Cæsar. The impression on that couch, and the two fresh honeysuckles in the leaves of those two books, would show, even to a stranger, that this room is peculiarly the master's. Are they sacred?

Lucullus. To me and Cæsar.

Cæsar. I would have asked permission —

Lucullus. Caius Julius, you have nothing to ask of Polybius and Thucydides; nor of Xenophon, the next to them on the table.

Cæsar. Thucydides! the most generous, the most un-prejudiced, the most sagacious, of historians. Now, Lucullus, you whose judgment in style is more accurate than any other Roman's, do tell me whether a commander, desirous of writing his *Commentaries*, could take to himself a more perfect model than Thucydides?

Lucullus. Nothing is more perfect, nor ever will be: the scholar of Pericles, the master of Demosthenes, the equal of the one in military science, and of the other not the inferior in civil and forensic ; the calm dispassionate judge of the general by whom he was defeated, his defender, his encomiast. To talk of such men is conducive not only to virtue but to health.

Cæsar. We have no writer who could keep up long together his severity and strength. I would follow him ; but I shall be contented with my genius, if (Thucydides in sight) I come many paces behind, and attain by study and attention the graceful and secure mediocrity of Xenophon.

*   *   *   *

Lucullus. This other is my dining-room. You expect the dishes.

Cæsar. I misunderstood, — I fancied —

Lucullus. Repose yourself, and touch with the ebony wand, beside you, the sphynx on either of those obelisks, right or left.

Cæsar. Let me look at them first.

Lucullus. The contrivance was intended for one person, or two at most, desirous of privacy and quiet. The blocks of jasper in my pair, and of porphyry in yours, easily yield in their grooves, each forming one partition. There are four, containing four platforms. The lower holds four dishes, such as sucking forest-boars, venison, hares, tunnies, sturgeons, which you will find within ; the upper three, eight each, but diminutive. The confectionery is brought separately, for the steam would spoil it, if any should escape. The melons are in the snow, thirty feet under us : they came early this morning from a place in the vicinity of Luni, so that I hope they may be crisp, independently of their coolness.

Cæsar. I wonder not at any thing of refined elegance in Lucullus ; but really here Antiochia and Alexandria seem to have cooked for us, and magicians to be our attendants.

Lucullus. The absence of slaves from our repast is the luxury, for Marcipor alone enters, and he only when I press a spring with my foot or wand. When you desire his appearance, touch that chalcedony just before you.

Cæsar. I eat quick and rather plentifully; yet the valetudinarian (excuse my rusticity, for I rejoice at seeing it) appears to equal the traveller in appetite, and to be contented with one dish.

Lucullus. It is milk: such, with strawberries, which ripen on the Apennines many months in continuance, and some other berries of sharp and grateful flavour, has been my only diet since my first residence here. The state of my health requires it; and the habitude of nearly three months renders this food not only more commodious to my studies and more conducive to my sleep, but also more agreeable to my palate than any other.

Cæsar. Returning to Rome or Baiæ, you must domesticate and tame them. The cherries you introduced from Pontus are now growing in Cisalpine and Transalpine Gaul ; and the largest and best in the world, perhaps, are upon the more sterile side of Lake Larius.

Lucullus. There are some fruits, and some virtues, which require a harsh soil and bleak exposure for their perfection.

Cæsar. In such a profusion of viands, and so savoury, I perceive no odour.

Lucullus. A flue conducts heat through the compartments of the obelisks ; and, if you look up, you may observe that those gilt roses, between the astragals in the cornice, are prominent from it half a span. Here is an aperture in the wall, between which and the outer is a perpetual current of air. We are now in the dog-days ; and I have never felt in the whole summer more heat than at Rome in many days of March.

Cæsar.   Usually you are attended by troups of domestics and of dinner-friends, not to mention the learned and scientific, nor your own family, your attachment to which, from youth upward, is one of the higher graces in your character. Your brother was seldom absent from you.

Lucullus.   Marcus was coming; but the vehement heats along the Arno, in which valley he has a property he never saw before, inflamed his blood, and he now is resting for a few days at Fæsulæ, a little town destroyed by Sylla within our memory, who left it only air and water, the best in Tuscany.   The health of Marcus, like mine, has been declining for several months: we are running our last race against each other, and never was I, in youth along the Tiber, so anxious of first reaching the goal.   I would not outlive him: I should reflect too painfully on earlier days, and look forward too despondently on the future.   As for friends, lampreys and turbots beget them, and they spawn not amid the solitude of the Apennines.   To dine in company with more than two is a Gaulish and a German thing. I can hardly bring myself to believe that I have eaten in concert with twenty; so barbarous and herdlike a practice does it now appear to me — such an incentive to drink much and talk loosely; not to add, such a necessity to speak loud, which is clownish and odious in the extreme. On this mountain-summit I hear no noises, no voices, not even of salutation; we have no flies about us, and scarcely an insect or reptile.

Cæsar.   Your amiable son is probably with his uncle: is he well?

Lucullus.   Perfectly.   He was indeed with my brother in his intended visit to me; but Marcus, unable to accompany him hither, or superintend his studies in the present state of his health, sent him directly to his Uncle Cato at Tusculum — a man fitter than either of us to direct his education, and preferable to any, excepting yourself and Marcus Tullius, in eloquence and urbanity.

Cæsar.   Cato is so great, that whoever is greater must be the happiest and first of men.

Lucullus.   That any such be still existing, O Julius, ought to excite no groan from the breast of a Roman citizen. But perhaps I wrong you; perhaps your mind was forced reluctantly back again, on your past animosities and contests in the Senate.

Cæsar.   I revere him, but cannot love him.

Lucullus.   Then, Caius Julius, you groaned with reason, and I would pity rather than reprove you.

On the ceiling at which you are looking, there is no gilding, and little painting — a mere trellis of vines bearing grapes, and the heads, shoulders, and arms, rising from the cornice only, of boys and girls climbing up to steal them, and scrambling for them : nothing over-head; no giants tumbling down, no Jupiter thundering, no Mars and Venus caught at Mid-day, no river-gods pouring out their urns upon us; for, as I think nothing so insipid as a flat ceiling, I think nothing so absurd as a storied one. Before I was aware, and without my participation, the painter had adorned that of my bed-chamber with a golden shower, bursting from varied and irradiated clouds. On my expostulation, his excuse was that he knew the Danaë of Scopas, in a recumbent posture, was to occupy the centre of the room. The walls, behind the tapestry and pictures, are quite rough. In forty-three days the whole fabric was put together and habitable.

The wine has probably lost its freshness : will you try some other ?

Cæsar.   Its temperature is exact; its flavour exquisite. Latterly I have never sat long after dinner, and am curious to pass through the other apartments, if you will trust me.

Lucullus.   I attend you.

Cæsar.   Lucullus, who is here? What figure is that on the poop of the vessel? Can it be —

Lucullus.   The subject was dictated by myself; you gave it.

Cæsar.   Oh how beautifully is the water painted! How vividly the sun strikes against the snows on Taurus! The gray temples and pier-head of Tarsus catch it differently, and the monumental mound on the left is half in shade. In the countenance of those pirates I did not observe such diversity, nor that any boy pulled his father back : I did not indeed mark them or notice them at all.

Lucullus.   The painter in this fresco, the last work finished, had dissatisfied me in one particular. "That beautiful young face," said I, "appears not to threaten death."

"Lucius," he replied, "if one muscle were moved, it were not Cæsar's : beside, he said it jokingly, though resolved."

"I am contented with your apology, Antipho; but what are you doing now? for you never lay down or suspend your pencil, let who will talk and argue. The lines of that smaller face in the distance are the same."

"Not the same," replied he, "nor very different : it smiles, as surely the goddess must have done at the first heroic act of her descendant."

Cæsar.   In her exultation and impatience to press forward, she seems to forget that she is standing at the extremity of the shell, which rises up behind out of the water ; and she takes no notice of the terror on the countenance of this Cupid who would detain her, nor of this who is flying off and looking back. The reflection of the shell has given a warmer hue below the knee ; a long streak of yellow light in the horizon is on the level of her bosom, some of her hair is almost lost in it ; above her head on every side is the pure azure of the heavens.

Oh! and you would not have led me up to this? You, among whose primary studies is the most perfect satisfaction of your guests!

Lucullus. In the next apartment are seven or eight other pictures from our history.

There are no more : what do you look for?

Cæsar. I find not among the rest any descriptive of your own exploits. Ah, Lucullus! there is no surer way of making them remembered.

This, I presume by the harps in the two corners, is the music-room.

Lucullus. No, indeed; nor can I be said to have one here: for I love best the music of a single instrument, and listen to it willingly at all times, but most willingly while I am reading. At such seasons, a voice or even a whisper disturbs me ; but music refreshes my brain when I have read long, and strengthens it from the beginning. I find also that if I write anything in poetry (a youthful propensity still remaining), it gives rapidity and variety and brightness to my ideas. On ceasing, I command a fresh measure and instrument, or another voice ; which is to the mind like a change of posture, or of air to the body. My health is benefited by the gentle play thus opened to the most delicate of the fibres.

Cæsar. Let me augur that a disorder so tractable may be soon removed. What is it thought to be?

Lucullus. There are they who would surmise and signify, and my physician did not long attempt to persuade me of the contrary, that the ancient realms of Æætes have supplied me with some other plants than the cherry, and such as I should be sorry to see domesticated here in Italy.

Cæsar. The gods forbid ! Anticipate better things ! The reason of Lucullus is stronger than the medicaments of Mithridates ; but why not use them too? Let nothing be neglected. You may reasonably hope for many years of life : your mother still enjoys it.

Lucullus. To stand upon one's guard against Death exasperates her malice and protracts our sufferings.

Cæsar. Rightly and gravely said : but your country at this time cannot do well without you.

Lucullus. The bowl of milk, which to-day is presented to me, will shortly be presented to my Manes.

Cæsar. Do you suspect the hand?

Lucullus. I will not suspect a Roman : let us converse no more about it.

Cæsar. It is the only subject on which I am resolved never to think, as relates to myself. Life may concern us, death not ; for in death we neither can act nor reason, we neither can persuade nor command ; and our statues are worth more than we are, let them be but wax.

XXVII.

THE APOLOGUE OF CRITOBULUS.

" I WAS wandering," says Critobulus, " in the midst of a forest, and came suddenly to a small round fountain or pool, with several white flowers (I remember) and broad leaves in the centre of it, but clear of them at the sides, and of a water the most pellucid. Suddenly a very beautiful figure came from behind me, and stood between me and the fountain. I was amazed. I could not distinguish the sex, the form being youthful and the face toward the water, on which it was gazing and bending over its reflection, like another Hylas or Narcissus. It then stooped and adorned itself with a few of the simplest flowers, and seemed the fonder and tenderer of those which had borne the impression of its graceful feet ; and, having done so, it turned round and looked upon me with an air of indifference and unconcern. The longer I fixed my eyes on her — for I now discovered it was a female — the more ardent I became and the more embarrassed. She perceived it, and smiled. Her eyes were large and serene ; not very thoughtful as if perplexed, not very playful as if easily to be won ; and her countenance was tinged with so delightful a colour, that it appeared an effluence from an irradiated cloud passing over it in the heavens. She gave me the idea, from her graceful attitude, that, although adapted to the perfection of activity, she felt rather an inclination for repose. I would have taken her hand : 'You shall presently,' said she ; and never fell on mortal a diviner glance than on me. I told her so. She replied, 'You speak well.' I then fancied she was simple and weak, and fond of flattery, and began to flatter her. She turned her face away from me, and answered nothing. I declared my excessive love : she went some paces off. I swore it was impossible for one who had ever seen her to live without her : she went several paces farther. ' By the immortal gods !' I cried, ' you shall not leave me !' She turned round and looked benignly ; but shook her head. ' You are another's then ! Say it ! say it ! utter the word once from your lips — and let me die !' She smiled, more melancholy than before, and replied, ' O Critobulus ! I am indeed another's : I am a god's.' The air of the interior heavens seemed to pierce me as she spoke ; and I trembled as impassioned men may tremble once. After a pause, ' I might have thought it !' cried I : ' why then come before me and torment me ? ' She began to play and trifle with me, as became her age (I fancied) rather than her engagement, and she placed my hand upon the flowers in her lap without a blush. The whole fountain would not at that moment have assuaged my thirst. The sound of the breezes and of the birds around us, even the sound of her own voice, were all confounded in my ear, as colours are in the fulness and intensity of light.   She said many pleasing things to me, to the earlier and greater part of which I was insensible ; but in the midst of those which I could hear and was listening to attentively, she began to pluck out the gray hairs from my head, and to tell me that the others too were of a hue not very agreeable.   My heart sank within me.   Presently there was hardly a limb or feature without its imperfection. ' Oh !' cried I in despair, ' you have been used to the gods ; you must think so : but among men I do not believe I am considered as ill-made or unseemly.'   She paid little attention to my words or my vexation; and when she had gone on with my defects for some. time longer, in the same calm tone and with the same sweet countenance, she began to declare that she had much affection for me, and was desirous of inspiring it in return.   I was about to answer her with . rapture, when on a sudden, in her girlish humour, she stuck a thorn, wherewith she had been playing, into that part of the body which supports us when we sit.   I know not whether it went deeper than she intended, but, catching at it, I leaped up in shame and anger, and at the same moment felt something upon my shoulder.   It was an armlet inscribed with letters of bossy adamant, ' Jove to his daughter Truth.'

" She stood again before me at a distance, and said gracefully, ' Critobulus !   I am too young and simple for you ; but you will love me still, and not be made unhappy by it in the end.   Farewell.'"

XXVIII.

THE PENTAMERON.

IT being now the last morning that Petrarca could remain with his friend, he resolved to pass early into his bed-chamber. Boccaccio had risen, and was standing at the open window, with his arms against it. Renovated health sparkled in the eyes of the one; surprise and delight and thankfulness to heaven, filled the other's with sudden tears. He clasped Giovanni, kissed his flaccid and sallow cheek, and falling on his knees, adored the Giver of life, the source of health to body and soul. Giovanni was not unmoved: he bent one knee as he leaned on the shoulder of Francesco, looking down into his face, repeating his words, and adding,

"Blessed be thou, O Lord! who sendest me health again! and blessings on thy messenger who brought it."

He had slept soundly; for ere he closed his eyes he had unburdened his mind of its freight, not only by employing the prayers appointed by Holy Church, but likewise by ejaculating; as sundry of the fathers did of old. He acknowledged his contrition for many transgressions, and chiefly for uncharitable thoughts of Fra Biagio: on which occasion he turned fairly round on his couch, and leaning his brow against the wall, and his body being in a becomingly curved position, and proper for the purpose, he thus ejaculated:

"Thou knowest, O most Holy Virgin! that never have I spoken to handmaiden at this villetta, or within my mansion at Certaldo, wantonly or indiscreetly, but have always been, inasmuch as may be, the guardian of innocence ; deeming it better, when irregular thoughts assailed me, to ventilate them abroad than to poison the house with them. And if, sinner that I am, I have thought uncharitably of others, and more especially of Fra Biagio, pardon me, out of thy exceeding great mercies ! And let it not be imputed to me, if I have kept, and may keep hereafter, an eye over him, in wariness and watchfulness ; not otherwise. For thou knowest, O Madonna ! that many who have a perfect and unwavering faith in thee, yet do cover up their cheese from the nibblings of vermin."

Whereupon, he turned round again, threw himself on his back at full length, and feeling the sheets cool, smooth, and refreshing, folded his arms, and slept instantaneously. The consequence of his wholesome slumber was a calm alacrity: and the idea that his visitor would be happy at seeing him on his feet again, made him attempt to get up: at which he succeeded, to his own wonder. And it was increased by the manifestation of his strength in opening the casement, stiff from being closed, and swelled by the continuance of the rains. The morning was warm and sunny: and it is known that on this occasion he composed the verses below:

> My old familiar cottage green !
> I see once more thy pleasant sheen ;
> The gossamer suspended over
> Smart celandine by lusty clover ;
> And the last blossom of the plum
> Inviting her first leaves to come ;
> Which hang a little back, but show
> 'T is not their nature to say no.
> I scarcely am in voice to sing
> How graceful are the steps of spring ;
> And ah ! it makes me sigh to look
> How leaps along my merry brook,
> The very same today as when
> He chirrupt first to maids and men.

Petrarca. I can rejoice at the freshness of your feelings: but the sight of the green turf reminds me rather of its ultimate use and destination.

> For many serves the parish pall,
> The turf in common serves for all.

Boccaccio. Very true; and, such being the case, let us carefully fold it up, and lay it by until we call for it.

Francesco, you made me quite light-headed yesterday. I am rather too old to dance either with Spring, as I have been saying, or with Vanity: and yet I accepted her at your hand as a partner. In future, no more of comparisons for me! You not only can do me no good, but you can leave me no pleasure: for here I shall remain the few days I have to live, and shall see nobody who will be disposed to remind me of your praises. Beside, you yourself will get hated for them. We neither can deserve praise nor receive it with impunity.

Petrarca. Have you never remarked that it is into quiet water that children throw pebbles to disturb it? and that it is into deep caverns that the idle drop sticks and dirt? We must expect such treatment.

Boccaccio. Your admonition shall have its wholesome influence over me, when the fever your praises have excited has grown moderate.

*   *   *   *

Petrarca. Turn again, I entreat you, to the serious; and do not imagine that because by nature you are inclined to playfulness, you must therefore write ludicrous things better. Many of your stories would make the gravest men laugh, and yet there is little wit in them.

Boccaccio. I think so myself; though authors, little disposed as they are to doubt their possession of any quality they would bring into play, are least of all suspicious on the side of wit. You have convinced me. I am glad to have been tender, and to have written tenderly : for I am certain it is this alone that has made you love me with such affection.

Petrarca. Not this alone, Giovanni ! but this principally. I have always found you kind and compassionate, liberal and sincere, and when Fortune does not stand very close to such a man, she leaves only the more room for Friendship.

Boccaccio. Let her stand off then, now and for ever ! To· my heart, to my heart, Francèsco ! preserver of my health, my peace of mind, and (since you tell me I may claim it) my glory.

Petrarca. Recovering your strength you must pursue your studies to complete it. What can you have been doing with your books ? I have searched in vain this morning for the treasury. Where are they kept ? Formerly they were always open. I found only a short manuscript, which I suspect is poetry, but I ventured not on looking into it, until I had brought it with me and laid it before you.

Boccaccio. Well guessed ! They are verses written by a gentleman who resided long in this country, and who much regretted the necessity of leaving it. He took great delight in composing both Latin and Italian, but never kept a copy of them latterly, so that these are the only ones I could obtain from him. Read : for your voice will improve them.

TO MY CHILD CARLINO.

Carlino ! what art thou about, my boy ?
Often I ask that question, though in vain,
For we are far apart : ah ! therefore 't is
I often ask it ; not in such a tone
As wiser fathers do, who know too well.
Were we not children, you and I together ?
Stole we not glances from each other's eyes ?

Swore we not secrecy in such misdeeds ?
Well could we trust each other.   Tell me then
What thou art doing.   Carving out thy name,
Or haply mine, upon my favourite seat,
With the new knife I sent thee over sea ?
Or hast thou broken it, and hid the hilt
Among the myrtles, starr'd with flowers, behind ?
Or under that high throne whence fifty lilies
(With sworded tuberoses dense around)
Lift up their heads at once, not without fear
That they were looking at thee all the while.

   Does Cincirillo follow thee about,
Inverting one swart foot suspensively,
And wagging his dread jaw at every chirp
Of bird above him on the olive-branch ?
Frighten him then away ! 't was he who slew
Our pigeons, our white pigeons peacock-tailed,
That fear'd not you and me — alas, nor him !
I flattened his striped sides along my knee,
And reasoned with him on his bloody mind,
Till he looked blandly, and half-closed his eyes
To ponder on my lecture in the shade.
I doubt his memory much, his heart a little,
And in some minor matters (may I say it ?)
Could wish him rather sager.   But from thee
God hold back wisdom yet for many years !
Whether in early season or in late
It always comes high-priced.   For thy pure breast
I have no lesson ; it for me has many.
Come throw it open then ! What sports, what cares
(Since there are none too young for these) engage
Thy busy thoughts ?   Are you again at work,
Walter and you, with those sly labourers,
Geppo, Giovanni, Cecco, and Poeta,
To build more solidly your broken dam
Among the poplars, whence the nightingale
Inquisitively watch'd you all day long ?
I was not of your council in the scheme,
Or might have saved you silver without end,
And sighs too without number.   Art thou gone

> Below the mulberry, where that cold pool
> Urged to devise a warmer, and more fit
> For mighty swimmers, swimming three abreast?
> Or art thou panting in this summer noon
> Upon the lowest step before the hall,
> Drawing a slice of watermelon, long
> As Cupid's bow, athwart thy wetted lips
> (Like one who plays Pan's pipe), and letting drop
> The sable seeds from all their separate cells,
> And leaving bays profound and rocks abrupt,
> Redder than coral round Calypso's cave?

Petrarca. There have been those anciently who would have been pleased with such poetry, and perhaps there may be again. I am not sorry to see the Muses by the side of childhood, and forming a part of the family. But now tell me about the books.

Boccaccio. Resolving to lay aside the more valuable of those I had collected or transcribed, and to place them under the guardianship of richer men, I locked them up together in the higher story of my tower at Certaldo. You remember the old tower?

Petrarca. Well do I remember the hearty laugh we had together (which stopped us upon the staircase) at the calculation we made, how much longer you and I, if we continued to thrive as we had thriven latterly, should be able to pass within its narrow circle. Although I like this little villa much better, I would gladly see the place again, and enjoy with you, as we did before, the vast expanse of woodlands and mountains and maremma; frowning fortresses inexpugnable; and others more prodigious for their ruins; then below them, lordly abbeys, overcanopied with stately trees and girded with rich luxuriance; and towns that seem approaching them to do them honour, and villages nestling close at their sides for sustenance and protection.

Boccaccio. My disorder, if it should keep its promise of

leaving me at last, will have been preparing me for the accomplishment of such a project. Should I get thinner and thinner at this rate, I shall soon be able to mount not only a turret or a belfry, but a tube of macarone, while a Neapolitan is suspending it for deglutition.

What I am now about to mention, will show you how little you can rely on me ! I have preserved the books, as you desired, but quite contrary to my resolution : and, no less contrary to it, by your desire I shall now preserve the *Decameron.* In vain had I determined not only to mend in future, but to correct the past ; in vain had I prayed most fervently for grace to accomplish it, with a final aspiration to Fiammetta that she would unite with your beloved Laura, and that, gentle and beatified spirits as they are, they would breathe together their purer prayers on mine. See what follows.

Petrarca. Sigh not at it. Before we can see all that follows from their intercession, we must join them again. But let me hear anything in which they are concerned.

Boccaccio. I prayed ; and my breast, after some few tears, grew calmer. Yet sleep did not ensue until the break of morning, when the dropping of soft rain on the leaves of the fig-tree at the window, and the chirping of a little bird, to tell another there was shelter under them, brought me repose and slumber. Scarcely had I closed my eyes, if indeed time can be reckoned any more in sleep than in heaven, when my Fiammetta seemed to have led me into the meadow. You will see it below you : turn away that branch : gently ! gently ! do not break it ; for the little bird sat there.

Petrarca. I think, Giovanni, I can divine the place. Although this fig-tree, growing out of the wall between the cellar and us, is fantastic enough in its branches, yet that other which I see yonder, bent down and forced to crawl along the grass by the prepotency of the young shapely walnut-tree, is much more so. It forms a seat, about a cubit above the ground, level and long enough for several.

Boccaccio.   Ha! you fancy it must be a favourite spot with me, because of the two strong forked stakes wherewith it is propped and supported!

Petrarca.   Poets know the haunts of poets at first sight; and he who loved Laura — O Laura! did I say he who *loved* thee? — hath whisperings where those feet would wander which have been restless after Fiammetta.

Boccaccio.   It is true, my imagination has often conducted her thither; but here in this chamber she appeared to me. more visibly in a dream.

"Thy prayers have been heard, O Giovanni," said she.

I sprang to embrace her.

"Do not spill the water! Ah! you have spilt a part of it."

I then observed in her hand a crystal vase. A few drops were sparkling on the sides and running down the rim; a few were trickling from the base and from the hand that held it.

"I must go down to the brook," said she, "and fill it again as it was filled before."

What a moment of agony was this to me! Could I be certain how long might be her absence? She went: I was following: she made a sign for me to turn back: I disobeyed her only an instant: yet my sense of disobedience, increasing my feebleness and confusion, made me lose sight of her. In the next moment she was again at my side, with the cup quite full. I stood motionless: I feared my breath might shake the water over. I looked her in the face for her commands — and to see it — to see it so calm, so beneficent, so beautiful. I was forgetting what I had prayed for, when she lowered her head, tasted of the cup, and gave it me. I drank; and suddenly sprang forth before me,

many groves and palaces and gardens, and their statues and
their avenues, and their labyrinths of alaternus and bay, and
alcoves of citron, and watchful loopholes in the retirements
of impenetrable pomegranate. Farther off, just below where
the fountain slipt away from its marble hall and guardian
gods, arose, from their beds of moss and drosera and
darkest grass, the sisterhood of oleanders, fond of tantalis-
ing with their bosomed flowers and their moist and pouting
blossoms the little shy rivulet, and of covering its face with
all the colours of the dawn. My dream expanded and moved
forward. I trod again the dust of Posilipo, soft as the
feathers in the wings of Sleep. I emerged on Baia; I
crossed her innumerable arches; I loitered in the breezy
sunshine of her mole; I trusted the faithful seclusion of her
caverns, the keepers of so many secrets; and I reposed on
the buoyancy of her tepid sea. Then Naples, and her
theatres and her churches, and grottoes and dells and forts
and promontories, rushed forward in confusion, now among
soft whispers, now among sweetest sounds, and subsided,
and sank, and disappeared. Yet a memory seemed to come
fresh from every one : each had time enough for its tale, for
its pleasure, for its reflection, for its pang. As I mounted
with silent steps the narrow staircase of the old palace, how
distinctly did I feel against the palm of my hand the cold-
ness of that smooth stone-work, and the greater of the
cramps of iron in it.

"Ah me! is this forgetting?" cried I anxiously to
Fiammetta.

"We must recall these scenes before us," she replied :
"such is the punishment of them. Let us hope and believe
that the apparition, and the compunction which must follow
it, will be accepted as the full penalty, and that both will
pass away almost together."

I feared to lose anything attendant on her presence : I

feared to approach her forehead with my lips : I feared to touch the lily on its long wavy leaf in her hair, which filled my whole heart with fragrance. Venerating, adoring, I bowed my head at last to kiss her snow-white robe, and trembled at my presumption. And yet the effulgence of her countenance vivified while it chastened me. I loved her — I must not say *more* than ever — *better* than ever ; it was Fiammetta who had inhabited the skies. As my hand opened toward her,

"Beware !" said she, faintly smiling ; "beware, Giovanni ! Take only the crystal ; take it, and drink again."

"Must all be then forgotten ?" said I sorrowfully.

"Remember your prayer and mine, Giovanni. Shall both have been granted — O how much worse than in vain !"

I drank instantly ; I drank largely. How cool my bosom grew ; how could it grow so cool before her ! But it was not to remain in its quiescency ; its trials were not yet over. I will not, Francesco ! no, I may not commemorate the incidents she related to me, nor which of us said, "I blush for having loved *first;*" nor which of us replied, "Say *least*, say *least*, and blush again."

The charm of the words (for I felt not the encumbrance of the body nor the acuteness of the spirit) seemed to possess me wholly. Although the water gave me strength and comfort, and somewhat of celestial pleasure, many tears fell around the border of the vase as she held it up before me, exhorting me to take courage, and inviting me with more than exhortation to accomplish my deliverance. She came nearer, more tenderly, more earnestly ; she held the dewy globe with both hands, leaning forward, and sighed and shook her head, drooping at my pusillanimity. It was only when a ringlet had touched the rim, and perhaps the water (for a sunbeam on the surface could never have given it such a golden hue), that I took courage, clasped it, and exhausted it.   Sweet as was the water, sweet as was the serenity it gave me — alas! that also which it moved away from me was sweet!

"This time you can trust me alone," said she, and parted my hair, and kissed my brow. Again she went toward the brook: again my agitation, my weakness, my doubt, came over me : nor could I see her while she raised the water, nor knew I whence she drew it. When she returned, she was close to me at once : she smiled : her smile pierced me to the bones : it seemed an angel's. She sprinkled the pure water on me ; she looked most fondly : she took my hand ; she suffered me to press hers to my bosom : but, whether by design I can not tell, she let fall a few drops of the chilly element between.

"And now, O my beloved!" said she, "we have consigned to the bosom of God our earthly joys and sorrows. The joys can not return, let not the sorrows. These alone would trouble my repose among the blessed."

"Trouble thy repose! Fiammetta! Give me the chalice!" cried I — "not a drop will I leave in it, not a drop."

"Take it!" said that soft voice. "O now most dear Giovanni! I know thou hast strength enough ; and there is but little — at the bottom lies our first kiss."

"Mine! didst thou say, beloved one? and is that left thee still?"

"*Mine*," said she, pensively; and as she abased her head, the broad leaf of the lily hid her brow and her eyes ; the light of heaven shone through the flower.

"O Fiammetta ! Fiammetta !" cried I in agony, "God is the God of mercy, God is the God of love — can I, can I ever?" I struck the chalice against my head, unmindful that I held it ; the water covered my face and my feet. I started up, not yet awake, and I heard the name of Fiammetta in the curtains.

Petrarca. Love, O Giovanni, and life itself, are but dreams at best.

*   *   *   *

Boccaccio. What is that book in your hand?

Petrarca. My breviary.

Boccaccio. Well, give me mine too — there, on the little table in the corner, under the glass of primroses. We can do nothing better.

Petrarca. What prayer were you looking for? let me find it.

Boccaccio. I don't know how it is: I am scarcely at present in a frame of mind for it. We are of one faith: the prayers of the one will do for the other: and I am sure, if you omitted my name, you would say them all over afresh. I wish you could recollect in any book as dreamy a thing to entertain me as I have been just repeating. We have had enough of Dante : I believe few of his beauties have escaped us : and small faults, which we readily pass by, are fitter for small folks, as grubs are the proper bait for gudgeons.

Petrarca. I have had as many dreams as most men. We are all made up of them, as the webs of the spider are particles of her own vitality. But how infinitely less do we profit by them! I will relate to you, before we separate, one among the multitude of mine, as coming the nearest to the poetry of yours, and as having been not totally useless to me. Often have I reflected on it; sometimes with pensiveness, with sadness never.

Boccaccio. Then, Francesco, if you had with you as copious a choice of dreams as clustered on the elm-trees where the Sibyl led Æneas, this, in preference to the whole swarm of them, is the queen dream for me.

Petrarca. When I was younger I was fond of wandering

in solitary places, and never was afraid of slumbering in woods and grottoes. Among the chief pleasures of my life, and among the commonest of my occupations, was the bringing before me such heroes and heroines of antiquity, such poets and sages, such of the prosperous and the unfortunate, as most interested me by their courage, their wisdom, their eloquence, or their adventures. Engaging them in the conversation best suited to their characters, I knew perfectly their manners, their steps, their voices: and often did I moisten with my tears the models I had been forming of the less happy.

Boccaccio. Great is the privilege of entering into the studies of the intellectual; great is that of conversing with the guides of nations, the movers of the mass, the regulators of the unruly will, stiff, in its impurity and rust, against the finger of the Almighty Power that formed it : but give me, Francesco, give me rather the creature to sympathise with ; apportion me the sufferings to assuage. Ah, gentle soul! thou wilt never send them over to another ; they have better hopes from thee.

Petrarca. We both alike feel the sorrows of those around us. He who suppresses or allays them in another, breaks many thorns off his own ; and future years will never harden fresh ones.

My occupation was not always in making the politician talk politics, the orator toss his torch among the populace, the philosopher run down from philosophy to cover the retreat or the advances of his sect ; but sometimes in devising how such characters must act and discourse, on subjects far remote from the beaten track of their career. In like manner the philologist, and again the dialectician, were not indulged in the review and parade of their trained bands, but, at times, brought forward to show in what manner and in what degree external habits had influenced the conformation of the internal man. It was far from unprofitable to set passing events before past actors, and to record the decisions of those whose interests and passions are unconcerned in them.

Boccaccio. This is surely no easy matter. The thoughts are in fact your own, however you distribute them.

* * * *

Petrarca. Allegory, which you named with sonnets and canzonets, had few attractions for me, believing it to be the delight in general of idle, frivolous, inexcursive minds, in whose mansions there is neither hall nor portal to receive the loftier of the Passions. A stranger to the Affections, she holds a low station among the handmaidens of Poetry, being fit for little but an apparition in a mask. I had reflected for some time on this subject, when, wearied with the length of my walk over the mountains, and finding a soft old molehill, covered with grey grass, by the wayside, I laid my head upon it, and slept. I can not tell how long it was before a species of dream or vision came over me.

Two beautiful youths appeared beside me; each was winged; but the wings were hanging down, and seemed ill adapted to flight. One of them, whose voice was the softest I ever heard, looking at me frequently, said to the other,

"He is under my guardianship for the present: do not awaken him with that feather."

Methought, hearing the whisper, I saw something like the feather on an arrow; and then the arrow itself; the whole of it, even to the point; although he carried it in such a manner that it was difficult at first to discover more than a palm's length of it: the rest of the shaft, and the whole of the barb, was behind his ankles.

"This feather never awakens anyone," replied he, rather petulantly; "but it brings more of confident security, and more of cherished dreams, than you without me are capable of imparting."

"Be it so!" answered the gentler—"none is less inclined to quarrel or dispute than I am. Many whom you have wounded grievously, call upon me for succour. But so little am I disposed to thwart you, it is seldom I venture to do more for them than to whisper a few words of comfort in passing. How many reproaches on these occasions have been cast upon me for indifference and infidelity! Nearly as many, and nearly in the same terms, as upon you!"

"Odd enough that we, O Sleep! should be thought so alike!" said Love, contemptuously. "Yonder is he who bears a nearer resemblance to you : the dullest have observed it." I fancied I turned my eyes to where he was pointing, and saw at a distance the figure he designated. Meanwhile the contention went on uninterruptedly. Sleep was slow in asserting his power or his benefits. Love recapitulated them ; but only that he might assert his own above them. Suddenly he called on me to decide, and to choose my patron. Under the influence, first of the one, then of the other, I sprang from repose to rapture, 'I alighted from rapture on repose — and knew not which was sweetest. Love was very angry with me, and declared he would cross me throughout the whole of my existence. Whatever I might on other occasions have thought of his veracity, I now felt too surely the conviction that he would keep his word. At last, before the close of the altercation, the third Genius had advanced, and stood near us. I can not tell how I knew him, but I knew him to be the Genius of Death. Breathless as I was at beholding him, I soon became familiar with his features. First they seemed only calm ; presently they grew contemplative ; and lastly beautiful : those of the Graces themselves are less regular, less harmonious, less composed. Love glanced at him unsteadily, with a countenance in which there was somewhat of anxiety, somewhat of disdain; and cried, "Go away! go away! nothing that thou touchest lives."

"Say rather, child!" replied the advancing form, and advancing grew loftier and statelier, "Say rather that nothing of beautiful or of glorious lives its own true life until my wing hath passed over it."

Love pouted, and rumpled and bent down with his forefinger the stiff short feathers on his arrow-head; but replied not. Although he frowned worse than ever, and at me, I dreaded him less and less, and scarcely looked toward him. The milder and calmer Genius, the third, in proportion as I took courage to contemplate him, regarded me with more and more complacency. He held neither flower nor arrow, as the others did; but, throwing back the clusters of dark curls that overshadowed his countenance, he presented to me his hand, openly and benignly. I shrank on looking at him so near, and yet I sighed to love him. He smiled, not without an expression of pity, at perceiving my diffidence, my timidity: for I remembered how soft was the hand of Sleep, how warm and entrancing was Love's. By degrees, I became ashamed of my ingratitude; and turning my face away, I held out my arms, and felt my neck within his. Composure strewed and allayed all the throbbings of my bosom; the coolness of freshest morning breathed around; the heavens seemed to open above me; while the beautiful cheek of my deliverer rested on my head. I would now have looked for those others; but knowing my intention by my gesture, he said, consolatorily,

"Sleep is on his way to the Earth, where many are calling him; but it is not to these he hastens; for every call only makes him fly farther off. Sedately and gravely as he looks, he is nearly as capricious and volatile as the more arrogant and ferocious one."

"And Love!" said I, "whither is he departed?   If not too late, I would propitiate and appease him."

"He who can not follow me, he who can not overtake and pass me," said the Genius, "is unworthy of the name, the most glorious in earth or heaven.   Look up!   Love is yonder, and ready to receive thee."

I looked : the earth was under me : I saw only the clear blue sky, and something brighter above it.

XXIX.

PERICLES AND ASPASIA.

PERICLES TO ASPASIA.

THERE are things, Aspasia, beyond the art of Phidias. He may represent Love leaning upon his bow and listening to Philosophy; but not for hours together: he may represent Love, while he is giving her a kiss for her lesson, tying her arms behind her; loosing them again must be upon another marble.

PERICLES TO ASPASIA.

Do you love me? do you love me? Stay, reason upon it, sweet Aspasia! doubt, hesitate, question, drop it, take it up again, provide, raise obstacles, reply indirectly. Oracles are sacred, and there is a pride in being a diviner.

ASPASIA TO PERICLES.

I will do none of those things you tell me to do; but I will say something you forgot to say, about the insufficiency of Phidias.

He may represent a hero with unbent brows, a sage with the lyre of Poetry in his hand, Ambition with her face half-averted from the City, but he cannot represent, in the same sculpture, at the same distance, Aphrodite higher than Pallas. He would be derided if he did; and a great man can never do that for which a little man may deride him.

I shall love you even more than I do, if you will love
yourself more than me.   Did ever lover talk so?   Pray tell
me, for I have forgotten all they ever talked about.   But,
Pericles! Pericles! be careful to lose nothing of your glory,
or you lose all that can be lost of me; my pride, my happiness, my content ; everything but my poor weak love.   Keep
glory, then, for my sake !

PERICLES TO ASPASIA.

Send me a note whenever you are idle and thinking of
me, dear Aspasia!   Send it always by some old slave,
ill-dressed.   The people will think it a petition, or something as good, and they will be sure to observe the pleasure
it throws into my countenance.   Two winds at once will
blow into my sails, each helping me onward.

If I am tired, your letter will refresh me; if occupied, it
will give me activity.   Beside, what a deal of time we lose in
business !

ASPASIA TO PERICLES.

Would to heaven, O Pericles! you had no business at all,
but the conversation of your friends.   You must always be
the greatest man in the city, whoever may be the most
popular.   I wish we could spend the whole day together ;
must it never be?   Are you not already in possession of all
you ever contended for?

It is time, methinks, that you should leave off speaking in
public, for you begin to be negligent and incorrect.   I am to
write you a note whenever I am idle and thinking of you!

Pericles! Pericles! how far is it from idleness to think of
you!   We come to rest before we come to idleness.

In our republic it is no easy thing to obtain an act of divorce from power. It usually is delivered to us by the messenger of Death, or presented in due form by our judges where the oyster keeps open house.

Now, oysters are quite out of season in the summer of life; and life, just about this time, I do assure you, is often worth keeping. I thought so even before I knew you, when I thought but little about the matter. It is a casket not precious in itself, but valuable in proportion to what Fortune, or Industry, or Virtue, has placed within it.

CLEONE TO ASPASIA.

We have kept your birthday, Aspasia! On these occasions I am reluctant to write anything. Politeness, I think, and humanity, should always check the precipitancy of congratulation. Nobody is felicitated on losing. Even the loss of a bracelet or tiara is deemed no subject for merriment and alertness in our friends and followers. Surely then the marked and registered loss of an irreparable year, the loss of a limb of life, ought to excite far other sensations. So long is it, O Aspasia! since we have read any poetry together, I am quite uncertain whether you know the Ode to Asteröessa.

> Asteröessa! many bring
> The vows of verse and blooms of spring
>   To crown thy natal day.
> Lo, *my* vow too amid the rest!
> Ne'er mayst thou sigh from that white breast,
>   "*O take them all away!*"
>
> For there are cares and there are wrongs,
> And withering eyes and venom'd tongues;
>   They now are far behind;

> But come they must : and every year
> Some flowers decay, some thorns appear,
>   Whereof these gifts remind.
>
> Cease, raven, cease ! nor scare the dove
> With croak around and swoop above ;
>   Be peace, be joy, within !
> Of all that hail this happy tide
> My verse alone be cast aside !
>   Lyre, cymbal, dance, begin !

Although there must be some myriads of odes written on the same occasion, yet, among the number on which I can lay my hand, none conveys my own sentiment so completely.

Sweetest Aspasia, live on ! live on ! but rather, live back the past !

ASPASIA TO CLEONE.

In ancient nations there are grand repositories of wisdom, although it may happen that little of it is doled out to the exigencies of the people. There is more in the fables of Æsop than in the schools of our Athenian philosophers ; there is more in the laws and usages of Persia, than in the greater part of those communities which are loud in denouncing them for barbarism. And yet there are some that shock me. We are told by Herodotus, who tells us whatever we know with certainty a step beyond our thresholds, that a boy in Persia is kept in the apartments of the women, and prohibited from seeing his father, until the fifth year. The reason is, he informs us, that if he dies before this age, his loss may give the parent no uneasiness. And such a custom he thinks commendable. Herodotus has no child, Cleone ! If he had, far other would be his feelings and his judgment. Before that age how many seeds are sown, which future years, and distant ones, mature successively ! How much fondness, how much generosity, what hosts of other virtues, courage, constancy, patriotism, spring into the father's heart from the cradle of his child !   And does never the fear come over him, that what is most precious to him upon earth is left in careless or perfidious, in unsafe or unworthy hands ?   Does it never occur to him that he loses a son in every one of these five years ?   What is there so affecting to the brave and virtuous man as that which perpetually wants his help and cannot call for it !   What is so different as the speaking and the mute !   And hardly less so are inarticulate sounds, and sounds which he receives half-formed, and which he delights to modulate, and which he lays with infinite care and patience, not only on the tender attentive ear, but on the half-open lips, and on the eyes, and on the cheeks ; as if they all were listeners.   In every child there are many children ; but coming forth year after year, each somewhat like and somewhat varying.   When they are grown much older, the leaves (as it were) lose their pellucid green, the branches their graceful pliancy.

Is there any man so rich in happiness that he can afford to throw aside these first five years ? is there any man who can hope for another five so exuberant in unsating joy ?

O my sweet infant !   I would teach thee to kneel before the gods, were it only to thank 'em for being Athenian and not Persian.

PERICLES TO ASPASIA.

I am pleased with your little note, and hope you may live to write a commentary on the same author.   You speak with your usual judgment, in commending our historian for his discretion in metaphors.   Not indeed that his language is without them, but they are rare, impressive, and distinct. History wants them occasionally ; in oratory they are nearly as requisite as in poetry ; they come opportunely wherever

the object is persuasion or intimidation, and no less where
delight stands foremost.   In writing a letter I would neither
seek nor reject one ; but I think, if more than one came
forward, I might decline its services.   If, however, it had
come in unawares, I would take no trouble to send it away.
But we should accustom ourselves to think always with
propriety, in little things as in great, and neither be too
solicitous of our dress in the house, nor negligent because
we are at home.   I think it as improper and indecorous to
write a stupid or a silly note to you, as one in a bad hand or
on coarse paper.   Familiarity ought to have another and
worse name, when it relaxes in its attentiveness to please.

We began with metaphors, I will end with one. — Do not
look back over the letter to see whether I have not already
used my privilege of nomination, whether my one is not
there.   Take, then, a simile instead.   It is a pity that they
are often lamps which light nothing, and show only the
nakedness of the walls they are nailed against.

ASPASIA TO PERICLES.

When the war is over, as surely it must be in another
year, let us sail among the islands of the Ægean, and be
young as ever.   O that it were permitted us to pass together
the remainder of our lives in privacy and retirement !   This
is never to be hoped for in Athens.

I inherit from my mother a small yet beautiful house in
Tenos : I remember it well.   Water, clear and cold, ran
before the vestibule ; a sycamore shaded the whole building.
I think Tenos must be nearer to Athens than to Miletus.
Could we not go now for a few days ?   How temperate was
the air, how serene the sky, how beautiful the country ! the
people how quiet, how gentle, how kind-hearted !

Is there any station so happy as an uncontested place in
a small community, where manners are simple, where wants

are few, where respect is the tribute of probity, and love is the guerdon of beneficence ! O Pericles ! let us go ; we can return at any time.

ANAXAGORAS TO ASPASIA.

Be cautious, O Aspasia ! of discoursing on philosophy. Is it not in philosophy as in love? the more we have of it, and the less we talk about it, the better. Never touch upon religion with anybody. The irreligious are incurable and insensible ; the religious are morbid and irritable : the former would scorn, the latter would strangle you. It appears to me to be not only a dangerous, but, what is worse, an indelicate thing, to place ourselves where we are likely to see fevers and frenzies, writhings and distortions, debilities and deformities. Religion at Athens is like a fountain near Dodona, which extinguishes a lighted torch, and which gives a flame of its own to an unlighted one held down to it. Keep yours in your chamber ; and let the people run about with theirs ; but remember, it is rather apt to catch the skirts. Believe me, I am happy : I am not deprived of my friends. Imagination is little less strong in our later years than in our earlier. True, it alights on fewer objects, but it rests longer on them, and sees them better. Pericles first, and then you, and then Meton, occupy my thoughts. I am with you still ; I study with you, just as before, although nobody talks aloud in the school-room.

This is the pleasantest part of life. Oblivion throws her light coverlet over our infancy; and, soon after we are out of the cradle we forget how soundly we had been slumbering, and how delightful were our dreams. Toil and pleasure contend for us almost the instant we rise from it ; and weariness follows whichever has carried us away. We stop awhile, look around us, wonder to find we have completed the circle of existence, fold our arms, and fall asleep again.

ASPASIA TO CLEONE.

A pestilence has broken out in the city, so virulent in its character, so rapid in its progress, so intractable to medicine, that Pericles, in despite of my remonstrances and prayers, insisted on my departure. He told me that, if I delayed it a single day, his influence might be insufficient to obtain me a reception in any town, or any hamlet, throughout the whole of Greece. He has promised to write to me daily, but he declared he could not assure me that his letters would come regularly, although he purposes to send them secretly by the shepherds, fumigated and dipped in oil before they depart from Athens. He has several farms in Thessaly under Mount Ossa, near Sicurion. Here I am, a few stadions from the walls. Never did I breathe so pure an air, so refreshing in the midst of summer. And the lips of my little Pericles are ruddier and softer and sweeter than before. Nothing is wanting, but that he were less like me and more like his father. He would have all my thoughts to himself, were Pericles not absent.

ASPASIA TO PERICLES.

Now the fever is raging, and we are separated, my comfort and delight is in our little Pericles. The letters you send me come less frequently, but I know you write whenever your duties will allow you, and whenever men are found courageous enough to take charge of them. Although you preserved with little care the speeches you delivered formerly, yet you promised me a copy of the latter, and as many of the earlier as you could collect among your friends. Let me have them as soon as possible. Whatever bears the traces of your hand is precious to me : how greatly more precious what is imprest with your genius, what you have meditated and spoken ! I shall see your calm thoughtful face while I am reading, and will be cautious not to read aloud lest I lose the illusion of your voice.

PERICLES TO ASPASIA.

Aspasia ! do you know what you have asked of me ? Would you accept it, if you thought it might make you love me less ?   Must your affections be thus loosened from me, that the separation, which the pestilence may render an eternal one, may be somewhat mitigated ?   I send you the papers.   The value will be small to you, and indeed would be small to others, were it possible that they could fall into any hands but yours.   Remember the situation in which my birth and breeding and bent of mind have placed me ; remember the powerful rivals I have had to contend with, their celebrity, their popularity, their genius, and their perseverance.   You know how often I have regretted the necessity of obtaining the banishment of Cimon, a man more similar to myself than any other.   I doubt whether he had quite the same management of his thoughts and words, but he was adorned with every grace, every virtue, and invested by Nature with every high function of the soul. We happened to be placed by our fellow-citizens at the head of two adverse factions.   Son of the greatest man in our annals, he was courted and promoted by the aristocracy ; I, of a family no less distinguished, was opposed to him by the body of the people.   You must have observed, Aspasia, that although one of the populace may in turbulent times be the possessor of great power, it rarely has happened that he retained it long, or without many sanguinary struggles. Moroseness is the evening of turbulence.   Every man after a while begins to think himself as capable of governing as one (whoever he may be) taken from his own rank.   Amid all the claims and pretensions of the ignorant and discontented, the eyes of a few begin to be turned complacently toward the more courteous demeanour of some well-born citizen, who presently has an opportunity of conciliating many more, by affability, liberality, eloquence, commiseration, diffidence, and disinterestedness. Part of these must be real, part may not be. Shortly afterward he gains nearly all the rest of the citizens by deserting his order for theirs: his own party will not be left behind, but adheres to him bravely, to prove they are not ashamed of their choice, and to avoid the imputation of inconsistency.

Aspasia! I have done with these cares, with these reflections. Little of life is remaining, but my happiness will be coetaneous with it, and my renown will survive it; for there is no example of any who has governed a state so long, without a single act of revenge or malice, of cruelty or severity. In the thirty-seven years of my administration I have caused no citizen to put on mourning. On this rock, O Aspasia! stand my Propylæa and my Parthenon.

ASPASIA TO PERICLES.

Gratitude to the immortal gods overpowers every other impulse of my breast. You are safe.

Pericles! O my Pericles! come into this purer air! live life over again in the smiles of your child, in the devotion of your Aspasia! Why did you fear for me the plague within the city, the Spartans round it? why did you exact the vow at parting, that nothing but your command should recall me again to Athens? Why did I ever make it? Cruel! to refuse me the full enjoyment of your recovered health! crueller to keep me in ignorance of its decline! The happiest of pillows is not that which Love first presses; it is that which Death has frowned on and passed over.

ASPASIA TO CLEONE.

Where on earth is there so much society as in a beloved child? He accompanies me in my walks, gazes into my eyes for what I am gathering from books, tells me more and better things than they do, and asks me often what neither I nor they can answer. When he is absent I am filled with reflections ; when he is present I have room for none beside what I receive from him. The charms of his childhood bring me back to the delights of mine, and I fancy I hear my own words in a sweeter voice. Will he (O how I tremble at the mute oracle of futurity !), will he ever be as happy as I have been ? Alas ! and must he ever be as subject to fears and apprehensions? No ; thanks to the gods ! never, never. He carries his father's heart within his breast : I see him already an orator and a leader. I try to teach him daily some of his father's looks and gestures, and I never smile but at his docility and gravity. How his father will love him ! the little thunderer ! the winner of cities ! the vanquisher of Cleones !

ASPASIA TO PERICLES.

Never tell me, O my Pericles ! that you are suddenly changed in appearance. May every change of your figure and countenance be gradual, so that I shall not perceive it; but if you really are altered to such a degree as you describe, I must transfer my affection — from the first Pericles to the second. Are you jealous ! if you are, it is I who am to be pitied, whose heart is destined to fly from the one to the other incessantly. In the end it will rest, it shall, it must, on the nearest. I would write a longer letter; but it is a sad and wearisome thing to aim at playfulness where the hand is palsied by affliction. Be well ; and all is well : be happy ;

and Athens rises up again, alert, and blooming, and vigourous, from between war and pestilence. Love me : for love cures all but love. How can we fear to die, how can we die, while we cling or are clung to the beloved ?

PERICLES TO ASPASIA.

The pestilence has taken from me both my sons. You, who were ever so kind and affectionate to them, will receive a tardy recompense, in hearing that the least gentle and the least grateful did acknowledge it.

I mourn for Paralos, because he loved me ; for Xanthippos, because he loved me not.

Preserve with all your maternal care our little Pericles. I cannot be fonder of him than I have always been; I can only fear more for him.

Is he not with my Aspasia ! What fears then are so irrational as mine? But oh ! I am living in a widowed house, a house of desolation; I am living in a city of tombs and torches; and the last I saw before me were for my children.

PERICLES TO ASPASIA.

It is right and orderly, that he who has partaken so largely in the prosperity of the Athenians, should close the procession of their calamities. The fever that has depopulated our city, returned upon me last night, and Hippocrates and Acron tell me that my end is near.

When we agreed, O Aspasia ! in the beginning of our loves, to communicate our thoughts by writing, even while we were both in Athens, and when we had many reasons for it, we little foresaw the more powerful one that has rendered it necessary of late. We never can meet again : the laws forbid it, and love itself enforces them. Let wisdom be heard by you as imperturbably, and affection as authoritatively, as ever ; and remember that the sorrow of Pericles can arise but from the bosom of Aspasia. There is only one word of tenderness we could say, which we have not said oftentimes before ; and there is no consolation in it. The happy never say, and never hear said, farewell.

Reviewing the course of my life, it appears to me at one moment as if we met but yesterday ; at another as if centuries had passed within it ; for within it have existed the greater part of those who, since the origin of the world, have been the luminaries of the human race. Damon called me from my music to look at Aristides on his way to exile ; and my father pressed the wrist by which he was leading me along, and whispered in my ear :

"Walk quickly by; glance cautiously; it is there Miltiades is in prison."

In my boyhood Pindar took me up in his arms, when he brought to our house the dirge he had composed for the funeral of my grandfather ; in my adolescence I offered the rites of hospitality to Empedocles ; not long afterward I embraced the neck of Æschylus, about to abandon his country. With Sophocles I have argued on eloquence ; with Euripides on polity and ethics ; I have · discoursed, as became an inquirer, with Protagoras and Democritus, with Anaxagoras and Meton. From Herodotus I have listened to the most instructive history, conveyed in a language the most copious and the most harmonious ; a man worthy to carry away the collected suffrages of universal Greece ; a man worthy to throw open the temples of Egypt, and to celebrate the exploits of Cyrus. And from Thucydides, who alone can succeed to him, how recently did my Aspasia hear with me the energetic praises of his just supremacy !

As if the festival of life were incomplete, and wanted one great ornament to crown it, Phidias placed before us, in ivory and gold, the tutelary Deity of this land, and the Zeus of Homer and Olympus.

To have lived with such men, to have enjoyed their familiarity and esteem, overpays all labours and anxieties. I were unworthy of the friendships I have commemorated, were I forgetful of the latest. Sacred it ought to be, formed as it was under the portico of Death, my friendship with the most sagacious, the most scientific, the most beneficent of philosophers, Acron and Hippocrates. If mortal could war against Pestilence and Destiny, they had been victorious. I leave them in the field : unfortunate he who finds them among the fallen !

And now, at the close of my day, when every light is dim and every guest departed, let me own that these wane before me, remembering, as I do in the pride and fulness of my heart, that Athens confided her glory, and Aspasia her happiness, to me.

Have I been a faithful guardian? do I resign them to the custody of the gods undiminished and unimpaired? Welcome then, welcome, my last hour ! After enjoying for so great a number of years, in my public and my private life, what I believe has never been the lot of any other, I now extend my hand to the urn, and take without reluctance or hesitation what is the lot of all.

HELLENICS.

XXX.

THE HAMADRYAD.

RHAICOS was born amid the hills wherefrom
Gnidos the light of Caria is discern'd,
And small are the white-crested that play near,
And smaller onward are the purple waves.
Thence festal choirs were visible, all crown'd
With rose and myrtle if they were inborn;
If from Pandion sprang they, on the coast
Where stern Athenè rais'd her citádel,
Then olive was entwined with violets
Cluster'd in bosses, regular and large;
For various men wore various coronals,
But one was their devotion; 't was to her
Whose laws all follow, her whose smile withdraws
The sword from Ares, thunderbolt from Zeus,
And whom in his chill caves the mutable
Of mind, Poseidon, the sea-king, reveres,
And whom his brother, stubborn Dis, hath pray'd
To turn in pity the averted cheek
Of her he bore away, with promises,
Nay, with loud oath before dread Styx itself,
To give her daily more and sweeter flowers
Than he made drop from her on Enna's dell.
    Rhaicos was looking from his father's door
At the long trains that hastened to the town

From all the valleys, like bright rivulets
Gurgling with gladness, wave outrunning wave,
And thought it hard he might not also go
And offer up one prayer, and press one hand,
He knew not whose.   The father call'd him in
And said, " Son Rhaicos! those are idle games;
Long enough I have lived to find them so."
And ere he ended, sighed; as old men do
Always, to think how idle such games are.
" I have not yet," thought Rhaicos in his heart,
And wanted proof.
                         "Suppose thou go and help
Echion at the hill, to bark yon oak
And lop its branches off, before we delve
About the trunk and ply the root with axe :
This we may do in winter."
                         Rhaicos went;
For thence he could see farther, and see more
Of those who hurried to the city-gate.
Echion he found there, with naked arm
Swart-hair'd, strong-sinew'd, and his eyes intent
Upon the place where first the axe should fall :
He held it upright.   " There are bees about,
Or wasps, or hornets," said the cautious el'd,
" Look sharp, O son of Thallinos !"   The youth
Inclined his ear, afar, and warily,
And cavern'd in his hand.   He heard a buzz
At first, and then the sound grew soft and clear,
And then divided into what seem'd tune,
And there were words upon it, plaintive words.
He turn'd, and said, " Echion! do not strike
That tree: it must be hollow ; for some god
Speaks from within.   Come thyself near."   Again
Both turn'd toward it: and behold! there sat

Upon the moss below, with her two palms
Pressing it, on each side, a maid in form.
Downcast were her long eyelashes, and pale
Her cheek, but never mountain-ash display'd
Berries of colour like her lip so pure,
Nor were the anemones about her hair
Soft, smooth, and wavering like the face beneath.
  "What dost thou here?" Echion, half-afraid,
Half-angry cried.   She lifted up her eyes,
But nothing spake she.   Rhaicos drew one step
Backward, for fear came likewise over him,
But not such fear : he panted, gasp'd, drew in
His breath, and would have turn'd it into words,
But could not into one.
                    "O send away
That sad old man!" said she.   The old man went
Without a warning from his master's son,
Glad to escape, for sorely he now fear'd,
And the axe shone behind him in their eyes.
  Hamad.   And wouldst thou too shed the most
      innocent
Of blood?   No vow demands it; no god wills
The oak to bleed.
  Rhaicos.   Who art thou? whence? why here?
And whither wouldst thou go?   Among the robed
In white or saffron, or the hue that most
Resembles dawn or the clear sky, is none
Array'd as thou art.   What so beautiful
As that gray robe which clings about thee close,
Like moss to stones adhering, leaves to trees,
Yet lets thy bosom rise and fall in turn,
As, touch'd by zephyrs, fall and rise the boughs
Of graceful platan by the river-side?
  Hamad.   Lovest thou well thy father's house?

Rhaicos.   Indeed
I love it, well I love it, yet would leave
For thine, where'er it be, my father's house,
With all the marks upon the door, that show
My growth at every birthday since the third,
And all the charms, o'erpowering evil eyes,
My mother nail'd for me against my bed,
And the Cydonian bow (which thou shalt see)
Won in my race last spring from Eutychos.
   Hamad. Bethink thee what it is to leave a home
Thou never yet hast left, one night, one day.
   Rhaicos. No, 't is not hard to leave it: 't is not hard
To leave, O maiden, that paternal home
If there be one on earth whom we may love
First, last, for ever; one who says that she
Will love for ever too. To say which word,
Only to say it, surely is enough.
It shows such kindness — if 't were possible
We at the moment think she would indeed.
   Hamad. Who taught thee all this folly at thy age?
   Rhaicos. . I have seen lovers and have learnt to love.
   Hamad. But wilt thou spare the tree?
   Rhaicos.   My father wants
The bark; the tree may hold its place awhile.
   Hamad. Awhile? thy father numbers then my days?
   Rhaicos. Are there no others where the moss beneath
Is quite as tufty? Who would send thee forth
Or ask thee why thou tarriest? Is thy flock
Anywhere near?
   Hamad. I have no flock: I kill
Nothing that breathes, that stirs, that feels the air,
The sun, the dew. Why should the beautiful
(And thou art beautiful) disturb the source
Whence springs all beauty? Hast thou never heard

Of Hamadryads?

   Rhaicos.   Heard of them I have:
Tell me some tale about them.   May I sit
Beside thy feet?   Art thou not tired?   The herbs
Are very soft; I will not come too nigh;
Do but sit there, nor tremble so, nor doubt. .
Stay, stay an instant: let me first explore
If any acorn of last year be left
Within it; thy thin robe too ill protects
Thy dainty limbs against the harm one small
Acorn may do.   Here's none.   Another day
Trust me; till then let me sit opposite.

   Hamad.   I seat me; be thou seated, and content.

   Rhaicos.   O sight for gods! ye men below! adore
The Aphroditè.   *Is* she there below?
Or sits she here before me? as she sate
Before the shepherd on those heights that shade
The Hellespont, and brought his kindred woe.

   Hamad.   Reverence the higher Powers; nor deem
      amiss
Of her who pleads to thee, and would repay—
Ask not how much — but very much.   Rise not:
No, Rhaicos, no!   Without the nuptial vow ___
Love is unholy.   Swear to me that none
Of mortal maids shall ever taste thy kiss,
Then take thou mine; then take it, not before.

   Rhaicos.   Hearken, all gods above!   O Aphroditè!
O Herè!   Let my vow be ratified!
But wilt thou come into my father's house?

   Hamad.   Nay: and of mine I cannot give thee part.

   Rhaicos.   Where is it?

   Hamad.   In this oak.

   Rhaicos.   Ay; now begins
The tale of Hamadryad: tell it through.

Hamad. Pray of thy father never to cut down
My tree; and promise him, as well thou mayst,
That every year he shall receive from me
More honey than will buy him nine fat sheep,
More wax than he will burn to all the gods.
Why fallest thou upon thy face? Some thorn
May scratch it, rash young man! Rise up; for shame!
  Rhaicos. For shame I cannot rise. O pity me!
I dare not sue for love — but do not hate!
Let me once more behold thee — not once more,
But many days: let me love on — unloved!
I aimed too high : on my own head the bolt
Falls back, and pierces to the very brain.
  Hamad. Go — rather go, than make me say I love.
  Rhaicos. If happiness is immortality,
(And whence enjoy it else the gods above?)
I am immortal too: my vow is heard —
Hark! on the left — Nay, turn not from me now,
I claim my kiss.
  Hamad.   Do men take first, then claim?
Do thus the seasons run their course with them?

Her lips were seal'd; her head sank on his breast.
'T is said that laughs were heard within the wood:
But who should hear them? and whose laughs? and why?

Savoury was the smell and long past noon,
Thallinos! in thy house; for marjoram,
Basil and mint, and thyme and rosemary,
Were sprinkled on the kid's well roasted length,
Awaiting Rhaicos. Home he came at last,
Not hungry, but pretending hunger keen,
With head and eyes just o'er the maple plate.
"Thou seest but badly, coming from the sun,
Boy Rhaicos!" said the father. "That oak's bark

Must have been tough, with little sap between ;
It ought to run; but it and I are old."
Rhaicos, although each morsel of the bread
Increased by chewing, and the meat grew cold
And tasteless to his palate, took a draught
Of gold-bright wine, which, thirsty as he was,
He thought not of, until his father fill'd
The cup, averring water was amiss,
But wine had been at all times pour'd on kid.
It was religion.

              He thus fortified
Said, not quite boldly, and not quite abash'd,
" Father, that oak is Zeus's own; that oak
Year after year will bring thee wealth from wax
And honey.   There is one who fears the gods
And the gods love — that one "

                         (He blush'd, nor said
What one)

          " Has promised this, and may do more.
Thou hast not many moons to wait until
The bees have done their best; if then there come
Nor wax nor honey, let the tree be hewn."
  "Zeus hath bestow'd on thee a prudent mind,"
Said the glad sire : " but look thou often there,
And gather all the honey thou canst find
In every crevice, over and above
What has been promised ; would they reckon that?"
  Rhaicos went daily; but the nymph as oft,
Invisible.   To play at love, she knew,
Stopping its breathings when it breathes most soft,
Is sweeter than to play on any pipe.
She play'd on his: she fed upon his sighs;
They pleased her when they gently waved her hair,
Cooling the pulses of her purple veins,

And when her absence brought them out, they pleased.
Even among the fondest of them all,
What mortal or immortal maid is more
Content with giving happiness than pain?
One day he was returning from the wood
Despondently.   She pitied him, and said
"Come back!" and twined her fingers in the hem
Above his shoulder.   Then she led his steps
To a cool rill that ran o'er level sand
Through lentisk and through oleander, there
Bathed she his feet, lifting them on her lap
When bathed, and drying them in both her hands.
He dared complain; for those who most are loved
Most dare it; but not harsh was his complaint.
"O thou inconstant!" said he, "if stern law
Bind thee, or will, stronger than sternest law,
O, let me know henceforward when to hope
Thē fruit of love that grows for me but here."
He spake; and pluck'd it from its pliant stem.
"Impatient Rhaicos!   Why thus intercept
The answer I would give?   There is a bee
Whom I have fed, a bee who knows my thoughts
And executes my wishes: I will send
That messenger.   If ever thou art false,
Drawn by another, own it not, but drive
My bee away: then shall I know my fate,
And — for thou must be wretched — weep at thine.
But often as my heart persuades to lay
Its cares on thine and throb itself to rest,
Expect her with thee, whether it be morn
Or eve, at any time when woods are safe."
　Day after day the Hours beheld them blest,
And season after season: years had past,
Blest were they still.   He who asserts that Love

Ever is sated of sweet things, the same
Sweet things he fretted for in earlier days,
Never, by Zeus! loved he a Hamadryad.

   The nights had now grown longer, and perhaps
The Hamadryads find them lone and dull
Among their woods; one did, alas!   She called
Her faithful bee: 't was when all bees should sleep,
And all did sleep but hers.   She was sent forth
To bring that light which never wintry blast
Blows out, nor rain nor snow extinguishes,
The light that shines from loving eyes upon
Eyes that love back, till they can see no more.
Rhaicos was sitting at his father's hearth:
Between them stood the table, not o'erspread
With fruits which autumn now profusely bore,
Nor anise cakes, nor odorous wine; but there
The draft-board was expanded; at which game
Triumphant sat old Thallinos; the son
Was puzzled, vex'd, discomfited, distraught.
A buzz was at his ear: up went his hand
And it was heard no longer.   The poor bee
Return'd (but not until the morn shone bright)
And found the Hamadryad with her head
Upon her aching wrist, and show'd one wing
Half-broken off, the other's meshes marr'd,
And there were bruises which no eye could see
Saving a Hamadryad's.
                 At this sight
Down fell the languid brow, both hands fell down.
A shriek was carried to the ancient hall
Of Thallinos: he heard it not: his son
Heard it, and ran forthwith into the wood.
No bark was on the tree, no leaf was green,
The trunk was riven through.   From that day forth

Nor word nor whisper sooth'd his ear, nor sound
Even of insect wing; but loud laments
The woodmen and the shepherds one long year
Heard day and night; for Rhaicos would not quit
The solitary place, but moan'd and died.

Hence milk and honey wonder not, O guest,
To find set duly on the hollow stone.

XXXI.

ACON AND RHODOPÈ; OR, INCONSTANCY.

(*A Sequel.*)

THE Year's twelve daughters had in turn gone by,
Of measured pace though varying mien all twelve,
Some froward, some sedater, some adorn'd
For festival, some reckless of attire.
The snow had left the mountain-top; fresh flowers
Had withered in the meadow; fig and prune
Hung wrinkling; the last apple glow'd amid
Its freckled leaves; and weary oxen blink'd
Between the trodden corn and twisted vine,
Under whose bunches stood the empty crate,
To creak ere long beneath them carried home.
This was the season when twelve months before,
O gentle Hamadryad, true to love!
Thy mansion, thy dim mansion in the wood
Was blasted and laid desolate: but none
Dared violate its precincts, none dared pluck
The moss beneath it, which alone remain'd
Of what was thine.
                         Old Thallinos sat mute
In solitary sadness. The strange tale
(Not until Rhaicos died, but then the whole)

Echion had related, whom no force
Could ever make look back upon the oaks.
The father said, " Echion ! thou must weigh,
Carefully, and with steady hand, enough
(Although no longer comes the store as once !)
Of wax to burn all day and night upon
That hollow stone where milk and honey lie :
So may the gods, so may the dead, be pleas'd ! "
Thallinos bore it thither in the morn,
And lighted it and left it.
                                        First of those
Who visited upon this solemn day
The Hamadryad's oak, were Rhodopè
And Acon ; of one age, one hope, one trust.
Graceful was she as was the nymph whose fate
She sorrowed for : he slender, pale, and first
Lapp'd by the flame of love : his father's lands
Were fertile, herds lowed over them afar.
Now stood the two aside the hollow stone
And look'd with stedfast eyes toward the oak
Shivered and black and bare.
                                        " May never we
Love as they loved ! " said Acon.   She at this
Smiled, for he said not what he meant to say,
And thought not of its bliss, but of its end.
He caught the flying smile, and blush'd, and vow'd
Nor time nor other power, whereto the might
Of love hath yielded and may yield again,
Should alter his.
                          The father of the youth
Wanted not beauty for him, wanted not
Song, that could lift earth's weight from off his heart,
Discretion, that could guide him thro' the world,
Innocence, that could clear his way to heaven ;

Silver and gold and land, not green before
The ancestral gate, but purple under skies
Bending far off, he wanted for his heir.
 Fathers have given life, but virgin heart
They never gave ; and dare they then control
Or check it harshly? dare they break a bond
Girt round it by the holiest Power on high?

 Acon was grieved, he said, grieved bitterly,
But Acon had complied — 't was dutiful !
 Crush thy own heart, Man ! Man ! but fear to wound
The gentler, that relies on thee alone,
By thee created, weak or strong by thee ;
Touch it not but for worship ; watch before
Its sanctuary ; nor leave it till are closed
The temple doors and the last lamp is spent.
 Rhodopè, in her soul's waste solitude,
Sate mournful by the dull-resounding sea,
Often not hearing it, and many tears
Had the cold breezes hardened on her cheek.
 Meanwhile he sauntered in the wood of oaks,
Nor shunn'd to look upon the hollow stone
That held the milk and honey, nor to lay
His plighted hand where recently 't was laid
Opposite hers, when finger playfully
Advanced and push'd back finger, on each side.
He did not think of this, as she would do
If she were there alone. The day was hot ;
The moss invited him ; it cool'd his cheek,
It cool'd his hands ; he thrust them into it
And sank to slumber. Never was there dream
Divine as his. He saw the Hamadryad.
She took him by the arm and led him on
Along a valley, where profusely grew

The smaller lilies with their pendant bells,
And, hiding under mint, chill drosera,
The violet, shy of butting cyclamen,
The feathery fern, and, browser of moist banks,
Her offspring round her, the soft strawberry;
The quivering spray of ruddy tamarisk,
The oleander's light-hair'd progeny
Breathing bright freshness in each other's face,
And graceful rose, bending her brow, with cup
Of fragrance and of beauty, boon for gods.
The fragrance fill'd his breast with such delight
His senses were bewildered, and he thought
He saw again the face he most had loved.
He stopp'd: the Hamadryad at his side
Now stood between; then drew him farther off:
He went, compliant as before: but soon
Verdure had ceased: although the ground was smooth,
Nothing was there delightful.   At this change
He would have spoken, but his guide repress'd
All questioning, and said,

                          "Weak youth! what brought
Thy footstep to this wood, my native haunt,
My life-long residence? this bank, where first
I sate with him — the faithful (now I know
Too late!) the faithful Rhaicos.   Haste thee home;
Be happy, if thou canst; but come no more
Where those whom death alone could sever, died."

   He started up: the moss whereon he slept
Was dried and withered: deadlier paleness spread
Over his cheek; he sickened: and the sire
Had land enough; it held his only son.

XXXII.

THE DEATH OF ARTEMIDORA.

" Artemidora !　Gods invisible,
While thou art lying faint along the couch,
Have tied the sandal to thy veinèd feet,
And stand beside thee, ready to convey
Thy weary steps where other rivers flow.
Refreshing shades will waft thy weariness
Away, and voices like thine own come nigh,
Soliciting, nor vainly, thy embrace."
Artemidora sigh'd, and would have press'd
The hand now pressing hers, but was too weak.
Fate's shears were over her dark hair unseen
While thus Elpenor spake : he look'd into
Eyes that had given light and life erewhile
To those above them, those now dim with tears
And watchfulness.　Again he spake of joy
Eternal.　At that word, that sad word, *joy*,
Faithful and fond her bosom heav'd once more,
Her head fell back : one sob, one loud deep sob
Swell'd through the darken'd chamber ; 't was not hers :
With her that old boat incorruptible,
Unwearied, undiverted in its course,
Had plash'd the water up the farther strand.

XXXIII.

THE WRESTLING MATCH.

[From *Gebir*.]

" 'T was evening, though not sunset, and the tide
Level with these green meadows, seem'd yet higher :
'T was pleasant, and I loosen'd from my neck
The pipe you gave me, and began to play.
O that I ne'er had learnt the tuneful art !
It always brings us enemies or love.
Well, I was playing, when above the waves
Some swimmer's head methought I saw ascend ;
I, sitting still, survey'd it with my pipe
Awkwardly held before my lips half-closed.
Gebir ! it was a Nymph ! a Nymph divine !
I cannot wait describing how she came,
How I was sitting, how she first assumed
The Sailor ; of what happen'd there remains
Enough to say, and too much to forget.
The sweet deceiver stepp'd upon this bank
Before I was aware ; for with surprise
Moments fly rapid as with love itself.
Stooping to tune afresh the hoarsen'd reed,
I heard a rustling, and where that arose
My glance first lighted on her nimble feet.
Her feet resembled those long shells explored
By him who to befriend his steed's dim sight
Would blow the pungent powder in the eye.
Her eyes too ! O immortal gods ! her eyes
Resembled — what could they resemble ? what
Ever resemble those ? Even her attire
Was not of wonted woof nor vulgar art :

Her mantle show'd the yellow samphire-pod,
Her girdle the dove-colour'd wave serene.
'Shepherd,' said she, 'and will you wrestle now,
And with the sailor's hardier race engage?'
I was rejoiced to hear it, and contrived
How to keep up contention : could I fail
By pressing not too strongly, yet to press?
'Whether a shepherd, as indeed you seem,
Or whether of the hardier race you boast,
I am not daunted ; no ; I will engage.'
'But first,' said she, 'what wager will you lay?'
'A sheep,' I answered : 'add whate'er you will.'
'I cannot,' she replied, 'make that return :
Our hided vessels in their pitchy round
Seldom, unless from rapine, hold a sheep.
But I have sinuous shells of pearly hue
Within, and they that lustre have imbibed
In the sun's palace-porch, where when unyoked
His chariot-wheel stands midway in the wave :
Shake one and it awakens, then apply
Its polish'd lips to your attentive ear,
And it remembers its august abodes,
And murmurs as the ocean murmurs there.
And I have others given me by the nymphs,
Of sweeter sound than any pipe you have ;
But we, by Neptune ! for no pipe contend;
This time a sheep I win, a pipe the next.'
Now came she forward eager to engage,
But first her dress, her bosom then survey'd,
And heaved it, doubting if she could deceive.
Her bosom seem'd, inclosed in haze like heaven,
To baffle touch, and rose forth undefined :
Above her knee she drew the robe succinct,
Above her breast, and just below her arms.

'This will preserve my breath when tightly bound,
If struggle and equal strength should so constrain.'
Thus, pulling hard to fasten it, she spake,
And, rushing at me, closed: I thrill'd throughout
And seem'd to lessen and shrink up with cold.
Again with violent impulse gush'd my blood,
And hearing nought external, thus absorb'd,
I heard it, rushing through each turbid vein,
Shake my unsteady swimming sight in air.
Yet with unyielding though uncertain arms
I clung around her neck; the vest beneath
Rustled against our slippery limbs entwined:
Often mine springing with eluded force
Started aside and trembled till replaced:
And when I most succeeded, as I thought,
My bosom and my throat felt so compress'd
That life was almost quivering on my lips.
Yet nothing was there painful : these are signs
Of secret arts and not of human might;
What arts I cannot tell; I only know
My eyes grew dizzy and my strength decay'd;
I was indeed o'ercome — with what regret,
And more, with what confusion, when I reach'd
The fold, and yielding up the sheep, she cried,
'This pays a shepherd to a conquering maid.'
She smiled, and more of pleasure than disdain
Was in her dimpled chin and liberal lip,
And eyes that languish'd, lengthening, just like love.
She went away; I on the wicker gate
Leant, and could follow with my eyes alone.
The sheep she carried easy as a cloak;
But when I heard its bleating, as I did,
And saw, she hastening on, its hinder feet
Struggle, and from her snowy shoulder slip,

One shoulder its poor efforts had unveil'd,
Then all my passions mingling fell in tears ;
Restless then ran I to the highest ground
To watch her ; she was gone ; gone down the tide ;
And the long moonbeam on the hard wet sand
Lay like a jasper column half uprear'd."

XXXIV.

TO IANTHE.

1.

IT often comes into my head
That we may dream when we are dead,
　But I am far from sure we do.
O that it were so ! then my rest
Would be indeed among the blest ;
　I should for ever dream of you.

2.

Ianthe ! you are call'd to cross the sea !
　　A-path forbidden *me !*
Remember, while the sun his blessing sheds
　　Upon the mountain-heads,
How often we have watch'd him laying down
　　His brow, and dropp'd our own
Against each other's, and how faint and short
　　And sliding the support !
What will succeed it now ?　Mine is unblest,
　　Ianthe ! nor will rest
But on the very thought that swells with pain.
　　O bid me hope again !
O give me back what Earth, what (without you)
　　Not Heaven itself can do,

One of the golden days that we have past ;
    And let it be my last !
Or else the gift would be, however sweet,
    Fragile and incomplete.

3.

Your pleasures spring like daisies in the grass,
    Cut down and up again as blithe as ever ;
From you, Ianthe, little troubles pass
    Like little ripples in a sunny river.

4.

Well I remember how you smiled
    To see me write your name upon
The soft sea-sand, — "O ! what a child !
    You think you 're writing upon stone !"
I have since written what no tide
    Shall ever wash away, what men
Unborn shall read o'er ocean wide
    And find Ianthe's name again.

XXXV.

ROSE AYLMER.

Ah what avails the sceptred race,
    Ah what the form divine !
What every virtue, every grace !
    Rose Aylmer, all were thine.
Rose Aylmer, whom these wakeful eyes
    May weep, but never see,
A night of memories and of sighs
    I consecrate to thee.

XXXVI.

A FIESOLAN IDYL.

Here, where precipitate Spring with one light bound
Into hot Summer's lusty arms expires,
And where go forth at morn, at eve, at night,
Soft airs that want the lute to play with 'em.
And softer sighs that know not what they want,
Aside a wall, beneath an orange-tree,
Whose tallest flowers could tell the lowlier ones
Of sights in Fiesole right up above,
While I was gazing a few paces off
At what they seem'd to show me with their nods,
Their frequent whispers and their pointing shoots,
A gentle maid came down the garden-steps
And gathered the pure treasure in her lap.
I heard the branches rustle, and stepp'd forth
To drive the ox away, or mule, or goat,
Such I believed it must be.   How could I
Let beast o'erpower them? when hath wind or rain
Borne hard upon weak plant that wanted me,
And I (however they might bluster round)
Walk'd off?   'T were most ungrateful: for sweet scents
Are the swift vehicles of still sweeter thoughts,
And nurse and pillow the dull memory
That would let drop without them her best stores.
They bring me tales of youth and tones of love,
And 't is and ever was my wish and way
To let all flowers live freely, and all die
(Whene'er their Genius bids their souls depart)
Among their kindred in their native place.
I never pluck the rose ; the violet's head
Hath shaken with my breath upon its bank

And not reproach'd me ; the ever-sacred cup
Of the pure lily hath between my hands
Felt safe, unsoil'd, nor lost one grain of gold.
I saw the light that made the glossy leaves
More glossy ; the fair arm, the fairer cheek
Warmed by the eye intent on its pursuit ;
I saw the foot that, although half-erect
From its gray slipper, could not lift her up
To what she wanted : I held down a branch
And gather'd her some blossoms ; since their hour
Was come, and bees had wounded them, and flies
Of harder wing were working their way thro'
And scattering them in fragments under foot.
So crisp were some, they rattled unevolved,
Others, ere broken off, fell into shells,
Unbending, brittle, lucid, white like snow,
And like snow not seen through, by eye or sun :
Yet every one her gown received from me
Was fairer than the first.   I thought not so,
But so she praised them to reward my care.
I said, " You find the largest."

                            " This indeed,"
Cried she, " is large and sweet."   She held one forth,
Whether for me to look at or to take
She knew not, nor did I ; but taking it
Would best have solved (and this she felt) her doubt.
I dared not touch it ; for it seemed a part
Of her own self ; fresh, full, the most mature
Of blossoms, yet a blossom ; with a touch
To fall, and yet unfallen.   She drew back
The boon she tender'd, and then, finding not
The ribbon at her waist to fix it in,
Dropp'd it, as loth to drop it, on the rest.

XXXVII.

UPON A SWEET-BRIAR.

My briar that smelledst sweet
When gentle spring's first heat
  Ran through thy quiet veins, —
Thou that wouldst injure none,
But wouldst be left alone,
Alone thou leavest me, and nought of thine remains.

What ! hath no poet's lyre
O'er thee, sweet-breathing briar,
  Hung fondly, ill or well?
And yet methinks with thee
A poet's sympathy,
Whether in weal or woe, in life or death, might dwell.

Hard usage both must bear,
  Few hands your youth will rear,
  Few bosoms cherish you ;
Your tender prime must bleed
Ere you are sweet, but freed
From life, you then are prized ; thus prized are poets too.

And art thou yet alive ?
And shall the happy hive
  Send out her youth to cull
Thy sweets of leaf and flower,
And spend the sunny hour
With thee, and thy faint heart with murmuring music lull?

Tell me what tender care,
Tell me what pious prayer,
  Bade thee arise and live.

The fondest-favoured bee
Shall whisper nought to thee
More loving than the song my grateful muse shall give.

XXXVIII.

THE MAID'S LAMENT.

I LOVED him not; and yet now he is gone
  I feel I am alone.
I check'd him while he spoke; yet could he speak,
  Alas! I would not check.
For reasons not to love him once I sought,
  And wearied all my thought
To vex myself and him: I now would give
  My love, could he but live
Who lately lived for me, and when he found
  'T was vain, in holy ground
He hid his face amid the shades of death.
  I waste for him my breath
Who wasted his for me: but mine returns,
  And this lorn bosom burns
With stifling heat, heaving it up in sleep,
  And waking me to weep
Tears that had melted his soft heart: for years
  Wept he as bitter tears.
Merciful God! such was his latest prayer,
  These may she never share.
Quieter is his breath, his breast more cold,
  Than daisies in the mould,
Where children spell, athwart the churchyard gate,
  His name and life's brief date.
Pray for him, gentle souls, whoe'er you be,
  And oh! pray too for me.

XXXIX.

TO ROBERT BROWNING.

THERE is delight in singing, though none hear
Beside the singer ; and there is delight
In praising, though the praiser sit alone
And see the prais'd far off him, far above.
Shakspeare is not our poet, but the world's,
Therefore on him no speech ! and brief for thee,
Browning !   Since Chaucer was alive and hale,
No man hath walk'd along our roads with step
So active, so inquiring eye, or tongue
So varied in discourse.   But warmer climes
Give brighter plumage, stronger wing : the breeze
Of Alpine highths thou playest with, borne on
Beyond Sorrento and Amalfi, where
The Siren waits thee, singing song for song.

XL.

TO THE SISTER OF ELIA.

COMFORT thee, O thou mourner, yet awhile !
        Again shall Elia's smile
Refresh thy heart, where heart can ache no more :
        What is it we deplore ?

He leaves behind him, freed from griefs and years,
        Far worthier things than tears,
The love of friends without a single foe :
        Unequalled lot below !

His gentle soul, his genius, these are thine ;
        For these dost thou repine ?
He may have left the lowly walks of men ;
        Left them he has ; what then ?

Are not his footsteps followed by the eyes
    Of all the good and wise?
Though the warm day is over, yet they seek
    Upon the lofty peak

Of his pure mind the roseate light that glows
    O'er death's perennial snows.
Behold him! from the region of the blest
    He speaks: he bids thee rest.

XLI.

ON DIRCE.

STAND close around, ye Stygian set,
    With Dirce in one boat convey'd,
Or Charon, seeing, may forget
    That he is old, and she a shade.

XLII.

I will not love!
   .   .   .   These sounds have often
    Burst from a troubled breast;
Rarely from one no sighs could soften,
    Rarely from one at rest.

OLD AGE AND DEATH.

XLIII.

How many voices gaily sing,
"O happy morn, O happy spring
Of life!" Meanwhile there comes o'er me
A softer voice from Memory,
And says, "If loves and hopes have flown
With years, think too what griefs are gone!"

XLIV.

THE place where soon I think to lie,
In its old creviced nook hard-by
 Rears many a weed: .
If parties bring you there, will you
Drop slily in a grain or two
 Of wall-flower seed ?

I shall not see it, and (too sure !)
I shall not ever hear that your
 Light step was there ;
But the rich odour some fine day
Will, what I cannot do, repay
 That little care.

XLV.

TO AGE.

WELCOME, old friend ! These many years
 Have we lived door by door :
The Fates have laid aside their shears
 Perhaps for some few more.

I was indocile at an age
 When better boys were taught,
But thou at length hast made me sage,
 If I am sage in aught.

Little I know from other men,
 Too little they from me,
But thou hast pointed well the pen
 That writes these lines to thee.

Thanks for expelling Fear and Hope,
　One vile, the other vain ;
One's scourge, the other's telescope,
　I shall not see again :

Rather what lies before my feet
　My notice shall engage.
He who hath braved Youth's dizzy heat
　Dreads not the frost of Age.

XLVI.

ON HIS SEVENTY-FIFTH BIRTHDAY.

I STROVE with none, for none was worth my strife,
　Nature I loved, and next to Nature, Art ;
I warmed both hands before the fire of life,
　It sinks, and I am ready to depart.

XLVII.

ON HIS EIGHTIETH BIRTHDAY.

To my ninth decade I have totter'd on,
　And no soft arm bends now my steps to steady ;
She, who once led me where she would, is gone,
　So when he calls me, Death shall find me ready.

XLVIII.

DEATH stands above me, whispering low
　I know not what into my ear :
Of his strange language all I know
　Is, there is not a word of fear.

NOTES.

3 I. **Achilles and Helena** (1853). Helen's meeting with Achilles, in answer to his prayer .to Aphrodite and Thetis, is an incident in a lost epic anciently attributed to Homer, based on early traditions of the Trojan war. Though this colloquy is not Homeric, nor are the speakers especially lifelike, yet various traits — the distinctness of the scene, the references to familiar incidents in the *Iliad*, the implication of the effect produced by the hero and the beauty on each other, the refined reticence, the sureness of touch — render the dialogue an adequate specimen of Landor's characteristically measured treatment of short heroic themes from the Greek mythology.

Landor was fond of these subjects, and handled them as only he could. There are several dialogues like this, some in verse, others — of which this is one — originally in prose and afterward versified. As the prose versions are the better, this scene may here suffice to represent the class to which it belongs — a class which even Landor's treatment can make interesting only to those who can find the certain, if not quite spontaneous, pleasure which lies hidden in all work where technical merit reaches excellence. The point, which is worth dwelling on for a moment at the outset as marking a radical difference between two ways of estimating Landor's work, may be illustrated by reference to a remark of one of his best critics, who believes that in the scene between Peleus and Thetis, which is a worthy companion of this between Achilles and Helen, he "unites with the full charm of Hellenic mythology the full vividness of human passion." That is attempted: to say that the attempt is successful is to claim for the scene dramatic power of the first order, and so to set the doubter rummaging his recollection for scenes which have actually moved him. That parts of Landor's work are suffused with human feeling, few of his readers deny; but fewer still would admit the mythological dialogues to be more than a cool reflection of the antique fire which kindled Landor's own emotion.   His mythical Greeks, we must concede, do not rival the true creatures of the art of Greece; at most they are like pale marbles wrought by a foremost student of Greek modes.   Grudging though such praise as this may sound, it ranks them above modern rivals.

The dainty passage about " trees and bright-eyed flowers " (p. 6) is in tune with Landor's line:

> Flowers may enjoy their own pure dreams of bliss.

9 II.   **Æsop and Rhodopè** (1846).   Of Rhodope, the "rose-faced," a fellow-slave, according to Herodotus, with Æsop, to whom she became attached, nothing is known beyond a few legendary details, some of which are here used.   The two Conversations between them are so nearly equal in ease and grace that, rather than exclude either, I prefer, even at the risk of mutilation, to give part of each.   There is great flexibility in the treatment of both characters, with an abundance. of beautifully modulated passages.

Æsop's reflections, near the beginning (pp. 9–10), on the desirability of early death — " It is better to repose in the earth betimes," with the several lines preceding and following — may be compared with the somewhat similar reflections contained in a quatrain of Landor's :

> Is it not better at an early hour
> ¸ In its calm cell to rest the weary head,
> While birds are singing and while blooms the bower,
> Than sit the fire out and go starved to bed?

Here the prose passage is more imaginative than the verse, more original, developed with greater ease and freedom, more essentially poetic, more harmonious to the ear, and quite free from any such feebly frigid conventional touch as ends the third line of the quatrain.

The incident related by Rhodope in the latter part is of Landor's invention.   The song of the Fates (p. 18) alludes to the story that she became queen of Egypt, which is thus quaintly told by Burton : "*Rhodope* was the fairest Lady, in her days, in all *Egypt;* she went to wash her, and by chance (her maids meanwhile looking but carelessly to her clothes) an Eagle stole away one of her shoes, and laid it in *Psammetichus* the King of *Egypt's* lap at *Memphis:* he wondered at the excellency of the shoe, and pretty foot, but more *aquilae factum*, at the manner of the bringing of it: and caused, forthwith, proclamation to be made, that she that owned that shoe should come presently to his Court; the Virgin came and was forthwith married to the King." *Anatomy of Melancholy*, Part. IIL Sect. II. Mem. V. Subs. V.

19 III. **Tiberius and Vipsania** (1828). Suetonius is authority for this interview, of which Landor says: " Vipsania, the daughter of Agrippa, was divorced from Tiberius by Augustus and Livia, in order that he might marry Julia, and hold the empire by inheritance. He retained such an affection for her, and showed it so intensely when he once met her afterward, that every precaution was taken lest they should meet again."

Mr. Swinburne, in his article on Landor in the *Encyclopædia Britannica*, remarks that " his utmost command of passion and pathos may be tested by its transcendent success in the distilled and concentrated tragedy of *Tiberius and Vipsania*, where for once he shows a quality more proper to romantic than classical imagination, — the subtle and sublime and terrible power to enter the dark vestibule of distraction, to throw the whole force of his fancy, the whole fire of his spirit, into the 'shadowing passion' (as Shakespeare calls it) of gradually imminent insanity." This exalted estimate is only Mr. Swinburne's inimitable way of saying definitely what others had vaguely felt before him — Julius Hare, for instance, declaring the dialogue to be the "greatest English poem since the death of Milton." Landor himself thought it superlatively good, and tells in his letters how he tried again and again before he got it right, shedding copious tears in the attempt. Feeling so real is respectable. Yet few of the present critical generation can share it, or can allow that the tragic pang fully vitalises Landor's Romans. Mr. Swinburne's maladroit allusion to one of the tremendous moments in *Othello* does Landor an ill turn, by suggesting a comparison which his *Tiberius and Vipsania* cannot bear. Cooler consideration, while noting Landor's limitation, as thus unwittingly implied in his eulogist's unmeasured words, yet need not hesitate to recognise in the scene artistic qualities so high and rare, so distinctive of its author, as to entitle it to a place in the first rank of its class. Precisely what that class is, it seems worth while to try to indicate. A random remark of Mr. A. J. C. Hare's may help to a true discrimination between the type of beauty which does exist in some of Landor's most highly wrought scenes and that which does not. He casually mentions Landor's habit of sitting long silent in "impassioned contemplation" — a phrase which recalls Landor's own saying that he " walked alone on the far eastern uplands, meditating and remembering." Here, it would appear, is a suggestion of the mood in which such a scene as this may have been composed, and which it may induce in an imaginative reader. The dominant note, in short, is contemplative and meditative, rather than actively and tragically passionate. On page 195 of this volume

Petrarch and Boccaccio, speaking for Landor, support the view here advanced.

23 IV. **Metellus and Marius** (1829). Strikingly characteristic, and therefore worth attentive examination. The first speech of Metellus accurately describes Marius as in the course of the action he is shown to be. The reply of Marius, exhibiting his promptness, also implies the adjacent outlook ; his next is full of youthful eagerness and intrepidity. The third speech of Metellus, in two parts, shows, without mentioning it, what Marius has done while he was speaking. Then follow the suggestion of Metellus that the centurion is afraid, the indifference of Marius to that insinuation in surroundings which might well justify fear, and presently the recognition by the tribune of his junior's fearlessness. The reader may, on these hints, pursue for himself the examination of the method and mark the result. IIe will find strict attention throughout to minute detail both of incident and of language, which is so shown and so arranged as to produce a precise picture of all that Marius sees, as well as of the effect on Metellus of his account of his experiences. It is as vivid as Rebecca's account of the storming of Front de Bœuf's castle, differing from that in the extreme verbal compression and in the exclusion of all irrelevance. The "civic fire" (p. 27), which is rightly accounted a powerful stroke of imagination on Landor's part, though greatly heightening the effect, it is yet possible to regard as bordering on that province of the grotesque which Mr. Rider Haggard rules. The concluding monologue of Marius, referring to a story of Plutarch's to the effect that Scipio, having noticed an act of valor performed by Marius, had singled him out as his own possible successor, makes a resounding climax to a peculiarly coherent and telling dialogue.

Plutarch and Appian furnish the facts relating to Marius and to the reduction by famine of Numantia ; and Landor supplies the imaginative treatment whereby the speakers and the scene, obviously very distinct to himself, become so to the attentive reader who is willing to make a slight effort. The whole thing seems as typically Landorian as almost any other equal number of consecutive pages.

28 V. **Marcellus and Hannibal** (1828). Appian and Plutarch give the facts on which this scene is based; Landor, characteristically, prolongs the life of Marcellus till Hannibal reaches him, and thus renders possible a dialogue embodying the dauntless pride of the Roman and the generosity of his victorious foe. Nothing better illustrates Landor's method of adapting history to his purpose ; and few of his scenes more fully justify the procedure than this one, which is, to an unusual degree,

animated by the spirit of traditional Roman haughtiness and martial dignity. These traits are perfectly matched by the style, which is direct, elevated, controlled, statuesque, not quite mobile.

33 VI. **Henry VIII. and Anne Boleyn** (1824). Of the various laudatory comments made on this vigorous scene by Landor's admiring friends, the one best worth recording is Julius Hare's just remark that a "fine peculiarity" consists in the simplicity of the language, which tells the whole story almost without imagery. Yet Coleridge asserted, in 1834, that Landor had "never learned to write simple and lucid English."

Especially in the case of scenes from English history, it would be out of place in these notes to discuss Landor's conception of characters over which historians contend. His own comments, however, may still be read with interest by such as care to put themselves for the moment at his point of view, which he is never averse to stating with clearness. Among his utterances on the subject of Henry are these bits of sarcasm : " Henry was not unlearned, nor indifferent to the costly externals of a gentleman; but in manners and language he was hardly on a level with our hostlers of the present day." " His reign is one continued proof, flaring and wearisome as a Lapland summer day, that even the English form of government, under a sensual king with money at his disposal, may serve only to legitimize injustice." " The government was whatever the king ordered; and he a ferocious and terrific thing, swinging on high between two windy superstitions, and caught and propelled alternately by fanaticism and lust." " It does not appear that the Defender of the Faith brought his wife to the scaffold for the good of her soul, nor that she was pregnant at the time, which would have added much to the merit of the action, as there is the probability that the child would have been heretical." Whether historically sound or not, the feeling which animates those sentences is unquestionably embodied with keen zest in this fictitious interview between the father and the unfortunate mother of Elizabeth.

41 VII. **Roger Ascham and Lady Jane Grey** (1824). The touch of pedantry in the master, his ominous foreboding, his solicitude for his pupil, her winning innocence and trustfulness, all expressed in musically cadenced sentences, give to this slight scene a dainty tenderness of pathetic suggestion.

A glance at the subjoined passage from the *Scholemaster* will show between Ascham's style and Landor's a wide dissimilarity not incompatible with charm which the two pictures have in common : " Before

I went into *Germanie*, I came to Brodegate in Le[i]ceſterſhire, to take my leaue of that noble Ladie *Iane Grey*, to whom I was exceding moch beholdinge.   Hir parentes, the Duke and Duches, with all the houſhold, Gentlemen and Gentlewomen, were huntinge in the Parke: I founde her, in her Chamber, readinge *Phædon Platonis* in Greeke, and that with as moch delite, as ſom ientlemen wold read a merie tale in *Bocaſe*.   After ſalutation, and dewtie done, with ſom other taulke, I aſked hir, whie ſhe wold leeſe ſoch paſtime in the Parke? ſmiling ſhe anſwered me: I wiſſe, all their ſporte in the Parke is but a ſhadoe to that pleaſure, that I find in *Plato*: Alas good folke, they neuer felt, what trewe pleaſure ment.   And howe came you Madame, quoth I, to this deepe knowledge of pleaſure, and what did chieflie allure you vnto it: ſeinge, not many women, but verie fewe men haue atteined thereunto.   I will tell you, quoth ſhe, and tell you a troth, which perchance ye will meruell at.   One of the greateſt benefites, that euer God gaue me, is, that he ſent me ſo ſharpe and ſeuere Parentes, and ſo ientle a ſcholemaſter.   For when I am in preſence either of father or mother, whether I ſpeake, kepe ſilence, ſit, ſtand, or go, eate, drinke, be merie, or ſad, be ſowyng, plaiyng, dauncing, or doing anei thing els, I muſt do it, as it were, in ſoch weight, meſure, and number, euen ſo perfitelie, as God made the world, or elſe I am ſo ſharplie taunted, ſo cruellie threatened, yea preſentlie ſome tymes, with pinches, nippes, and bobbes, and other waies, ‧which I will not name, for the honor I beare them, ſo without meaſure miſordered, that I thinke my ſelfe in hell, till tyme cum, that I muſt go to *M. Elmer*, who teacheth me ſo ientlie, ſo pleaſantlie, with ſoch faire allurementes to learning, that I thinke all the tyme nothing, whiles I am with him.   And when I am called from him, I fall on weeping, becauſe, what ſoeuer I do els, but learning, is ful of grief, trouble, feare, and whole miſliking vnto me: And thus my booke, hath bene ſo moch my pleaſure, and bringeth dayly to me more pleaſure and more, that in reſpect of it, all other pleaſures, in very deede, be but trifles and troubles vnto me.   I remember this talke gladly, both bicauſe it is ſo worthy of memorie, and bicauſe alſo, it was the laſt talke that euer I had, and the laſt tyme, that euer I ſaw that noble and worthie Ladie."

Mr. Leslie Stephen remarks that Landor's antipathy to Plato leads him to deprive Jane of her favourite author, allowing her only Cicero and Epictetus and Plutarch and Polybius.

44 VIII.   **Princess Mary and Princess Elizabeth** (1846).   This is the most natural and most entertaining of the three Conversations in which Elizabeth takes part.

In the group of scenes laid in the time of Elizabeth, the one between
Mary Stuart and Bothwell has merit. Its blemish is that Landor's
Queen of Scots, meant to be winsomely feminine, unluckily comports
herself at moments with the pert self-consciousness of an underbred
little girl flustered by the attentions of her first beau. Some of Landor's women are among his most satisfactory personages. Such are
Jane Grey, Anne Boleyn, Alice Lisle and Elizabeth Gaunt, Godiva,
Catharine, Leonora, Aspasia, Giovanna,[1] each one of whom in her own
way justifies these words of his in a letter to Southey: " I delight in
the minute variations and almost imperceptible shades of the female
character, and confess that my reveries, from my most early youth,
were almost entirely on what this one or that one would have said or
done in this or that situation. Their countenances, their movements,
their forms, the colours of their dresses, were before my eyes." His
comments on Virgil's treatment of the character of Dido are in keeping
with the feeling here expressed. But he does not always give to his
reveries on the female character, in its "minute variations and almost
imperceptible shades," a body that breathes and moves like a true
woman. Those who are animated by some set purpose in a crisis are
far more apt to call forth his best powers than those who merely behave
like the ladies of one's acquaintance. When he attempts the casual
in his treatment of the feminine nature, he sometimes lapses into the
commonplace or the trivial. His mind was of a cast so essentially
heroic that a sense of something out of keeping is liable to mar the
effect of his pictures of the usual or incidental — especially in the conduct of women. At the precise point where Jane Austen falls only
just short of supremacy Landor dwindles almost to insignificance.
He is cited by Mr. Locker-Lampson as saying prettily of Addison that
there was "coyness in his style, the archness and shyness of a graceful
and beautiful girl " — the very qualities in which his own style is deficient. The gracious figure of Assunta, in the *Pentameron*, tends to
belie the somewhat comprehensive generalisation made above ; but she
is quite exceptional, if not unique.

· 54 IX. **Essex and Spenser** (1834). Drummond of Hawthornden
says Ben Jonson told him, "That the Irish having rob'd Spenser's
goods, and burnt his house and a litle child new born, he and his wyfe
escaped ; and after, he died for lake of bread in King Street, and re-

[1] " How few hands since Shakespeare," exclaims Professor Dowden with enthusiastic
exaggeration, " could have drawn so difficult and delicate a portrait as that of Giovanna ! " Aspasia and Giovanna are on a larger scale than Landor's other female figures,
and both have moments of life. ·

fused 20 pieces sent to him by my Lord of Essex, and said, He was sorrie he had no time to spend them "—some of which statements probably far exceed the facts.

The early part of the dialogue, here omitted, deals with the disturbances in Ireland, and leads naturally to Spenser's account of his own calamity. The bearing of both speakers under increasing emotion is so admirably indicated as to come near stirring real emotion in the reader.

59 X. **Leofric and Godiva** (1829). So enchanting a scene, so fragrant and wooing, so musically pleading, so human, needs no comment. The only flaw — if that can be called a flaw which is almost an inherent attribute of work in this form — is the occasional perhaps slightly too obvious intrusion into the dialogue of implied stage directions for the reader's information.

Leofric's picture of Godiva mounting her horse (p. 64) brings to mind Landor's line:

> Calm hair meandering in pellucid gold.

"May the peppermint," etc., recalls Newman wistfully remembering, after he had joined the Church of Rome, the snap-dragon which used to grow opposite his freshman's rooms at Trinity College.

"Among the moderns," writes Landor in his essay on Theocritus, "no poet, it appears to us, has written an Idyl so perfect, so pure and simple in expression, yet so rich in thought and imagery, as the *Godiva* of Alfred Tennyson," which Emerson calls "a noble poem that will tell the legend a thousand years." Landor's treatment of the subject preceded Tennyson's in publication by thirteen years.

65 XI. **The Lady Lisle and Elizabeth Gaunt** (1829). Lady Alice (more properly *Mrs.*) Lisle, widow of one of the Regicides, was beheaded at Winchester, and Elizabeth Gaunt was burned at Tyburn, for harboring persons concerned in the Duke of Monmouth's insurrection. Macaulay calls the execution of Elizabeth Gaunt "the foulest judicial murder which had disgraced even those times." Burnet's *History of the Reign of James II.* gave Landor the incidents and the characters, but this meeting in prison is of his own imagining. The scene, vividly picturing the interaction of contrasted personalities in the shrinking widow and the courageous matron, is one of the most natural and lifelike that he has written; it abounds in delicate touches, and is throughout sustained at a high level.

A daughter of Alice Lisle was wife of Dr. Leonard Hoar, third President of Harvard College, and afterward of Mr. Hezekiah Usher, a merchant of Boston. See Sewall's *Diary*, I. 104 (Nov. 13, 1685).

69 XII. **The Empress Catharine and Princess Dashkof** (1829). Of this scene Landor says: " It is unnecessary to inform the generality of readers that Catharine was not present at the murder of her husband; nor is it easy to believe that Clytemnestra was at the murder of hers. Our business is character." Catharine's is presented with satiric force, and an instinctive sense of temperament. The only recorded performance of a scene of Landor's on any stage is the recitation of *Pelens and Thetis* by Epicurus and Ternissa, toward the close of their stroll with Leontion in the garden of Epicurus near Athens. Sardou might be fancied adapting for Sarah Bernhardt the material here furnished by Landor, and she making a melodramatic hit in the part of the fiercely arbitrary and emotional empress. The scene is full of suggestion and implication of incident, and abrupt transitions expressive of overstrained nervous tension seeking relief, with complete mastery of language. It leads nowhere in particular; but that is usually the case with Landor's sculpturesquely isolated moments. Its companion piece, *Peter the Great and Alexis*, equally inspired by hatred of tyrants, is less subtle than this concentrated essence of feminine malignity.

77 XIII. **John of Gaunt and Joanna of Kent** (1829). Landor's note is: " Joanna, called the Fair Maid of Kent, was cousin of the Black Prince, whom she married. John of Gaunt was suspected of aiming at the crown in the beginning of Richard's minority, which, increasing the hatred of the people against him for favouring the sect of Wickliffe, excited them to demolish his house and to demand his impeachment." In the light of those facts thus clearly stated, this rather unusually intricate Conversation becomes less difficult to follow. It is coupled by Mr. Colvin with that of *Tancredi and Constantia*, published seventeen years later, as typical of mediæval chivalry. Both are among the most highly finished, though perhaps not most natural, of Landor's short episodical scenes.

82 XIV. **Tancredi and Constantia** (1846). The following succinct statement of facts is taken from E. A. Freeman's article on Sicily in the *Encyclopædia Britannica.* " The brightest days of Sicily ended with William the Good. His marriage with Joanna, daughter of Henry of Anjou and England, was childless, and William tried to procure the succession of his aunt Constance and her husband, King Henry the Sixth of Germany, son of the Emperor Frederick the First. But the prospect of German rule was unpopular, and on William's death the crown passed to Tancred, an illegitimate grandson of King Roger, who figures in English histories in the story of Richard's crusade." The capture and release of Constance by Tancred, after Henry had become

emperor, form an episode such as Landor delights to treat, and treats with freedom and spirit.

Forster prints this curious extract from a letter written to himself years afterward: " While writing the Tancredi dialogue I had the greatest difficulty to prevent my prose running away with me. Sundry verses I could not keep down, nor could I afterwards break them into prose. Here is a specimen, not in the Conversation as it stands at present, which was written while I fancied I was writing prose :

> Can certain words pronounced by certain men
> Perform an incantation which shall hold
> Two hearts together to the end of time ?
> If these were wanting, yet instead of these,
> There was my father's word, and there was God's."

Here is a shorter specimen, from the Peleus and Thetis dialogue, which seems to have escaped his notice :

> Doth not my hand enclasp that slender foot,
> At which the waves of Ocean cease to be
> Tumultuous . . . ?

87 XV. **The Maid of Orleans and Agnes Sorel** (1846). The meeting is not historic. Though the treatment is slightly stiff, and the change produced in Agnes by Jeanne's appeal lacks plausibility, yet the " Demoiselle de Seurelle, Dame de Beauté," the inscription on whose tomb in the quiet chapel at Loches describes her as "une douce et simple colombe plus blanche que les cygnes, plus vermeille que la flamme," is, on the whole, well contrasted with "Joan the Maid," through whose words runs a strain of visionary exaltation. In this Conversation occur — what is rare in Landor's prose — several iambic lines, of which the prettiest is :

> Life is but sighs ; and, when they cease, 't is over.

See previous note.

96 XVI. **Bossuet and the Duchess de Fontanges** (1828). This scene has variously affected different people. Forster, for instance, grows solemnly enthusiastic over " Bossuet, sent by the king to compliment one of his child-mistresses on her elevation to the rank of duchess, listening with a half mournful, half smiling gravity to the giddy, vain, wild, gentle, childish, joyous girl, until at last the very danger of the good-hearted simple little creature moves him to tell the truth to her, and as the courtier drops from him the God rises and speaks "; and he adds, in all seriousness, that there is "hardly a finer thing than this in

the whole of the conversations." Others, more light-minded, single it out as Landor's signal success in what Emerson would have called his "gamesome mood." Still other readers, though pleased by the diverting irony of the dialogue and the distinctness of the speakers, yet fancy they detect a slight lapse in taste, with some lack of lightness in the touch ; so they pronounce Landorian density of style ill suited to a vein of pleasantry. Equally ironical, but less diverting, is the dialogue of Louis XIV. and his confessor.

104 XVII. **Dante and Beatrice** (1846). Miss Kate Field writes in the *Atlantic Monthly*, May, 1866 : "Landor has conceived the existence of a truly ardent affection between Dante and Beatrice, and it was my good fortune to hear him read this beautiful imaginary conversation. To witness the aged poet throwing the pathos of his voice into the pathos of his intellect, his eyes flooded with tears, was a scene of uncommon interest. 'Ah!' said he, while closing the book, 'I never wrote anything half as good as that, and I never can read it that the tears do not come.'" It is recorded that Tennyson used likewise to be affected to tears at his own reading of passages from his works which left his hearers unmoved. This scene between Dante and Beatrice, fervid and tender as it is, scarcely has power to stir in a reader emotion such as Miss Field describes in its author. It has a pretty sequel in the interview between Dante and Gemma Donati soon after the birth of their seventh child, a girl whom the mother names Beatrice.

113 XVIII. **Beniowski and Aphanasia** (1828). See Mr. Crump's note for facts concerning Beniowski, a Hungarian who, taken prisoner by the Russians and banished to Siberia, fell in love, though already married, with the daughter of the Governor of Kamscatka, his pupil Aphanasia. This genuine little love duo, in a major key, is as distinctive and individual as the utterly dissimilar one, in a minor key, between Dante and Beatrice.

118 XIX. **Leonora di Este and Father Panigarola** (1853). Mr. Crump furnishes the following translation from Serassi's *Vita di Torquato Tasso:* "In those days the famous Father Panigarola came to Ferrara, where he had preached the Lent before with much applause ; he was high in favour with the Duke and the Princesses ; and to him Tasso wrote asking that he would be good enough to visit him. Then Tasso begged that Panigarola would kiss Leonora's hand for him, if she were better, and tell her that he grieved much for her illness, which he had not lamented in verse by reason that to do so was repugnant to his nature ; but that if he could serve her in any other way he was very ready, especially if she desired to hear any glad songs. I do not know

if Panigarola was in time to do this kindness." The companion piece to this exquisite scene, a Conversation between Tasso and his sister Cornelia, represents him across the border-line between feigned and real insanity, and her humouring him. It is less simple and less successful than the one here given, which is plaintive and haunting, truly feminine.

120 XX. **Admiral Blake and Humphrey Blake** (1853). Landor's substitution of Humphrey for Benjamin, another of Admiral Blake's brothers, is immaterial, since the story on which the Conversation is founded is not true. See Mr. Crump's note, and Professor Laughton's article on Blake in the *Dictionary of National Biography*.

The conflicting emotions of the hero in a trying situation are particularly well shown. A really dramatic moment is dramatically treated.

In the Conversation between Penn and Peterborough, first published twenty-four years before this one, is a fine tribute to Blake.

124 XXI. **Rhadamistus and Zenobia** (1837). Abrupt and agitated, full of action, not always fortunate in choice of words, occasionally stiff in turn of phrase, this, though not one of the best of Landor's short scenes, is sufficiently rapid and vivid to have a place near them.

Zenobia, who lived in the first century, was, as a matter of fact, rescued by some shepherds.

129 XXII. **Epicurus, Leontion, and Ternissa** (1829). The parts selected, forming a small fraction of the whole, are pervaded by an atmosphere of leisurely dalliance in which Epicurus, who is Landor thinly veiled, turns easily from one topic to another with his fair pupils. Ternissa, an almost imaginary character, does much to add grace and lightness to the dialogue, which becomes at times pretty drowsy, when Theophrastus, for instance, is under discussion. It is easy to see why Landor was fond of this discursive Conversation, in which thoughts on various subjects deeply interesting to him are strung on a thread of pleasing talk in a pretty place; and which is a sort of idealised confirmation of Browning's remark, made some thirty years later, that, "whatever he may profess, the thing he really loves is a pretty girl to talk nonsense with." The dialogue is a good one to open at random, for, with little coherence and no dramatic development, it abounds in choice bits of reflection and dainty play of fancy.

This Conversation first appeared when Landor was fifty-four. A dialogue between Menander and Epicurus, written when he was past eighty, contains tender reminiscences of Ternissa. It is worthy of remark that much of his late work, like Tennyson's, has all the freshness of his best period.

138 XXIII. **Walton, Cotton, and Oldways** (1829). Forster is not far wrong in describing this Conversation as an idyl "fresh as a page of Isaak's own writing ; a natural country landscape overrun with charming thoughts; and with a sweet soberness in its cheerfulness and sunshine." It is also an elaborate and skilful experiment in style. Walton's manner is not copied; rather his temper and tone are assimilated, and reproduced with Landor's impress. Oddly enough, though we may miss, on comparison, what Lowell calls "that charm of inadvertency with which Walton knew how to make his most careful sentences waylay the ear," we shall detect no discord between this choicely good strain of fancy and its illustrious predecessor of the seventeenth century. Technically different as is Landor's style from Walton's, the honest angler's refreshing innocency is by no means all lost in the transposition to another key.

Is it fantastic to please oneself with the notion that in writing the lines beginning, "She was so beautiful" (p. 150), which are strongly reminiscent of Donne, Landor may have had in mind the youthful heroine of Donne's *Anatomy*, whose .

> "Pure and eloquent blood
> Spoke in her cheeks, and so distinctly wrought
> That one might almost say, her body thought"?

Oldways, representing Landor's tutor, Mr. Langley, is a quaintly charming sketch of kindliness and pedantry. The fiction of Margaret Hayes gives a pretext for the motive of the Conversation. Further introduction to a scene the full enjoyment of which may be had for the reading appears needless.

It is a pleasure to find elsewhere in Landor tributes which show the sincerity of his regard for Walton. Horne Tooke is made to speak of the "perpetually pleasant light . . . reflected from every thought and sentence "; and Johnson to say, " Fortunate is he who in no hour of relaxation or of idleness takes up to annex or pamper it, a worse book than Walton."

155 XXIV. **William Penn and Lord Peterborough** (1829). This extremely long and superbly written dialogue is one of the most highly esteemed of Landor's rambling discussions. "Peterborough's freakish delight," says Mr. Crump, "in turning the conversation on to subjects likely to provoke Penn into enthusiastic indignation is as natural as Penn's piety." The aristocrat at odds with aristocracy, and in sympathy with the element of common sense in the Quaker religion, is obviously Landor himself speaking behind the mask of Peterborough. "Profligate,

unprincipled, flighty as he was," says J. R. Green, " Peterborough had a genius for war."   Macaulay's Essay on Mahon's *War of the Succession* contains a spirited sketch of him.   His visit to Pennsylvania, though mentioned in Spence's *Anecdotes,* is not fully authenticated.   Whether the Quaker character is truly drawn by Landor, let none but a Philadelphian presume to say.

167 XXV.   **Epictetus and Seneca** (1828).   Sufficiently characterised by Forster as " very striking for its contrasts as well in the character as in the philosophy of the high-bred man of learning and the low-born slave, and enforcing admirable rules of simplicity and naturalness in writing "; and picked out by Lord Houghton for its aptness of language.   Between Epicurus and Epictetus, it will be remembered, Landor aspired to walk through life.

172 XXVI.   **Lucullus and Cæsar** (1829).   Plutarch describes the sumptuous villa of Lucullus and his mode of life in it.   This is one of the Conversations mentioned by Lord Houghton as showing how much at home Landor was with the Romans; it is the most entertaining of the Roman undramatic scenes.

180 XXVII.   **The Apologue of Critobulus** (1826).   Among the Roman philosophical discussions, that between Cicero and his brother holds the foremost place.   The fitness of style and the urbanity have been remarked on by critics.   It contains several eloquent passages, but it is long and not very lively.   The allegory here given, which was added in the second edition of the dialogue, ranks scarcely below those in the *Pentameron.*   Similar in kind and quality is the dream of Euthymedes, an allegory of Love, Hope, and Fear, in the dialogue of Scipio, Polybius, and Panætius.

183 XXVIII.   **The Pentameron** (1837).   From 1829 to 1835 Landor, happy with his family, his friends, his pets, and his flowers, lived near Fiesole at the Villa Gherardesca, "master of the very place," he writes, "to which the greatest genius of Italy, or the Continent, conducted those ladies who told such pleasant tales in the warm weather."   Something of the spirit of the place and of its associations for Landor is conveyed in his poems relating to this period, and in some of Boccaccio's descriptive interludes introducing the days of the *Decameron.*   Here is a specimen bit from Payne's English version of the opening of Day the Seventh : " Never yet had the nightingales and the other birds seemed to them to sing so blithely as they did that morning, what while, accompanied by their carols, they repaired to the Ladies' Valley, where they were received by many more, which seemed to them to make merry for their coming.   There, going round about the place and reviewing it all

anew, it appeared to them so much fairer than on the foregoing day as
the season of the day was more sorted to its goodliness. Then, after
they had broken their fast with good wine and confections, not to be
behindhand with the birds in the matter of song, they fell a-singing
and the valley with them, still echoing those same songs which they did
sing, whereto all the birds, as if they would not be outdone, added new
and dulcet notes."

Given Landor's preference of Boccaccio to all other modern writers
except Shakespeare and Milton, what wonder that in such a spot he
conceived the idea of the *Pentameron, or Interviews of Messer Giovanni
Boccaccio and Messer Francesco Petrarca, when said Messer Giovanni
lay infirm at his Villetta hard by Certaldo ; after which they saw not
each other on our Side of Paradise* — as the title affectionately runs ! The
Fifth Day's Interview — from which excerpts are here made — contains
a notable poem to his son, written in England after he had left his
family and his beloved Italy ; it concludes with the allegorical dreams
of Boccaccio and Petrarch, on which has been lavished encomium which
it is difficult to call over-enthusiastic. Any one who cares at all for
Landor will prize these closing strains of his most charming composition ; one who does not feel their serene imaginative loveliness may in
vain turn his pages in search of anything more delightful.   -

A competent critic lays stress on the superiority of these dreams to
De Quincey's *Ladies of Sorrow* and *Daughter of Lebanon.* One question naturally suggested by that comparison — a question which may
arise concerning much of the most highly finished work of any but the
few supreme spirits — is whether in either case the undisputed excellence of workmanship diverts attention from the equally undisputed
beauty of thought ; whether conscious admiration of the process pre-
dominates over spontaneous delight in the result ; whether, in a word,
the artificer supersedes the artist. As between Landor's most delicate
prose with its cadences as perfect as Handel's, and De Quincey's with
its harmonics as mysterious as Chopin's, any one's preference will be
a matter largely of individual temperament until experimental psy-
chology shall determine by what common unit to measure emotional
effects so different in kind as these two masters produce.

200 XXIX. **Pericles and Aspasia** (1836). A few letters can only
partially indicate some of the qualities which together cause this to be
generally regarded as its author's masterpiece. To be caught in its
"strong toil of grace," one should read at random a good many pages
at a sitting. A reader with the knack of skipping luckily may easily
find hidden in the letters the heart of Pericles and of Aspasia. As a

whole, the book, though not equal in sustained human interest to the *Pentameron*, is the richest in thought of Landor's works, and his noblest in point of English.

Mrs. Browning enthusiastically calls *Pericles and Aspasia* and the *Pentameron* " books for the world and for all time, whenever the world and time shall come to their senses about them; complete in beauty of sentiment and subtlety of criticism." Horne's *New Spirit of the Age.*

215 XXX–XXXII. **Hellenics** (1846-47). At Lady Blessington's instance, Landor translated into English some of his *Idyllia Heroica;* these translations, together with certain of his English poems on kindred subjects, he entitled *Hellenics.* There can be no more fitting introduction to them than the following lines from Lowell's *Rhoecus*, a version of the story — a story dating from the fifth century B.C. — on which the *Hamadryad* is founded:

> " Hear now this fairy legend of old Greece,
> As full of freedom, youth, and beauty still
> As the immortal freshness of that grace
> Carved for all ages on some Attic frieze."

The *Hamadryad* (p. 215) and its sequel, *Acon and Rhodopè* (p. 224), were not translated from the Latin, but were written originally in English.

For technical criticism on the "fine filed phrase" of the *Death of Artemidora* (p. 228), which is like an outline of Flaxman's, see Colvin's *Landor*, pp. 193-4. The poem was first published in *Pericles and Aspasia*, in the form here given; afterward, with several changes and the omission of the last three lines, in *Hellenics.* In the *Hellenics* version the change of " Fate's shears were " (l. 11) to " Iris stood " is clearly a gain, and the lopping off of the last three lines is not commonly reckoned a loss. On the second point, however, a word may be said. Though the abbreviated form, it is true, more strictly encloses the picture within its frame, yet the discarded lines, appropriately carrying on the main idea rather than introducing a new one, give a ray of light in the prevailing gloom; as verse, too, they are among the best of the twenty-two, and close the poem naturally with a well modulated cadence more agreeable than the abrupt and rather harsh phrase, " 't was not hers."

229 XXXIII. **The Wrestling Match** (1798). From the first book of *Gebir;* reprinted in the second edition of *Hellenics.* To Gebir, a Spanish prince, his shepherd brother Tamar confides his love for a sea-nymph. For the passages in Wordsworth and Byron similar to

Landor's description of the shell, see Colvin's *Landor*, pp. 168–9.
Those melodious lines were first composed in not less melodious Latin:

> At mihi caeruleae sinuosa foramina conchae
> Obvolvunt, lucemque intus de sole biberunt,
> Nam crevere locis ubi porticus ipsa palati
> Et qua purpurea medius stat currus in unda.
> Tu quate, somnus abit: tu laevia tange labella
> Auribus attentis, veteres reminiscitur aedes,
> Oceanusque suus quo murmure murmurat illa.

Aubrey de Vere, writing of a visit he made in 1854 to Tennyson, at
Farringford, says: "Alfred and I had many a breezy walk along the
Downs and as far as the Needles, sometimes with a distant view of the
coast flushed by sunset, sometimes with a nearer one of the moon-
beams 'marbling' the wet sea-sands, as the wave recoiled, which last
always reminded me of Landor's lines:

> 'And the long moonbeam on the hard wet sand[s]
> Lay like a jasper column half uprear'd.'"
>
> *Alfred Lord Tennyson, A Memoir by His Son*, I. 378.

232 XXXIV. **To Ianthe.** A score of pretty little pieces referring
to Ianthe, written and published at various times, have been grouped
by Mr. Colvin.

233 XXXV. **Rose Aylmer** (1806). If anything Landor wrote may
be said to approach popularity, it is this. A few verbal improvements
were made after the first publication; the present text dates from 1831.
See Colvin's *Landor*, pp. 43–4.

Lord Aylmer's daughter, a friend of Landor's at Swansea, lent him
Clara Reeve's *Progress of Romance*, in which he found the kernel of
Gebir. Born in 1779, she died of cholera in India in 1800. Mr. Stephen
Wheeler, whose *Letters and Other Unpublished Writings of Walter
Savage Landor* tells more about her than is elsewhere accessible, thinks
the following lines of Landor's may also refer to her:

> My pictures blacken in their frames
>   As night comes on;
> And youthful maids and wrinkled dames
>   Are now all one.
>
> Death of the day! a sterner Death
>   Did worse before;
> The fairest form, the sweetest breath,
>   Away he bore,

234 XXXVI. **A Fiesolan Idyl** (1831). Landor's passionate fondness for flowers, to which his writings abundantly testify, is nowhere more pleasingly phrased than in this attractive little poem.   Some one speaks of his regarding women as a more delicate sort of flowers. Perhaps this piece of a letter to Crabb Robinson, with its unconsciously prophetic allusion to the present culture of polychrome orchids, lends colour to that dainty fancy: "I like white flowers better than any others; they resemble fair women. Lily, tuberose, orange, and the truly English syringa are my heart's delight. I do not mean to say that they supplant the rose and violet in my affections, for these are our first loves, before we grew too fond of considering and too fond of displaying our acquaintance with others of sounding titles."   H. C. Robinson's *Diary*, II. 518, Ed. 1869.

Curiously interesting similarities and differences in detail may be discovered on comparison of this with Tennyson's idyl, *The Gardener's Daughter*, published eleven years later. The two well show, respectively, the restraint of the classic manner and the efflorescence of the romantic, with its emotional reaction, in describing nature and persons. Tennyson's highly wrought miniature of Rose, "full and rich," as he said it must be, is, if more individual, less distinct than Landor's intaglio of the nameless "gentle maid."

236–7 XXXVII. XXXVIII. From the *Examination of Shakespeare.*

238 XXXIX. **To Robert Browning** (1846). A letter to Forster contains this concise and apt remark on Browning: "You were right as to Browning. He has done some admirable things. I only wish he would atticise a little. Few of the Athenians had such a quarry on their property, but they constructed better roads for the conveyance of the material."   In another letter to Forster, in 1845, Landor calls him "a great poet, a very great poet indeed, as the world will have to agree with us in thinking. . . .   God grant he may live to be much greater than he is, high as he stands above most of the living : *latis humeris et toto vertice.*"

238 XL. **To the Sister of Elia** (1846). "The death of Charles Lamb has grieved me very bitterly. Never did I see a human being with whom I was more inclined to sympathize. There is something in the recollection that you took me with you to see him which affects me greatly more than writing or speaking of him could do with any other. When I first heard of the loss that all his friends, and many that never were his friends, sustained in him, no thought took possession of my mind except the anguish of his sister. That very night before I closed my eyes I composed this." *Extract from a letter to H. C. Robinson, enclosing the poem.*

Contrast with Landor's verses Wordsworth's "monumental portrait"
— as Professor Dowden calls it — of Lamb, ending with the lines
referring to his sister's loneliness :

> " The sacred tie
> Is broken ; yet why grieve? for Time but holds
> His moiety in trust, till Joy shall lead
> To the blest world where parting is unknown."

Closely in keeping with Landor's feeling, though more religious, is
Cardinal Newman's on the sudden death, in 1828, of his own sister.
His poem on the occasion closes with the stanza :

> " Joy of sad hearts, and light of downcast eyes !
>   Dearest, thou art enshrined
> In all thy fragrance in our memories ;
>   For we must ever find
>   Bare thought of thee
> Freshen this weary life, while weary life shall be."

239 XLI, XLII. From *Pericles and Aspasia.*
239–41 XLIII–XLVIII. Neither Mrs. Barbauld's " Life! I know
not what thou art," Browning's *Prospice* or his Epilogue to *Asolando,*
Tennyson's *Crossing the Bar*, nor Stevenson's *Requiem* expresses a
more natural feeling with regard to meeting death than Landor's
unstudied verses.

www.ingramcontent.com/pod-product-compliance
Lightning Source LLC
Chambersburg PA
CBHW020944120726
47905CB00008B/2666